W9-CMP-752

DARKNESS OF THE LIGHT

DARKNESS

OF THE

LIGHT

PETER DAVID

A TOM DOHERTY ASSOCIATES BOOK
NEW YORK

DARKNESS OF THE LIGHT

Copyright © 2007 by Peter David

Edited by James Frenkel

A Tor Book
Published by Tom Doherty Associates, LLC
175 Fifth Avenue
New York, NY 10010

www.tor.com

Tor® is a registered trademark of Tom Doherty Associates, LLC.

Library of Congress Cataloging-in-Publication Data

David, Peter (Peter Allen)
    Darkness of the light / Peter David.
        p. cm.
    "A Tom Doherty Associates book"—T.p. verso.
    ISBN-13: 978-0-7653-1173-3
    ISBN-10: 0-7653-1173-9
    I. Title.
    PS3554.A92144D37 2007
    813'.54—dc22

                                        2006102690

First Edition: June 2007

Printed in the United States of America

0 9 8 7 6 5 4 3 2 1

TO KATHLEEN,
the light to my darkness

ACKNOWLEDGMENTS

Thanks to my agent, Matt Bialer, and editor, Jim Frenkel, without whom the Earth would remain hidden.

DARKNESS OF THE LIGHT

THE BATTLE PLAIN OF MARSAY

i.

Mandraques do nothing in half measures.

That had always been the unofficial motto of the Five Clans. Aside from their mutual contempt, it might well have been the only thing that united them. It was a motto that applied to all things, all dealings, all clanwars. And it very much applied to the battlefield, which was running green with Mandraque blood.

The field was flat and lifeless, with the bodies of hundreds of Mandraques scattered in various places and assorted pieces. Nothing was moving except the flies, and the air was thick with the stench of bodies, decay, and waste. There had been choruses of groaning, cries for help, moans of "My leg!" and "Help me, damn you!" and "I'll kill you all for this!" Eventually they had tapered off. Only the corpses remained.

One Mandraque in particular had not gone down easily. His sword was clenched tightly in his clawed hand. His armor was in tatters, and through the holes one could see the blue-green scales that were the typical skin covering for the species. He had been massively muscled. Like most Mandraques, his scaled head was round, his eyes were little more than slits, his parallel nostrils were cruel lines in the middle of his face. His mouth, in death, was drawn back in a sneer, which actually mirrored the way it had normally appeared in life.

Insects were gathering upon his forehead, working their way into his nostril slits, as he stared lifelessly at the sky above. It was a gorgeous day if one was willing to discount the smoke that hung in the air from the various fires . . . fires that had resulted from the flaming arrows filling the air like so many shooting stars.

Those arrows had been largely responsible for the aroma of cooked meat hanging heavy in the still air.

A slender hand, fingernails thick with dirt, skin abraded on the back, reached over and brushed the flies away from his forehead. The hand's possessor slowly hauled herself forward on her hands and knees. She had only just come around, shaking off the darkness that had claimed her. She could not have been more different from the dead Mandraque supine upon the ground. Her skin was smooth and tanned, and copious amounts of thick black hair hung in her face. Her eyes peered through the strands, and reflected in them was a soul with the frailty of a crippled sparrow. The various stenches assaulted her as her full senses began to come around, and she coughed in violent spasms, her breasts heaving as she did so.

She was bloodied from having been thrown around during the fighting. Her mind was a blur . . . images tumbling one over the other . . . blood flying, teeth tearing and ripping, terrifying and unrecognizable roars of defiance and death, death all around her . . .

"Greatness?" she said softly. Her hand hesitated over him, because she was never supposed to touch him without his permission. Nevertheless, this time she took the risk and rested her fingers tentatively upon him. Her fingers were tinted green with blood.

No response.

A bit more boldly, she shook the Mandraque as she whispered his title into his earhole. "Greatness?" she repeated. "Greatness . . . what do you wish me to do now?"

Still no answer.

Caution dissolved within her. She grabbed the dead Mandraque with both hands and shook him violently. "Greatness! *What do you wish me to do! Tell me! Greatness . . . !*"

Her cries were so loud that she didn't hear the footsteps behind her, crunching across the ash and rubble-strewn land. She continued to shout at the dead Mandraque, pounding with a combination of mounting fury and terror upon his chest, and would have continued to do so until she'd collapsed in exhaustion had she not been alerted by a loud clearing of a throat.

She turned, jumping back, startled. She rubbed some stray soot from her eyes and wiped dirt from her face, leaving smears from the back of her hand. She squinted at the new arrival and had no idea what to make of him.

He was neither as tall nor as wide as the Greatness had been. His visage was fearsome and feral, but surprisingly it was mingled with a gentleness such as she had never seen in all her life. She didn't truly know how many years old she actually was. She had once asked, and the Greatness had told her she was between fifteen and twenty cycles around the sun. He couldn't be more specific beyond that.

The newcomer's skin was similar to her own, but an even darker hue. He had a mop of curly brown hair that hung in ringlets around his triangular face. He looked at her, tilting his head from side to side in curiosity, and the curls bounced around as he did so. Save for a large, thick band of leather that wrapped around him from waist to shoulder, he was naked from the waist up, displaying a flat stomach and taut chest. It was a warm day, so his relative lack of apparel didn't surprise her terribly. She herself was not wearing much: scraps of cloth to accentuate the curves of her body, gauzy and filmy and out of place in the blood-soaked environs.

What did surprise her was that, from the waist down, he was covered with thick brown fur. His legs bent at an odd angle to the knees, and tapered down into cloven feet.

"I don't think he's in much of a position to respond," he said. His voice was rough, but there was amusement in it. He glanced around the scene with obvious interest. "He certainly gave an accounting of himself in his final moments."

"Final . . . moments?" she said slowly.

"Well . . . yes. Look," and he pointed at the devastation in the area immediately around the Greatness.

She studied where he was indicating, truly seeing it for the first time. There were other Mandraque bodies strewn about, their weapons broken and scattered. Even the least damaged of them were ripped up or gutted. Most of them were missing pieces of their bodies: arms, legs, tails, and such. There were still trickles of blood from some of the severed limbs. She saw that there was a Mandraque with his teeth sunk into the Greatness's leg.

She looked back up at the newcomer. "Final moments?" she said again.

He stared at her, clearly disbelieving. "Yes. He's . . . dead. You *do* understand that, don't you?" He took a step toward her. "You're a human, aren't you? A human female. I've never seen one of you living before. Does your kind have names? What's your name?"

"Final . . . moments?"

Blowing out air through tight lips in annoyance, he said, "Are you . . . mentally deficient in some way? I don't mean to be insulting. It's just, well . . . if you are I can probably save myself some time. I'm Karsen, by the way. Karsen Foux." He paused for a moment, frowning, looking as if he was trying to recall something. Then he smiled, having mentally retrieved it, and he extended a hand with the palm sideways. "This is how your sort greets, does it not?"

As he approached her she stepped back reflexively. She crisscrossed her breasts

protectively, twisting herself around to keep clear of him despite his lack of outward aggression. "He is the Greatness! His . . . his kind does not have final
moments!"

"He is flesh and blood, my sweet," said Karsen. "I assure you, he has final moments, just like the rest of us." He looked around at the corpses. "Quite a fight this
was, I'll grant you. Brutal, too. A number of them cut down by blades, but others . . . look at this. Their throats torn out. Necks broken. I'll give your Greatness
credit, he was certainly versatile in the way he killed his enemies. Now what's your
name?"

She began shaking her head ferociously. She was starting to look less like a human rational being and more like a trapped beast. Her eyes were hot and glowering. "Keep away from him," she said.

"I don't have to actually," he told her. "He's fair game, under the Treaty. So why
not let me do my job, and you can go and do yours . . . whatever that might be."

He approached her with slow, measured strides. She wanted to remain where
she was; she wanted to find some way to stop him. She kept looking down at the
Greatness for hints or a measure of guidance, and nothing was forthcoming.
Instead her mind was gradually pointing her down a road that she had no desire
to travel.

She now realized the Greatness's hide was cold beneath her fingers. No life
pulsed within his frame.

She was alone.

She had never been alone. Not since she had first come to the Greatness's court,
so far back that she could not recall a time when she hadn't been there.

Panic began to seize her. She started trembling, shaking her head as if she
could deny what was occurring. Karsen, concerned, drew closer. "Are you . . . all
right?"

She turned and bolted.

Immediately she nearly tripped over a fallen arm, righted herself, and ran from
the scene, hoping that she could expunge the hideous sights she had seen from her
memory, knowing that she never could.

Soot was settling upon the ground, and her delicate feet were leaving a trail of
prints behind her. She risked a glance over her shoulder. There was no sign of the
creature calling itself "Karsen."

She let out a sigh of relief that she wasn't being followed, and then shrieked as she
nearly plowed straight into Karsen, now inexplicably in her path. As it was she lost
her balance, staggered and fell. Karsen stood over her, looking down impassively.

"In answer to what you're probably thinking . . . no, you didn't run in a circle or circumnavigate the globe," Karsen assured her. He advanced on her, his patience ebbing away. "Now if you'd just allow me to—"

The instant he came within range, she drove a foot straight up and into the area of his loins. The impact had the same effect on Karsen as it did on males of her own race. He doubled over, his face becoming pale, and he clutched at his groin, cradling something thankfully unseen deep within the fur.

She did not wait to see if the attack had any further results. Instead she ran.

She ran over the battle-scarred land. She ran past the fallen Mandraques, past the tents that were still smoldering, past the makeshift fortresses and the trenches that had been dug but presented only minimal protection. She ran and ran, her heart pounding as if intending to flee the protection of her bosom. She could barely breathe; her throat sore and rasping from the smoky, stale air. She was sobbing, but her eyes were dry of tears. She had no idea what she was running toward. All she knew was to follow her impulse to get as far from the scene of the Greatness's death . . .

The Greatness's death!

It was the first time she had actually said those repellent words to herself, and she still couldn't believe them. The Greatness couldn't die. He was . . . he was the Greatness! He . . .

She tripped.

She didn't simply trip. Her foot hit something, the exact nature of which she never knew. Perhaps it had been a stray rock or random piece of a body. Either way, it sent her sprawling, hurtling through the air flat with her arms outstretched as if she were flying. She did not remain airborne. Instead she crashed to the ground, tearing her skin even further, slamming her jaw down with such force that it jarred her brain. She skidded several more feet before grinding to a stop. The world was swirling around her. She was sure from the tightening of her stomach muscles that she was going to vomit. She did not, although it might have made her feel better if she'd done so.

She closed her eyes to block out the spinning. Then she heard footsteps in front of her. It seemed impossible. She had dealt him a fearsome blow, had run as fast as she could. How could he conceivably have caught up with her?

She tried to pull herself upward, to keep going in the vain hope that he hadn't spotted her somehow, when suddenly rough hands were yanking her to her feet. She gasped and was twisted around to face two Mandraques. She recognized them immediately, more from their signs of rank and various ribbons of lineage than their faces.

They looked battered and bloodied, both relieved to be alive and also a bit chagrined. One was taller than the other, and the shorter one said, "Ranzell . . . I think I recognize this one. What's her name . . . ?"

The one addressed as Ranzell snagged her free hand and shook her, snapping the arm as if cracking a whip. He carried no sword, but she saw an impressively large war hammer strapped to his back. Its handle was half as long as Ranzell himself, and the rough-hewn stone head was flecked with Mandraque blood. Ranzell's associate was busy tossing aside his own, broken sword, and was hefting a sword picked up from a corpse, swinging it this way and that to gauge the weight. Ranzell flinched away slightly, scowling in an annoyed way that indicated the sword had come a bit too close to him for comfort. "What's your name, girl? One of your betters has asked you."

Her mouth moved with no sound emerging at first. The two Mandraques didn't seem sympathetic. Tokep, the shorter one, grinned in a way that only made him look sinister. "I recall now. Her name is Jepp. She's the Greatness's pleasure toy, aren't you, Jepp."

She managed a nod. They didn't seem particularly friendly, but that was certainly normal for the entirety of their race. "Yes . . . I am . . . I am the Greatness's. I have always belonged to the Greatness."

"Good t'hear," said Ranzell. "And now you're ours."

"No," she told him, trying to pull away. "I am the Greatness's . . ."

"We passed the Greatness. He's dead. You belong to—"

"To me."

They turned and there was Karsen. He was a few feet away, and he must have moved like a demon to get there, but he didn't seem especially tired out.

"What's a Laocoon doing way out here?" said Tokep. His body was tense in a manner that suggested he was going to attack if he didn't get an answer he liked.

"Finding things," replied Karsen. "In this case, I found her first. First, my friends. And the laws of salvage, as laid out by the Treaty, say she's mine."

Tokep processed the information, and then he visibly relaxed. The two Mandraques looked at each other and shared a laugh. "It's a Bottom Feeder," snorted Tokep. "A godsdamned Bottom Feeder."

"I've always preferred the term 'reclamation expert,' " Karsen said.

Ranzell was nodding in recognition. "We've even encountered each other before, haven't we? Yes . . . it was after the Battle of the Shifting Plains. You were there scrounging, just like all your ilk. You ran away at the first sign of trouble, as I recall."

"My ilk prefers discretion to foolish altercation."

"You mean cowardice to bravery."

"Just so."

Jepp wasn't entirely sure how any of this was going to play out, but she knew she'd prefer to be elsewhere when it did. Still lying on the ground, she started to edge away, hoping that no one would notice. The hope lasted for as long as it took Ranzell's thick round tail to snap around viciously, extending to its full length and slamming down in front of her, cutting off her retreat. "Stay where you are, pleasure girl," warned Ranzell. "This won't take long. We just have to send the Bottom Feeder on his way . . ."

"But I found her first!" Karsen said, sounding not a little whiny. His tone of voice was distressing to Jepp. It certainly didn't come across as that of someone she could count on.

Tokep didn't seem any more impressed by Karsen than Jepp had been. "*Balls!*" snarled Tokep. "Why'd we find her alone, then?"

"She ran off. I just now caught up with her." He spoke with uncertainty, as if fishing for explanations.

"Too bad," said Ranzell. "Not that it would have made much difference. Even if she'd been with you, we'd still have taken her off your hands."

"Don't you have any respect for the Firedraque Treaty?" asked Karsen.

Ranzell spat on the ground nearby. The liquid was thick and viscous and sizzled slightly when it struck the dirt. "That for the Firedraques and for their damned treaty. And that for you as well."

"That's not very respectful," said Karsen. "Now, I'm sure you don't want me to register a formal complaint . . ."

Ranzell turned to the Mandraque standing next to him. "Tokep. Make this idiot stop talking. Knock him out or rip off his head. It makes little difference to me."

Karsen stepped back, fear flickering in his eyes. "Well, I . . . I have to say it makes something of a difference to *me*. I . . . I really don't want to fight."

"Then go away," said Ranzell.

"*No!*" Tokep abruptly spoke up. "I don't want to let him off that easily. I've lost a brace of kinsmen this day, almost got killed myself, and now I've had to stand here and listen to a Bottom Feeder spout off? Enough! I'm looking for someone to hurt and this fool is it."

"No, look!" and Karsen was trembling. He forced a smile, backing up. "I'll . . . just be on my way, all right? She's not worth it. You're not worth it," he said to Jepp. "No offense."

The girl looked from Karsen to the grinning Mandraques, and back to Karsen. "You're . . . you're not going to leave me with them . . ."

"Yes, he is," growled Ranzell.

"Yes, I am," Karsen affirmed.

"But . . . you need to save me!"

Karsen sighed heavily. "The truth of the matter, girl, is that I am exactly what they say. It's a great fool who doesn't know the reality of himself, and I am many things, but a great fool is not one of them." He bowed to the Mandraques, his hands clasped palm-to-palm. "War be with you."

And then, just like that, he was gone, propelled from the scene by his powerful legs, moving with startling silence.

"Please, don't!" Jepp cried out, having no clue as to whether her voice was even reaching him. "You have to save me! You have to be Great for me! I know you have it in you to . . . !"

Part of her was stunned at her own aggressiveness. It was not within the purview of one such as she to tell others what to do. In fact, she could not remember ever having done it before. Then again, she had always been under the command of, and subject to the whims of, the Greatness. So it had simply never come up.

"He was just trying to salvage you so he can trade you for goods and services," Ranzell informed her. "If he wasn't planning to have you service him in addition. His type is the lowest of the low, girl. You're better off with us. Trust me."

Jepp studied him tentatively, and then withdrew from him. She saw vast amounts of cruelty within him, far more than in even the Greatness. Tokep didn't seem any different. They frightened her. She wanted nothing but to distance herself from them as soon as possible.

They were disinclined to cooperate. Tokep advanced, swinging his newfound jagged sword in Jepp's direction. "Where do you think you're going, girl?" he demanded.

She had no idea why she cried out. But she did, and what she said was *"Karsen!"*

"You idiot human!" snarled Ranzell. "He's gone! He won't help you!"

Except he wasn't. And he did.

For Karsen was suddenly in the middle of the clearing. Confusion flickered upon Karsen's face for a moment, but then the certainty of his actions clarified for him what he was about to undertake. He was crouched low, his legs coiled, one hand touching the ground. His face was twisted in what seemed grim amusement.

Tokep needed no further urging. He switched targets and moved. The sword swung viciously toward him, and Karsen easily vaulted not only over the sword, but over Tokep himself . . . and landed on Ranzell's shoulders. Ranzell grabbed at him, but Karsen's powerful legs pushed off, like those of a swimmer moving through air rather than water. He vaulted away from Ranzell and landed directly behind him.

Ranzell yelped and grabbed at his back, his frantic fingers confirming what the loss of weight had already told him: Karsen had ripped the war hammer off his back. He spun just as Karsen twisted at the waist, whipping around the war hammer. Ranzell ducked under it. Tokep turned around to find out what all the yelling was about. The hammerhead slammed against Tokep's skull. The Mandraque's head practically exploded from the impact, bits of blue matter and green blood spattering everywhere, including Jepp's leg. She let out a disgusted shriek and brushed it away.

Karsen faced Ranzell, and Jepp saw that the war hammer was covered with much fresher blood than it had been before.

Ranzell grabbed up Tokep's fallen sword and the Mandraque charged, bellowing in a voice so deafening that Jepp clapped her hands to her ears. This time Karsen did not leap out of the way, probably because the Mandraque was expecting it. Instead he swung the hammer to meet the arc of the sword. The two weapons came together with a resounding clang, and the sword's blade snapped in three pieces. Ranzell stared dumbly at the hilt with a bit of steel protruding from it that wasn't more than an inch.

Karsen didn't stop moving. He spun in place and brought the hammer down, around and up. It caught Ranzell squarely in the chest and Jepp heard something crack within Ranzell. The Mandraque fell backward, his arms flailing, a deep wheezing in his chest.

Karsen took a step back and coldly regarded his handiwork. He didn't appear to have exerted any effort. He nodded once, and then dropped the war hammer. Ranzell watched him approach and actually forced a smile.

"You're . . . skilled," he said. "And merciful. That is a—"

At which point Karsen began to kick him with his hard-edged, cloven hooves. He kicked him in the face, the chest, anywhere he could reach. The Mandraque's scaled hide provided some protection, but huge welts were rising wherever Karsen's hooves came into contact. Even after Ranzell lapsed into unconsciousness, Karsen continued to beat him for a time, either to make sure he was really unconscious, or else because he didn't feel like stopping.

Finally he tired of his activities. He crouched and fumbled at the straps upon Ranzell's chest for a few moments before pulling the straps free that served as the hammer's harness. Then he buckled them onto himself, picked up the hammer, and sheathed it on his back. He turned and scowled fiercely at Jepp, and she shrank back. And then, like the passing of a summer squall, the ferocity was gone. He looked around at what he had wrought, and there was regret and even chagrin upon his face.

Then he turned and started to walk away.

Jepp lay there, watching him, and then slowly got to her feet. He kept on walking, stepping over the strewn bodies, paying her no mind at all.

She should have taken the opportunity to flee, to get as far away from him as possible. She surprised herself again with the sound of her own voice saying, "Am . . . am I supposed to come with you now? I . . . I thought you . . ."

He stopped. He did not turn to look at her. Instead he sounded rather tired as he said, "Do what you want."

He kept going.

She hesitated for a time that seemed far longer than it was, and then she fell in behind him.

ii.

It wasn't easy for her to keep up with him. His stride was far longer, and he seemed to move with a sort of bounce of his legs. There were so many things she wanted to ask him, but it was taking all her effort and breath just to maintain the pace, so she remained silent.

At one point, Karsen picked up an equipment bag lying next to one of the corpses and slung it over his shoulder. After that, every so often, he would stop without warning and study one of the bodies, removing trinkets or particularly well-tended weapons. He was limited in the number of swords he could transport, but a goodly number of daggers found their way into the bag.

At one point he was hunched over a pair of warriors who had cleaved each other's skulls, taking some ornate wristbands off them. Then he looked up in surprise as Jepp reached down and into the armor chest plating of one of them. She fished around, the tip of her tongue visible as she concentrated, and then she extracted a small leather bag. She handed it to Karsen, who tugged open the restraints and up-ended the contents onto his open palm. A variety of precious stones spilled out.

"Mandraques usually have small hidden compartments inside their chest plating in which they store their valuables," said Jepp.

Karsen stared at her. Then a small smile played across his lips.

"*Karsen!*"

A high loud voice rang across the field. Jepp blinked in surprise.

It was a female of the same species as Karsen. Like him, she was nude from the waist up. Her breasts were small and hard, and the lines in her face indicated that she was considerably older than Karsen.

She was also much larger. Her shoulders were wide, her arms thick and muscled, and her face was blocky with a pitiless expression. Her hair was tinged with gray. Several large sacks were slung over her shoulders, each sack stuffed to bursting. Jepp didn't think she would have been able to manage even one of the bags. This female was toting at least five with what appeared to be little effort.

"Karsen!" she said again. "What the hell are you doing with that?"

"It's a human." Karsen glanced at her up and down to double-check. "A female, I'm fairly sure."

"I know it's a human female! What are *you* doing *with* it?"

He smiled and said with what appeared to be great hope and eagerness, "She followed me home, Mother. Can I keep her?"

It is a warm, humid day in prehistory, and the small herd of grazing creatures that dominate the planet are aware of their world's newness and purity only in the most abstract of ways. They are oblivious of the notion that change may be forthcoming, or imminent, or even that the beginning of their demise will be arriving within moments to set their eventual extinction into motion. They know only of the great hanging fronds upon which they contentedly munch, and of the sun that bathes them in its generous rays.

On this particular day, they are heading in leisurely fashion toward the water, the ground trembling beneath each downward thrust of their massive feet. They do not have names for themselves. They don't think in such terms. They simply exist and, to their knowledge, have always existed, and always will. They will not have names until they are long gone. The descendants of the small furred creatures perched in the trees and watching with rapt attention will do the naming.

The water is cool and refreshing, and it is their intent to lower the small heads upon their imposing necks and lap up as much of the liquid as possible. Very likely they will ease their bulk into the waters, with the gentle waves lapping against the shore, and be further cooled.

They know that danger exists in their world. They know there are others of their kind who would turn upon them, attack them, leap on them and try to tear great, dripping strips of meat from their carcasses. They don't take offense at it. They fear it, watch for it, but they understand that it is the natural order of things. One survives the best one can.

The mighty creatures take a bit more time at the trees, selecting which leaves are the greenest and most inviting to consume. As they do this, they start to become aware of a change in the air. They do not exactly know what it is. The faint whiff of something called "ozone" (also to be named at some future date by the cringing primates' descendants) makes them think that perhaps a lightning storm is imminent. Not that they have any clear idea what causes bolts of untapped electricity to lance across the skies at random intervals, or their tiny ears to be assaulted by waves of rolling thunder. It is, yet again, something that is simply natural and to be accepted.

Nevertheless, it is not a lightning storm. They do sense that much. And they sense something else as well.

It is not natural. For they are nature's own beauties, the dominant life-form. They know what is and what isn't, what should and should not be. Their nostrils twitch as other, unfamiliar smells float through the air, the faint ozone aroma overwhelmed by something else, something unknowable and unnamable.

Vast billowing clouds sweep across the skies, blocking the sun's rays, ushering an early darkness. They don't seem to be coming from any one place in particular, but instead are everywhere, a great shroud being drawn across all living things.

The creatures' small heads swivel toward one another in mutual concern. They are all aware that something has changed.

Then comes the thunderous explosion, as if all the assorted smells and sensations had been building toward it. It is the single loudest noise they have ever heard. And considering that they have been witnesses to a world still in its infancy, with infant squalling consisting of the rumbling of earthquakes and the distant explosions of volcanoes, this is an impressively loud noise by which to be startled.

They open their mouths, confused ululation warbling through the previously still air. The deafening sound continues to echo through the air for long moments and then trails off as if riding away into the horizon.

Everything stops.

Everything is the same, and yet . . . everything is different.

Then, from the near distance, they hear an all-too-familiar cry.

It is one of the death bringers, one of the great monsters similar to them but opposite, with its mouth full of sharp, vicious teeth that rend and tear at their flesh. A monster with small, cruel eyes and tiny arms and huge legs that can propel it across the air and onto the back of its prey in a heartbeat. The death bringer's screech erupts from behind a thick grove of lazily swaying trees, and immediately the herd of creatures starts for the water, seeking safety.

Then they pause as they realize the sound of the death bringer is different from that to which they are accustomed. The cry such monsters cut loose with is designed to freeze prey in its place, to short-circuit the impulse to run long enough for the death bringer to cover the distance between them and sink its fearsome teeth into their hide.

That is not what they're hearing this time. This time . . .

. . . the death bringer is afraid.

The death bringer, which fears nothing, is afraid.

This realization is enough to trigger mounting panic in the normally placid creatures, and the death bringer suddenly emerges into the open. It is moving as quickly as it can. It sees the herd a distance away, makes as if to start toward it, and then pivots with the intention of heading in another direction.

The moment's hesitation is enough to cost it its life.

The newly arrived creatures emerge from the greenery around the death bringer. They are unlike anything that any in the herd has ever seen. They are small, with skin pale as the moon. They lope in a two-legged manner not dissimilar from that of the furred, tree-hugging creatures beholding their arrival. But they move from side to side, thrusting themselves forward with their knuckles to gain greater speed.

They descend upon the death bringer, encircling him to cut him off. The death bringer attempts to crush them beneath his clawed feet, or sweep them away with his tail. It does no good. He manages to pick off one or two of the slower-moving ones as they disappear beneath his feet . . . literally disappear, ground to a fine powder. But the rest are all over him. He is covered with a sea of undulating white, and they suck out the creature's lifeblood. His skin begins to pucker and shrivel, and he staggers toward the herd, howling as if seeking their help.

It doesn't work that way. The death bringer knows it, and they know it. The herd joins its own forces against the death bringer. It does not join with the death bringer. That would be against the laws of nature, laws that they could never articulate but know nevertheless.

And the first and foremost law of nature is survival.

The death bringer stumbles, tries to right himself, and then falls, hitting the ground violently. Death has been brought to him.

Until that moment the herd had remained paralyzed, watching in astonishment. The shock of the impact, the vibrations rippling through the ground and the finality in that "thud" are enough to break the spell. The herd runs toward the water, its traditional safe haven. The death bringer despised the water, although they never knew why, and he was certainly never in any position to explain.

The herd splashes into the water. Despite the urgency of the situation, they move with grace and majesty. The water surges around them, the waves lapping. Their huge feet sink into the muck, but they pull each foot free with ease as they move farther out to perceived safety.

Within minutes the entire herd is in the water, moving away from the shore. They cannot swim, but they have never needed to before. Some distance away from the shoreline, they stand and watch impassively as the corpse of the death bringer lies there. The small white creatures have drained it, and are now experimentally chewing on the meat. They do nothing beyond that. It seems that the rest of the death bringer is not to their taste. Its fluids have sated them, at least for the moment.

The newcomers turn toward the herd. Their eyes are glistening, their mouths drawn back to reveal ridges of sharp teeth that are not as formidable as those of the fallen death bringer, but are nonetheless impressive enough. They approach the water's edge, but do not enter. They look at the sweeping waves suspiciously.

The herd believes it is safe.

They sense it before they see it, a tidal change that cannot be ascribed to anything normal. Something is coming, displacing water at a staggering clip.

The water surges around them and the herd starts to back up. Then it stops, realizing collectively the danger that awaits it upon the shore. The small predators are stalking back and forth, eyeing the herd, searching out weaknesses.

Higher and higher surges the surf, and then something tears upward from below, blasting out of the water and releasing a challenging bellow that is louder than anything any member of the herd has ever encountered. It dwarfs the herd, and the small white creatures are jumping up and down in appreciation of the monstrosity's entrance, their own kill lying shriveled and pathetic nearby. The newly arrived water monster growls a second time, and then its head stabs forward, its mouth opening wide. A member of the herd is snatched up, the monster's teeth sinking in. Then the mammoth head tilts back, bites down, and swallows the herd member in two deftly bisected pieces.

And then it attacks again, and again; its appetite seems insatiable.

The herd is now in full panic. Some of the herd makes it to shore and finds itself in a life-and-death struggle for survival as the small white creatures surge forward, eager for fresh sustenance. The rest of the herd tries to cope with the monster from below. A few of them just stand there, helpless and hopeless. They have the right idea. In the end, none of it matters, because they are all going to die, and it's only the how of it that's to be determined.

The air is filled with the crunching of bones, and slurping, and death cries. The remains of the death bringer are already attracting flies and smaller insects seeking an easy meal.

The small white creatures and the being from the depths take no notice of the furry animals clinging to their treetop havens, watching with wide eyes. They are witnessing something truly historic at a time when the only capability of history being recorded is on a subconscious level. That is what happens now. The spectacle of otherworldly death and destruction being introduced to the still unnamed world is so traumatic that it fashions the beginnings of racial memory.

They, and their kind, will witness the advent of these otherworldly beings, and more besides. Beings that will become the basis for legends, the rudiments of those things which go bump in the night.

Relatively speaking, the newcomers are a mere handful. Yet they will annihilate the dominant species, turn upon each other, and eventually wipe out one another.

They are the First Wave.

There will be two more.

THE COUNTRY OF FEEND

i.

Nagel, king of the Ocular, loved the quiet time he took to do research. He liked the smell of it especially.

He would sit at his desk as the dark hours rolled one into the next, with some ancient tome stretched out in front of him. His study was simple and unassuming, as was the king himself. The desk was a family heirloom, constructed from large slabs of stone found on the Salsbree Plain, the original home of the Ocular. That was before the Ocular had relocated to Feend because of the appeal of the long dark.

Nagel lived in a castle that was likewise an heirloom, although it had actually predated the arrival of the Ocular themselves. The story went that there had been an outpost of Morts (short for "Mortals," or "humans," which was the manner in which some others chose to refer to them) in the castle—somehow overlooked during earlier conflicts—who had tried to stave off the Ocular incursion. They had lasted for a while, but not all that long, and eventually the Ocular had triumphed, as they always did.

The only drawback was that the castle, like the book, had been designed for the far smaller Morts. Renovation had been performed on Castle Skops (as it had been renamed, after one of the earliest and greatest of Ocular warriors) over the years, but every so often, Nagel still managed to bump his head on a low doorframe.

Nor was turning the pages in the books easy for him. Nagel, stood at fifteen feet high. So naturally the rest of him was likewise sizably proportioned, and the books were intended for far smaller creatures than he.

Nagel leaned back in his chair, and rubbed his eye tiredly. There was nothing else in the room to distract him, aside from piles of books stacked on shelves in the gray bricked corner of the otherwise unadorned chamber. Nagel had a long hank of silky black hair, braided, which began in the middle of his otherwise bald skull, arched slightly upward, and then hung halfway down his back. His ears were elegant and pointed, surprisingly delicate in contrast to the almost crude roughness of the rest of his broad face and muscular body. He was bare-chested, as was his habit, wearing a large brown woven kilt around his middle and thick sandals on his feet. When he sighed, as he did now in annoyance, it sounded like a tornado trapped inside of a cave.

Not only was the annoying smallness of the book getting to him, but also the scribbling upon the pages continually frustrated him. Sheet after sheet was decorated with small, black markings that he knew were the equivalent of what the Morts used for written language.

If it weren't for the translation texts pioneered by one of his more scholarly ancestors, he would have been completely stumped. His ancestor, Clowdus, had worked with a Mort slave of the time to develop a written text that would translate Mort words into Ocular writing and vice versa. Unfortunately the Mort had died, as Morts were wont to do, before Clowdus could complete the job. Furthermore, even with the Mort's aid, there had been only so much Clowdus could do because the texts were in a variety of scripts and the Mort knew only one of them. So Nagel struggled along with the translation texts as best he could, reading those volumes that were decipherable while staring at the others with boundless yearning.

It made no sense at all to Nagel that the Morts conversed in a variety of languages. The entire point of language was to communicate in both written and oral manners. If one person in one area was saying something incomprehensible to someone in another area, how could the creatures inhabiting the world ever have a hope of pulling together? Particularly at times of global threat?

Well, the answer to that was obvious, wasn't it.

They hadn't been able to. As far as Nagel was concerned, that had made all the difference.

But if the Morts were gone, or at least mostly gone (he knew some survived to this day, although he'd never seen one himself), their odor remained.

Any text he encountered always had that deep, almost intoxicating smell. It was thick and musty and full of promise, although the promise would never truly be fulfilled. Sometimes Nagel would spread a text in front of him, close his single great eye, flip through the pages quickly so that the aroma actually rose up from the pages, and breathe in through his nose so deeply that he fancied he might actually inhale the printed scribbling right off the paper.

It made him feel like a time traveler, giving him a much more visceral sense of the creatures who had written the books than merely looking at the text possibly could. The text was incomprehensible, but scent was universal.

He had not been around during those long gone days; it had been much before his time. All he knew of the Morts was what he'd learned as he'd grown up and been groomed for his position as king of the Ocular. Unfortunately what he'd learned of them hadn't been all that flattering, and his continued studies had gone a long way toward explaining just why the Morts had been so easily overcome. If they couldn't even communicate something as simple as "Help me!" without the aid of a translator, then one was forced to conclude that it had been a miracle they'd lasted as long as they had.

"Still becoming misty-eyed over the Morts?" came a sardonic voice from behind him.

Nagel did not even bother to turn his head. "No, honored Phemus," he replied. "Not misty-eyed at all. I shed no tears for them as a race. Only for the knowledge they possessed that's now lost to us."

Two medium-sized strides, both several yards long, and Phemus had come around the other side of the desk. Phemus was a head shorter than Nagel, but still reasonably tall for an Ocular. His face was more square than the generally triangular shape of Nagel's skull, and the tips of his ears drooped a bit as a result of his age. His head was shaved, and his single eye was deep blue, as was every other Ocular's eye . . . except Nagel's, which was brown. He wore thick robes of red and purple, and when he stood—as he was now doing in front of Nagel—he was absolutely immobile.

"Your quaint nostalgia . . . even your curious empathy . . . for an all-but-extinct race is admirable, my king. It nicely underscores the compassion for which you're so well known. But really . . . I think you give them far too much credit. They were here, and now they're all but gone. The stronger race won out and, in the end, all that matters is strength."

"Yet you describe me as compassionate, which is the antipathy of strength," Nagel pointed out.

"In you, it's a strength."

"Very smooth, Phemus. Very smooth."

"Well," said Phemus, smiling politely, "I did not become this polished overnight. I had many years practice as your father's advisor."

"As you will have with me, I daresay." Nagel leaned back in his chair; it creaked slightly under his weight. "My father loved this place," he said wistfully. "This room, I mean. He would be in here for hours. When I was younger, I'd sometimes come in here and couldn't see him."

"Couldn't . . . see him?"

"Because he'd vanished behind the stacks of books."

Phemus looked dubious at that. "Your father wasn't the smallest of individuals. How did he manage to do that?"

"That's how high the books were stacked, I suppose."

Clearly Phemus still doubted the scenario that Nagel was describing, but then he tilted his head slightly in deference to Nagel's recollection. Changing the subject, he said, "I thought you might want to look out the window."

Nagel studied him for a moment in puzzlement, then shrugged and rose from the chair. He walked across the study to the large window, carved from the rough-hewn stone, and looked out and down.

It was dark outside, as it was more often than not in Feend. Nagel leaned out, and saw a hundred of so of his subjects milling about. They had not ventured far from their homes, though. There were vast, green fields where the Ocular could assemble, play games, cluster in large groups to hear minstrels sing songs of great deeds. Those fields were not far from the castle or the small, simple homes that studded the general castle proximity. No one was on the fields. Instead they were gathered into small groups of three or four, standing around just outside their houses. Presumably they were chatting, talking peacefully. Strangely there was no sense of celebration, no joviality.

"They're afraid," said Nagel. "I can smell it from here."

"Yes."

"Afraid of the Piri."

"Yes," Phemus said again.

"Damn them," Nagel muttered, and then, stepping back from the window, he shouted "*Damn them!*" and slammed one of his massive fists against the wall. The wall didn't shake from the impact, but a few bits of loose brickwork fell.

"By 'them' can I assume you mean the Piri rather than our own people?"

"Of course," said Nagel impatiently as he leaned against his desk. He shook his head wearily. He'd been feeling much older than his relative youth lately. He had left adolesence behind, but not very far behind, and still felt naked and unsure in a world that expected much of him. "It's so unfair, Phemus. So blasted unfair. Feend should be a paradise for our people. The sunlight is minimal in this country . . ."

"Meaning our people can see most of the time," agreed Phemus, "since in the harsh light of day, we are all blind . . . all save you."

"All save me. You know, Phemus . . . sometimes I feel guilt over that. The happenstance of birth that gave me sight at all times while my people can only see in darkness."

"It's foolishness, my king . . . although I say that with all respect," Phemus added hastily.

Nagel didn't notice the apparent slight. "Why do things have to be this way, Phemus? Why is it that we cannot simply embrace the darkness that our nature drives us toward? Why do there have to animals like the Piri who exist only to prey upon us? To torment us? To force us to live in fear?"

"No one forces us to do anything, my king. We're presented with a situation. The way we respond to that situation . . . that is a choice."

"I do not choose this," Nagel said angrily, pointing in the direction of the window. "And my people should not have to choose this. This is supposed to be a day of celebration. The fiftieth anniversary of the day we took this castle, and of our settling in Feend. And they huddle and cower, no doubt jumping at the slightest shadow. This is . . ."

He was becoming more and more angry, and now it seemed as if the study could no longer contain his mounting ire. Nagel spun on his heel abruptly and stalked through the corridors of the castle. Phemus followed quickly, doing his best to keep up.

"Merrih!" he bellowed, and again, *"Merrih!"* When no immediate reply came to his shout, he stopped, turned, and said to a guard, "Where is Merrih? Have you seen her?"

"Perhaps her chambers, my king?" Phemus suggested.

"Yes, of course," said Nagel, and he started off in another direction, only to be halted in midstep as a young female Ocular sprinted toward him. She was adjusting the shoulders of her white gown laced with gold filigree, and her long braid of hair—similar to Nagel's own—swung wildly back and forth. A twinkling red pendant—a gift from her late mother—dangled around her neck. Her eye was the deepest blue of any in the kingdom, or at least Nagel thought as much. She reached barely up to his shoulders, but she was young, and Nagel had the feeling that she was going to wind up taller than he when she reached her full growth years from now.

"Uncle, how you shout!" she said in exasperation.

Phemus's brow furrowed. "Have respect for your king, young lady."

With a slightly mocking expression, she repeated herself but genuflected while she said it. This drew an even fiercer scowl from Phemus, but Nagel merely chuckled softly. Then, his face growing more serious, he said, "Merrih. Why are you not out with the citizens? It's a night of celebration."

"I know that, Uncle, but . . ." She shrugged.

"What? What is it?"

"Well . . . you know. The Piri . . ."

"Ahhh, the Piri," he said, as if encountering the notion for the first time. "We are nearly three times as big as the average Piri. Do you think it meet that we should be afraid of them?"

"I haven't thought of the . . . the 'meetness' of it. I just . . . I . . ." Her hand fluttered against the pendant.

"We have to set an example, Merrih." He took her by the shoulders. "Our people look to us for guidance. For leadership. We cannot let them down."

"I suppose not. It's just . . ."

"Just what?"

She looked from right to left as if afraid that she was being observed. Then, very softly, she said, "I dream of them."

"Oh, Merrih." He rolled his eye.

"I do! I dream of them coming at night, of attacking me, of . . ."

"Merrih, you have to face your fears," he said in exasperation.

She stared at him defiantly. In her attitude and posture, he could see so much of his late sister. It made his heart ache sometimes, just to look at her. "I don't see you out there. I don't see you facing any fears. I just see you standing here, lecturing me."

"And that's something I'm going to attend to right this very moment." He extended an elbow to her and said challengingly, "Coming along?"

Phemus looked from one to the other, and it seemed to Nagel that Phemus was judging him. And guards and various castle servants who'd been passing by were looking as well. Nagel suddenly felt very uncomfortable. Through sheer stupidity and impulse, he'd placed himself in an indelicate position. If Merrih defied him, left him standing there with his elbow out, he'd look like a great weak fool who couldn't even control his own niece. It wasn't as if Nagel was concerned with being perceived as ineffective and therefore subject to violent overthrow or assassination. Such activities were relegated to the Ocular's past. They had grown beyond that . . . or at least had been forced to by Firedraque treaties and other impositions.

Still, a king ruled by respect willingly given. If Merrih brushed him off . . .

But she didn't. Instead, she wrapped one of her slender arms around his and gazed up at him with polite patience, waiting for him to lead the way.

He stifled his sigh of relief, nodded as if he had fully expected her to cooperate, and then headed for the nearest stairs. The guards bowed their heads slightly as he passed, as was the custom and due deference to the king.

Phemus followed as always, gliding across the floor so quietly that one would almost have wondered if his feet were even touching it.

ii.

The night was cool, as it so often was in Feend. The citizens reacted with pleasure to the approach of their king. He warmly greeted everyone he saw, addressing them by name and thus making them feel honored and special.

He knew that their acceptance of him was not the easiest of things. His father had ruled for a very long time. An entire generation of Ocular had been born and raised to adulthood during the reign of his father. So it was disconcerting for them to have to make the transition. Although it seemed trite, Nagel was grateful for the fact that he, too, had been named "Nagel." As preposterous as it sounded, it likely made it easier for his subjects to adapt since the king at least had the same name.

"My friends!" he called out, his voice carrying up and down the great pathways that stretched as far as the eye could see. People were massing, moving toward him, eager to hear what he had to say. "I notice little celebration among you! The fields are empty. You cluster closely, like grazing animals. There is tentativeness in your jubilation that would fly in the face of this great day's intent. If I did not know better," and his mouth twisted in an almost contemptuous sneer, "I would think that the mighty Ocular are afraid of something!"

There was much shifting from one foot to the other and there were many chagrined looks. He heard someone mutter something and he called out, "Did I hear someone complaining of the Piri?"

Nervous looks then, one Ocular to the other. More foot shifting. "They are as nothing to us!" Nagel said firmly. "They are animals! Animals to be exterminated, that is all!"

"But they are not cooperating with their extermination."

It was a single voice speaking out clearly, rising above the others. Nagel recognized the voice's owner immediately: an elderly Ocular named Riel. Wielding a walking staff for support, he moved toward the king with a steady lurching manner, inevitable considering he only had one foot.

"When we first came here," growled Riel, "the Piri were few. Given time, they might even have died out. But they've grown in both number and strength because of us, Highness. Or were you under the impression that I lost this," and he pointed at the right ankle where a foot had once rested, "in a game of chance? The Piri took it." He turned and faced his audience. It didn't matter that he had told the tale so often that they'd all heard it who knew how many times. They still listened with respectful attention. "I was out there," and he pointed in the general direction of a forest in the distance. "Lying with my back against a tree, taking a rest, and suddenly two of the disgusting vermin were tearing at my ankle. I was damned lucky to get away in two pieces, leaving the one behind. And I'll never forget the disgusting noises coming from them as they devoured my foot."

Riel proceeded to replicate orally the slurping sounds as vividly as he could. Judging by the looks of disgust on the adults and even greater horror from the youngsters, he was succeeding admirably.

Exercising regal prerogative, Nagel said, "Yes, yes, we know. But it was, by your own admission, Riel, very far away. The Piri nest in the catacombs, and those are nowhere near here."

"But you never know when and where they'll be lurking," Riel pointed out.

Nagel's face darkened as if a great anger was seizing him. "And that is our destiny, then? To live not only in perpetual darkness, but perpetual fear? That is not who we are," and he thumped his chest. "Not unless you think we are soft! Perhaps we should resume our old warring ways. Firm up the softness. Take drastic steps so that we do not turn into frightened, mindless sheep, cowering near our homes. Look at us!" and he threw wide his arms to take in the entirety of the assemblage. "Are we not mighty? Are we not the things that should be lurking in the nightmares of the Piri? Should they not fear us? What sort of tribute are we to offer to our ancestors this day: a tribute tainted by our cowering, afraid of our own shadows? Is this how we honor their bravery? Their heroism? Their warrior spirit? By letting those . . . those blood-sucking terrorists dictate where we will and will not go?"

"No."

It was Merrih who had spoken, and Nagel looked at her with barely contained surprise. She had a ready smile upon her lips, and she was nodding approvingly. "You speak effectively and with great passion, Uncle," she said, and then spoke quietly so only he could hear and added, "Although, as always, you use a hundred words where ten would do." He smiled at that even as she raised her voice and called out, "I, for one, am ashamed that I even hesitated to enjoy the night."

And with that, her long braid swaying, Merrih headed toward the fields. With three great strides, Nagel was by her side. He laughed merrily as if she had said something remarkably witty and then, in a low tone, asked nervously, "Are they following us?"

Merrih risked a sidelong glance and then smiled. "You should have more confidence in your people, Uncle."

Sure enough, the Ocular were following their one-eyed king. They were doing so in silence, giving the proceeding more of a funereal air than a celebration of a joyous time. But at least they were following him. Or perhaps they were following Merrih. Either way, there was some forward motion occurring, and that was more than enough to cause relief to flood through Nagel.

They arrived at the field, and Merrih immediately slipped out of her footwear, tying the laces together and slinging it around her neck. Then she ran across the grass, clearly enjoying the feel of the green blades against her bare feet. She sang a traditional song of Ocular triumphs over their enemies, dancing in a small circle, her arms thrown wide and her head tilted back, basking in the moonlight. The moon was at the time of what the Ocular called "Open Eye," its full glowing radiance shining down upon them. It remained that way for several days every month, and was considered a time of good luck.

The adults hung back, and Nagel was about to say something to them. But then some of the very young Ocular, with whom Merrih had always been extremely popular, slipped from their parents' grasping hands and ran to join Merrih in her dance. Several of the parents cried out in alarm. Then they quickly silenced themselves. Nagel knew exactly why: They were concerned over how it would look if full-grown members of the Ocular race were acting in a tentative fashion while their children boldly indulged in celebration without the slightest care of threats or monsters. One could chalk it up to the childrens' naïveté . . . but also to cowardice on the part of the parents.

So instead they watched and worried as more and more young Ocular pranced and cavorted on the field. And then, slowly, one by one and then by the dozens, the adults came out to join them.

Within an hour the entire populace of Feend was enjoying itself upon the great field, displaying nary a care in the world.

Looking every inch the confident and vindicated ruler, Nagel strolled through the proceedings, his arms draped behind his back. His people greeted him or nodded to him or smiled at him in such a generous way that it was as if there had been no hesitation in their festivities. As if they had been out here all this time, and were beginning to wonder when in the world their leader would be joining them.

Food was trotted out in short order, and the air was filled with the pungent scent of cooking meat. Nagel's nostrils flared in anticipation. Various groups were engaging in assorted games, and over in one corner a well-known troupe of court thespians were performing one of their most beloved playlets, a retelling of a long-ago confrontation between one of the oldest and greatest of the Ocular, Polyphemus, and a pissant little Mort named Oolissus. Nagel was fascinated by the rendition, and they were just getting to the part where Polyphemus was about to roast Oolissus on a spit when he sensed his own advisor at his side. "Enjoying the tales of your namesake, Phemus?" he asked.

Phemus shrugged. "I have heard it many times before. Truly, my king, although I know the tale gives great amusement to the masses, I don't understand the allure. It tells the story of a triumph over a Mort, and an ancient Mort, for that matter. It's as if an adult went on at length boasting over the outwitting of a child."

"Don't dismiss such triumphs so lightly," Nagel replied. "Some of those children were extremely crafty."

"I'll grant you that," Phemus said with a rare smile. "But still . . . we have other, more potent challenges to worry about. Potential allies or potential enemies, depending upon—"

Nagel rolled his eye in exasperation. "Don't start, Phemus. It was yeoman's work encouraging my people to set aside their concerns for the Piri and enjoy themselves . . ."

"I'm not speaking of the Piri," Phemus said. "The Piri are animals *and* enemies, first and last. I'm speaking of those who have the potential to be either enemies *or* allies. The fact is that the Mandraques . . ."

"Oh, the Mandraques," said Nagel dismissively. "They are far too obsessed with trying to lay waste to each other to worry about us."

"And what of the Trulls . . . ?"

"The Trulls?" Nagel looked positively bewildered. "What of them? They maintain neutrality in all matters. The Trulls pose no threat . . ."

"Presuming their neutrality is legitimate." Phemus lowered his voice, glancing around as if worried that someone was listening in on them. "I have word through channels that their claims of neutrality may not be all that they appear. That they may be just that: claims. But that they were working in secret to better position themselves for dominance . . ."

"And who might these 'channels' be?" Nagel said skeptically.

"I regret that I cannot tell you at this time."

"You regret?" Nagel's brow darkened. He could display a fearsome scowl when he was of a mind to. "Honored Phemus, I wish to remind you of who you are . . . and who I am. Your 'regrets' mean nothing, while your refusal to answer a direct question from your liege means far, far more."

"With all respect, my king, my 'regrets' mean everything and more. I have constructed a very delicate web of intelligence gathering. The information that I have obtained in this way has served you in good stead in the past . . . nor did you find fault with the way in which I gathered it. When I speak in confidence with my sources, then in confidence it must remain, for I have given my word. Would you have me, whom you address as 'honored,' violate trust?"

"It's not a matter of that," Nagel began, "it's . . ."

That was when the screams began.

Nagel knew instantly. He knew from the direction they were coming in. He knew in the pit of his stomach, in the darkest and blackest reaches of his soul, he knew. Yet he had to go through the motions of not knowing, for if he allowed himself to succumb to the knowledge, he would have collapsed right then and there.

He sprinted across the field, Phemus trying to keep up with him and failing utterly. The children were backing up, their arms waving in terror, and they were all howling at once. Parents were charging forward, grabbing up their youngsters in their arms, and looking just as panicked as their offspring. They were running away from the source of the horror, while Nagel and a number of other Ocular were trying to push through. Nagel shouted commands as loudly as he could, so loudly that the tops of the highest trees were shaking, and still it was all he could do to shove through the stampeding crowd.

"No further! No further, Highness!" someone was shouting, and he skidded to a halt several feet shy of the hole. He stared down at it, gasping for breath, still unable to process fully what it was he was seeing.

It was more than a hole. It was a pit, at least four feet across and who knew how deep. There were still pebbles and clods of dirt rolling down into it. From the pit itself there was only darkness.

At the edge of the pit were Merrih's shoes. The ones she had removed and was carrying slung around her neck. There was, however, no sign of Merrih.

Nagel let out a roar liked the damned, a roar so thunderous that children who were already upset began to howl even louder. And then, ignoring cries of "No, Your Highness!" and "Sire, don't!," Nagel lunged toward the hole, throwing himself flat, and trying to clamber into it.

His shoulders were far too wide for the diameter of the hole, but still Nagel managed to get his head and one arm down into it. Surrounded as he was by pitch blackness, he was able to see perfectly.

So he had a clear view of the Piri who were coming right at him.

They were not moving upright. There wasn't room for them to do so. Nagel was able to make out a network of what appeared to be tunnels, like something carved by a great ant infestation, and Piri were slithering toward him from all sides, gliding along on their bellies while pulling themselves forward with their clawed hands. Their skin was pale and pasty, their eyes were blazing with nightfire, their thin lips were drawn back in that hideous death's head grimace that haunted many an Ocular child in his sleep. Their teeth were slightly extended from their mouths, clicking together eagerly.

"*Give her back!*" howled Nagel, and he grabbed at the nearest Piri. The parasitic creature dodged around and clawed at Nagel's arm. Nagel felt a deathly chill where the nails cut into his flesh, and then the Piri darted forward and sank its teeth into Nagel's outstretched arm.

With a roar of pain, his movements constricted, Nagel waved his arm about until the Piri shook loose. But there were more coming from all directions, and the only thing that saved him was that they were getting in each other's way trying to reach him. If they had been able to attach themselves to him en masse, he might well have been drained dry before he could do anything to prevent it.

The closest Piri made another try at Nagel's arm, but this time Nagel snapped his hand around quickly and it clamped across the Piri's head. Nagel's hand was so large in comparison with the creature's skull that it totally encompassed it. The Piri tried to pull loose, but it was too late. Nagel fiercely twisted his hand and ripped the Piri's head clear of its shoulders. The Piri's body fell down and away, and the others in Nagel's immediate sight line backed off, retreating into the depths of the tunnels they'd burrowed.

"Give her back!" he continued to shout, even as strong hands grabbed him around the upper body and hauled him back to the surface. There were horrified gasps from all onlookers as they saw the Piri's head in his hand, pale blood dripping from the base of its throat.

"Are you satisfied, O mighty king!" It was the contemptuous voice of Riel, limping toward him, and he was pointing to his leg that ended at the ankle. "What they did here, to me, wasn't enough for you, was it?" He stabbed a finger angrily at Nagel. "You denied the danger! You thought you were above it, that we could pretend we were safe. And your niece has paid for your blindness! She got what she deserved for trusting you, and you—"

Later, try has he might, Nagel would not remember the next few seconds. All he knew was that one moment, Riel was ranting at him, and the next moment, he had Riel pinned on the ground with both hands wrapped around the elder's throat. Riel was gasping for air, his skin turning blue, his eye bulging out of its socket. He was slapping ineffectually at Nagel's arms. The head of the Piri was lying nearby, having fallen out of Nagel's grasp. Other Ocular were upon Nagel, trying desperately to pry him off Riel during the mere seconds of life that remained to the old one.

It was not without effort that Nagel forced himself to release his grip on Riel's throat. He allowed himself to be pulled away and, hauled to his feet. As he stood there staring down at the fallen Ocular, the only sound that could be heard at that moment was Riel's desperate gasping for air.

"To your homes. All of you," commanded Nagel, and the Ocular needed no further urging. They vacated the area within seconds, leaving only Nagel, Phemus, and a handful of guards who clearly felt that their presence was better served there than anywhere else.

"We have to go down after her," Nagel said. His words sounded like a death knell in the darkness.

"But . . . my king . . ." Phemus began.

"Don't say it."

"It has to be said, my king! She cannot be retrieved! The Piri have her. She is gone."

"There must be a way."

Phemus glanced tentatively down the hole. "Who would have thought they would have been able to tunnel this far? Or perhaps the catacombs extend much further than we previously thought . . ."

"Do not speak of these things as if they are purely academic matters, Phemus!" growled Nagel. "Merrih's *life* is at stake!"

"Merrih's life is ended, my king, and the sooner you accept that—"

Nagel started to advance on him, and automatically Phemus took a cautious step back, almost making a misstep and tumbling down into the pit himself. "The tunnels down there," he said with urgency. "Were they large enough for you to enter to pursue them? For any Ocular, save children? Were they?"

Nagel's teeth rubbed against each other, making a disturbing grinding noise. "No," he finally conceded.

"And are you planning to convince your people that their children should be sent in to attack the Piri?"

"Of course not."

"Then let them be, my king. Let your people live their lives as they wish, huddled in their homes . . ."

"Live their lives in fear, you mean?"

"At least they're living!"

"*No!*" roared Nagel. "That is no life! It's a . . . a mockery of life, a half life! To life in the shadow of perpetual terror? Afraid that some . . . some vermin might snatch them away at any time? It cannot be allowed to continue! Don't you see that, Phemus?"

"I see that we are in a tragic situation . . ."

"If that is all you see, then you see nothing," Nagel said fiercely. "If these creatures are truly burrowing around under our feet, how long before they come up beneath our very homes, eh? Like the vermin they truly are? How long before they come to us in the cover of darkness and steal away more of us, before . . ." He put a hand to his brow and moaned softly, as if all the energy had been drained from him. "Gods . . . Merrih . . . I . . . I promised to protect her . . . I swore an oath, always to look after her, to . . ."

"I . . . am truly sorry, my king."

Nagel stood there like a great one-eyed statue. "Your sorrow means nothing, honored Phemus," he said finally. "Nor does mine. The only thing that will mean anything . . . is the end of these things." And he turned and brought down his foot upon the head of the Piri that was lying near him. It crushed easily beneath his weight, a mass of pale red spreading outward from under his foot. "And I will find that way, Phemus. I swear to the gods, and on Merrih's soul, I will find it."

THE CITY-STATE OF VENETS

i.

{Gorkon watches his brethren float in a pleasant haze. He watches his father, in particular, look at him with an utter lack of recognition, and not caring in the slightest who he is, and for the first time in his life, something within him snaps.}

{He does not know what it is during this particular tide that causes him to come to the end of his endurance. He had thought it would become easier, not progressively more difficult, to see his brethren drifting blissfully in a Klaa-induced twilight state; his parents, his two sisters, his friends, all wrapped neatly and tidily in the arms of Klaa, looking at him blankly when they look at him at all. They cannot share the place in which their minds dwell, nor do they have any interest in doing so. Even when they look at each other, they do so in such a way that Gorkon cannot tell for certain if their mutual presence is actually registering upon them. Either way, it does not especially seem to matter to them.}

{But it matters to him. He had not realized until just now, just this moment, how much it matters to him.}

{His people are graceful beneath the water as they float, frolic, and play with one another. They are more powerfully built than almost anything that dwells beneath the waves, and thus fear nothing. But that is not because of the power that pulses beneath their sleek, gray hides. It is because they are oblivious to any danger, thanks to the Klaa. Once it was the sea that nurtured them, supported them, blessed them with its all-encompassing presence. Now it is the Klaa, and they are unaware of the sea or each other or anything.}

{For the life of him, Gorkon doesn't know whether his roiling emotions stem from frustration or jealousy. Does he despise his people because of what they are? Or because of what he is not, and cannot ever be?}

{In the end, it really doesn't matter. All that matters is that Gorkon has reached his breaking point, and action must be taken. As the lifespan of the Markene is measured, Gorkon is not at all old. Just barely out of his adolescence. But he resolves that he will grow no older.}

{Like all the Markene, his legs are powerful beyond measure when it comes to propelling him through the water. They are quadruple-jointed so that, when he moves through the water, his legs almost undulate in their up-and-down rhythmic kicking motion. In terms of land use they are inefficient, but the Markene have no interest in existing on land anyway. That is the province of the Merk, something that the Markene are more than happy to leave to them. The Markene have the sea, they have their Klaa, and all are content.}

{All save for Gorkon, who must attend to this burning frustration in his heart immediately, before another moment passes.}

{Fortunately, he knows exactly where to go: The Resting Point.}

{The Resting Point, little more than a strip of grass and rock protruding from the water, is not large, and not far. Once upon a time, when the Markene were concerned about such things as hopeless love or extreme age to the point where existence was intolerable, the Resting Point was where Markene went to dispose of themselves once and for all. It was not a difficult undertaking. The water surrounding the Resting Point was nice and deep. All one had to do was go toward the bottom of the seabed, head toward the surface with sufficient velocity, launch at the proper angle, and one could beach oneself nicely upon the Resting Point and then just . . . lie there. The tide never brings the water high enough to immerse the Resting Point, so it was just a matter of allowing nature to take its course.}

{At first, as Gorkon approaches the Resting Point, he does so with a heavy soul. The closer he draws to it, though, the more relaxed he feels, and the more his heart sings with joy. If there is any doubt in his mind as to the rightness of his actions, all he has to do is envision his brethren floating around in their Klaa-induced haze and it is sufficient to steel his resolve once more.}

{It wasn't as if they'd always been absorbed into the nerveless joys of Klaa. Gorkon seems to remember that, in his youth, Klaa had been only an occasional pastime. He is sure there had been other things. At least, he thinks he is sure of it. As he has gotten older, however, Klaa had seemed to dominate all their waking time, and even much of their sleeping time. As a result, Gorkon had felt more and more isolated. Indeed, some might argue that this moment, this final act of Gorkon's life, is no shock at all, but instead inevitable.}

{By the change in the water around him, Gorkon knows that he is coming to the Resting Point. He has swum past there any number of times, and is familiar with the reefs and topography of the area underwater, as well as the fact that the current turns warm there for no discernible reason. He angles down, down toward the bottom, and rests there a moment contemplating his fate. He had wondered if, when faced with the final instant of decision, his resolve would waver. Such does not seem to be the case. He feels utterly alone in the world. If he ended his life, none would miss him, so what was the point in prolonging it?}

{He pauses a moment before making the final leap. His feet sink into the silt. He used to find the shifting of dirt beneath his webbed toes to be amusing. Now such hollow entertainment feels exceedingly quaint, even trivial, harking back to halcyon times when he knew nothing about nothing. The truth is, he still knows nothing about nothing. He's just more willing to admit it now, and further, admits the futility of trying to learn. He attempts picturing the faces of his loved ones in his mind. He tries to envision their individual expressions, but is not able to. Each one seems much like the other. Pure, bland bliss. No aspiration. No individuality. And the worst part is, whenever they're not that way, they are cranky and irritable until such time that they can be that way again. They are with him, and all they want to be is away from him and back with the Klaa. He means that little to them.}

{With that serving as the final impetus, he springs from the bottom of the sea. He almost imagines that it pulls at his feet, trying to drag him back, to make him reconsider his decision. He does not do so. The efficient undulation of his legs sends him higher, faster, the water hurtling past him. The drag against his sleek body is almost stimulating, a trill of pleasure working its way through him. The sea is caressing him, kissing him farewell. It is the single most exotic, and erotic, moment of his life, and then he bursts from the sea in a swell of water, angling through the air. He throws his arms to either side, his webbed fingers flexing and grasping at nothing, and then lands heavily. The impact jolts him and he feels that familiar heaviness settling into his chest. It's the heaviness that always occurs whenever he emerges from the water. Occasionally his kind are known to bask in the sun, but they can only do so for short periods before the sheer weight of their massive bodies makes it impossible for them to remain. He can breathe the air for a time, but not forever, and his body will dry out in short order either way. It will be a race to see whether his body collapses under its own weight before the lack of water proves fatal for his respiratory system.}

{He lies flat upon the grass, making no effort to turn his head. His great black eyes remain open, although a thin, clear shell of an eyelid clicks open and closed over them to protect them. His gray skin is hairless, his snout is small but round and not unattractive. His mouth is slightly open, drawing in air in large gulps in hopes of hastening his end. On his back, his dorsal fin quivers slightly, the only outward manifestation of the fear that is beginning to suffuse him. The wisdom of his course of action is starting to elude him, but he refuses to let himself be swayed by last minute uncertainties.}

{He bids a silent good-bye to his family and wonders if they will even notice that he is gone. Probably not.}

{And that is when he hears the voice.}

"What the scorch are you doing there?"

The voice was that of an older man, although not that old. It sounded more confused than anything else, as if it could not fathom what Gorkon might possibly be doing in this place . . . while at the same time knowing precisely what was going on, but just not wanting to make an issue out of it. Moreover, the voice sounded vaguely familiar, but Gorkon couldn't quite place it. Gorkon felt embarrassed. He didn't know why he should, for he was about to die, so, embarrassment should not have been a prominent concern for him. Yet it was.

He wanted to keep his face staring up at the sky. He wanted his body to shut down soon, sooner, immediately. He felt the beginning of pressure upon his respiratory and circulatory system. It was not, however, transpiring quickly enough. In the meantime the voice of the newcomer was continuing to wheedle at him, and finally he looked to see who it was that was speaking and ruining the elegance of his suicide.

Gorkon was both impressed and horrified by the answer.

The individual who had been speaking to him, and who now seemed quite pleased that Gorkon had deigned to look at him, was a stark contrast to Gorkon. Gorkon's people wore no clothing, save for a few random ornaments signifying their heritage or representing awards presented them by the rulers of the Sirene. Clothing would simply serve as a useless drag as they traversed the currents. It was very different for the Merk, the species that—along with the Markene—constituted the race known as the Sirene. The Merk traversed both land and water with equal facility. They were the thinkers, the rulers, the aristocrats. Most of all, they controlled the Klaa, and had always done so for as long as Gorkon knew.

It was a Merk who was now gazing upon Gorkon with a bemused air. He was clearly a noble, but wore his nobility as a beggar wore rags: it hung upon him in a shapeless fashion, unattended to and unpleasant to contemplate. His upper torso lacked definition and was flabby. If he was or once was a warrior, he had done nothing to maintain whatever fighting form he once had. Both species of the Sirene possessed webbed fingers and toes, but that was the only resemblance that the newcomer and his kind bore to the heavyset, water-bound Markene. The

Merk's scaled skin was deeply brown, colored by the sun that was unforgiving to the more sensitive hide of the Markene. The Merk's legs bent only at the knees, making his kind far less efficient swimmers than the Markene, and the dorsal fin that the Merk possessed was merely a small, almost vestigial bit of flesh and bone on his back.

The Merk also sported hair, unlike the Markene. Their hair did not resemble traditional hair so much as it did seaweed. Despite appearances, it was not plant growth, but merely thick strands of pale green hair that had a seaweedlike appearance. Merk had black, pitiless eyes like the Markene, but they were heavily shielded by extended brows that were thick bone ridges, reducing whatever problem the sun might represent.

This particular Merk, gazing upon Gorkon with such unabashed curiosity, was floating not far from the Resting Point. He was sitting in a small, one-man boat that he was moving by means of a foot-operated propeller device. At the moment, however, he was allowing it to float nearby, apparently so he could simply stare at Gorkon and find some mild amusement in him.

"Did you not hear me?" he prompted. He never raised his voice, nor spoke in a tone that indicated anything other than genteel befuddlement. "What are you doing out here?"

"I am attempting to kill myself." He felt a bit sheepish, since his stated intention sounded so preposterous, bordering on inane.

If the Merk had formed an opinion about him, and that opinion was somehow diminished by Gorkon's intent on self-demise, he did not indicate it as such. "Ah. Well. Don't let me get in your way then." He then leaned back in his one-occupant vessel and watched, as if waiting to be entertained at some sort of performance.

"You are . . . making me uncomfortable," Gorkon said at last.

This did not seem to bother the floating Merk particularly. "Ah. Well. I daresay your discomfort will cease once you have died. How long do you think your death will require?"

"I . . . do not know," Gordon admitted.

"Well, I do have other places to be and other things to do, so if you could find a way to hurry it up, I would be most obliged."

Gorkon was becoming cross with the situation. He even propped himself up slightly. "I have never come to the Resting Point to die before!"

"Is there somewhere else you usually go?"

"You mock me!"

"Never! I would never do such a thing. Never in . . . all right, yes, I mock you. But only because you are about to destroy yourself and therefore will not survive to make me pay for my disrespect."

Now Gorkon's ire was truly beginning to rise to the breaking point and beyond. His despair was not being accorded the dignity for its release that he felt it was due. "Why, you . . . I don't care if you are nobility, you—"

"I would have thought," replied the noble, whoever he was, "that you wouldn't have cared about anything at all. That is the point of suicide, is it not? That you are beyond caring?" He shrugged. "Or perhaps I am misunderstanding that. Please clarify it for me, if you wish, for it is something with which I do not have a great deal of familiarity."

Gorkon sighed heavily, his breath rattling around in his chest. "I . . . I suppose it could be argued that way, yes," he admitted.

"Ah. And yet you care what I think. Care so much what I, a total stranger, think of you, that you're becoming positively incensed about it." His chair continued to bob in the water, like a floating and taunting conscience. He tilted his head slightly, studying Gorkon with great thought. "You are strange for a Markene. I thought all your type drifted in the sea all day, dreaming of . . . well, I wouldn't presume to know of what. But in a sort of stupor."

This characterization of his people caused Gorkon to bristle slightly, but he felt a sort of inner deflation, as he had to admit to himself the accuracy of it. He prided himself on being reasonable, and using his brain in a way that his brethren deliberately chose not to. Was he to castigate or attack this . . . this taunter . . . for the unthinkable act of speaking the truth? With a heavy resignation, he said, "Yes. So my kind does."

"But you do not."

"No."

"Why?"

"I choose not to."

The floating Merk scratched his head thoughtfully with his long fingers. "Is that so?"

That was all he said, with no implication beyond that. Yet Gorkon unaccountably felt shame, because he knew it was not so, and he couldn't help but feel that this person somehow knew it wasn't so as well. "No," he admitted. "I am . . . I have violent reactions to Klaa. I tried it, I did. But there was nothing pleasurable in it for me. My head felt as if it were about to explode. I had seizures, and awful visions of . . . of darkness and misery. I did not see what the others saw. I have no idea what I saw."

"The truth, perhaps?"

Gorkon looked at him oddly, not sure what to make of that comment. "What truth? What are you talking about?"

"Oh, don't worry about it," said the Merk dismissively. "No one knows what

I'm talking about. Ask my wife. Ask anyone. Even I don't know what I'm talking about half the time, and the other half, I only pretend to."

"I see," said Gorkon, who didn't.

A long moment of silence passed, and then the Merk said, in a voice so dripping with sympathy that Gorkon wasn't entirely certain whether he was being sarcastic or not, "It must be terrible to be so lonely in the midst of a crowd."

"It is," Gorkon allowed.

"I can see why it would drive you to this."

"You do? So you understand."

"Oh, no," said the Merk quickly. "No, I don't understand it. You have other options, so I don't understand why you take the one option that permits no others. But, as you've made quite clear, it's your business, not mine. Do as you wish. Good day . . . or at least may what's left of yours be good."

With that he began to paddle, angling the rudder so that the little boat started to move away.

Gorkon had felt nothing but irritation and humiliation from the moment the Merk had shown up, unasked and undesired, and began speaking in that taunting and derisive manner. With the Merk departing, Gorkon had exactly what he'd wanted: solitude and the opportunity to let nature take both its course and his life. However, as was so often the case, *having* something was turning out to be not as rewarding as *wanting* it.

The result was that Gorkon unaccountably felt abandoned. Before he gave full thought to what he was doing, he had pushed himself off the rock and eased his bulk back into the water. "Wait!" he called, his voice burbling water since half his face had submerged before he could splash back up to the surface. A fast kick of his legs and he was beside the boat. The Merk looked at him with guarded curiosity. "What options?"

"Options?"

"Yes. You said I had other options."

"Did I?" The Merk frowned, looking thoughtful, as if he were scrounging around for some tidbit of something rattling around in his skull. "Oh. Yes. I suppose I did."

"What are they?"

"How would I know?"

"How—?" Gorkon suddenly felt ready to climb back out onto the rock. "How would you know? *You're* the one who told me . . . !"

"I said there were options because there are always options . . . unless, of course, you foolishly kill yourself, in which event there no longer are, as I believe I mentioned."

"Yes, you did. But I don't know what they are . . ."

"What do you call yourself?" the Merk demanded abruptly.

"G-Gorkon . . ."

"My dear Gorkon," said the Merk with a hint of scolding, "if you, with all your brain power completely unimpeded by the use of Klaa, are still unable to come up with any possibilities, then it really doesn't say much for your species, now, does it? Do you never think about things?"

"No. Never."

"Oh." The Merk blinked. "Well . . . your candor is commendable, I suppose." He pursed his lips, pondering the situation. "Well," he said finally, "now is as good a time as any to start, wouldn't you say? Tell you what, Gorkon: I'll strike a bargain with you. You come back to this place in five suns. I give you that long to come up with options. I'm willing to make the commitment of my time if you are."

"I . . ." Gorkon hesitated.

"What have you to lose? You can always take your own life five suns from now, can you not?"

"I suppose."

"Then it's settled."

"All right . . ."

"I shall see you in five suns. Do not disappoint me." He began to paddle away in his boat.

"And what if I do disappoint you?" demanded Gorkon.

"Then you'll disappoint yourself as well."

"Wait!"

The Merk stopped the small boat, tossing a glance over his shoulder, his face puckered in question.

"You . . . did not tell me your name."

"Ruark," the Merk said.

"That's interesting. We have a ruler by the same name."

"An astounding coincidence," Ruark deadpanned as he paddled his boat away. "I never get tired of hearing about it."

ii.

Tulisia Sydonis was not in a good mood. She was, however, in a typical mood.

"Where the depths have you been, Ruark?" she demanded of her husband.

Ruark, for his part, smiled and bobbed his head and said, "Yes, my dear," as he padded across the floor of their bedchamber.

Her idiot husband's response had been a non sequitur, but she was used to that. Once she would have reamed him out for it; now it didn't even warrant a comment. Tulisia had slept late, as she often did, and was rising from the watery enclosure that was her bed. She rubbed the water from her eyes and ran her webbed fingers through her seaweed hair. She muttered, "I can already tell, I'm not going to be able to do a damned thing with it today."

"You worry far too much, my dear," Ruark assured her. "You are the standard of beauty for all Venets. If you were to do nothing with your hair save to leave it in a great hanging clump, all female Merks throughout the land would emulate your daring new style."

She eyed him suspiciously as she eased herself out of the enclosure. Standing naked and dripping on the floor, she demanded, "Are you mocking me? I believe you are mocking me."

"Alas," he said sadly, "I hear that often. I'm beginning to think I'm incapable of giving a compliment and having it understood as such."

"What are you *talking* about?"

"Nothing. That's what I always talk about."

"Yes, I know," she said impatiently. "Where were you?"

"Out thinking."

"You don't think."

"Yes, I know," said Ruark. "I was hoping to remember how to go about it. It did not come. Maybe it shall another day."

"I wouldn't hold out any great hopes of it."

Clearly having heard the conversation, her servants knocked at the door. Tulisia bade them enter, and two young females padded in quickly, each holding large towels. Tulisia held her arms straight up as they proceeded to rub her down. A third servant rolled in a large mirror so that Tulisia could study her naked body with a keen and unforgiving eye, as she did every morning.

Despite her age . . . indeed, because of her age . . . she decided she was satisfied with her body's state this day. She still possessed the roundness and hardness of a Merk half her age. Any Merk male in his right mind would thirst to take advantage of her body. That naturally explained why Ruark, as always, displayed no interest. This suited Tulisia just fine. She had other, bigger things to worry about.

"Unpleasant dreams last night?" he asked out of the blue.

The fact that he inquired at all startled Tulisia. Dried of her overnight moisture, she was being fitted by her aides with the gown she'd be wearing that day. It was mostly a single bolt of purple cloth that wrapped around her, leaving one breast exposed, as was the current fashion. "How did you know?" she demanded suspiciously.

"You splashed around and cried out. It wasn't all that difficult to determine," he said. "What was bothering you?"

"Do you care?"

"No," he said with his usual, insufferably cheerful tone. "But I figured it would be polite to ask."

"If you must know . . ."

"Which I don't," he was quick to assure her.

". . . I was having nightmares about the Travelers," she continued as if she hadn't spoken. Since she rarely paid attention to him when he did speak, ignoring him came easily to her.

"The Travelers?" he echoed.

"Yes," she said impatiently, "the Travelers." She turned this way and that, intently regarding her image in the mirror. She was delicately placing combs in her hair, each glimmering with a delicate, translucent pinkish glow. "It was brutal."

"I daresay. They certainly give me nightmares."

"Of course they do. And I am not certain how much longer I will choose to allow them to have that sort of control over me."

Her words were so forceful, her manner so threatening, that her fearful servants slightly backed away from her. She noticed their cowering and bristled in anger. "What manner of Sirene are you," she demanded of them, "that merely mentioning the Travelers causes you to shrink in terror?" When they didn't respond, she swung her hand sweepingly and bellowed, "Go! Just go!" Offering no argument, they hustled from the room, almost dropping various towels and clothing items. Tulisia Sydonis watched them go, and then she turned toward Ruark Sydonis while pointing with quivering finger. "You see! You see what we have to tolerate? It is wrong, Ruark. Wrong in every aspect, wrong no matter how it's regarded."

"My dear, is it not early in the day for this sort of discussion?" he said pleadingly. "You've only just awoken. You know you're not at your best when you've first dried. Become aware of the—"

"I'll tell you what I'm aware of, Ruark," she told him. Several long, tapering pieces of cloth were draped from her wrists, and they brushed across the floor as she swung her arm about. "I am aware that three-quarters of this godsforsaken sphere is water. I am aware that we absolutely, unequivocally, control the waters. Do you understand that? As the 'Draques battle each other and lay waste to one another with mind-boggling ferocity, quarreling over every scrap of terrain they can, no one dares to challenge us for supremacy of the seas and oceans. No one . . . save for the Travelers. And they go where they wish and do what they want without offering us anything in tribute. Not a single damned thing. How dare they?"

"Well, my dear," he said coolly, "I suppose they dare because they serve the Overseer. And they know that none would go against the Overseer. I mean, I know you, milady Tulisia, and I know not even you would . . ."

His voice trailed off as he saw the defiant look in her eyes. He cocked his head slightly as if he had lifted a rock and were staring with great fascination at the life scuttling around beneath it. "You know . . . I wanted to talk to you about the party you're planning for a few suns from now. I thought it might be nice to—"

"Don't change the subject," she told him, advancing on him. "You're the one who brought it up."

"Did I?" His eyes were wide with innocence. "I intended to bring up nothing. I chat. I talk. I blather. That's what I do. That's all I do. I know this of a certainty because you've told me that any number of times."

"I'm aware of that, you fool," she snapped. "But you started discussing the Travelers and the Overseer. If you do not have the nerve to see the discussion through . . ."

"See it through to where?" he asked helplessly. "The Travelers are the Travelers. They are who they are, and go where they wish, and none can gainsay them. It has always been that way, and will always be that way as much as we might desire otherwise. The Twelve Races assembled cannot stand against the Travelers or the Overseer."

"The Twelve Races are scrambling for the crumbs that the Overseer and his slaves leave in their wake. They are too divided to be of any threat."

"They would be of no threat even if united."

"We do not know that."

"We do not?" he asked.

"No. For none have ever stood up to them. Can you imagine, Ruark Sydonis?" she said as she approached him. He flinched automatically, but she merely rested her hands upon his shoulders. She spoke with growing intensity. "Can you imagine if the Sirene led the way? If we defied the Travelers? Let them know that we will no longer be taken for granted or submit to them? That rather than treating us as prisoners on this world, and they our guardians, they instead realized that we are a force to be reckoned with?"

"But we *are* prisoners on this world," he pointed out. "The fact that we are a force to be reckoned with is why we're here in the first place, isn't it? Is why our ancestors were sent here, marooned here . . ."

"That's the way it was," she said fiercely, "but it is not the way it always has to be. At what point does the Damned World become ours?"

"Well . . . I suppose never."

"I suppose differently," she replied. "I need to know right here, right now, whether you will be with me or not."

"With you in what, my dear? I do not even understand what it is that we're discussing . . ."

"*Ohhh!*" Her hands had been resting on his shoulders, but now she shoved him away and stepped back, shaking her head. "Are you completely feeble-minded? Do you not understand anything?"

"No. Well . . . yes, and no . . . actually," he frowned, "I'm not entirely sure how to answer that question because of the way it's phrased. Perhaps if you . . ."

"Oh, shut up," she snapped.

"All right," he said, instantly agreeable. "If that's what you desire, that's what I'll do."

She was no longer paying him any mind. She was, instead, envisioning the Travelers. Mighty, invincible, striding the Damned World, certain in their dominance. For a very long time, the frustration had eaten away at her like a cancer, giving her no peace in her waking or her sleeping moments.

She strode away from him, threw open the great doors that opened onto their balcony. She stepped out, closing her eyes, feeling the sea breeze in her face, and sniffing the moist air. Above, the sun's rays beamed down caressingly. She looked out upon the city-state of Venets. The canals stretched beneath her, with the Merk swimming or boating along, going about their business. Several of them spotted her standing there, looking down upon them, and they waved eagerly in hope that she would notice them. Tulisia did so, smiling and nodding and waving her hand in response.

Tulisia couldn't help but dwell on what it would be like if it were more than just the Sirene who looked up to her reverently and sought her blessing. What if it were members of all the Twelve Races? What if their dominance of the water upon the Damned World could be made to have real significance?

She looked contemptuously at the man she'd married in order to acquire power. He smiled in his typically vacant manner. She snorted and turned away from him, waved once more to the throngs below and imagined the canals, the courtyards, every square inch of Venets crowded with members of the Banished from every corner of the Damned World. All of them, calling her name, singing their praises, blessing her for freeing them of the constant oppression of the Overseer and his Travelers.

Whether they walked and swam and flew forward together in unity, or destroyed one another in one great, final conflagration, it would be their decision to make and their future to chart.

She stood there upon the balcony, drinking in the future that had yet to be writ, as her husband—whom she intended to dispose of at the earliest opportunity—continued to smile beatifically.

THE UNDERGROUND

She kneels before the Orb. It is hers and no one else's. It is both her strength and her weakness. Her distorted features are even more distorted in its gleaming, curved surface.

She gazes at it lovingly, longingly. It is a gift from the gods, her only gift. When she speaks to it, she likes to pretend that it is a direct line to the gods themselves. That they are listening to her when they have forsaken all others.

"Give me the will," she whispers, delicately placing her hands on either side. It is smooth and cold to the touch. "Give me the will to deal with my sons . . . the will to love them, to help them. And the will not to kill them with my own hands."

The Orb makes no reply save that which is in her own imagination. But, for the time being, it serves.

i.

Ulurac kept his head down as the tunnel walls rushed past him. His helmet was low to his head, and his long brown hair—braided and normally hanging to the small of his back—was tucked up and around and shoved underneath the helmet. He squinted against the blast of dank air that hammered at his face, his broad, flat nose twitching as it always did uncontrollably when he was apprehensive. He clutched the sides of the small but speedy vehicle with his meaty fists and kept waiting for the car to fly off the track and crash headlong into the nearest slab of rock. He knew deep down that it wouldn't happen. Never in the long history of Trulling—the art of riding a Trull car—had there been such a mishap. That didn't prevent him from continuing to white-knuckle it the entire ride, silently cursing the name of his mother as he did so. Always silently, though. Never, ever aloud. He was terrified, but he wasn't insane.

Now Eutok . . . Eutok never had such concerns. Ulurac, in a sideways manner that was theoretically supposed to take his mind off his concerns, cast his thoughts back to the days when he and his brother, Eutok, would go Trulling together. Even in those days Ulurac would be seized with barely controlled panic. Not Eutok, no. He would open his mouth and roar and holler like the damned . . . providing the damned were in an exceptionally good mood. His voice would echo through the tunnels, and every Trull within earshot would know when the two young princes were on their way to some new misadventure.

Since that time, Ulurac and Eutok had gone in very different directions, become very different people. There was not much about Eutok that Ulurac would have desired to emulate, but . . . that reckless fearlessness was certainly one of the few things.

Knowing that he was approaching the termination point, Ulurac began to massage the brake handle. The Truller car automatically started to slow. Ulurac realized that he'd been holding his breath for some time, and tried to force himself to inhale and exhale normally. He was only partly successful. "Breathe, breathe," he muttered to himself, for it certainly wouldn't do to have him step off the Truller and look like a ghost. Or worse, trembling and frightened over a ride that young Trulls would have enthusiastically experienced.

The Truller rolled on its tracks off to one side and bumped to a gentle halt. The hiss of air being released from the brakes was drowned out by the loud and prolonged "phewwwwww" that came from Ulurac's lips.

He vaulted from the Truller, took several steps, then mentally chastised himself and reached back into the Truller. His hand wrapped around his walking staff as he withdrew it. His fingers slid over the intricate carvings that featured stylized representations of all those who had gone before him and had borne the position he now had: Spiritu Sanctum, the spiritual leader of the Trulls. Eventually, he knew, his own likeness would be carved onto the staff when his successor took over the position. He hoped that, at the very least, it would be someone who had an easier time Trulling than he.

He made his way through the caves, and as he drew closer to the Hub, he encountered more and more of his people. Without exception they bowed to him, greeted him, whispered his name in reverence. Some went so far as to kneel, bending their stubby legs and bowing their heads in earnest supplication of receiving his favor. They asked for his blessing for some thing or another: a new child, a new tool, a new hole in which to reside. All these and more besides, with such frequency and to such a degree that he was beginning to wonder if it was healthy. The way in which they asked for his "blessings" wasn't all that different from the way one might pray to a god. Ulurac did not for one instant desire his people to think of him as a god, or even remotely godlike. He had far too many things to worry about to contemplate such a blasphemy.

So to each of them he muttered a few words, occasionally while placing a hand on his or her head, and then off he would go. He'd brought a cloak with him, more as a symbol of his calling than out of any need for protection. Now he raised the hood to help obscure his face so that, while his fellow Trulls would know a man of faith walked among them, they might not realize it was Ulurac himself until he was already gone.

He moved through the Hub, and wondered why it seemed a bit dimmer than he'd recalled. He looked to the glowing lanterns that lined the wall, all of them powered by hotstar chips. He tapped one of them lightly with his finger and the lantern flickered a bit, flaring a shade brighter before returning to its previous brightness.

Although the Trulls resided in the underground, they had never developed the sort of eyes that could see perfectly in the dark. That had been as much by choice as anything else, for those would have made them uncomfortably similar to the Piri, and that was a resemblance no Trull wanted. The lanterns had always been there to provide a comforting luminescence. It concerned Ulurac a bit that the lanterns didn't seem as bright as before. But the hotstars never varied in their energy output, which meant the problem was in his eyes. That did not sit well with Ulurac at all.

In the distance he could hear the continued clanking and clanging of Trulls hard at work. When he had lived in the Hub full-time, the constant and steady noises had become so much a part of his daily existence that he had ceased noticing them. Whenever he made the occasional return, as he was doing now, the overwhelming and incessant noise presented itself anew. It made him wonder if Trulls who lived in the Hub weren't slowly going deaf and they just hadn't figured it out yet. His eyes beginning to fade, his people losing their hearing. The future of the Trulls did not appear as bright as it once was. And the sad truth for Ulurac was that there was no one he could talk to about it. He carried this burden, as he did all burdens, deep in his heart.

There were guards at the main gates of the Hub; each was armed with gargantuan axes that had heads carved from the hardest stone. Ulurac slogged forward, one massive foot in front of the other, his staff making a steady clacking noise on the rocky tunnel floor.

The guards did not even seem to look at him, and yet in unison they snapped their axes around so that they were holding them firmly crosswise across their chests at attention. They turned to face each other in perfect synchronization, as if operating via some sort of mutual cue. Then they stepped back, gripping the gate handles and swinging them wide so that Ulurac could enter unmolested. The stone gates swung open on oiled hinges, and Ulurac entered displaying a swagger that exuded a confidence he didn't feel.

What does she want? The thought kept rattling through his brain. *What does she want and what did I do? Or, even better, what did Eutok do that I'm going to be blamed for?*

As if capable of reading his very thoughts . . . an attribute that Ulurac would have ascribed to his brother on any number of occasions . . . Eutok strode toward him as the gates swung noiselessly shut behind Ulurac.

Through long years of habit, Ulurac tended to move slowly, even ponderously, as if the weight of years hung heavily upon him. He wasn't entirely sure when he had acquired that habit. Perhaps it stemmed from the fact that so many people asked him to stop and give of his time that he'd conditioned himself not to walk very fast.

Eutok was quite the opposite. Built similarly to his older brother, Eutok moved with his shoulders hunched and his head down, almost as if he was prepared to walk right over anyone unfortunate enough to drift into his path. What he lacked in subtlety, he more than made up for in an air of self-importance. He was clad in black and brown leathers, his stone ax strapped to his back and his sling dangling from his hip. He looked ready to go to war, which was his typical mode of dress. His eyes snapped with the sort of amusement that Ulurac rarely, if ever, felt. Ulurac resented the hell out of him for it, and felt guilty about that resentment . . . but not too guilty.

Without preamble, before Eutok could get a word out, Ulurac waddled toward his brother and demanded, "What did you do?"

Eutok affected a look of bewildered hurt. "Do? What did *I* do?" he grunted. "What makes you think I did anything at all?"

"Because Mother summoned us," shot back Ulurac, hands on his hips, "and typically when she summons us, it's because you've been up to some mischief. A mischief that I invariably get blamed for because she still thinks that I'm supposed to be riding herd on you."

"I don't need anyone to ride herd on me!" Eutok informed him. "I'm Chancellor of the Trulls! I ride herd on others!"

"Yes, well," and Ulurac swaggered past Eutok, disdaining to cast a glance at him, "since I'm the older brother, apparently Mother feels I have that added responsibility of attending to you, no matter what sort of exalted title you take."

"You're older by ten minutes, and I didn't 'take' the title," Eutok protested as he

fell into step just behind Ulurac. "It was given me by our people after my prede-
cessor passed away."

"Said passing away occurring thirty seconds after your ax was found buried in
his skull."

"Pure coincidence."

Ulurac snorted at that. It was not Eutok's naked ambition that bothered him so
much as it was his wide-eyed protests that he was not responsible for the trail of
violence that lay behind him in his career. "As you say," he said, and waved dismissively.

Any Trulls they passed scrambled to get out of their way. Most of them lowered
their gazes, for it was considered to be a sacrilege to look upon both the Chancellor and the Spiritu Sanctum. Worse than sacrilege, for none was truly fit to gaze
upon that much glory at one time. The only Trulls who met Ulurac's gaze were
the very young, who stared at them with the sort of innocence that only children
could muster. If their parents happened to notice they were looking, they quickly
cuffed their heads and made them look away.

This bothered Ulurac. It seemed to him lately that there had been a growing
gap between himself and his people, and this sort of behavior only widened that
gap. Unfortunately, he had no time to dwell on it. The queen, their mother, had
summoned them, and concerns over the relations between nobility and the
masses would have to wait for another day.

If only the damned hammering would stop . . .

ii.

Eurella rubbed softly at either side of her head, trying to ease the distant pain that
she had to deal with almost daily.

It was not the constant sound of the hammers. She was used to that. Eurella
didn't know whence the pain had originated, or why it was being inflicted upon
her. Healers had been baffled over it and prescribed increased and fervent prayers
to the gods, but none of it seemed to make any difference. So Eurella had resigned
herself to the concept that the gods simply hated her, wanted her to suffer, and she
was required to withstand all that they wished to foist upon her. Why? Because
apparently having her people, as well as eleven other races, dumped upon this
forsaken Damned World wasn't enough to atone for whatever offenses they might
have committed.

As she waited for her sons to show up, she drummed her fingers idly on the
arm of her chair that had been carved entirely out of a rock wall. Certainly it

seemed to her that they were taking their own sweet time getting here. Then again, she couldn't be entirely sure. She'd started to notice these days that she was forgetting things, or having less awareness of them. Things like time, for instance. The truth was that she wasn't entirely sure just how much time had passed. For all she knew, they actually were going to get there reasonably swiftly and she had no cause for complaint.

But she was the queen of the Trulls, and the last thing she could afford was to present any air of uncertainty.

So it was that when Ulurac and Eutok marched into her throne room—a spartan affair as befitted a leader of Trulls—Eurella lurched up off her throne to greet each of them with a sharp blow to the head. The swing of her right hand caught Ulurac by surprise and staggered him so thoroughly that only by leaning upon his staff did he avoid tumbling over and landing comically on his backside. It took her only a half second to pivot and swing her other hand back toward Eutok. That was all the time he needed to brace himself. She hated to admit it to herself, but his swift reaction impressed her even as she smacked him on the side of his head as well. Having prepared for the impact, Eutok rocked back slightly on his wide heels but otherwise managed to hold his ground.

"*What the blazes . . . ?*" Ulurac sputtered as he hauled himself to his feet. Eutok merely shook his head with the air of one who was often put-upon but chose to suffer in silence.

Eurella flopped back into her throne and allowed her head to sag back as if what she had just done had been a tremendous exertion. She sighed heavily and then scratched the thin fuzz of beard that covered her chin.

"Mother!" Ulurac demanded her attention but she waved him off, choosing instead to pick a few scavenging bugs out of her beard before looking at him. "Why did you do that? What possible reason—?"

"I want to know which one of you did it," she said coolly but with an undercurrent surging with the ferocity of a lava flow.

Ulurac and Eutok exchanged looks of silent confusion and then suspicion. Clearly each one thought the other knew what Eurella was referring to, and was resenting the other for having landed them in some sort of trouble. Either that or one of them—or both—were putting on an exceptionally effective pretense.

They simultaneously began to speak and then both promptly fell silent so that the other could proceed. A couple more of these false starts, and finally Eutok made a point of bowing deeply and gesturing that Ulurac should go first. The Spiritu Sanctum took a cautious step forward and asked tentatively, "Mother . . . which one of us did what?"

"Did you think I would not hear? Did you think I would not summon you immediately upon learning of this travesty of a development?" she demanded, her voice beginning to rise. "And by the way, considering how long ago I summoned you, you certainly both took your leisure in responding!"

"Our leisure?" Eutok spoke up, annoyed by the accusation. "I'll have you know . . ."

"*You'll . . . have . . . me . . . know?*" she demanded, stretching out each single-syllable word so that it consumed three, even four beats. She interlaced her fingers and cracked the knuckles so that the sound echoed around them. "And what, pray tell, will you have me know?"

"He forgets," Ulurac cut in before Eutok could open his mouth and sink himself even further. "He forgets what he would have you know."

"Do you?" she demanded of Eutok.

He stared at her with a carefully blank expression. "I can't recall."

"Mother, with all respect," Ulurac continued before Eurella had time to decide whether Eutok was being sarcastic or not, "we are both uncertain as to what, specifically, you're referring to."

"You cannot play dumb with me," Eurella said, waggling a finger at them.

Eutok squatted on his haunches, which was his preferred position when there were no chairs around to support his muscular bulk. "Oh, no, Mother, our ability to play dumb pales in comparison with your own skills at—"

With a low groan, Ulurac interrupted once more, gaining him a fairly nasty look from his brother. "Mother, again must I respectfully ask for specifics as to—"

"You want specifics? Very well. I shall give you specifics," she said, rubbing her hands together briskly and feeling most satisfied that she had kept the two of them sufficiently off balance. "The Piri."

Yet again blank expressions were exchanged. "What about the Piri?" Eutok asked cautiously.

"Did you think I would not hear?"

"You heard the Piri?" Ulurac asked, totally lost. "How could you . . . they are nowhere near here . . . are they?"

Immediately Eutok's defensive instincts kicked in. "If they are," he said warily, "I'll marshal the Trull lords at once. We will be fully armed and ready to—"

"*Stop pretending!* I want to know which one of you was behind it!"

The clueless faces of her offspring were beginning to grate on her, and when her demands only resulted in further protests of ignorance, Eurella began to think she might have to accept said protests at face value . . . at least if she had any desire for the conversation to proceed further.

She leaned forward on her throne, her gaze darting from one to the other, looking for the slightest sign of dissembling from either as she said, "The Piri have struck against the Ocular."

Eutok was the first to speak. "That is hardly a ground-shattering event, Mother. Have they not historically . . . ?"

"This is a different matter. They burrowed."

"Burrowed?"

"Yes, Ulurac, burrowed. Underground."

"That would certainly be easier than burrowing aboveground," Eutok remarked, and received only an angry scowl in response. He took a step back and stared at the tops of his feet with fixed interest.

"Merrih has been taken."

"Merrih!" Ulurac looked genuinely upset at that. "Nagel's niece? I met her once! When the Ocular negotiated with us for that supply of stone clubs we made for them. And that sword Nagel ordered . . ."

"I remember that sword," said Eutok, and naturally he would. If there was one thing Eurella knew that Eutok had, it was an eye and fondness for weaponry. "Crafters worked on it for a month. The way it gleamed in the forge fires . . . I've never seen the like."

"Nagel inspires that in people," Eurella said with grudging respect. "More than I ever did, damn him. He is wise and decent, and he deserves better than to have his niece carried off by the Piri."

"Then we will help him!" Eutok declared. "I will summon the lords, and—"

"No!" Eurella snapped at him, seeing that Ulurac was about to respond to him and interrupting before he could do so. "We maintain neutrality, Eutok! That is our way! We sell to almost all sides and give none any advantage over another. That way all continue to require our services. That is best."

"But Mother . . ."

"That is best!"

Eutok was growling deep in his throat, his fists clenched and trembling slightly in repressed fury, but he managed to rein himself in . . . albeit barely. Meanwhile understanding began to flare in Ulurac's eyes. "You think," he said slowly to the queen, "that we provided burrowing equipment to the Piri."

"She doesn't!" Eutok protested, but then he comprehended as well and stared at his mother. "You do?"

"The Piri creep about within their caves, like animals, the way that grizzes roam the forests," she said. "If grizzes, when they treed their prey, pulled out axes from their furry asses and started chopping the trees down, you wouldn't think the grizzes suddenly developed weaponry. You'd know that someone gave them those axes."

"And you think," Ulurac said, slowly pacing back and forth while his gaze never wavered from his mother, "that Ulurac or I might have given the Piri digging tech? Is that what you think?"

"I consider that a possibility, yes," she replied stiffly.

"Well, don't."

Eurella tilted her head and studied Ulurac in a manner similar to the way she would study a microbe. "You would tell the queen in such a way what she can and cannot do?"

Ulurac did not back down. In a way, that pleased her. In another way, it annoyed her. "I would tell the queen that to accuse either her Chancellor or her Spiritu Sanctum of what is effectively high treason—especially without a shred of proof—is wildly inappropriate. I would also tell our mother that to think such of her sons is distressing, to say the least."

"What makes you think I have not a shred of proof?" she challenged.

"Because," Ulurac said calmly, "you cannot have proof of that which is not true."

Eutok snorted, a phlegmatic wheeze. "As if no one in history has ever condemned someone with falsified evidence. You, brother, are to be admired for your continued naïveté."

Ulurac pointedly turned his back and ignored him. "I do not believe you have proof that any Trull—us or any other—has given digging equipment to the Piri. As you say, they are merely animals. Parasites. They have nothing with which to purchase anything from us in any event. No means of barter, no nothing. Digging technology belongs to the Trulls alone. We know that. All know that. In order to violate that rule, a huge incentive would have to be provided, and the Piri have none to give. In every way, shape, and form . . . in every conceivable way . . . this is not something that any Trull would do, much less the two of us."

"And why accuse the two of us, for that matter?" Eutok demanded. "When it could be any member of our people?"

"It's not!" Ulurac said sharply.

"But it could be, even though it's not!"

"That makes no sense at all, you fool!"

Eutok pointed a trembling finger at Ulurac, remained that way for a brief time, and then admitted, "All right . . . no. No, I suppose it didn't make sense. But still—"

Eurella put up her hands to quiet them both. "My belief that it could only be one of the two of you was because you, in your duties, go much further afield than any other Trull. Only you would have reasonably had any interaction with the Piri."

"Even if that were the case," demanded Ulurac, "why would either of us do such a thing?"

"I don't know." She glowered at one and then the other. "I was hoping you would tell me that."

"Well, we didn't. So we can just stop this foolishness right now," said Ulurac. "And frankly, Mother, considering how long it has been since the three of us were together, it is tragic that this reunion could not have been anything other than a series of baseless accusations."

"Oh, of all the pompous . . ."

Ulurac turned and walked away. Instantly Eurella was on her feet as she called out, "You have not been given permission to depart!"

"I did not ask for it," he replied, his voice icily calm.

The shock to Eurella was such that for a few moments she felt a numbing in her face and she didn't even dwell upon the ceaseless ringing in her ears. Mute, she looked to Eutok. He merely shrugged. "When you consider that our laws say that the Spiritu Sanctum is allowed to come and go as he pleases in the Underground, he's really not doing anything beyond asserting his rights. In fact," he added, struck by the notion, "as I recall, the same law exists for the Chancellor as well. Good tremors to you, Mother," and with that he tossed off a vague salute and walked out of the room as well.

Eurella sagged back into her chair, grateful at first that no one had been present to witness such disrespect and insubordination.

And then, after long moments, as her mind processed all that had just transpired, she grudgingly realized that there was at least one thing to appreciate about this minor uprising.

For the first time that she could recall, her sons weren't fighting with each other. They were actually in accord.

Dark gods take the Piri. Perhaps they had developed a few tunneling tricks on their own. At least the things that really mattered—the mutual cooperation of her sons—was finally, after all these ages, coming into clearer focus. And if what it took for that to transpire was for them to be united against a common enemy . . . her . . . then she would be satisfied with that development.

iii.

Eutok emerged from the throne room and glanced around, wondering to where Ulurac had gotten.

Suddenly Eutok was seized with the dizzying sensation that the far wall was rushing toward him. It took him a second or two to realize that a pair of firm hands had grabbed him from behind and were, instead, shoving him forward at high speed.

He brought his hands up just in time, marginally cushioning his slam against the wall. Nevertheless his body and face crashed up against it, and his skull rang from the concussive force of it.

Under ordinary circumstances, Eutok would have fought like a madman against whoever was attacking him. In this case, Eutok knew exactly who it was and what was going on. So instead of taking an aggressive course of combat, Eutok did that which he knew would be most annoying: He chuckled.

It had exactly the desired effect. "Shut up," snarled Ulurac, and, for good measure, shoved Eutok up against the wall a second time.

"What's the matter, brother?" Eutok inquired silkily. "That pacifist cloak you wrap yourself in beginning to itch? Your true nature asserting itself again?"

Ulurac twisted Eutok around so that he was facing him, slamming his back against the wall. "If I find out," he snarled, right in Eutok's face, "that you had any-thing . . . *anything* . . . to do with this . . . with the Piri . . . I'll . . ."

"You'll what? Gut me? Like this?"

Ulurac had no clue of the jeopardy he was in until he felt the point of Eutok's knife jabbing ungently against his belly. He looked down and saw it and grunted in acknowledgment of his vulnerability. Eutok's distended brow was low and his dark eyes were barely visible as he continued, with the hilt of his knife gripped se-curely in his right hand, "General rule: When you're threatening someone, it's al-ways best to keep them facing away from you. Turn them around and they can produce weapons out of the strangest hiding places."

"Point . . . taken," said Ulurac as he released Eutok and stepped back, putting distance between the two of them. Eutok smiled but did not put the knife away, instead twirling it between the palms of both hands. The blade spun and glittered wildly in the pale light of the nearby lanterns. "But you take my point as well."

"Why would I have truck with the Piri?" Eutok scoffed. "They give us a bad name. The 'Draques and their ilk . . . they lump us together as one. Even as they come to us for weapons, even as they depend on us . . . they think that because Trulls and Piri both shun the above, we are indistinguishable one from the other. That we're the same as those . . . those vermin. So why . . . ?"

"I don't know why, Eutok," Ulurac admitted. "But I just want you to know that if I find out . . ."

"Yes, yes, you've made your position abundantly clear." Eutok was not espe-cially impressed. He tilted his head slightly on his thick neck and inquired, "Did Mother get the idea from you? That we were involved somehow? Were you spilling poisons in her ear?"

"Our beloved queen mother needs no poisonous sources outside of what she herself can conjure," said Ulurac.

Eutok nodded at that, but still continued to study his brother. "It *has* been a long time, hasn't it. You look well, Spiritu."

"As do you, Chancellor."

Showing his wide, dirty teeth, Eutok inquired, "Kill anyone lately?"

With an angry snarl and a sweep of his cape, Ulurac stomped away on his large, bare feet, leaving behind a snickering Eutok, spinning his knife on one finger while wondering if—in taking the niece of the Ocular king—the Piri had not bitten off more than even they could chew.

SUBTERROR

Merrih, for as far back as she could remember, had never had to do anything that ran counter to her first impulse.

As the niece of Nagel, ruler of the Ocular, she had lived a life of pleasure and privilege, and there had been nothing that she had ever wanted or desired that had been denied her. If she saw something that intrigued her, some object that struck her fancy, then all she had to do was request it and it would be given her.

It didn't matter how casual a comment it was. On one occasion she had noticed a charming bauble, a pendant, hanging about the neck of a young girl. She had commented on the loveliness of it, and the girl's mother had promptly snatched it from around her daughter's neck and presented it to Merrih, bowing and scraping the entire time. The child had howled in protest, and Merrih had tried to demur but the mother would not hear of it. Mortally embarrassed over the situation, Merrih had eased matters by offering the girl a trade of a glittering ring she was wearing. The captivated youngster's tears had quickly dried and the swap was made. The swap had infuriated Nagel, considering that the ring was an heirloom and worth easily twenty times what the pendant had been. But a deal was a deal, and there was nothing for it but to live with it.

Nagel had told her to take that as a lesson to watch what she said. Merrih instead had considered it further proof that she could pretty much do whatever she wanted. Giving the girl the ring, really, had just been a sop to her conscience. Instead of suppressing her desires and instincts, Merrih preferred to work on suppressing her conscience. She'd gotten fairly good at it, too.

The moment she had been pulled under the ground, her first instinct had been to scream and scream and keep on screaming . . . to scream and not stop. To yield utterly and totally to the panic that had overwhelmed her, the acidic fear that rose in her throat and that she could taste like rotting lemons.

At first she had screamed, gods above and below, how she had screamed. The world she knew had been pulled rapidly and horrifically away from her, and she had felt things grabbing at her ankles, dragging her down. Disoriented, she had understood within several heartbeats what was happening, and the level of danger that she was in. She'd heard the cries of her people, heard Nagel yelling down after her, felt the stink of the underworld, the disgusting moistness and mildew. Her back and legs had scraped viciously against the walls, for they were dug wide enough to accommodate the Piri but not quite wide enough for an Ocular.

All during the initial drag-down she had screamed, and then suddenly the tunnel widened and she thudded down into some sort of antechamber. There, in the utter, abysmal darkness, her single eye widened even more than it had in the night above, and she was able to see everything.

The walls were literally crawling with Piri, so many that it seemed as if the wall was actually made of the vermin. They skittered about, impossibly thin, their ribs and spines visible, their deathly white skin a latticework of blue veins. Their claws, from both their fingers and toes, cracked and crackled against the walls. The antechamber was lined with some sort of rock, as opposed to the thick, crusty dirt of the tunnels. Merrih couldn't determine whether the chamber had been carved right from rock or had somehow been lined with it to provide additional support.

Most of them barely wore anything resembling clothing. Mere tatters at best, and she suspected that they were items not made by the Piri themselves, but instead were taken off the bodies of their victims. A number of them were just naked, but were eyeing her in a way that made her think they were planning to use her clothing as their next trophies.

Her impulse was to continue to scream, to cower, even to plead for her life. To sob and cry about how much she just wanted to go home, return to the surface, forget that this hideous nightmare had ever been thrust upon her. She wanted to curse the name of Nagel as loudly as she could, for it had been he and his foolish determination to fly in face of fear that had resulted in her being hauled bodily into this living hell.

As she stood there, frozen, arms outstretched in either direction, she clamped her mouth tightly and—for the first time in her recollection—fought back her impulses. Because she could tell from the anticipatory gleam in their eyes, the way they licked their chops, the snickering and muttered animalistic sounds between them, that protest was exactly what they were expecting her to do. They probably wanted her to display fear. The dismay of their victims, the total loss of pride and the last shreds of dignity . . . the creatures undoubtedly drew pleasure from all of it.

She was very likely going to wind up providing them sustenance, for they were many and she was but one, and she did not for a moment believe that she could overwhelm them. She had even given up the notion that she would ever be able to make it to the surface again. Her life was over. All that mattered now was the way in which it was to end.

Some of the Piri looked at each other in confusion at her sudden silence. Then they began to creep toward her. It was at that moment that Merrih let out a roar.

It was a very different noise from the screams of panic she had made earlier. The full-throated bellow of the Ocular, a battle cry of sheer defiance, was something that creatures such as the Piri were not often faced with. They were craven beasts that cowered in the dark, grabbed small and petrified victims, and devoured them. A bold Ocular who was not afraid to go down fighting was something very different.

It wasn't that Merrih was not afraid. She was. But she allowed her anger and indignation to overcome it. Her challenge resounded through the antechamber, through the tunnels, down into the darkest hidey-holes of the Piri. The ones around her mewled and grabbed the sides of their narrow heads, covering their ears. Several of them fell off the wall, writhing about. Without hesitation, still bellowing inarticulate defiance, Merrih charged the ones that had fallen and brought her feet crashing down.

There was a loud crunching noise as her huge foot—crushed the head of one of them. She looked down and saw the goo and ooze seeping from beneath her foot.

At which point her resolve, her show of strength, completely evaporated. She felt her insides twisting and turning, and she tried desperately to control it. She failed utterly and she vomited up everything that was in her stomach. It blasted from her mouth, splattered everywhere, and the Piri scampered to get out of her way. She lurched, clutching at her stomach, and moaned wretchedly, for this was certainly not the way she wanted to go. Not with the smell of her own spew wafting up her nostrils.

That was when they came at her, and she didn't care about anything else for she had completely disgraced herself. All she could think was *Let it just end quickly, let it be done, let it—*

"Stop."

She thought at first the voice was her own, coming out of her head, but then realized that was obviously not the case. Whoever it was that had spoken, it had been a female. The order had been made with no sense of urgency, no thundering demand as a commander would shout at an army. The word had been spoken calmly, almost conversationally.

Yet the Piri had halted. They were all looking off in the direction from which the voice had come . . . that direction being several feet behind Merrih.

Slowly, cautiously, Merrih turned in place like a tentative dancer. Her eyes widened as she saw something that made no sense to her.

She was being eyed with mild amusement by a female who was taller than the other Piri . . . perhaps half as tall as Merrih herself. She was definitely Piri, but she was not like the others. Whereas the other Piri, both male and female (for she could see withered breasts hanging pathetically on the fronts of some of them) had mere strings of hair hanging randomly from their head, this one had long, lustrous hair that was as pale white as the rest of her. It flowed elegantly all around her. Her only clothing was long, fluttering pieces of cloth that hung front and back from her waist, held in place by a glittering gold belt that was studded with fine green jewels such as Merrih had never seen. She appeared to be naked from the waist up, but her hair was so thick that it fell over her chest and provided cover for whatever breasts she might have had.

She wrinkled her nose slightly as the odor from Merrih's spew reached her. "Well well well," she said with a scolding tone. "We've made a bit of a mess here, haven't we."

Unaccountably, Merrih's first notion was to apologize for her action. Then she realized that her foot was still atop the crushed skull of the Piri, and the realization was almost enough to set off another wave of nausea.

The new arrival looked in the direction of Merrih's foot and said, "Oh my. Oh, oh my. Yes, a mess indeed. Come this way, please, my dear," and she clapped her hands briskly. When Merrih didn't move at first, the female prodded her with, "Yes, dear, I was addressing you."

Merrih was beginning to think that this was more than just a nightmare in the sense that it was horrific. It might well have been a nightmare in the sense that she was asleep and dreaming all of this insanity. Piri didn't speak. Everyone knew they had no language beyond animalistic grunts and growls. This . . . this Piri woman had to be some sort of dream construct, a combination of Piri and Ocular that her mind had cooked up.

But . . . what sort of dream, even nightmare, included something as vivid as smell of any kind, much less the spell of something as pungent as her own sickness?

"I'm not accustomed to repeating myself, dear," said the Piri woman, and she extended one hand in a firm, commanding manner. Almost as an afterthought, she added, "Unless you wish to remain here and be torn to shreds. I doubt that would be much fun for you, would it?"

"N-None at all," Merrih admitted, and then mentally chided herself for the lapse. There was no advantage at all to confessing to any sort of weakness, even if that weakness was fear of—as the woman had said—being torn to shreds. Screwing her courage firmly down, she inquired in a preemptory fashion, "Who are you? What is your name? Does your kind even have names?"

"As much as your kind does. I would suggest," she said, pointing to a large stone positioned nearby, "that you wipe your foot on that. No need to track such . . . unpleasant . . . things along with you."

Trying not to think about what she was doing, Merrih moved over to the rock and dragged the sole of her foot across it repeatedly, trying to ignore the thick, gelatinous bits of matter that were being removed from it. When she was as satisfied as she was going to be, Merrih lowered her foot and then turned back to face the female. The rest of the Piri—thirty or forty of them, at least—continued to remain immobile.

"They obey you. You are their queen?"

"I am their leader. We here in Subterror don't indulge in royal appellations. That tends to be more the province of . . ." and she tilted her head to indicate the surface world.

"Subterror . . . ?"

"That's what we call our land."

"But you . . . you don't *have* a land," Merrih protested. "You just . . . you hide underground and . . . you're parasites. Animals."

"All point of view, my dear. All point of view. Sunara."

"Su . . . ?"

"Sunara," and the woman tapped her chest lightly. "That would be my name. You wished to know."

"Oh. Yes. I did."

"Sunara Redeye," and she bowed majestically, waving her one hand as if to a crowd of worshippers. Merrih heard sharp intakes of breath from the Piri all around her. They seemed to respond to the mere mention of her name, in the way that the truly devout trembled before the speaking of the name of a powerful god. "Mistress Sunara is my hereditary reference. As I said, we disdain titles . . . but we appreciate good lineage as well as the next 'animalistic parasites.' That is what you just said your kind calls us, is it not? Animals? Parasites?" The edges of her lips twitched in amusement as if she found the notion amusing . . . but not amusing enough to garner laughter.

Sunara led the way out of the antechamber, pausing at the exit and gesturing grandly that Merrih should precede her. Merrih hesitated, suspecting a trap, but then realized the absurdity of such a concern. Enemies surrounded her. She'd already been dragged into the trap. She could make the most of her defense, make certain that even more Piri paid with their lives, but ultimately they were many and she was one. She had nothing to lose by following this "Mistress Sunara" wherever she chose to lead, since matters could hardly become any worse. At least, that was her theory. There was always the chance that subsequent events would prove her tragically overoptimistic.

"You have not shared, my dear," said Sunara as she rounded the corner of one tunnel. Oddly, even though she was a fraction of Merrih's size, she seemed to cover more ground than Merrih did, or at least with greater efficiency. It was almost as if Sunara was floating across the ground rather than treading upon it.

"Shared?" Merrih was keeping her eye fixed upon Sunara, but her ears were attuned to noises behind her. She heard nothing, however.

"Your name." She sounded faintly scolding. "You know mine, but I do not know yours. What do you call yourself, or what do others call you, if it 'twere not the same thing."

"Why would it not be the same thing?"

Sunara stopped and turned to face her, looking surprised that she would have to ask. Her dark eyes seemed to glitter, which was odd considering there was absolutely no source of light. "Because there are names, my dear, and then there are *names*. There are the names that you tell the world so that they are able to address you in casual conversation. And there are names, true names, names of power, that you keep buried deep in here," and she touched a long-fingered hand to her breast, "so no others may have power over you."

"Names have power?"

"They can. Whether one utters a name, or even uses a name, indicates the significance of that name. Look at the planet we live on."

"The Damned World?"

"Do you know its true name?"

Merrih frowned at that, stepping carefully over a stone outcropping, trying not to bang up her legs. "Is that not its true name?"

"Who's to know?" She shrugged. "My people tell the tale of the final battle of the Third Wave. Supposedly when the last of the true Mort defenders tried to hold his position against an overwhelming force, he stood upon a high mountain and—as the Banished clambered toward him—raked them with weapons and howled in their language, *'Get off the damned world!'* And they took that to be the actual name . . . which, when you think upon it, makes as good a name as any."

"I suppose."

"But it may be that we never will fully rule this world until we do know its true name . . . whatever that may be. Or perhaps," and she shrugged once more, "it is all merely superstition, stuff and nonsense. Who could say? So . . . your name, my dear . . . ?"

She hesitated, quickly trying to decide whether she should fabricate a moniker on the spot. But lying did not come readily to Merrih. As a daughter of privilege, she'd never needed to develop a talent for it, since she was accustomed to saying whatever she wanted and doing whatever she wanted without fear of consequence. After the briefest of pauses, she said, "Merrih."

"Merrih." Sunara rolled the name over in her mouth as if she was tasting an appetizer. She rolled the double "r" so that it almost sounded as if she were purring it. "Your true name?"

"My name."

"Do not concern yourself. If you have another, truer name buried within you, it shall be revealed to me sooner or later."

They had been heading steadily downward, not at a sharp incline, but a noticeable one nevertheless. Several times during their journey, Merrih considered the fact that she could try to attack Sunara at any moment. Try to use her as a hostage, force the Piri to release her. But she kept coming back to the folly of such an approach. Sunara was all that was keeping her alive. Merrih had no idea where she was, here in the depths. If she just killed Sunara, she'd never find her way out before the Piri found her and descended upon her. True, there was an attraction to the prospect of fighting to the death, but Merrih was still young and really didn't want to have to die out at all. So she restrained herself even as the pathway opened wider in front of them. Several times they arrived at splits in the cavern tunnels, and the Piri mistress made her way through with confidence. Merrih followed as best she could.

"Tell me what you think of this."

Sunara was just ahead of her, around a corner, and her voice echoed. Once more Merrih tensed, concerned about some sort of . . . of something designed to lure her in. She glanced behind herself. No Piri followed her. She could make a run for it . . . but to what end? *Probably your own,* she thought grimly, and walked around the corner.

She gasped at the sight before her.

This corridor, unlike others which had been narrow, twisting and turning, stretched far into the distance. Furthermore, there was some light. This was not moonlight, however. The rocks themselves lining the walls seemed to be glowing.

It was not the rocks, though, nor even the distance spanned by the rocky corridor that surprised her so. It was what was propped against the cave walls on either side: a series of pictorial representations of creatures that she was reasonably sure were Morts, although she had never actually seen one of them in person. The

Morts were wearing a variety of odd costumes, and the presentations varied wildly in style. She wasn't discerning enough to be able to comprehend exactly how they differed, but she knew instinctively diverse hands had produced them.

She had seen drawings, of course. Her people made their own pictorial renditions of themselves or others of the Banished on the Damned World. But they were inevitably simple renderings, straight line etchings. Nothing this elaborate, filled with so many colors . . . how was it even possible? How had the colors been applied?

Merrih leaned close to one and reached toward it. But her hand was brought up short by Sunara, who was abruptly at her side and gripping her wrist gently but firmly. "They do not do well with being touched," she cautioned. "It damages them."

"What . . . *are* they?"

"They are called 'paintings,'" Sunara told her. Certain that Merrih was going to pay heed to her wishes, Sunara released her wrist and focused her attention on her treasures. She smiled and Merrih noticed the array of pointed teeth protruding from just under her upper lip. Inwardly she shuddered. "It is rather an advanced art form. None of the surface races practice it, although it is my understanding that the Overseer has been known to dabble."

"The . . ." Merrih flinched at the very mention of the name and inadvertently glanced skyward. Her voice dropped to a whisper, as was typical whenever anything having to do with the Overseer was brought up. "The Overseer?"

"That is what I've heard."

"How?" she demanded skeptically. "How could you have heard such a thing? How would you know, you who . . . who crawl about down here while the Overseer . . . he resides far off in the Spires! He is as far above you as . . . as . . ."

"Are these paintings not beautiful?" Sunara interrupted her.

Merrih tried to keep her focus on what she was saying, but wasn't successful. Instead she only nodded and admitted, "They are . . . amazing."

"They are. You have a good eye . . . which is fortunate, what with only possessing the one." Sunara's arms were draped behind her back. She was walking silently across the floor, casually moving in a sideways manner by drawing one long leg back behind the other and then stretching. If she'd done it faster, to a beat, her movements were so graceful that she would have been dancing. "I personally am particularly enamored of this one," she said, pausing in front of one. It was still in one piece, but the surface was riddled with minute cracks. It was, Merrih saw, a simple portrait of a Mort female clad mostly in dark colors. "Her little smile," continued Sunara. "Slightly imperious expression. Sallow skin. It would not surprise me if she were one of us. A Piri."

"What would a Mort be doing painting a Piri?" scoffed Merrih.

"Creating this," Sunara replied, and Merrih had to concede the point. The picture—the "painting," as she'd called it—was an end to itself.

"All right, but . . . how did this come to—?"

"Be here?" When Merrih nodded, Sunara shook her head with an air of woe. "The battles during the Third Wave were brutal. The Twelve Races did not exactly . . . how best to put it? Distinguish themselves . . . when it came to discernment."

"I don't understand."

"I mean that the Third Wave was so intent on taking the Damned World . . . of driving the Morts into the oblivion that many felt they so richly deserved . . . that they paid no attention to what they were destroying, but instead simply annihilated it because it was there, and because they could. They saw Morts as animals. Perhaps even parasites, much in the way that we are seen. That may well be one of the reasons that my people felt something of an affinity for the Morts. They were despised and underestimated. They were cast down from the paradise that they once inhabited, much as we Piri were driven underground."

"You weren't driven here," Merrih said. "Catacombs, caves . . . that is where the Piri prefer to be."

"Why, thank you ever so, my dear Ocular, for claiming to know the Piri mind far better than I."

"I . . . did not mean to . . ."

But Sunara wasn't waiting for her response. Instead she turned away and continued down the corridor. "Sunara?" Merrih called after her, but she kept going. Merrih was left alone in the portrait-filled hall. She looked back the way she had come, but again could see no point in essaying the darkness on her own. Then she glanced left and right, making certain that she wasn't seen, and touched the painting of the woman with the odd smile.

A piece flecked off the canvas, from a section of the background. Merrih gasped, convinced she had somehow broken the portrait, worried that the rest of the pieces were going to follow suit and there would be nothing remaining but a large blank space. As it turned out, she didn't have worried. The remainder of the painting stayed where it was supposed to. In wonderment, Merrih studied the tiny piece in her hand. It was miraculous to her. It was as if color itself—in this case, a sort of pale yellow—had developed its own texture. To Merrih, it was no different than if she had happened upon a rainbow and removed a bit of it to examine more closely. A piece of the ephemeral given substance . . . it was almost impossible to believe.

It made her wonder about the Morts, and even more, wonder about the Piri.

She heard splashing up ahead and padded after it. The ceiling was getting lower. Walking space that more than accommodated the Piri was problematic for an Ocular, and Merrih was convinced she was soon going to have to bend herself in half in order to proceed . . . and even that might not suffice.

She paused in front of an archway directly in front of her. It might have started out as a natural formation, but studying it more closely, she saw that carvings had been etched into the rock. She could discern immediately that they represented various Piri, and there was an eerie, sinewy sexuality to them. The carvings were all naked Piri, of both genders, intertwined one with the other so that it was impossible to determine where one began and another ended. The sculpture hewn from rock started at one side of the arch and continued all the way across to the other side in one unbroken array of exquisitely posed bodies. Was it supposed to be a representation of sexuality? A mass grave? She couldn't tell for sure, although she was leaning more in the direction of the former than the latter.

The splashing continued and the air just ahead seemed warmer. Thus far the air had been cold, and she had fancied she could feel it creeping into her bones, into her joints. The tips of her fingers and toes were starting to numb. Anything that might serve to warm her up would be a blessing.

She stepped through the arch into a chamber that was huge beyond anything that she had imagined.

Vast columns of solid stone went from floor to ceiling; it was impossible for her to tell if they were of natural design or if they had been carved and shaped. There was the steady flow of water nearby, some sort of underground stream.

Merrih turned in Sunara's direction and then looked away with an exclamation of shock. That only lasted for a few moments, however, as, Merrih felt compelled to look back once more at the Mistress of the Piri.

There was a pool of bubbling liquid some feet away, and Sunara was standing there with several attendants, two male, two female. The attendants, although obviously Piri, didn't appear quite as emaciated as the ones Merrih had seen earlier. None of them was as tall or robust as Sunara, but they were clearly in a good deal better shape than their "brethren."

Sunara was stepping out of her sole garment, allowing it to drop to the rocky floor where one of the women immediately picked it up and delicately set it aside. Merrih's gaze was drawn, in spite of herself, to the area of Sunara's femininity.

She had never seen anything like it. Sunara's pubic region was devoid of any sort of hair growth. Instead Merrih could see, even from where she was standing, that the entire area of her pubic swell was viciously burned and scarred, as if someone had taken a blazing torch and thrust it cruelly between Sunara's legs. Merrih tried to imagine the excruciating pain that Sunara had undergone and could scarcely conceive it. It had obviously occurred some time ago, since the scars had healed over. What Sunara must have endured during the long, slow healing process . . .

If Sunara was aware of the impact the sight of her nether regions was having upon Merrih, she gave no indication of it. One of the male attendants was rubbing some sort of cream upon the area. A salve perhaps. Maybe it pained her to this day. Sunara did not seem to be feeling discomfort from the activity of the male attendant. Instead her head was tilted back slightly, her breathing relaxed and steady, and she was making a soft "cooing" noise that seemed to indicate she was finding the tactile sensation pleasurable.

Sunara swept her hair back and away, and once more Merrih was startled by what she saw. Sunara had no breasts. Rather, she'd had them at one time, but in place of where they once had been, there were more scars. There were two of them, twin scars running horizontally across her chest, indicating that someone had expertly removed her breasts via some type of surgical process.

The warmth of the place was starting to pervade Merrih, relaxing her, enabling her to shake the numbing cold from her limbs. She made no pretense of not staring at Sunara's body. Sunara noticed, as it would have been impossible not to, and gestured for Merrih to sit. There were no chairs or couches or cushions of any sort, so Merrih simply sank to the stony ground. It was warm as well, and filled her with a sense of security in the disorienting, fearsome environment.

She said nothing as Sunara eased herself into the liquid pool. Vapor wafted upward. It might have been Merrih's imagination, but it seemed to her as if the pool bubbled even more zealously once Sunara's body was immersed. One of the male and one of the female attendants slid into the pool on the opposite side and approached her with sponges. The female gently swathed Sunara's upper body with the sponges. The male took a breath and then sank under the water. Sunara repositioned herself and Merrih could tell that Sunara was spreading her legs to accommodate the ministrations of the now-unseen male. A faint smile spread across her lips. Merrih was feeling extremely uneasy, as if she was witnessing something far more intimate than she should be allowed to see. At the same time, the general warmth and security suffusing her helped to allay whatever nagging sense of embarrassment and discomfort she might be feeling.

"What happened to you . . . ?" Merrih asked at last. It sounded to her own ears as if her voice was coming from very, very far away. She didn't dwell upon it, though, for her interests lay elsewhere.

"Happened?" Sunara appeared not to know what Merrih was referring to.

"Your b—" It required long moments and several tries to get the word out. "Your body. You have . . . the scars, and the . . ."

"Oh. That."

Merrih couldn't tell if Sunara was pretending to have no idea what Merrih was referring to, or if Sunara was just adopting a "seen it all" tone that made her sound removed and above concerns over such petty matters as mutilation.

Sunara's fingers strayed over the soft white scars that marked where her breasts had once been. "That was a very long time ago . . . and it was necessary."

"Necessary? Why?"

She leaned back and allowed her long hair to sink under the water. The male attendant came up for air, or perhaps was just thrown off by the sudden repositioning of her body. After a moment he took another gulp and submerged once more. "Because it is the honored responsibility of the Mistress to serve the needs of all Piri, male and female. So it is tradition that, once a Mistress—or a Master, if such there be—reaches a certain age, and has already produced an heir, all outward sign of gender be . . . how do I put this?"

"Butchered?"

"Made obsolete," Sunara said. "That way no preferential treatment may be given, and the Mistress will serve as the living symbol of all Piri. What gives us uniformity of spirit, after all, is this," and she tapped her head, "and this," and she touched the area of her heart. "Gender can, and often does, lead to divisiveness. We can only be strong if we are united. I, as Mistress, represent that."

"But that's . . . I mean . . . didn't it hurt . . . ?"

"I don't think 'hurt' is the word I would use."

"What then?"

She stared at Merrih, her eyes luminous and bright with remembered pain. "There are no words for it. There are no words to encapsulate what it's like knowing that most of who you are is being . . . taken from you forever. The pain and the fear . . . fear of knowing only who you have been all this time, and having no clue what it is you're going to wind up as. No, my dear . . . no words at all. But," and her face softened, "I endured. It was my responsibility, and I fulfilled it, as have those before me."

"And your mate? How did he . . . ?"

"He was . . . not a factor."

"Why?"

"He was not," she said, her voice carefully modulated and controlled. "And that is all I wish to speak of in that regard." She raised her hands, cupping them, sipping the liquid that she had gathered between them, and then allowed it to trickle through her fingers. Something about the water did not look right. It appeared slightly rusty in color. That was when a chill thought breezed through Merrih's mind.

"Are you . . . ?" Her voice caught, even as the warmth continued to spread through her. "Are you . . . bathing in . . . in blood?"

Sunara's response was to laugh in a way that sounded almost musical to Merrih's ears. "Oh, my dear, how you do go on so. Bathe in blood? Something so vital, so difficult to come by at times . . . how excessively self-indulgent would such an act be? No, no," and she stirred the water lazily with one finger, "it comes in this manner out of whatever underground fissures are its source. Oh, we have some minerals, some plants we add in. It helps to revitalize and refresh. Cleanses the body inside and out."

By this point the male attendant had emerged once more and floated back and away, remaining in position should his mistress have any desires. The female attendant was scrubbing Sunara's back.

The scent from the water was everywhere to Merrih. She could not remember when she had ever been so relaxed. She realized that there was a silly smile upon her face, and her single eye was beginning to lose focus. But she only thought of these things in an "Oh by the way" manner rather than feeling any alarm from it.

"Do you have a desire to join me here?" Sunara's voice floated to her.

She thought about it . . . about what it would be like to have the water caressing her bare skin. Thought about the pleasure of seeing Sunara seated across from her, smiling at her, perhaps reaching through the water and touching her in a way that would bring her joy . . . a joy that she had, in all her years, yet to experience.

But she remained where she was . . . not out of a reluctance to move to the pool and join Sunara, but rather from an inability to rise from where she was. In the entirety of her existence, she'd never been as comfortable as she was just then.

There was some small part of her mind that was crying a warning to her, telling her that she should not be lying immobile and content. It was a faint buzzing in her brain, threatening to distract her from her newly relaxed state of mind. She paid it no heed.

"Nooo," she sighed. "I believe I'll be fine . . . right here."

"Suit yourself." The voice of the Mistress had become even more mellifluous, golden honeyed tones that teased Merrih into giggling inwardly.

Merrih almost wanted to weep thanks to this feeling, for she had never felt this way before, and she mourned the stretch of her life when she hadn't known such pleasure, such relaxation. She began to view her existence as a long, barely endurable tragedy, that it had been absent sensations such as this.

The fear that she had felt, the anger, the resentment when she had first been pulled beneath the ground into Subterror . . . it all seemed as if had happened to someone else. Some poor, pathetic individual who could not possibly have dreamt, in her wildest imaginings, of all that she was missing in her life.

"How can we be these feckless animals of which you speak?" the Mistress inquired. There were fingers, loving fingers, running the length of Merrih's body now, pressing her flesh ever so gently, working their way under her garments. She loved it, wanted more, couldn't wait. "You see our love of art . . . our love of the sensual . . . is that the mind-set of animals? Is it?"

"No," whispered Merrih.

"I didn't quite hear that . . ."

"No," slightly louder this time.

"We have been misjudged, my dear Merrih. Misjudged by the Banished. Misjudged by you. There is so much more to us than any of them can and will believe. But you will come to understand us. Won't you?"

Sunara's voice prodded and poked at all Merrih's innermost secret places in her psyche, penetrating with ruthless and yet delicate efficiency. "Won't you?" she inquired again, and Merrih could no longer tell if the voice was coming from within her or outside of her. Nor did it matter. In, out, they were one and the same.

"Yes. Yes, I . . . will understand," Merrih said, and that small warning voice in her was finally silenced against the flow of warmth and love and intimacy that flooded through Merrih.

She sensed something moving against her then. Her eyes were closed, but she opened one lazily and saw a Piri rubbing himself against her body. And there was another licking her bare leg, and still another, and they were moving slowly in on her from all sides. They were smiling. She smiled back.

"You poor Ocular," Sunara said in a voice laced with sympathy. "Each of you, living alone, trapped within your own body. No sharing. No connection. Oh, you may meld your bodies from time to time for brief intervals . . . but you have no true bond. You are not genuinely family, one mind, one spirit. But that is going to change for you, my sweet, oh yes indeed. You will have a family. You will have us. We will provide you with what you have been missing . . . and you will do the same for us. All will win. All will benefit. All will be happy."

"Oh yes," sighed Merrih, who had never realized how desperately unhappy a creature she was until just this moment. "Yes, I would so like that."

The Piri, writhing, enveloped her, their teeth sinking into her, and she brought her arms around and embraced her new family of lovers.

THE OUTER PLAINS OF MARSAY

i.

Jepp, the wayward pleasure slave of the late Mandraque she called "the Greatness," followed at a respectful distance behind the creature "Karsen" who had saved her from all manner of things that she could not imagine . . .

Actually, she could imagine them. She, as well as anyone and better than most, knew full well the atrocities that Mandraques could inflict upon slaves of any race, much less a race as irrelevant as humans. She had witnessed them, seated or crouched at the Greatness's side while he had bantered or partied or plotted or otherwise been engaged with other Mandraques, oblivious of her presence except at those times he had need of her services. She had watched others of her kind, or of similar status to her, brutalized in the most creative ways that the Mandraques could conceive. All that time, she had been unable to do anything other than sit there and watch it, or wince and turn away. She had been able to say nothing about it, for to whom was she to speak? Other slaves or servants envied her her status, for the Greatness was many harsh and terrible things, but he never abused her in the manner that other Mandraques did with their possessions. This was not out of any respect for her, or care as to her feelings, but simply because she was his property, and the Greatness cared about his property. He kept her in pristine functioning condition in the same way that he kept his sword in pristine functioning condition. His sword was clean and polished and always by his side should he need it, and so was Jepp. She accepted that and was grateful for it. And if it was no way to live, well, it was the only way she knew, and so she adjusted.

However, she could not speak to the Greatness about her feelings over the way she saw others of her kind treated, nor would he think for a moment that he should do something about it. What others did with their property was their business, not his.

For that matter, she wasn't entirely sure she had any feelings on the subject. She understood on some basic level that she should be more upset than she was about witnessing such brutalities. In some very vague, distant way, she had wished that matters could be otherwise. She knew, though, that was not to be. She was what she was, the others were what they were, and the Mandraques . . .

Well, the Mandraques were dead, now, weren't they.

Not all of them, certainly. There were still many Mandraques walking and stalking the Damned World. Right here and now, however, there were none. There were only Jepp and Karsen and the equally odd creature that was apparently his mother.

It was Karsen's mother who was making the most noise now as they trudged toward wherever it was they were all going. She was speaking in low tones, which was seemingly an unusual habit for her, and one she was having a good deal of difficulty maintaining. Her normal state was to be speaking very, very loudly. That was clear even to Jepp, a female to whom most things were obscure. The only reason Zerena was making the slightest endeavor to keep her voice down was due to the pleadings of Karsen.

"You want to hondle with this . . . thing?" Zerena demanded loudly. "Then do so, be done with it, dump it and go on about your business!" As she spoke, she cast fiery, irritated glances over her shoulder in Jepp's direction, and then tried to make a point of pretending that she wasn't looking at Jepp at all. It was a strange little game that Jepp couldn't begin to understand.

"She's a she, Mother, not an it," Karsen protested. "Please do not speak of her so."

"You're a fool," Zerena assured him.

"That may be. But she's spoils of war, Mother. The law says I found her, and I can do whatever I wish with her. My wish is for her to stay with me."

Zerena stopped in her path, turned, and faced him, and there was something extremely unpleasant in her expression. "You seem to forget, Karsen, that that is not a decision you get to make alone. You are not the head of our clan. That would be me. Any final decision in regards to . . . *that* . . . is in my hands, not yours."

Karsen flinched and looked back at Jepp. She had no idea what she should say or do. If Karsen tossed her aside, as he could very easily do, then she didn't know what her next step would be. She couldn't imagine anything other than just standing right where she was and waiting for someone else to come along and . . . well, she didn't like to think about what the next person coming along would do. She was aware that she had been tremendously lucky insofar as Karsen was concerned, and was certain that her luck wouldn't hold out twice.

"Dispose of her now," Zerena continued, unknowing and uncaring of what was going through Jepp's head, "or dispose of her later, but not much later. We don't need an extra mouth to feed. As head of this clan, that is my final word." She waited for some response from him, and when none was forthcoming, she started to walk away.

"Then I'll form my own clan."

Karsen looked as surprised at the words that had just come out of his mouth as Zerena was. She halted once more, and Jepp could see the tensing of the muscles in her back. This time when she turned to stare at Karsen, it was with the same attitude she would have had if she'd lifted up a rock and became entranced with the insect life scuttling around beneath it.

"Your own clan."

Everything in Karsen's face and attitude indicated that he wanted to back down immediately. Yet he nodded with a definite vigor that belied any hesitation or second thoughts.

"Your *own clan*," she said again.

He seemed to be gaining strength from her incredulity. "Yes, my own clan, Mother."

"*Your own clan!*"

As loud as she got, that was as soft as he got. "If you keep repeating it at increasing volume, is that supposed to change my mind somehow?"

She looked like she wanted to laugh, but it choked in her throat, and suddenly it wasn't funny anymore. "You wouldn't last ten turns," she said. "No . . . make that five! And who is going to take care of you? Defend you? Her?" and she pointed at Jepp, barking that distinctive odd laugh of hers. She continued her rant, this time directed at Jepp. "That's how it would have to be, you know! Because he's useless when it comes to—"

Karsen's face crimsoned, but before he could interrupt, Zerena advanced on Jepp. "Don't hurt her!" he cried out.

Zerena uttered an annoyed growl deep in her throat as if he was speaking idiocy, and grabbed Jepp by the elbow. Jepp gasped at the strength in her grip, and noticed the older Laocoon's thick, broken fingernails, and she thought Zerena Foux was going to rip her arm off at the socket in anger. Instead Zerena only pulled her a few feet and then, as if the marginally increased distance between herself and her son somehow assured privacy, she said, "There's something you have to understand about Karsen. He gets interested in things. Random things. Intensely interested. There's no telling what's going to be his next obsession. In this case, it happens to be you. And he will be intrigued with you for whatever period of time you continue to hold his fancy. At which time he will then get bored with you and in short order probably won't even remember your name . . ." She paused and scowled. "Do you have a name?"

"Yes. It's . . ."

"Don't tell me. I don't actually care. There's no point in remembering it because you won't be around all that long. Furthermore, I meant it when I said that—if he truly maintains this daft notion of forming his own clan—*you'll* be the one who has to protect *him*."

"You do realize I'm standing right here, Mother!" Karsen protested.

"I have no secrets from you, Karsen," she replied. "I'm simply telling the girl what she has to look forward to. Perhaps she's foolish enough to think you would afford her some sort of protection, and I'm disabusing her of—"

"He did protect me! From two Mandraques."

That piece of information clearly caught Zerena off guard. She looked back at Jepp and for the first time there was genuine surprise on her face, rather than simple hostility. "What? What do you mean . . . ? You mean the two of you hid . . .?"

"No! I mean they . . ." She stopped and looked to Karsen for guidance. "Is it acceptable to you that I speak of this? I . . . I would not wish to overstep my bounds."

"You have no bounds here," Karsen said, sounding generous. Zerena briefly rolled her eyes in exasperation, but then returned her expectant gaze to Jepp.

"All right. Well . . . there were two Mandraques. They had survived the battle. They wished to make me their prize. And Karsen . . . he fought them. Killed them."

"He what? You what?" She gaped at Karsen. "Fought and killed? Since when? In all you life, I never . . . you *fought* them? Killed them? Were they ill in some way?"

"No."

"Had limbs or even their heads chopped off, perhaps?"

"They were actually impressive specimens," Jepp spoke up. "But Karsen dispatched them most handily. He used the war hammer he now has on his back. See? The blood of the Mandraques is upon it still."

Zerena let go Jepp's hand as if she no longer mattered. She strode to her son, gripped him by the shoulders, and then turned him around. She stared at the war hammer, apparently truly seeing it for the first time. Or perhaps, Jepp reasoned, Zerena had just figured that Karsen had taken it a souvenir or for its resale value, without any intention of ever using it in combat.

The blood upon the hammerhead had nearly dried to a pale green. Zerena touched it tentatively, and then raised her finger to her mouth. Her tongue darted out, tasting it, as if she thought its presence on the weapon was merely a trick and it was actually some type of condiment.

"You know, Mother," Karsen said, leaning in sideways toward Zerena, who seemed lost in thought, "she knew secret pouches and such that the Mandraques had upon them. Helped me acquire some valuable trinkets. Very useful in that regard, I should think."

Zerena seemed in the process of reassessing Jepp. Finally she shrugged, feigning indifference. "Let the others have their say. Then we shall see what we shall see. The camp is just ahead." As a warning to Jepp, she added, "Don't expect us to walk slowly or wait for you to catch up. Keep up with us, don't keep up with us, it's on your head, not mine."

"Yes, milady."

Upon hearing the title, Zerena made another loud noise that was probably supposed to be some sort of laugh. Jepp couldn't be sure. When she'd recovered herself sufficiently, Zerena said, "Save the high-flown titles, human. They mean nothing to us. The high-flown die just as readily as any Bottom Feeders. The only thing makes them think they're better than we are those fancy titles, so apply them to those who take stock in them and leave the rest of us the hell alone. Understood?"

"Yes, mi—"

"Zerena. Just . . . Zerena, if you feel that you must address me for some reason, and I'd rather you didn't."

She turned and strode away from Jepp, and Karsen sidled over to her with a ready smile. "Well done."

"Is it true?" she asked, as they began walking once more, and she could immediately see that Karsen was indeed slowing himself to allow her to remain near him. "What she said? About that you become interested in things and then get bored and forget about them?"

"I really can't recall," he said. She assumed at first that was supposed to be a joke, but when he said nothing beyond that, she realized he was serious. Rather than press the matter, she wisely decided to let it go.

They soon reached an incline. Zerena had gone ahead and Karsen was able to navigate it with animal-like confidence. For Jepp it was a bit more of an endeavor. She had to climb carefully, and fell several times, skinning herself badly. But when Karsen reached back to try and help her, she remembered Zerena's words and—more importantly—her attitude, and waved him off. Instead she gritted her teeth and even forced herself to smile as if it were all some grand adventure.

She made it to the top of what turned out to be a plateau. The Bottom Feeders had made camp there, and she could see why. The elevation gave them a decent view of the surroundings so that it would be difficult for anyone trying to surprise them. Several tents dotted the plateau, and there was a small fire going in the middle of the encampment. What impressed Jepp, however, was the vehicle parked at the far end of the plateau. It was large, very large, boxy, white, edged with windows, and it possessed not wheels, as Jepp had seen on most means of conveyance, but instead two long strips of metal, with treads, running along either side. She guessed that they were the means of locomotion, although she had trouble imagining exactly how they functioned. However they did it, they obviously did so with great efficiency, because they had managed to propel the large vehicle up the side of the plateau and onto this place.

It also seemed that something had spilled nearby the vehicle. Jepp couldn't quite make out what it was, but it appeared to be some sort of thick, viscous fluid, sitting in a puddle about two feet across. She wondered what kind of stuff it was, and then worried that perhaps it was some sort of strange Laocoon secretion or something like that.

Zerena was inspecting the fire to make sure it was in no danger of burning out. Once she was satisfied, she turned to Jepp and said, "Do you cook?"

"Food?"

"No, yourself," she snapped back with no pretense of patience. "Throw yourself on the fire and let's see how you taste."

"Mother!" Karsen said in annoyance upon seeing the obvious look of concern on Jepp's face.

"No wonder your kind is mostly extinct," Zerena said to Jepp. "No sense of humor. At all." She went into one tent and reemerged with a small closed bag, and a knife. She threw them at Jepp's feet. "Skin them, cook them. We're going to continue to forage. If any other members of our clan show up, feel free to introduce yourself."

"And what if more Mandraques show up?"

"I gave you a knife," she smirked. "Kill them or, failing that, kill yourself. It makes no difference to me."

"Mother, I should stay with her . . ."

"You would have someone that helpless travel with us?"

Karsen began to offer further protest, but Jepp stopped him. She put a hand gently on his shoulder and said, "Your mother is correct, Karsen. I should not require constant protection. You do as you need. I shall be fine here."

"You're sure," he said uncertainly.

She held up the knife and smiled gamely. "I'm armed. What could go wrong?"

It took several more assurances, but eventually Karsen accompanied Zerena out of the camp. He cast a few glances over his shoulder at Jepp before he moved out of sight. She was surprised to discover that she missed him almost immediately, not out of a desire to be protected, but simply because she liked him.

Jepp went to the bag and pulled it open. Her nose wrinkled against the immediate smell that emerged. She upended it and the corpses of several small, furry creatures tumbled out of it. She didn't know what they were, but it didn't matter. Her job was to skin them and prepare them to be eaten, so whatever names they might have borne were beside the point.

She set gamely to work. Jepp had not been lying about having some rudimentary knowledge of cooking. But it didn't extend to food preparation, and she mangled the first small corpse rather badly before she got the fur off it in jagged strips. She was, however, a fast learner, and so managed to get the remaining creatures skinned with increasing skill and speed. At least the knife was sharp, thus making the job a good deal easier.

Jepp could easily have just spitted the creatures and sat there, carefully dangling their fleshy corpses over the flame. She decided, however, to be a bit more ambitious. She went into the tent from which the food had been fetched and found, among other utensils, a cooking pan. Using the knife and a flat wooden board on which to balance it, she meticulously peeled the flesh off the bones and then carved it up into small cubes. This prompted her to smile with self-satisfaction, and then she scraped them into the pan. Once this was accomplished, she held the pan over the fire, flipping the meat cubes with growing confidence so they would cook evenly.

"This is how you do it," she said to herself. The aroma from the meat was starting to carry, wafting on the wind in such a way that she hoped it would prompt Foux mother and son to smell it and come running.

And as the meat continued to sizzle, cooking up nicely, Jepp became aware of some type of motion nearby her, just noticed out the corner of her eye, nearby the large treaded vehicle. She turned her head and let out a scream as the massive gelatinous mass she'd noticed earlier was moving right toward her, oozing with a life of its own, and she knew without any question that the thing was alive and about to envelop her and swallow her whole.

ii.

Mingo Minkopolis, a sack of swag hanging over his broad, hairy shoulder, was making his way back to camp when several aromas reached his nostrils all at once, intermingled one with the other. Such was the sensitivity of his snout, however, that Mingo could sort out each scent, determining the source and what precisely each smell signified.

It had not been easy for the aroma to get through the overall charnel smell of burnt flesh that continued to drift in from the field of battle. Long had he stood upon that field, surveying the remains of the folly that the Mandraques had brought upon themselves in their obsessive need for self-destruction. Mingo had known that there had been no way he himself could possibly have prevented the mutual massacre. Yet such was his view of the world that he continued to carry guilt, in perpetuity.

He would step gingerly between the corpses, his wide, bare feet moving with surprising delicacy considering their size. His legs were bare, as were his torso and arms. He wore tanned animal skins as a cloth around his loins. All of his exposed skin was a hardened, leathery brown, not easily penetrated by something as pedestrian as a blade.

Most impressive was his head. Many days he would simply sit with a brush or comb and comb out the fine, black shaggy hair—or perhaps some would call it fur—that covered the entirety of his face and head. His eyes were small, black and beady, set high and on either side of his head, and there was very little that they missed. Just above them were his horns, one on either side. Each horn was approximately a foot long, pointed and curved upward with an additional little twist at the tip. When he was charging, he was capable of impaling a victim on his horns and then lifting the victim up high and tossing him with a quick, efficient snap of his head. Showers of blood would spray in every direction. On those occasions when several opponents surrounded him, usually goring only one was required. The rest would experience a sudden diminution of nerve and abruptly discover that there were other, far more pressing matters that required their attention.

Now, as the smell of rotting Mandraques occupied his senses and his attention, something else was fighting for them as well. Something that was most definitely coming from the direction of the camp, and that naturally gave it far more priority. Fortunately he was downwind of it, so the passing breezes were making his life remarkably easy. He took a great whiff, his nostrils flaring to almost twice their normal size.

First and foremost was a scent that he had not detected in quite a long, long while. Fortunately he never forgot a smell once he had encountered it, and so Mingo knew without hesitation that he was scenting a human. A female human, if he was not mistaken . . . and, obviously, a male human if he *was* mistaken, but he didn't believe that was the case.

He also detected the smell of food cooking. Definitely the food that he, Mingo, had caught and killed for them. Mingo preferred his food raw. There was nothing like the animal flesh being torn to shreds by his teeth, the blood of the kill seeping down his throat. But he knew that most others opted for burning the flesh over flame and thus killing the true taste altogether. He did not understand it, and was even appalled by it, but had learned to tolerate it. So the human woman was cooking the food. Perhaps she had wandered into the camp and was trying to steal their supplies. The bristles on the back of his neck stood up to reflect his irritation over her effrontery.

He headed back toward the camp with great, loping strides. Karsen was fast, no question, but Mingo was swifter, and as he drew closer to the camp at high speed, he imagined the retribution he would inflict upon this upstart human, whoever she was, for daring to lay her fingers upon their supplies. Supplies that he, Mingo, had caught with his own two hands.

Just before he got to the plateau, he detected another smell that was hardly an olfactory challenge because it was supplemented by an audible cue. The smell was fear. Something had terrified the woman. The change in her bodily fragrance was palpable. However he didn't require his nose to tell him that, because the woman's outcries more than did the job.

Mingo barreled up the plateau, covering the last ten feet with a single, prodigious vault, and landed on the plateau's edge with a thud that actually caused the ground to shake. The female's back was to him, and she was too terrified of what she was seeing to notice his arrival.

A thick, gelatinous mass was looming in front of her. There were small flecks of purple throughout it, and it stood about a head higher than the woman, "looking" down at her even though it possessed no features that he could discern. Its viscous body was pulsing, although, again, there were no visible internal organs that would have explained what was causing the pulsation.

The woman tried to back up. In doing so, she tripped over a rock and her feet went out from under her. She hit the ground hard, knocking the breath out of her. The mass moved closer and actually grew taller (albeit narrower), and its top leaned down toward her as if trying to decide whether to envelop her.

She curled up into a ball, her arms wrapped around her head. It was the single most pathetic thing that Mingo had ever seen, and that was saying something. The campfire was between the mass and the girl, and it simply oozed around the fire, steering clear of it.

It was at that moment that a defiant roar sounded through the camp. The girl looked up just in time to see an aged Mandraque charge into the camp from the other side of the plateau. He was huffing and puffing mightily, the scales around his face tinged with white, his eyes a blazing red. His torso was festooned with ribbons and decorations, and he was gripping a sword in his left paw with such ferocity that one might have thought him prepared to do battle with death itself.

"Keep back, creature!" bellowed the Mandraque in a voice that was quavering but

still had iron strength to it. It was unclear to Mingo exactly to whom the Mandraque was addressing himself. His subsequent actions clarified it as he roughly pushed the woman back so that he could come between her and the gelatinous mass. The mass remained where it was, tilting its nonexistent head slightly, apparently curious about this new development. The Mandraque held his sword up and cried out, "You shall not have her, whatever you are!" When he spoke, it was with a deep, vibrant voice that was a marked contrast with his unimposing physical presence. It summarized the Mandraque, really: inwardly youthful and aggressive, outwardly . . . not quite as much.

Mingo moaned softly and then called out, "Kestor! Rafe Kestor! What the hell do you think you're doing?"

The Mandraque called Rafe Kestor froze and looked in Mingo's direction. When the woman saw Mingo, she gasped, her hand fluttering to her mouth, her eyes widened in . . . what? Shock? Fear? Mingo strode toward Rafe and repeated, "I said what the hell do you think you're doing?"

"This . . . this young woman," Rafe Kestor stammered indignantly, "she was being threatened by . . . by . . ."

"Think hard now," Mingo said, not unkindly. "Cogitate. Peruse as thoroughly as you desire the blue matter that comprises your brain. It will come to you. I can see it even now, drawing closer . . . closer . . . any moment now . . ."

"Gant."

"Ah, and the light dawns," sighed Mingo.

And the gelatinous mass, shimmering in a totally different manner, rumbled in a deep vibrato, "Idiot."

The word, emerging so unexpectedly from something so bizarre to her, caused the human woman to let out a startled yelp. The mass, apparently having lost interest in her, seeped away from her, undulating across the plateau and settling back to where it had been earlier. The woman was gasping for air, totally bewildered as to what she should say or do next. The Mandraque, Rafe Kestor, had gone from acting as her valiant savior to regarding her with overt suspicion. "Who are you?" he demanded. "What are you?" He pointed the sword in the general direction of her throat and continued, "Answer me quickly, creature! What happened to your scales? Your feathers or fur? Well? Speak up!"

"Rafe," sighed Mingo, touching the old Mandraque's sword arm and pushing it gently down. "Can't you see the brainless thing is terrified?"

"I . . . I'm not brainless!" the woman said. "And I'm not a . . . a thing! *That's* a thing!" She pointed at the mass.

"Suck yourself," the mass responded.

"Don't call him a thing. He's very sensitive about that," Mingo scolded her.

"And I'm not supposed to be sensitive?"

"There's a difference."

"What's the difference?"

"I don't care about your feelings."

"Oh." She considered that and then, to Mingo's surprise, seemed almost to deflate. "Well . . . yes, all right. I see how that makes sense. I am . . ." She bobbed her head deferentially. "I am sorry if I . . . if I spoke out of turn."

"We don't generally take turns speaking around here," said Mingo. "Whatever occurs to us, we simply blurt right out, and let the words fall as they may and where they will." He walked around her slowly, studying her thoughtfully. Then he glanced at the saucepan on the fire. "I'm hardly an expert in these matters, but I think you're burning that."

"Oh!" she cried out, grabbed up a cloth, wrapped it around the handle of the skillet and pulled it from the fire. "Thank you. You are too kind."

"I'm really not." He hunkered down and she, who was sitting, skittered back slightly, keeping a distance from him, eyeing him with concern. "You're a human, yes? A female, judging by the . . ." and he gestured toward her breasts, ". . . accouterments."

"Yes. I . . . am Jepp."

"I don't recall asking you your name," Mingo said.

"I'm sorry, milord," she replied, lowering her head in shame.

He stared at her, biting back amusement over being addressed with such a lofty title. "All right, well . . . Jepp . . . what are you doing here?"

"Cooking. Food."

"Is she in some sort of danger?" Rafe Kestor suddenly asked. He was seated on a boulder nearby and had been absorbed in using his sword to scratch his back when something called him back into the moment. "I seem to recall she was."

She glanced at Rafe Kestor and then looked at Mingo with uncertainty. "Is there something . . . wrong with him?"

"Nothing that death won't cure, sooner or later . . . sooner, ideally," Mingo muttered, although he looked sympathetically in Rafe Kestor's direction.

"And that . . . thing? It *talked*?" She couldn't understand, and there really was no reason that she should. "I . . . do not pretend to great thinking, milord, but I have some small knowledge of every race on the Damned World, even those I've never seen with mine own eyes, and he . . . it . . . is it a he or . . . ?"

"It is a 'he,' his name is Gant, and his situation is really none of your concern," Mingo told her.

"Thanks," Gant spoke up. His voice sounded much lower, now that he was spread thinner across the ground. "I appreciate . . . the notice," he added, his tone thick with sarcasm.

Jepp looked to him expectantly, and Mingo was helpless, caught up in the throes of being courteous in social situations where courtesy was called for. "And I am Mingo Minkopolis. I am a—"

"Minosaur, yes," Jepp said, openly interested, but then she quickly lowered her eyes as if feeling she'd overstepped herself. "My apologies. I did not mean to—"

"Don't worry about it," he assured her.

"But I do worry. I don't wish to offend."

"You're not offending!" Mingo said with mounting exasperation. Originally he'd been angry at her, seeing her as a trespasser. Now he had no further idea who she truly was or what the hell she was doing here, and his anger was coming from a totally different source. "You're not offending. You're simply . . . I . . ."

"You're annoying, is what you are."

Mingo let out a sigh of relief as Zerena trudged up onto the plateau. It was she who had spoken, and she had several more items of armor and knickknacks slung around her shoulders. She dumped them to the ground and glowered at Jepp. "I see you're making everyone's acquaintance. Has anyone tried to kill you yet?"

"I . . . am not sure," she said, casting a nervous glance in Gant's direction. For his part, Gant percolated slightly but otherwise ignored her.

"Zerena, do you know this . . . Jepp individual?" inquired Mingo.

"It's part of Karsen's salvage. He wants it to stay with us. What do the rest of you think?"

"Really." Mingo studied her thoughtfully. "You know, I'm not sure. Can't say I've ever had a pet before. Does it have any useful skills?" When Zerena shrugged, Mingo urged Jepp, "Well? Do you have any useful skills?"

"I was . . . am . . . *was*," she said, unsure of which tense to speak in, "a pleasure slave."

"*Really.*"

"Yes. For the Greatness," added Jepp with the slightest touch of pride.

"What greatness?"

"*The* Greatness. You know," she prompted. "The Greatness. All know the Greatness."

"Is he a Mandraque?" Mingo surmised.

"Yes."

"Where is he now?"

"He is . . . dead."

"Not so great then, was he."

Suddenly a hand cuffed Mingo on the back of the head. It was a resounding thwack, rattling Mingo's brain around. He snarled and his head whipped around to see Rafe Kestor standing there, and the clouds that were normally visible behind his eyes were gone.

"You will not speak so of the Greatness," Rafe Kestor warned him.

"You . . ." Mingo held the back of his head, trying to get the ringing to stop. "You stupid—!"

"You will not speak so of the Greatness!" To Mingo's utter shock, Kestor went for his sword, and Mingo was on his feet, poised, snarling, little flecks of foam flying from his mouth, Jepp all but forgotten. "She served the Greatness? I taught the Greatness! I taught him before he was the Greatness! *I made him Great!* So you will speak of him with respect, or the gods as my witness, I will render your neck lonesome for your head! Do you understand me, Mingo! Do you?!" Mingo stared at him, wide-eyed, astonished at the outburst, and Rafe Kestor waved the sword even closer to his face and repeated, "Do you?" Mingo managed a nod, but that was insufficient for Rafe Kestor. "Say you understand! Say it aloud! I want to hear it!"

"I . . . understand," Mingo said.

Rafe Kestor glowered at him for a moment, and then sheathed his sword. Slowly he turned to Jepp and his tone changed completely. He sounded gentle, even avuncular, as he asked, "The Greatness. How is he?"

The human girl, Jepp, was clearly bewildered. She had said only moments before that this "Greatness" that Rafe Kestor was so worked up over was dead. But she was not accustomed to the in-and-out of Kestor's brain as the others were. "Why . . . why he is . . ."

Zerena cleared her throat loudly, catching Jepp's attention. She looked to Zerena and, ever so slightly, Zerena shook her head. Mingo knew instantly what Zerena was trying to convey, and could only pray that the human's no doubt boundless stupidity would nevertheless allow her to comprehend.

Without missing a beat, Jepp—her eyes remaining fixed on Zerena—said, "He is . . . well. Quite well. He is . . . well, of course, he is the Greatness, so naturally how else could he be?"

Kestor took a step toward her, stretching his head forward on his thick neck, tilting his head with open curiosity. "Does he . . ." His voice wavered slightly. "Does he ever ask after me?"

This time Jepp did not need any cues from Zerena. Unhesitatingly, she said, "Of course! All the time! Why, just the other day, he was saying, 'You know . . . it has been ages since I have seen my old mentor, Raff Kestral . . .'"

"Rafe Kestor," Mingo breathed.

"Rafe Kestor," Jepp immediately corrected herself. Rafe Kestor didn't seem to notice the flub, even though—paradoxically—he was hanging on her every word. "Yes, my old mentor, Rafe Kestor, the . . . bravest and wisest and . . ." Zerena mouthed some words and Jepp promptly added, ". . . greatest worrier—"

"*Warrior,* you pale idiot!"

"Greatest warrior in the history of the Mandraques," Jepp finished all in a rush. She appeared as if she were about to add something else, but then thought better of it and simply waited for Rafe Kestor to say something in response.

"I should," Rafe Kestor finally announced, "stop by sometime, when we are next in the area." Absently he patted Jepp on the head, and then strolled away, his tail swishing behind him, to take up a conversation with Gant. Gant, in turn, paid him no mind at all, which didn't bother Rafe Kestor as he waxed nostalgic for the old days in the court of the Mandraques.

Zerena stepped in close to Jepp and Mingo heard her say, "Well, you almost made a complete muddle of that."

"My apologies, I should never have—"

"Oh, shut up," snapped Zerena, and then she sighed heavily as Rafe Kestor chattered away to Gant . . . who might well have been asleep for all Mingo knew. "You did well enough, I suppose. As much as was required, all things considered."

"Thank you, mil—" She caught herself and amended, "Zerena."

Zerena shook her head, her gaze still upon Rafe Kestor. "Believe it or not, he was once all that you said in your nattering just now. He was the bravest, the best. But time ravages us all, each in our own way."

"As you say, Zerena."

With faint disgust, Zerena looked back at Jepp. For a long moment nothing was said, and Mingo wondered what could be passing through Zerena's mind. Finally she said, "A pleasure slave, eh?"

Jepp nodded.

"Are you good at your vocation?"

"Are you asking for a demonstration, Zerena?" Jepp asked neutrally. Mingo couldn't begin to guess whether the notion was attractive to Jepp or not, or even if it made any difference to her.

"No, I'm not asking for a demonstration! I'm just asking . . . I mean, answer the damned question!"

"I am . . ." Jepp shrugged. "I am told I am satisfactory. Most satisfactory, in fact. I know many pleasuring techniques for the different races, since no two are precisely the same."

"You're conversant with what pleasures Minosaurs?" Mingo asked.

But the words were barely out of his mouth before Zerena said sharply, "You just get that right out of your head, Mingo, you understand me?"

"I was simply inquiring. I was curious from a . . . research and societal point of view."

"I'll bet you were," snorted Zerena. She turned toward Jepp. "And you . . ."

"Me?"

Zerena's gaze could be quite withering, and Mingo felt some grudging admiration for Jepp that she didn't appear taken aback by it. Instead she simply stared at Zerena and waited for her to speak. Zerena finally did, saying, "You bring pleasure to males."

"Yes."

"Do you have any idea of the power that gives you?"

Jepp appeared to be processing Zerena's words in her mind, but whatever it was she was thinking, it didn't seem to amount to anything. "Power?" she asked finally.

"Yes! Understand you nothing? Females have come to power in many ways. As a human female, you naturally could not, would not, rule in any capacity. But if you are indeed skilled, then you could use this talent to gain yourself a position of influence. Of wealth. A crafty female who is beloved of males can chart her own path. You, however . . . you don't seem to realize that. You bow, you scrape, you try not to offend. Whatever it is you do with your hands, there is power in them. And you are a fool for not having used that power to control your own destiny. Just a godsdamned fool."

"Such . . . aggression as you suggest, Zerena, is not part of the life that I, as a slave, was born and raised into," Jepp said. Yet again she did not sound at all angry, but merely matter-of-fact. Perhaps even a bit embarrassed for Zerena that something so self-evident to Jepp required explanation. "I am what I am. It has never occurred to me to aspire beyond my station."

"*Never?*"

"Is that so unusual?"

"Why would you not aspire to be greater than you are?"

"Zerena," and her eyebrows knit into curiosity. "You are a Bottom Feeder. From my understanding, the Twelve Races have lower regard for your social status than they do for anyone else on the Damned World. Why do you not aspire to be higher in rank than you are now?"

"Because I am carrying on the grand tradition of my clan and my forebears," Zerena snapped back with a good deal more heat than she'd intended. She heard a soft chuckle from Mingo, who had thought the point well taken and worth a laugh. She glowered at him.

"And I am continuing in the 'grand tradition' of my kind," said Jepp ruefully. "A tradition that was foisted upon us by you and your ilk."

"My ilk? My ilk did nothing to you."

"So you say."

"That's right, so I say, and how dare you have the temerity to—"

Mingo felt that there would be no better time to step in than right then. "Zerena," he noted, "first you castigate the girl for lack of character . . . and now you would chastise her when she first displays the sort of assertiveness you claim to value. Or do you only value it in yourself?"

Zerena was about to snap out an answer, and then clearly realized there was no easy response to that. Of course, Mingo silently reasoned, she could always go for something vulgar and obvious.

"Well?" he prodded. "Are you going to answer the que—"

"Shut up, half-man," Zerena snarled at him.

"Yes, I rather thought you'd say that."

"Zerena," Jepp spoke up. "I . . . do not think you understand. My skills . . . my gift for pleasuring, if you will . . . that is truly what it is. A gift. For me to utilize that gift in order to obtain personal gain, to get myself power and status . . . that would be an affront. Don't you see that? An affront. I could never do that. Not ever. Even if it means that I am never any more than what you see before you right now."

Zerena considered that, and then announced, "You're an idiot." She stood, stretching her legs, and headed over to the fire. The pan was still situated near it, basking in the warmth of the fire.

"I do not think she likes me much," Jepp muttered to Mingo.

"Actually, for her, telling you you're an idiot is perilously close to a term of endearment. Why, you should hear the things she calls her son, and her love for him is never in question."

"And Rafe Kestor? Does she bear love for him? And for you? And . . . what is the one you called 'Gant'? I do not understand any of—"

"Quiet!" shouted Mingo, suddenly on his feet, his nostrils searching the air. Zerena looked up from the food she was picking at. At first there was a questioning look upon her face, but that cleared immediately as she understood, without having it told to her, what was transpiring.

"Who or what?" she demanded. She tossed aside the food she'd been sampling. Jepp, oblivious to anything else that was going on, moaned as the food scattered all over the ground. Instantly she ran to it, her feet slap-slapping on the ground of the plateau, and tried to gather it and get it back into the pan. Zerena paid her no heed. "Who or what?" she said once more, and although there was no sound of worry in her voice, the concern was evident.

"Don't you smell them? Hear them? How can you not hear them?" said Mingo.

"What them is it? Is it Mandraques?"

Immediately Rafe Kestor had his sword out, snarling vicious defiance. "Let them come!" he shouted. "I will show them the true foolishness of . . ."

"*Not now,* Rafe!" Zerena snapped at him.

Mingo, meantime, began to shudder inwardly. The trembling came in response to something within him that was so primal, so basic to him, he knew what the source had to be even though he had not quite consciously identified the smell yet.

"Travelers," he whispered.

As if on cue, Karsen Foux abruptly scrambled up and over the edge of the plateau. While Mingo was just barely keeping himself contained, the effect their approach was having on Karsen was all too visible. "*Travelers!*" he cried out. "In the distance! Coming this way! Coming for *us!*"

And now all of them could feel the rumbling, bearing down upon them from the east. "Break everything down!" Zerena shouted. "Get everything in the jumpcar! *Hurry! Hurry!*"

There was no group alive capable of breaking down an encampment as fast as a group of Bottom Feeders. Furthermore there were no individuals on the Damned World that could move as fast as Bottom Feeders on the run. Combine the two, and the result was that they had their tents and equipment stowed inside the back end of the jumpcar—their oversized vehicle—in under a minute.

Yet during that minute the Travelers had drawn ever closer. The reverberations of their mounts had gone from a distant thunder to a storm of sound that threatened to envelop them. They clambered inside the jumpcar, all save Gant, who oozed up onto the top of the jumpcar and stretched himself as thin as he could. A strong aroma arose from him, pungent and eye-watering, as it usually did when he was faced with a hazardous situation. The rest of the Bottom Feeders had learned to live with it, but it was Jepp's first time, and Mingo saw that Jepp was squinting furiously and tears were running down her face. But she suffered in silence, which was fortunate.

What was unfortunate was that there was no room for Jepp in the jumpcar. There were only four seats and they were cramped in as it was. Jepp stood there, looking frightened and helpless.

"*Jepp!*" shouted Karsen, barely able to make himself heard over the pounding of the oncoming Travelers. Zerena cast a disinterested glance at her and then the large side door began to slide closed. Karsen wedged his hands in, preventing it from shutting. "Mother, we can't leave her—!"

"We're tight as it is, and she'll just slow us down!" Zerena snapped at him. "Get out of the doorway!"

"Mother, no!" He reached toward Jepp, trying to get to her.

And Jepp took several steps back, shaking her head. "Leave! Hurry! Get away from here! Don't let the Travelers get you, too! Go, just go!"

"Jepp!"

"Karsen!"

"*Oh, for the love of gods,* we don't have *time* for this melodramatic shit!" howled Mingo. And suddenly his large frame was in the opening, shoving the door wide, and he ripped his seat out of the jumpcar and tossed it onto the plateau. Jepp watched it bounce away in surprise, and then yelped as he reached out and grabbed her by the arm. One quick pull and she was in the jumpcar, scrunched tightly against Mingo, who was on the floor. "Now let's go! Come on! *Go!*"

The jumpcar roared to life, pulled back six inches . . . and stalled out.

For a long moment, nobody said anything. Then Zerena let out a frustrated howl and slammed the dashboard.

"You've got to be kidding me," said an incredulous Mingo.

Jepp tried to peer over Zerena's shoulder. "What's wrong?"

"We're not moving," Zerena snapped at her.

"You know," said Rafe Kestor, "I *thought* we weren't, but I was reluctant to say anything."

"*You've got to be kidding me!*"

"Stop saying that, Mingo, you're not helping," said Karsen.

"And how, precisely, *could* I help?"

"Care to get out and push?"

"*Both of you, shut up!*" Zerena was thrusting furiously on the ignition lever. The motor rumbled slightly but otherwise didn't seem inclined to start the vehicle moving again. "It's the hotstar. It's not delivering enough power to fire the engine."

"Why not?"

"I don't know, Mingo! I'm not a damned techwiz! I flip the switch, the jumpcar moves, that's all I've ever asked of it!" Zerena was fuming, and it was getting difficult for Mingo to hear her over the increasing pounding of the approaching Travelers on their draquons.

"Maybe . . . maybe they won't notice us?" Jepp sounded hopeful.

"Of course they'll notice us!" Zerena told her angrily. "And everyone knows how the Overseer feels about Bottom Feeders! They'll leave our guts strung out all over the field!"

"But . . . we did nothing wrong!"

"It's got nothing to do with right or wrong," Karsen said, sounding grim, "and everything to do with just being hated."

"But how do you know the Overseer—"

Fed up with Jepp's incessant questions, Mingo clamped a hand over her mouth. He made sure not to cover her nose, so that she could breathe. Her eyes widened in surprise, and Karsen looked alarmed and started to rise from his chair. But Mingo gave him a warning glance and Karsen remained where he was.

All talking ceased. Mingo's thoughts were filled with all the regrets that composed his life, a fairly sizable list. Closer came the Travelers, and closer still, and Mingo thought he was going to scream from the waiting, from the knowing that any second they would be here, would be everywhere . . .

. . . and then the draquons thundered past, down by the bottom of the plateau. He wasn't sure how many there were, for they were a mass of black, moving so quickly, and it was impossible to distinguish one from the other. He saw hints of their wings, which were rolled back and tight against their bodies since the beasts were galloping rather than flying, and the vague forms of the Travelers hunched down and low over them. He was able to make out, though, the glowing red of the draquons' eyes, and their mouths were wide open and screeching so loudly that Mingo thought he was going to go mad, that was all, just totally insane, that he would start clawing at the sides of his head until he'd ripped his skin off and be left a bleeding mess.

And then they were gone.

The screeching of the draquons slowly receded into the distance. The ground's rumbling lessened and eventually stopped altogether. The Bottom Feeders looked at one another with confusion and even a bit of awe, unable to believe that they were still there. The Travelers had totally ignored them.

Jepp was mumbling something incomprehensible, and it was only then that Mingo realized his hand was still covering her mouth. "Sorry," he muttered, and released his grip on her. She gulped in air as he asked, "What did you say?"

"I was asking you if you could remove your hand from my mouth now."

"Ah. Well . . . all right. That's moot, I suppose."

"They went right past us," Karsen said in amazement. "Did they not see us?"

"Oh, they saw us," Rafe Kestor spoke up with conviction. Mingo marveled at how the old Mandraque was able to fade in and out of situations, sometimes sounding evocative of the warrior he once was—as he did now—and other times like a doddering, errant fool. "They saw us. Rather, their draquons did. Whatever their mounts see, they see as well."

"How do you know their draquons saw us?" asked Jepp.

"Because," Rafe Kestor said darkly, "their mounts and my kind are not all that far removed, one from the other. I could sense them . . . sensing us. Oh, they knew we were here. They knew."

"But they ignored us," said Karsen.

"Yes. Yes, they did. And the why of that, young Karsen, I could not begin to know for sure. At a guess . . . they had something of more importance to deal with than a pack of Bottom Feeders like us."

"Then we should thank the gods for whatever that more important thing is," said Mingo. "Thank it . . . and pray for it on its behalf, whoever—or whatever— the poor thing is, to have so attracted the Travelers' attention."

FIREDRAQUE HALL, PERRIZ

i.

The shouting within Firedraque Hall was becoming so overwhelming that Nicrominus of the Firedraques finally quieted them as only he could.

Nicrominus was one of the oldest and most distinguished-looking Firedraques. His scaled skin was red where the Mandraques' skin was dusky green, and his jade eyes were mounted on either side of his head, swiveling independently of each other as they took in the entirety of the hall.

The hall was one of the few buildings in Perriz that remained standing after the Third Wave swept through the human city, annihilating all who attempted to resist them. For that matter, they annihilated even those who were presenting no resistance at all, which was, oddly enough, the case of many of the former residents of Perriz. They had tried their best to surrender to the forces of the Third Wave, and been slaughtered for their attempt. After that, the Third Wave had proceeded to destroy most of the buildings, not because it was necessary, but merely to display their contempt for creatures who would give up so easily.

Firedraque Hall, as it had been renamed, was one of the few structures that was spared, mostly through the heroic and determined efforts of a brace of Firedraques who kept their more bellicose brethren away. Nicrominus was reasonably certain it had once been a place of worship, where the humans had come to commune with their gods . . . gods who had obviously abandoned them, presuming that they'd ever been there in the first place. But the building had been an impressive accomplishment . . . the kind that humans had been capable of, and the kind that Mandraques and others of the Twelve Races generally liked to pretend were mere flukes, rather than proof that humans might have been a worthy or worthwhile race at some point. The ceiling of the hall stretched so high that Nicrominus had to squint to see it, and there were mighty colored windows through which the sun would filter. There were also, cleverly enough, troughs situated around the roof into which hot molten liquid could be dumped and sent cascading down upon enemies, making Firedraque Hall that much easier to protect.

Not many Firedraques actually resided there. It was the nature of their race to wander, to serve as sort of vagabond adjudicators and spreaders of the law. *Their* law. It was a slow, laborious process, but the brethren of Nicrominus were patient folk, willing to invest the time for the good of all the races upon the Damned World.

Nicrominus was one of the mainstays of the hall, however, and so it was left to him to deal with the situation when the Five Clans descended en masse upon him, each of them complaining of their ill use and demanding satisfaction.

He pondered the irony that, naturally, the fools had waited until it was too late. He knew full well that the plain of Marsay ran thick with Mandraque blood. He knew that they had violated the dictates of the laws that the Firedraques had set forth. They were laws that were supposed to govern Mandraque dealings and congress, and avoid precisely this pointless loss of life. But all the clan leaders were loudly accusing each other of provoking the situation, destroying the peace, and setting the bloody conflict into motion. They themselves were blameless, they insisted. They themselves had been ill used, had been pushed to the wall, had had no choice. As charges and countercharges flew past him like a swarm of bees on a hot summer's day, Nicrominus allowed their voices to merge into one indistinct buzzing, in hope that they might miraculously come to some sort of accord or—even simpler—just kill each other and get it over with.

Gorsh of Cheng was howling at the top of his lungs with such ferocity that Nicrominus thought Gorsh's eyes were going to explode. Thulsa Odomo was shouting right back, giving as good as he got. Pacing the table, circling uneasily, was Bazilikus, his malevolent gaze sweeping all who were seated there. Some maintained that leaders of his clan were able to cause enemies to drop dead with merely a glance. It was a claim that, to the knowledge of Nicrominus, had never been tested. Heading in the other direction around the table was Jormund, the largest and oldest of the clan leaders. He moved slowly and ponderously. Whenever he spoke he did so as if saying something remarkably portentous.

The one who caught Nicrominus's attention, however, was the youngest of the clan leaders. His name was Arren Kinklash, or at least, that was what he had named himself.

Unlike the others, he stood some feet away from the immediate disputes. He barely moved; indeed, to the casual observer, he might have seemed to be dead.

His eyes were lazily half-lidded, but Nicrominus was certain nothing in all these heated exchanges was going past him.

Gorsh pointed a trembling finger at Thulsa. *"You lie!"* he snarled. "I know perfectly well that your people entered our territory because they were trying to start a fight. They represented your interests in trying to take our land!"

"Why would we want your crap land?" Thulsa finally managed to get out a sentence longer than two words. "We have more than enough of our own!"

"No, you don't!"

Jormund snorted loudly at that assertion. "Are you looking to give them *reasons* for attacking you? Is that your plan? 'Thanks to Gorsh of Cheng, we now realize that we don't have enough land! So we're going to try and take his.' Most ingenious, Gorsh."

"Shut up, you! You covet our land as well!"

His voice suddenly hard and unpleasant, Jormund slammed the table with his open palm. "Oh, is that the excuse you're trotting out now? That we coveted your land? Is that why you sent out raiding parties on helpless settlements!" His spiked tail whipped around in agitation.

"Settlements that were on our land, blocking our progress!"

"With that attitude, is it any wonder that you attacked—"

"We attacked . . . ?!"

"Ah hah!" Thulsa spoke up, pointing at Gorsh. "You see, he admits it!"

"I admit nothing!"

"How typical since you so rarely take responsibility for anything that you—"

None of them noticed that Nicrominus was murmuring softly to himself as if in silent prayer. Only one of the clan heads noticed when, in the great closed hall, a wind current somehow began to stir. That one was Arren Kinklash, whose slitted eyes were narrowed in thought. He sniffed the air suspiciously and glanced toward Nicrominus, but said nothing. However, the slightest of smiles played at the edges of his mouth. And then, with remarkable prescience, Arren puts his hands over his earholes.

Seconds later, all shouting at the table was lost in howls of pain as thunderous clanging echoed from bells set high in a tower overhead. Powerful winds were swirling above, setting the bells tolling, and the peals smashed through the air with such force—as least as far as the Mandraques were concerned—that it seemed to them as if their heads would burst open like overripe fruit. Jormund, the heaviest of them, staggered about and then crashed heavily onto the table, upending it. The impact knocked back Gorsh, whose lower jaw was clipped by the edge of the table. Only his coiled tail prevented him from falling to the floor.

Arren, for his part, had made certain to distance himself from the table. He squeezed his eyes tightly to resist the thudding of the waves of sound against him. But since he'd had his ears covered from the outset, he'd been spared the initial shock and thus was in far less pain than his peers.

"*Stop it! Stop it!*" howled Bazilikus. Thulsa had yanked his sword from his sheath and was waving it about in almost comical fashion, as if he could cleave the bells high above with his blade.

Nicrominus was in no distress at all, since Firedraques were not nearly as sensitive to noise as Mandraques were. He was laughing softly, a noise like a faint rasp. Gripping his staff firmly, he was twisting it from side to side as if churning butter. The bells continued for as long as Nicrominus felt it necessary in order to drive his point home, and then he whispered the secret name of winds and they responded to him. Slowly they subsided and, as they did so, the bells began to taper off in their volume as well.

The leaders of the Five Clans, the most powerful and influential of the Mandraques, looked rather comical as they tried to pull themselves together. The only exception to that was Arren, who was studying the others with a clinical and amused eye while looking not at all nonplussed over what had just happened.

"You must understand . . ." Nicrominus began.

"We don't have to understand anything!" Gorsh snapped. Then to his surprise, Jormund slapped him in the back of the head, a caution to shut up and listen, and a mute reminder of just who it was who was speaking and the decorum required. Jormund was the only one who could have gotten away with such rude behavior when it came to Gorsh. He growled low in his throat in response, but made no other reply.

"You must understand," Nicrominus started again, not acknowledging in the slightest that Gorsh had spoken, "that other Firedraques are far more activist than I. It is they who put together the treaties that you willfully disobeyed by trying to exploit minuscule loopholes. It is they who created the laws under which we live . . . laws that have enabled us to survive the scrutiny of the Overseer. And it is they who, were they here instead of me, would very likely have slain the lot of you in response to your petty squabbles, and left your bones to bleach on the nearest rocks.

"Know you nothing? Remember you nothing? These pathetic displays, this warlike behavior, is part of what resulted in the lot of us being sentenced to this Damned World in the first place. It is part of what made us the Banished. It is why we were cast out. We of the Firedraques have endeavored to grow up, to mature. To set an example so that the rest of us can survive in this hostile realm."

"What did he say?" asked a still dazed Thulsa, thumping the side of his head with his hand, trying to restore his hearing.

"Nicrominus is right," Arren spoke up. The Firedraque looked at him with mild reproof, since he was not done speaking. But he opted to say nothing and allow the youngest clan leader to talk. "We united to destroy the Morts," continued Arren. "Why could that unity not remain? We must come together, if for no other reason than that we are stronger united than separate."

"You would like that, would you not," Gorsh said with a tone that did not sound especially sympathetic.

"Well, yes, Gorsh, I would," Arren replied. "I believe that's what I just said. So obviously, I would like it."

"You would like us to be united for your own ends!"

"Since my ends involve our mutual protection, then again, the answer is yes. However I'm not entirely sure what you're—"

And Gorsh was on his feet, spreading his arms wide, his voice bellowing through the hall. "Oh, he is not sure! Not entirely sure! Then allow me to clarify," and he pointed an angry, trembling finger at Arren. "I know all about you, Kinklash."

"Do you," Arren said calmly. He stepped away from Gorsh, and although there was nothing hurried in his steps, he nevertheless was keeping a wary eye on the larger, more powerful Gorsh. "I wasn't aware there was all that much to know. I am, after all, rather new to all of this . . ."

"I wish to point out," Nicrominus spoke up, "that I still had a few things to say."

Gorsh paid no attention to Nicrominus, either because he was too focused upon Arren Kinklash, or because his hearing was still a bit out of whack after the sonorous bells had done their work. "I have a son, you know, near grown. And he speaks to me of you. He says that your desire is to rule over the Five Clans! That we would all answer to you!"

"I think it obvious," Arren replied steadily, "that we need someone to rule over the Five Clans. How can we speak with one voice if there is not one voice speaking for us?"

"And you believe that ruler should be you!"

"I believe it should be whoever we five decide upon."

With utter contempt, Gorsh spat at Arren. Arren nimbly sidestepped it, and when the wad of spittle hit the floor, it erupted in a very small but visible puff of flame. Arren stared at the smoky remains in surprise. "All right, that's something I haven't seen before," he admitted, sounding impressed. "Interesting heritage you Chengs have."

Gorsh was acting like a beast that had spied an open wound upon another, weaker creature. Thulsa and Bazilikus were shouting at him that this behavior was inappropriate, that he should back away from Arren immediately. But Gorsh did not seem inclined to back away from anyone.

"You think you're more clever than I, don't you," Gorsh continued. Arren continued to retreat, and Gorsh to advance upon him. Nicrominus made no move to break up the confrontation, but instead remained in his chair with his armed folded, curious to see how matters would turn out. "More crafty, more cunning. You think you're the natural leader here."

"Do you even require me to participate in this conversation?" asked Arren with a carefully calculated air of openness. "I mean, you're doing quite well on your own . . ."

Gorsh's tail snaked to and fro behind him. Arren cast a glance toward it but didn't allow himself to be too distracted by it.

"What makes you think you can rule us, eh? What makes you so damnably superior!"

Still backing up, his arms to either side as if he were walking a narrow ledge, Arren said, "All right . . . if you insist . . . my superiority stems from my ability to think ahead." His forked tongue flashed out slightly, tasting the air. "And your lack of ability to do so is what holds you back."

"How dare you—!"

"You asked," Arren told him, sounding reasonable. He angled sharply to the right and Gorsh followed him, stalking him, waiting for Arren to make some sort of sudden move. "I wouldn't have told you had you not asked."

"Fool! Idiot!" shouted Gorsh, his voice rising. "You think you're far cleverer than I?"

"Honestly, yes."

"And can anticipate me? *Hah!*"

Arren had moved in a semicircle with Gorsh following in his track. Suddenly Arren stopped, apparently deciding to make a stand. He was positioned not all that far from the mammoth front doors. Gorsh, who had been following but was waiting for the exact right moment to make an attack, promptly halted. Arren automatically stopped as well, near the building's front south center. He hissed loudly, rocking back and forth on his heels and, occasionally, side to side.

"Did you anticipate that I would kill you this day?" Gorsh demanded.

"Gorsh, this is quite enough!" Jormund called out, but he made no attempt to advance on them.

"As a matter of fact, yes, I did anticipate that," Arren told him readily. "You see, I've been hearing things about you as well. Particularly that you were looking to make an example of one of the clan heads, and I was the most likely since you see me as the weakest."

"Well, I will credit you to be decent at information gathering," Gorsh said in grudging acknowledgment. He took two more steps forward. "If it makes you feel any better . . . I do not plan to kill you. I will, however, remove one or two of your limbs, just so you remember the lesson."

Abruptly, Arren placed his fingers between his lips and blew hard. A sharp, piercing whistle emerged from his lips, and Gorsh took a step back, shaking his head in annoyance. "Insolent fool! Did you think to *deafen* me just now?"

"No, not at all," replied Arren, lowering his fingers. "But since you're speaking of lessons being learned . . . I thought I would find a way to educate you as well, so you would be convinced that I do, indeed, think ahead."

"And how do you propose to do that?"

"Oh, if you think hard, I'm sure it will hit you."

That was the moment when a hellacious clanging erupted from above. The previous bell-related noises had at least been melodious to some degree, even if they were difficult for Mandraque ears to withstand. But they had been nothing compared with the hammering crashing noise that now filled the hall. Gorsh staggered with his hands clapped to either side of his head. There was an escalating cacophony of crashing and clanging and thudding, bells slamming into one another, and they were getting much closer, much faster.

Gorsh went to his knees, unable to bear the sounds, and then, in his agony, he decided to look up.

A huge bell was plummeting straight toward him. Its monumental clapper swung around within, sending peals of sheer noise pummeling into Gorsh. Gorsh tried to get to his feet but failed, and did not have time for a second attempt as the massive bell—weighing nearly thirty tons—crashed down upon him. Gorsh vanished beneath it as the bell kept right on going, the floor crumbling beneath it. Arren leaped back, an impressive vault that took him all the way to the meeting table as the section of floor beneath where he had stood vanished along with the bell. The other clan heads stared, stupefied, as the bell continued to fall beneath them before landing in the catacombs beneath, crashing to a halt. The echoes of the bell continued for long moments, and even long after they died away, they still said nothing, but just stared at one another. The only individual in the place who had not budged from his spot was Nicrominus, who simply looked amused.

There was the sound of thundering feet as several younger Firedraques, apprentices, students, and servants to Nicrominus, came running from all areas to determine what in the world had been the source of that calamitous racket. They stared in shock at the gaping hole in the floor.

The first one to arrive had been, as Nicrominus might have anticipated, Xeris. Xeris was tall and lean, with a narrow snout and eyes that sparkled with pure intelligence. It was an attribute that had prompted Nicrominus to pay Xeris a good deal of attention . . . partly because he appreciated a fine mind, and partly because he was cautious enough to see potential danger from Xeris in the future and so wanted to be able to keep a wary eye upon him.

"What . . . ?" Xeris finally managed to stammer out. "What . . . what did . . . ?"

"We were having negotiations, Xeris," Nicrominus informed him.

"But . . . what *happened*?"

"They fell through," said Arren Kinklash.

ii.

Arren Kinklash was savoring the looks of total astonishment upon the faces of everyone there. He saw now the opportunity to slam home a victory in as thorough and convincing a manner as he had slammed home the bell upon the hapless Gorsh.

Jormund was the first to recover his voice, although it was barely above a whisper. "Wh-What did you . . . just do?"

"Endeavored to make a point. Have I succeeded?" Arren asked quietly.

Nicrominus turned to his students and retainers. "I think it would be best," he told them gently, "if you would return to your duties. Xeris . . . we will need to repair the floor. You will see to that, won't you?"

"Y-Yes, Nicrominus," Xeris managed to say.

"You . . . you . . ." As the students and retainers filed out, Bazilikus kept looking up toward the highest reaches of the hall and then back down to the gaping hole that took up almost the entirety of the entranceway. "You . . . dropped that on him? How did you . . . ?"

"Because I knew, Bazilikus." Arren's attitude changed ever so subtly, the pleasant demeanor giving way to a tone of harsh cynicism. "I knew that Gorsh detested me. I knew he would try to move against me."

"But how . . . ?"

"Because that's what I do. I know things." Arren let that pronouncement hang there a moment, and then continued, "I know things, I figure things out, I anticipate things. I know precisely what others are going to do, and then I prepare for them. Are you beginning to understand that now? Because Gorsh didn't, nor would he ever have believed me if I'd told him. So I chose to use him to make my point and thus solve two problems with one stroke. And my point—in case you were wondering—is that of all the clan heads, I am the one whom you should take the greatest pains never to underestimate. Which means that if any of you is considering some sort of retaliation . . . you would be well advised to consider that I have already anticipated it and made preparations. Are any of you inclined to challenge me in that regard?"

The clan heads looked at one another uncomfortably. Jormund stepped forward, his tail twitching, his brow beetled and dark. "Have you considered your precipitous action will doubtless make you a target for Gorsh's son?"

"You mean Gorshen?" Arren made no attempt to hide his smile this time. "Gorshen despised his father . . . possibly from the first day Gorshen cracked his egg. Most of Gorsh's retainers and guards despised him as well, but none of them dared to make the first move against him. They feared what would happen to them if they failed."

Thulsa eyed Arren thoughtfully. "You are saying . . . that you and Gorshen have . . ."

"Come to an understanding, yes. He was well aware that his father might meet with a . . ." He glanced upward. ". . . freak accident . . . although there are those who would call the accident suspicious. But since Gorshen will be far too consumed with his duties as new head of the Cheng clan, I very much doubt that he will have any time to listen to them. At least . . . that is how he put it to me when he and I discussed it some time ago."

The clan heads looked at one another in a manner that Arren was easily able to read. He could see it going through their minds. *He outmaneuvered Gorsh. And Gorsh was the craftiest of us. What else does he have planned? What other trickery awaits us? Do we dare cross him? Is he able to read our very thoughts? Perhaps he is secretly in league with the Firedraques. If he has the backing of their elemental abilities, why . . . we may never leave here alive.*

"Listen to me very carefully, my fellow clan heads," Arren said. "We are stronger together than separately. These constant battles, the rising body counts . . . it must stop. It has to stop." He walked slowly around them, his voice rising with fervency. Nicrominus never took his eyes off him. The others continued to glance upward as if concerned they would be annihilated next. "Can't you sense them there?" he demanded. He pointed off in the general direction of the west, and their gaze followed where he was pointing. "Watching us. Looking down upon us. Laughing at us. Our exilers, the ones who sent us here. Represented by the Overseer, who keeps his Travelers moving through our midst, monitoring us, keeping us on guard and at each other's throats. The Firedraques have tried to show us the *way*. Gods know they have tried. And sooner or later, we must acknowledge that the way they have shown us is the *true* way. The *sane* way. So I feel the need to ask you, my friends . . . my peers, my . . ." He thumped Jormund, the nearest, on the arm. Jormund looked at him suspiciously. "My brothers-in-arms. I ask you, why should it not be sooner?

Why should we not set aside our destructive tendencies now? See each other as potential allies rather than potential foes."

"I made much the same observations," Nicrominus noted dryly, "and it did not seem to have much effect."

"With all respect, eldritch one," Arren said, clicking his heels and bowing slightly, "you are not one of us. Perhaps one of us has to say it . . . and, in so doing, open up possibilities for all of us." He let that sink in for a moment, and then said, "There can be no decision made here today. Merely . . . food for thought."

"And food for worms," commented Thulsa, nodding in the direction of the impromptu grave that housed the remains of Gorsh . . . or what remains there were after being hit by a falling object that was the weight of a hundred boulders.

The snide remark actually prompted some chuckling from the others, and Arren nodded approvingly. He was not surprised. He had known full well that Gorsh had no real supporters among the other clan heads, and that his demise would cause no Mandraque mourning.

And just as surely as he knew that, he also knew that he had to be the one who would be recognized as the central king. He could have pressed the matter right then, but his every instinct told him it was a poor idea, and so he restrained himself and instead said simply, "I suggest we return to our respective halls for now, to reconvene in . . . say . . . five turns? That should be sufficient time to discuss these matters, eh?"

This drew a hurried concurrence from the others. Arren knew that they were still shaken, and probably were grateful for the opportunity to take the time to consider all that had happened. Arren was perfectly fine with that.

He just didn't want them to take too long to consider it.

iii.

Norda Kinklash scampered around the upper reaches of the tower, giggling and whispering and having all manner of private conversations with herself. She was pleased with herself, ever so pleased, and could not wait to tell Arren just how pleased she was and why and all other sorts of things, if she could only remember them.

She halted her bounding around, pausing and frowning. Her passing thoughts about Arren reminded her that he wasn't here. She was waiting for him and becoming ever so cross that he was making her wait like this. She knew that he was the busy sort, always getting involved in this or that or the other thing, but she also knew that he depended upon her, and this was certainly no way to treat someone you depended upon. She might just have to punish him for it, since she was becoming oh so vexed. Provided she remembered long enough . . .

"Norda! What the hell are you doing up there?"

She froze where she was, hanging upside down, her tail wrapped around a high crossbeam. She wrapped her arms around herself, hugging herself joyously, and her long pink tongue slithered out and ran across the tops of her pointed teeth. "Did I do it right, Arren? Tell me if I did! I will be most upset if you say I didn't . . ."

Arren hauled himself up into the tower, huffing slightly from the long trek up the stairs. He forced a smile despite his exhaustion and said, "You did it exactly right, Norda. You cut through the ropes at exactly the right moment, when I whistled, just as I asked you to. I have to admit, I was nervous. I had no clue that Nicrominus would set the bells to ringing earlier. I had a vision of my whistling to you as we prearranged, and you—deafened from the bells—unable to hear the signal."

"You needn't have," she chortled. "I felt the winds, saw them start to move the bells. I knew before anyone what was going to happen. I got distance, covered my ears. I was clever, oh so clever . . ."

"I knew you would be," Arren said.

Suddenly she swung herself toward Arren, released her hold on the crossbeam, landed less than a foot away from him and snapped her jaws right at his face.

Arren flinched back, surprised and annoyed. "What was the purpose of that!"

"Just showing you. Just showing. Aren't my teeth wonderfully sharp?" She clacked her jaws repeatedly.

"Yes, wonderfully sharp, now be careful." He put one hand atop her jaws gently and one underneath.

For a heartbeat she felt annoyance at the way he was treating her. After all, he was only a few hundred turns older than she. Yet he tended to treat her as if she was much younger. She figured he probably thought she didn't notice, but she did. She wasn't sure why he treated her in that fashion, but mightily hoped that he would stop doing so.

"Bit right through the ropes, I did," she said proudly. She swept her spiked tail over his head and Arren practically had to flatten himself on the floor to avoid getting a spike in his head. She barely noticed. "And I used this to cut through, too. I had to move fast, you know. That's what you said. When I heard the whistle, I had to move fast."

"You moved wonderfully fast."

"So are you king yet?" She was eager to hear all about it. "Did they make you king of all the clans? Did they crown you? Did they walk you around upon their shoulders and sing little chants for you?"

"They did nothing of the sort. I advised them to return to their halls, and they did so."

She was surprised to hear that, cocking her head slightly and staring up at him with her slitted green eyes. "Why? I don't understand. Did you tell them that you are to be their king?"

He rested his hands upon her shoulders and spoke to her in a manner that he presumably thought came across as patient, but actually only served to annoy Norda. "These things must be handled delicately, Norda."

"Oh, must they." She did not sound impressed.

"If I press the matter, they will balk. They must have time to come to the conclusion themselves that my leadership is best for all concerned, and that they should all be united as one below me. If they feel that I am forcing them in that direction . . ."

"Then it might be you buried under a bell next time?" she asked, wide-eyed.

"Or with a knife in my back, yes. But don't worry," he said, patting her cheek. "It will not come to that. We will be united. And with all the Mandraques united, we will be able to provide a substantive force against the Travelers. We'll finally be able to take control of the Damned World and have control over our own destinies."

"Our own destinies!"

Delirious with the notion, Norda ricocheted backward. Within seconds she was a blur, rebounding this way and that, springing off with her legs or arms or tail from any one of a dozen directions. "Norda!" Arren kept shouting. "Norda!" She paid him no heed, far too caught up in her personal paroxysms of joy.

She bounded out of the tower, out onto the ledge. An alarmed Arren was right after her. He got there and let out a horrified yelp as he saw no sign of her. Quickly he crossed to the ledge, looking down, shouting, "Norda!"

It was only when he heard her self-satisfied snicker that he turned and looked with tremendous annoyance behind himself. Norda was perched above, clinging to a twisted statue of a creature that looked like a cross between a Trull and a draquon. There were a number of them, rocky guardians of the rooftop, or perhaps of the building itself.

"Norda, will you come down from there!" he ordered her with rapidly dwindling patience.

As if he hadn't spoken, she gazed into the distance with a distracted air. "Tell me, Arren," she asked, her voice abruptly filled with a clarity that it did not usually possess, "if the Travelers were to discover your plans . . . if they knew your aspirations, or if the Overseer were to learn of it . . . how do you think it would go for you?"

He snorted at the notion. "Not well. But they will not find out. You needn't concern yourself. I've thought of everything, left nothing to chance. You haven't the slightest reason to worry."

"I can think of one."

"And what," he asked with infinite patience, "would that be?"

For response, she pointed. He turned and looked where she was indicating.

A squad of at least half a dozen Travelers was coming up over the horizon line. It was usually hard to tell just how many Travelers there were when they were seen in a group. Somehow their numbers seemed to shift for no reason that anyone could determine.

But Travelers they most definitely were, their cloaks of bloodred and purple streaming out behind them, their draquons charging across the ground, propelled forward by their small but powerful wings. Travelers . . .

. . . and they were heading, with the precision and accuracy of an arrow, directly toward Firedraque Hall.

"Am I right?" Norda asked eagerly. "Is it a right reason to worry?"

Arren, trembling where he stood, was too terrified to reply.

SUBTERROR

Reality swirled around Merrih, except it was not reality. Or at least no reality with which she was familiar.

There were creatures gazing at her, as they were kissing her and licking her and making her feel warm, so warm. It was so strange, for she felt invigorated and exhausted all at the same time. Exhilarated but tired. She had no clue how she could have such mutually exclusive feelings. It made sense in the dream, but it was as if her mind had become split right down the middle. Half her mind was still in the dreaming, where all that was surreal and ridiculous was logical. The other half was struggling toward wakefulness, desperately trying to comprehend where she was, what had happened to her, and why none of it made any sense.

Very, very gradually, that part of her that was leaning toward wakefulness began to dominate. There was no one upon her now, no lips against her, no one nurturing her or drawing from her. She remembered . . . she remembered there had been that woman, that . . . strange female. What was she called? Sunara. The Mistress. Mistress Sunara, and she had said sweet things to her, things so sweet that Merrih had never imagined anything so erotic could be uttered, nor such glorious sensation be felt. Even now, as it spiraled into the furthermost reaches of her mind, it silently beckoned her to follow, and she almost abandoned her attempts at wakefulness so she could pursue that exquisite stimulation into whatever dark recesses of her mind it might care to hide.

But then she heard a voice. A female voice, and it was younger than Sunara's, and it said, "She awakens. May I talk to her?"

"Quiet. You hasten her at a time when she should not be hastened. There are delicacies at work here, Clarinda. I thought I had taught you better."

"My apologies, Mother," came the humble and appropriately chastened response.

Merrih fought herself to full consciousness and discovered that she was lying splayed upon an ornately decorated bed. No, not a bed . . . two beds that had been pushed together in order to accommodate her size. The mattresses were soft, and she almost sank into them. There were posts at either end of the beds that were intricately carved with designs that were—upon closer inspection—Piri bodies intertwined in an endless orgy of lust and hunger. It was imagery that would have repulsed Merrih not long ago. Now the niece of the Ocular king considered them to be attractively intriguing.

She reached down to discover that she was naked. She made vague attempts to cover herself with the bedding, but found that she had not the energy to move at all. In fact, she could barely lift her head. She blinked her eye to try and clear the cobwebs from her mind. Finally she was able to see who else was standing in the chamber.

There was no one else except the two Piri. She knew one of them, of course. That was Sunara Redeye. The other, however, was unknown to her. But there was no great mystery about her. She had addressed Sunara as "Mother" and Sunara had answered. Obviously this was her daughter.

Clarinda looked like a slightly smaller version of Sunara. Her face was a bit more angular, her chin more defiantly upthrust. Ultimately, however, she looked like Sunara redux . . . except for one major difference. Clarinda, scantily clad as she was, clearly had breasts. They were small, but they were there. Merrih had no idea whether she likewise was without scarring in her nether regions, but wasn't especially anxious to find out.

Sunara tilted her head slightly, looking sympathetic. "Ah. Well, it was inevitable. How was your sleep, child?"

"What did . . . you do to me?"

Sunara approached her, looking like she was gliding over the ground. She knelt next to the bed, where Merrih lay helpless, and she reached out and touched her face. Merrih trembled, but wasn't entirely sure why. She supposed it should have been from revulsion . . . and yet she didn't feel repulsed by Sunara at all. Instead the touch was oddly comforting. Perhaps, she reasoned, that was why she trembled: because she knew she should have been revolted, but wasn't.

"Ohhhh, is that how you see things? That they are done *to* you? It sounds to me as if you are content to think of yourself as a victim. How tragic."

"I . . . I'm not a victim."

"No, you're not," Clarinda spoke up. "You are a blessed one. You have been welcomed into our family by my mother," and she smiled beatifically, "the glorious Mistress Sunara. You should be grateful."

"I want to go home."

"You are home," Sunara said firmly.

"I'm a prisoner. I'm even . . ." She tried once more to move her limbs but was unable to do so. "I'm even a prisoner in my own body."

"My, how you *do* overdramatize. It's a temporary paralysis at worst, my dear. Your body is simply making . . . adjustments, shall we say . . . to its new reality. Before you know it, you'll be up and around. And maybe, just maybe, you'll be feeling a bit more generous toward your new brothers and sisters." She rose, stepping back and away from Merrih, and rested a hand gently on her daughter's shoulder. "Stay with Merrih, would you? Make her feel welcome. Make her feel at ease. I know you can."

"Thank you, Mother," said Clarinda, and she bowed her head slightly. Sunara patted her on the head as she would a faithful pet, and then glided noiselessly out of the room.

Clarinda kept her expression of serene calm, and Merrih started to open her mouth to say something. To Merrih's surprise, though Clarinda still maintained her look of peace, there was something in her eyes that changed at that moment. The look of dutiful daughter evaporated, and she put a finger to her pursed lips, indicating that Merrih should remain silent. Bewildered, Merrih did so, and then Clarinda tilted her head slightly, craftiness and cunning in her eyes. Understanding crept into Merrih's mind. Clarinda was waiting until she was sure that her mother was nowhere about. The finger that she had used to indicate Merrih should be quiet she now had raised in the air in a *wait until I say it's safe* manner. Aloud, she said, "The divine Mistress, my mother, is quite right. I should think that you would be deliriously happy to be down here with us. What does your old life have to offer you, really? You are a creature of darkness, as am I. As are all of us. Yet you live above as if you're something you're not. Your life is a lie . . . so welcome to the truth."

Finally she lowered her hand and let out a heavy sigh.

"At last," she said softly and knelt down next to Merrih. "I thought she'd never leave. Okay, let's try and move things along here." She slid her hands under Merrih's right arm and began to flex it. At first Merrih continued to feel nothing, but before long there was a faint tingling in her fingers. "You should be feeling something by now," Clarinda informed her.

"Yes. Yes, I . . . I am. I do. Thank you." She wiggled her fingers and nodded. As foolish as it seemed, she was filled with relief that she was able to do something as trivial and routine as that. She'd never felt so grateful for something that she'd so taken for granted as her ability to move. "How did you know I would be feeling anything?"

"Oh, I have a certain sensitivity when it comes to blood."

Merrih made a face. "Sensi . . . tivity . . . ?"

"I can smell it. Sense it. Hear it." Clarinda smiled in the way that anyone did who was discussing something near and dear to them. "I feel a little sorry for you, really, that you can't." As she spoke, she had moved down to the far end of the bed and picked up one of Merrih's feet. It was huge in Clarinda's hands, but nevertheless she began massaging it with expert efficiency.

"How can you . . . feel sorry for me?" demanded Merrih. "What you do . . . your whole attraction to blood . . . it's disgusting. You're . . . you're just a parasite . . ."

"We all have blood, Merrih," she sad with a trace of impatience. "Every one of the Twelve Races has it. It's just about the only thing we have in common, is blood. If more of the Twelve had a sense of that bond which should be bringing us together, you wouldn't see so many of us trying to kill each other. You think *I'm* disgusting? The most disgusting thing on this Damned World is that we're all constantly plotting and scheming to commit genocide on each other. And for what? Your toes."

Merrih peered at her in confusion.

"Your toes, move your toes on your right foot."

"Oh." Merrih did as she was told and was pleased to see that there was movement there once more.

Clarinda moved on to the other foot and began doing the same thing. "And for what?" she continued as if she hadn't interrupted herself. "For each other's land? There's more than enough to go around. For riches? Fighting over treasures and coins and glittering objects . . . it's pointless. We do it for the most ridiculous reason of all: It's what we've always done. Whatever the origins of our respective hostilities, they're buried with the corpses of ancestors generations back, and yet here we are, still acting as if there's any reason we should hate each other."

"We hate your people because you keep eating us!"

"We keep eating you because you think we're just animals and aren't willing to help us out."

"Why should we help you out?"

"So we won't keep eating you," Clarinda said as if it was the most obvious thing in the world.

Merrih tried to come up with a response but, to her surprise, none immediately suggested itself. So she tried a different approach. "For someone who feels that we should all be working to get on with one another and celebrates the notion of unity, you certainly don't seem particularly enamored of your mother."

"That," Clarinda told her testily, "is another matter entirely."

"How is it another matter?"

"Because my mother . . ." Then she stopped speaking, continuing to massage Merrih's feet as she frowned. "Why should I trust you?"

"I don't know. Why should I trust you?" responded Merrih. "After all, you might be trying to lure me into something. Present yourself as a friend or ally, just so you can . . . can . . ."

"Can what?" she asked impatiently. "Trap you? You're already down here. Sate myself on you? Already done that as well."

"You . . . you did?" Merrih felt faint. "You were . . . and there were others . . . they . . ."

"You're big," Clarinda told her with a shrug. "We can feast on you and then back off, and it can go that way for ages. You're a large supply. You'll last."

Tears began to coalesce at the edges of Merrih's eye, and Clarinda made an annoyed sound. "Oh, now, don't start."

"Well, what *else* am I supposed to do? You . . . you tell me these things, and . . . I . . . I want to go home . . ."

"So how is that my problem?"

"You can take me!"

Clarinda shook her head. "Too great a risk, too many ways watched, and besides, why in the world should I?"

"Because it . . ." Merrih's mind raced, and then inspiration hit her. "Because it would infuriate your mother."

"Well, that's true." Clarinda smiled slightly at that. She stopped rubbing Merrih's left foot and chuckled, the points of her teeth showing through her amused grimace. "It would drive her insane. Gods. I'm so sick of . . ."

"Sick of what?" Merrih prompted her.

Clarinda stared at her for a long moment, then glanced right and left as if concerned that the walls themselves had eyes and ears. For all Merrih knew, in the realm of Subterror that was very much the case. Finally, apparently convinced that no one was spying on them, she leaned forward and spoke to Merrih in low tones. "Sick of my mother lecturing me. Preparing me. 'Shaping' me, is what she calls it. It's just . . . it's so infuriating. Beyond infuriating. She's so pompous about it, and so smug and full of herself, and the life she's got laid out for me, wanting me to be like her. Not even caring what I want or think. It's never even occurred to her to ask how I feel about . . . about . . ."

Merrih didn't know what Clarinda was trying to say at first. And then some deep instinct cued her to what it was that Clarinda was getting at. "About . . . being mutilated?"

Clarinda looked at her in surprise, and then her face softened. Merrih couldn't help but think that—as alien to her own standards of beauty as Clarinda was— there was still, strangely enough, a certain degree of attractiveness in the Piri's face. Perhaps her lack of revulsion was due to some sort of psychological hold they had upon her. In feeding on her, they could have affected her mind somehow. Certainly Sunara had made inroads into her consciousness before, mucking with her, confusing her, rendering her helpless. Nevertheless, she still felt that her attitude toward Clarinda was genuine. The Piri had a certain beauty that she, Merrih, might not have been able to appreciate before, but could do so now.

"Yes. Exactly," Clarinda said, and when she spoke it was while heaving a sigh that sounded as if she were relieved to have someone she could confide in. There were still pinpricks of suspicion in Merrih's mind. Maybe this was all some grand ruse on Clarinda's part, engineered by Sunara. More and more, though, she believed that was not the case. "How did you know, Merrih? Was I . . . obvious?" Concern flickered in her eyes. "I hope to gods not. I wouldn't want Mother to know . . . she couldn't know . . ."

"Your mother doesn't know how you feel about her?"

"No, and I intend to keep it that way," Clarinda said firmly. "You don't know her, Merrih. You've seen her with all her pretty words and her seductive ways, but you don't know how she can get. You haven't seen her enraged. You don't *want* to, I can assure you. If she gets in a . . . certain way . . . no one is safe. But yes, you were right. I mean . . ." She cupped her breasts, a move that Merrih found both disturbing and yet . . . interesting. "They're not much, I admit, but I've no desire to see them hacked off."

"Is such a thing . . . imminent?"

"No," said Clarinda. "The ritual is not undertaken until the future Mistress has mated and produced an heir. Then the previous Mistress oversees the ritual. It's all very formalized and stylized and treated like some sort of . . . grand celebration. But I hate it. I hate the notion that the only way a Mistress can represent both genders of Piri is to have no gender herself. It's grotesque and unfair and it's . . ." Her voice choked. "It's going to hurt. A lot."

If the mighty Nagel, king of the Ocular, had ever told her that she would be in a position where she'd feel pity for a Piri, Merrih would have laughed in his eye. Yet that was exactly how she felt now. All worries that Clarinda was engaging in pretense or sham vanished.

"Did . . . did it hurt your mother?"

"Of course," Clarinda said, and she was no longer making the slightest attempt to hide her disdain. "But Mother—I'm sorry, our beloved Mistress—says it was a cleansing pain. That she was grateful for it, since it absolved her of all her sins and purified her for the job she was to undertake. Can you believe that nonsense?"

"I can believe that *she* believes it. So I wonder . . ."

"What do you wonder?"

"Well," Merrih said, and she reached up and stroked her chin thoughtfully. In doing so, she realized with great inner joy that she was in fact able to make that gesture, and that more and more control over her body was returning to her. "Well, I just wonder . . . two things, really. First, if the idea is so repulsive to you, why don't you leave?"

"Leave and go where?" Clarinda snorted. "It's not exactly as if we Piri are welcomed throughout the Damned World. Anywhere I would go, I would be hunted, feared, and despised. I doubt I could find enough blood to survive, and that's presuming that others of my kind don't track me down, find me, and drag me back here."

"What if you came with me? I mean," she said quickly when she saw Clarinda's incredulous look, "if you help me escape . . . certainly my uncle, the king, would welcome you into our home. Give you protection."

"Don't make me laugh," replied Clarinda. "Protect me? Sooner or later . . . and I'd be wagering on sooner . . . someone in your home would dispatch me in my sleep. And there would be much wailing and moaning and recriminations from your uncle, but secretly he'd be relieved, presuming he hadn't done it himself. I understand my choices, Merrih, even if you don't. To die whole . . . or live butchered." She shook her head, radiating a sense of hopelessness, and Merrih couldn't exactly say that she was wrong to feel that way. At length Clarinda glanced up at her and noted, "You said you were wondering about two things. What is the other?"

"Oh . . . yes. You mentioned about giving birth to 'only one heir'? What happens if the heir dies before completing the cycle and creating a new heir him- or herself."

"Then the title of 'Mistress' is given to another, chosen from the ranks of the Piri, and a new line is spawned. The line that my mother is a part of goes back at least ten generations."

"All right. So . . . so what if . . . a potential future Mistress were considered unworthy of the title. Has anything like that ever occurred?"

Clarinda looked at her askance "I don't know. Not to my knowledge, but . . . why?"

"Well, if you helped me escape, might not you be considered unworthy? Flying in the face of the desires of your mother, and the other Piri . . . that may prompt them to think that you could never do a decent job as Mistress, breastless or no."

"And do what? Live with my people in a state of disgrace?"

Merrih shrugged (another movement restored to her). "For a while, I suppose. But they would wind up getting another Mistress, as you said, and in time they would forget. After all, it takes a great deal of effort to continue to despise someone."

"How true. And yet," Clarinda said dryly, "those who reside on the surface continue to expend that effort with little difficulty when it comes to how our species, is viewed."

"Fair enough," Merrih admitted.

"Still . . ." Clarinda had risen from the bed and was now leaning against the wall, tapping it idly with her long fingernails that almost looked like—and might indeed have been—claws. "Still, it is an interesting notion that you suggest. Self-serving, to be sure."

"It serves me, but serves you as well," Merrih pointed out. "The best deals, alliances, and treaties in the world come from mutual self-interest, wouldn't you say?"

"Yes. Yes, I would." Her eyes narrowed, but a genuine smile countered it. "I shall have to give this thought, Ocular. A good deal of thought. But it has . . . potential, I have to say."

"Thank you," Merrih said graciously. "I thought it did as well."

Then Clarinda reached up and began massaging Merrih's thigh. Merrih, who should have shuddered in revulsion, instead nestled her head in the pillow and sighed with contented pleasure while Clarinda's hands continued to work their way upward.

THE CITY-STATE OF VENETS

Tulisia Sydonis, high lady of the Sirene in general and the Merk in specific, had been exceptionally careful when she had chosen her warlord, for she had had the foresight to look beyond the designation.

Traditionally "warlord" had been an honorary title, given to one who was charged with keeping the peace and looking after the health and welfare of the Sirene. He was not actually expected to wage war. As belligerent as the other members of the Twelve Races could be, none of them had attempted to go head-to-head with the Sirene. There were the occasional threats: The chest thumping, the spear rattling. But these were mostly for show, because the truth (or at least the truth as Tulisia saw it) was that none other of the Twelve Races was insane enough to stand against the Sirene. By the same token, there was little advantage to the Sirene trying some manner of assault on the others of the Banished.

Their respective environments served to keep them separate. In order to attack the Sirene, a water assault would be necessary. Although the Merk were not exactly what one would consider a formidable fighting force, the Markene most definitely were. On the other hand, for the Sirene to wage war against any of the other among the Twelve Races, they would have to find a means of mounting a ground assault, away from water for extended periods of time. The Sirene biology made that problematic at best for the Merk, and an impossibility for the Markene. The Merk required repeated immersion to survive, and the Markene flat-out couldn't move to any major degree out of water.

So the other eleven races and the Sirene tended to eye each other hungrily, driven by their nature to wage war, yet frustrated because their respective biologies made it unfeasible. Nor were the remaining eleven foolish enough to sail their vessels anywhere near Sirene territory, since the outcome would be both tragic and inevitable.

"Only one," she said to her warlord, "crosses Sirene borders with impunity. Just as they cross all borders with impunity."

Tulisia's warlord, whom she had handpicked, was named Orin Arn Oran. For someone who was designated as warlord of the Sirene, he was not as powerful looking or impressive at first glance as one would have thought. His body was compact; his hair was wilted a bit because he was not the youngest of Merk. Most surprisingly of all, as opposed to the aggressive and bellicose nature that one would have expected of a warlord, Orin Arn Oran was soft-spoken, his eyes surprisingly gentle. In addition to the weedlike hair atop his head, strands dangled from his chin as well, and he would occasionally absently wrap these around his fingers in thought.

But Tulisia knew that his mild appearance, while not a sham, was not all there was to him. She had seen Orin Arn Oran in battle situations on the rare occasions when errant members of the other races had been foolish enough to attempt an assault upon the Sirene. There had never been anything organized, no troop movements aimed at the Sirene. There were always foolish idiots, however, acting on their own and trying to prove that no one—even the water-bred Sirene—was impervious to attack.

When those occasions had arisen, it had been Orin Arn Oran who had been the first one providing a line of defense for the city-state of Venets. Those peaceful eyes had become as violent and intense as the seas during a tempest. He had moved with an efficiency and economy of movement that paradoxically made him seem as if he was moving very slowly . . . when, in fact, he was upon his opponent before the enemy even knew what hit him.

He was also politically savvy, careful and considered without being cowardly . . . and, not entirely by coincidence, someone whom the lady Tulisia found quite attractive and therefore wanted to keep in close proximity. Whether he was aware of her interest or not, he had yet to give any indication.

Tulisia had a small chamber that was entirely private and entirely hers. She maintained it for occasions such as these: when she wanted to have confidential meetings. She felt as if she were constantly under surveillance from members of the court who were curious about her latest plans. Certainly Ruark was the lord of Venets, but everyone knew where the true power was, so they tended to hang on her every word, her every movement. It could be most distracting.

The chamber had comfortable chairs filled with water, maintained inside clear material called "plastic" that the Morts had invented. The Sirene, having no more patience for such made-up words than any other member of the Banished, simply called the material "clear stuff." Tulisia lay back in her chair, bobbing up and down, her hands resting in her lap with her fingers interlaced. Orin Arn Oran sat opposite her, in a similar position, listening politely to her.

When he realized she was waiting for him to speak up, he said, "The Travelers, you mean."

"Yes. I mean the Travelers."

"You wished to speak with me, milady . . . because you want to discuss the Travelers?" Orin Arn Oran made no attempt to hide his confusion, although he was at least cordial about it. "I mean . . . I am honored, as always, to spend time with you. However, I don't exactly see the point. I mean, yes, the Travelers come and go as they please. Their draquons cannot swim, that's true, but they have very powerful wind vessels that they use to sail through our territory, whenever and wherever they wish. How is that anything that's appropriate for us to discuss?"

"I'm not interested in the appropriateness of it, Orin," she told him, leaning forward. A light of inner determination burned in her eyes. "I'm interested in the fact of it . . . and in possibly changing that fact."

He tried to process what she was saying to him, but had no luck doing so. Shaking his head, he said, "I'm not following, milady. I'm sorry, I . . ."

"Just because the Travelers take us for granted . . . lord it over us, act as if they're in charge . . ."

"They *are* in charge," he said matter-of-factly. "It's not a theoretical issue being debated. They are in charge, operating on behalf of the Overseer. Again, I don't exactly see what it is you're suggesting."

"Oh, you don't," she inquired in a challenging tone.

He continued to stare at her blankly. She was beginning to wonder whether she had erred in her selection of warlord those many months ago. And then, at long last, comprehension began to dawn upon him. She saw it in his eyes, in his demeanor. But it was comprehension mixed with a sense of growing dread.

"You . . . cannot be serious," he said.

"I have never been more so. I am curious, however, as to whether you fully understand what—"

He leaned forward, his face practically in hers. It was a rudely intimate posture for him to take with her, but it didn't bother her. He spoke in a hoarse whisper, not simply because he was trying to keep his voice down, but because something in his throat had tightened up. It was as if his own vocal apparatus was trying to strangle him in order to make certain he didn't speak of such things. "You wish to challenge the Travelers?" he demanded, his tone so soft that, even as close as they were, she could barely hear him.

"Does the thought frighten you?"

"It bewilders me, milady. I would almost think you can not be serious. That you are having some sort of jest."

"I do not jest about the future of my people."

"Nor do I," said Orin Arn Oran firmly. "And the future of my people would be, in great jeopardy if you were allowed to proceed with this plan."

"I don't see why."

Orin was rocked back in his chair, staring at her, his finned hands gripping the soft arms of the chair. "You don't see why? Milady . . . we are speaking of the Travelers! To challenge them is to challenge the Overseer himself!"

"And what of that?" she demanded indifferently.

"The power of the Overseer cannot be challenged!"

"Orin," said Tulisia, rubbing her palms together briskly as if she were warming to an interesting subject rather than discussing the potential annihilation of their race, "no great deed was every accomplished by those who proclaimed it could not be done."

"Then this deed will not be accomplished, and I will sleep soundly this night," shot back Orin Arn Oran. "How can you think such a thing is possible?"

"I do not know if it is possible," she admitted. "What I'm saying is that I am intrigued to find out. And if we do go forward, I will be looking to you to oversee the operation."

"I serve at your pleasure, as always," he said between gritted teeth, "but I am not inclined to risk the lives of my people simply to find out if some . . . some notion that's occurred to you is a viable one. Especially when I am certain it isn't."

"You do not know it's impossible."

"It's—"

"*You do not know!*" she interrupted him fervently. "The only reason you believe the Overseer cannot be challenged is because he never has been."

"He never has been because he has the power to destroy anyone who does try."

"So we've been taught! So we've been led to think! But we have not witnessed it, not ever!"

"That is because his power has its origins beyond this sphere. You know that, as do I, as does everyone else on the Damned World. It would be suicide."

"It would be intriguing."

Apparently realizing he wasn't going to get anywhere with Tulisia arguing the matter from the point of view of the Overseer, he doubled back and returned to the subject of the Travelers. "What you are suggesting, milady, in terms of challenging the Travelers, I . . ." Then he paused and frowned. "Actually, I'm not entirely clear on exactly what it is that you're suggesting. To challenge the Travelers . . . any reasonable person would say it is an act of madness . . ."

"Are you saying, Orin Arn Oran, that I am mad?"

"I do not think you mad, milady, no. But the actions you suggest, on the other hand . . ."

To his obvious surprise, she laughed. It was light, almost girlish, as if they were discussing matters of utter triviality, or he was a young swain offering her airy vanities. "Oh, very deft, Warlord. How you do manage to draw a fine line, seeking not to give offense." Then she lapsed into silence for such a long moment that Orin shifted uncomfortably in his seat. "How can you not be frustrated?" she asked at last.

"Frustrated, milady? I don't—"

She didn't allow him to finish the sentence. "This . . . Damned World . . . is mostly water, Orin Arn Oran. You must know that. While others of the races are restricted to their slabs of land, we can go anywhere. Anywhere. We are the rightful rulers of this world, not the Travelers and not the Overseer. Yet they look down at us with contempt."

"We do not know they do that—"

"Of course we do, Warlord," she said bitterly. "We are exiles here, for gods' sake! Exiles from our own sphere! Shunted here, unwanted, despised. Gathered up like so much refuse and dumped here on the Damned World. Their contempt for us is what resulted in our being here, so do not for an instant pretend that somehow that contempt is no longer felt."

"I . . . suppose it is, yes, milady," Orin admitted.

"And does that not eat at you? Does it not sit like bile in your mouth?" She rose lithely from her chair, the water within sloshing about. "Does it not make your heart cry out for justice? Don't tell me you have not thought about it. All of us think about it. It gnaws at our minds, at our souls, and we live in fear. I simply have the courage to give voice to it. You are our warlord. Why do you not have similar courage?"

Orin bristled at the challenge, as she knew he would. "I have the courage, milady, as I think you know. I have the courage to speak my mind and damned be the consequences. But my concerns lay with my people, with the Merk—"

"Ahhhh," said Tulisia, and she turned quickly to face him, a look of conspiratorial smugness on her face. "And now you cut to the heart of it, and open a portal to my thoughts on the matter."

"I don't understand."

She strolled around behind him. He began to rise from his chair but she rested her hands upon his shoulders and gently pushed him back down again. "Your people. The Merk. As you just said . . ."

"Yes, as I just said . . ."

"And what of the Markene? Are they not part of our race? Are they not as much Sirene as we?"

"Well, yes, of course," Orin allowed. "They are of our race. But—"

"But they are not our people. They are . . . what they are."

"I would not have phrased it in that manner, milady, but that is fundamentally correct, yes."

She pivoted quickly on the balls of her feet and swung herself around so that she was facing Orin, crouching down before him. She was quite close to him, and he shifted in his chair, suddenly overwhelmingly aware of the nearness of her. "They are unpredictable, the Markene, are they not? Their minds addled by their precious Klaa. They barely know their heads from their fins. They do what we tell them because all that matters to them is the Klaa, the supply of which we control. They will attack for us. They will die for us. They will even forget why they do such things for us. Is that not so?"

The full weight of what she was saying began to sink upon him. With a sharp intake of breath, he said, "You . . . mean to send the Markene after them?"

"Why not?" she said, shrugging carelessly. She rose once more, moving lightly as always. "The movements of the Travelers are not unknown to us. Their great vessels cruise through our waters with regularity as they proceed from land to land, spying upon the Twelve Races and intervening where they see fit. So what would be the outcome if a pod of the Markene converged upon one of the Travelers' vessels and assaulted it? Sank it, if they could. If they succeed, then we know for a fact that the Travelers are not remotely as invincible as they are believed to be. We parade their waterlogged carcasses for any and all to see, displaying to all the Twelve Races the clear supremacy of the Sirene. Our people will take the lead in ridding the Damned World once and for all of the Overseer and his Travelers. Or haven't you noticed that we mightily outnumber them. It is only our own fear and reluctance to alter the way of things that keeps us where we are."

"And if you're wrong?" Orin Arn Oran asked intently. Now he was on his feet as well, stroking the long weeds that hung from his chin. "I mean, you have more than made it clear that you believe in your vision of our future. But have you allowed for the possibility that the reputation of the Travelers is justified? What if they slaughter the Markene who assault them? Will they not then seek retaliation against—"

"Against whom?" Tulisia said in wide-eyed surprise. Her voice trembled like that of an innocent young girl. "Against us? But how were *we* to know the Markene would do such a thing. You said it yourself: One would have to be insane to think that the Travelers could be conquered. Why," and she shook her head sadly, as if relating the tale of a truly tragic fate which had overtaken distant relatives, "those Klaa-addled Markene must have come up with this ludicrous notion entirely on their own. Who knows what was going through their heads? Perhaps they mistook the Traveler vessel for a large Klaa reef and therefore attacked it. They are but poor, dumb, ungainly creatures who deserve our pity. I am certain that the all-powerful Travelers would be most willing to accept my apology for any inconvenience they suffered thanks to the rogue actions of a handful of pathetic Markene."

"That's . . ." He shook his head in astonishment. "That was . . . astoundingly impressive. I would never have known . . ."

"And neither would they," Tulisia said firmly, dropping the pretense of the young and abashed innocent. She reached over and took his hand. The gesture was enough to freeze him in place. "It is a perfect plan, Orin Arn Oran. We can be a great, shining beacon that will guide all our people. We will take charge of this Damned World. We will be united, all of the Twelve, even though the very fabric of our beings screams at us to indulge in futile interracial feuding. And once united, who knows? Perhaps we will find a way to mount a counterattack against our home sphere. Would that not be glorious? To be shoved out as refuse, but to return as conquerors? How stunningly delicious would that be."

"Very much so, milady. Very much so."

She reached over to him and drew the palm of one hand slowly across his face. He trembled at her touch and sucked in air sharply. "You will explore the notion, will you not? Quietly. Subtly. The Markene may be under my rule, but they are under your command as our first, best line of defense and offense against our enemies. You must make the plans. You must be prepared to point them in the correct direction so they will know where, when and how to destroy a group of Travelers. And after that . . ."

"Our gods will smile upon us," Orin Arn Oran said fervently.

Tulisia Sydonis looked appropriately contemptuous of the notion. "For all the times we've prayed to them and asked them for intervention, look at what their smiles have afforded us. I am hoping the gods will smile upon the Travelers. Let them be as damned to the depths as we . . . and they, at least, cannot breathe water."

She lowered her hand, turned, and walked away from Orin Arn Oran. She looked regal and confident. Still . . .

He could not entirely ignore the fact that she had just mocked the gods. And

Orin Arn Oran knew, from personal experience, that one mocked the gods at one's extreme peril. The fact that Tulisia had done so split his mind. On the one hand, he approved of her bravado. On the other hand, he couldn't help but pray that the gods just hadn't noticed her, lest the retribution be swift and brutal and . . . worst of all . . . spill over upon whoever might be standing near her.

THE COUNTRY OF FEEND

i.

The scream of Nagel, king of the Ocular, echoed and reverberated throughout Castle Skops with such intensity that servants trembled and hid, royal retainers feared for their lives, and Phemus, Nagel's chief advisor, worried for half a heartbeat that the castle itself would crumble around their ears.

Once having ascertained that the structure was not, in fact, in any danger of collapsing, Phemus hastened to the place where he knew that Nagel would be. Sure enough, Nagel was within his study, as he had been from the night that Merrih had been kidnapped by the Piri. Books were everywhere, and the clutter was horrifying to Phemus. Not that he gave a damn about the mess, the disorganization, or the lack of respect being paid toward leftover Mort artifacts. What worried him was that he knew full well that to Nagel these were major concerns. They always had been. He'd treated these dusty tomes as if they were holy relics, and had been fastidious in his care for them. So Phemus was extremely alarmed to find them tossed about as if a great windstorm had blown through the room.

Standing in the midst of the room, hands balled into fists, his head tilted back, bellowing an agonized scream that Phemus could only define as pure frustration, was Nagel. Directly in front of him was an Ocular whom Phemus immediately recognized as a royal messenger. The poor bastard was on his knees, his arms crossed over his head in a vain attempt to shield it, as if he was concerned that Nagel was about to smash his skull in with a club or perhaps just step on his head and crush it, grinding his brain between his toes.

"Nagel!" Phemus cried out, dispensing with his usual honorifics. "Nagel, what has—"

"*That bitch!*" Nagel shouted. He looked ready to smash apart the furniture, turned, and punched the wall, chipping a few pieces out of it.

"What . . . ?" Phemus looked around, trying to figure out who Nagel was referring to. The trembling messenger was hardly a female. "Merrih . . . ?" he ventured.

Nagel turned and fixed the gaze of his single eye upon him. "Don't be an idiot!" thundered Nagel. "Not Merrih! Never Merrih! She is an innocent victim in all this. No, it's Eurella! That bitch, that . . . that heartless—" He took aim at the messenger and swung a booted foot. Seeing it coming at the last instant, the messenger let out a terrified yelp and rolled out of the way so that the damage he sustained was minimal.

Immediately it all became clear to Phemus, and he wondered why he hadn't realized it sooner. "You sent this messenger to Eurella, the Trull queen. And she returned tidings that were not to your liking."

"*Do I look like they were to my liking?*"

The messenger looked up at Phemus with a silent, terrified plea in his eye. Protocol dictated that the messenger could not depart until he was given leave to. Nagel was too caught up in his rage to do so, and clearly the messenger was worried that Nagel was going to kill him in his towering anger. Phemus gave a hurried gesture, and that was close enough as far as the messenger's sense of etiquette was concerned. He stumbled to his feet and bolted from the room. Nagel's back was to him. He was too busy shouting out the window. Phemus could only imagine what must have been going through the minds of any Ocular below within hearing range, down in the darkness. Certainly they would be saying that the mighty Nagel had gone mad with grief. They would not be entirely wrong.

"I should have killed her! I should have killed that harridan years ago! Not a shred of compassion in her bones, not one! Either of her sons would be an improvement over—" Nagel turned and his head snapped around. "Where did he go?" he demanded.

"The messenger? I gave him leave to depart," Phemus said judiciously.

"Gave him leave! You cannot give him leave! Only I can do so!" Nagel was radiating cold, implacable fury, and he began to advance on Phemus.

For the first time in his career as an advisor, Phemus genuinely feared for his life. Nagel had been seized by a powerful rage that had near to made him mad, and it was entirely possible that he would annihilate Phemus before coming to his senses. Phemus, however, did not back down, nor allow to be seen the slightest hint of intimidation. Messengers might cower upon the ground, fearing the wrath of the One-Eyed King, but he would not follow that route.

"I allowed him to take leave of the room, since you have clearly taken leave of your senses," Phemus told him, his tone of voice as stiff as his back.

Nagel took two quick steps, and in that moment, Phemus was convinced that

Nagel was going to reach over and snap his neck like a dried twig. Nagel's jaw twitched, his eye glowered. There were so many emotions roiling within his un-blinking orb that, had there been a sailing vessel within, it would have sunk in no time.

Then, his voice sounding strangled, Nagel managed to say, "It is . . . probably better that you did."

He turned away from Phemus, presenting his back, and the royal advisor abruptly realized that he had been holding his breath. He let out an unsteady sigh and watched the king begin to pace, kicking books aside as he did so. "The Trulls were the most logical race to help us, Phemus. Who else among the Twelve can dig the way they do? They could root out the Piri for us in no time. They have dig-ging machines, tools. They have the tech. So I send a messenger to Eurella, and what does she say?"

"She says," Phemus told him with certainty, "that she regrets the actions taken by the Piri. That she regrets Merrih has been taken. However, the official posture of the Trull is neutrality and to service all sides equally. She will not provide us with the weaponry required to dispose of the Piri once and for all . . . unless, of course, we desire her to provide weaponry for the Piri to eliminate *us* once and for all. Normally they will not deal with the Piri, but to forestall genocide, she would be forced to make an exception."

"You know her all too well," Nagel said ruefully. "I don't understand her thinking."

"The Piri are one of the Twelve."

"They are one of the Twelve but in technicality only!" Nagel protested. "In re-ality, they are little more than animals! If we dealing with an animal infestation, would Eurella suffer the animals to live? I think not!"

"I think not as well, my king, but Eurella is unpredictable. The truth is, she might indeed suffer the animals to live. None know Eurella's mind."

"I wouldn't be willing to wager she has a mind at all," Nagel said. His anger was rising once more and it took a visible effort for him to keep it in check. Having nowhere else to place it, he turned and kicked over an entire table. It crashed to the floor. Phemus winced at the noise, and was about to scold Nagel firmly, albeit re-spectfully, but Nagel didn't look as if he would listen. Instead he sagged to the ground, shaking his head wearily. "What sort of king am I," he said with tragedy lac-ing his words, "who cannot even keep his niece safe, or his people safe? My father—"

"Your father could not have done more than you."

"Somehow I doubt that."

Phemus paused and then said, "Perhaps the Man—"

"No."

"The Mandraques, my king, if you'd only—"

"On his *deathbed*, Phemus!" Nagel said angrily, waving a finger in Phemus's face. "On his deathbed, one of the last things my grandfather said to me was 'Don't trust the Mandraques.' The look in his face, the intensity . . . he was trying to—"

"To carry on a hatred that has long—"

"He was trying to sear into me a lesson that he was convinced would save not only my life, but the entirety of our country!" Nagel's rage was so fervent that Phemus immediately stepped back to give him room. "Because he knew that at some point in the future there would be someone like you who would try to convince me to give the Mandraques a toehold in Feend!"

"I am trying to convince you of no such thing, Nagel," Phemus shot back, although he made no threatening move. "I am simply trying to tell you that you should consider all your options."

"Asking the Mandraques for help is not an option," Nagel said firmly. He turned his back to Phemus and leaned against a wall. Phemus initially thought of pressing him on the matter, but then simply chose to remain quiet and wait for Nagel to continue speaking. After a long silence, Nagel leaned down and picked up one of the fallen books. As was the case with most of the Mort texts, it looked remarkably small in his powerful hands. Phemus wondered how Nagel could even manage to page through it. "We so underestimate the Morts, you know. It's all in here."

"All in . . . ?" Phemus shook his head. "I don't understand, my king."

"The Morts had a device. A device of legendary power," and he waved the book around. "A device that, if used properly, could solve all my problems. Rid us of the Piri. Change to our advantage the very nature of the land that we live in. Then again," and with a heavy sigh he tossed the book onto a table, "for all I know, the power is legendary because the device itself is merely the stuff of legend, rather than reality. Who knows? It's always difficult to tell with the Morts. They wrote texts of utter fabrication, did you know that?"

"I did not," Phemus said.

"It's true. I have some here," and he picked up a couple of books from the floor, placing them back in their shelves. The floor was still a terrible mess, but he was making some feeble attempts to restore order. "Hard to tell what was truth with the Morts and what was fiction. Then again, I suppose that's to be expected, considering how many of their fictions stemmed from the fact of our ancestors' existence. Bastardized, of course, for the entertainment of the reading public. They called our kind 'cyclops,' did you know that? They had names for most of us, although none of the names were wholly accurate."

"I was actually aware of that, yes," Phemus assured him.

"The Mandraques," Nagel said abruptly, "betrayed us."

"Not exactly, my king."

"Are you denying—?"

"I deny nothing. What I am saying is that it was, in fact, the ancestors of Mandraques who betrayed our people's ancestors. That early betrayal has been more than enough to sustain the hostility between our people and the Mandraques."

"There is hostility because the Mandraques would just as soon kill someone as look at them," said Nagel. "And considering they oftentimes have done just that, I'd say that's a valid enough reason, wouldn't you?"

"Then what will you do, my king?"

"I don't know yet," said Nagel with mounting frustration. "I need to develop a plan that's actually workable. One that has no inherent negatives."

"I don't know that you'll find one. Consider, though, that an alliance with the Mandraques . . ."

"And even if I were to take that step," Nagel challenged, "what then? The Mandraques are smaller than us, true. What race isn't? But your suggestion, I assume, is that they would go into the labyrinths after the Piri." When Phemus nodded, Nagel continued, "They may still be too big for the job. They are larger than the Piri. If Mandraque warriors become trapped down there, our call for help—the alliance that you propose—may simply result in more captured sustenance for the Piri. We may be sending them their next year's worth of meals! Did you consider that?"

"I did," Phemus said. "And there is something that you have not considered." He didn't pause to allow Nagel to guess what that might be but instead continued, "Mandraque children."

Phemus wasn't quite sure how Nagel would react to that, but he certainly wasn't expecting Nagel to begin laughing uproariously. The king held his stomach as if he were concerned that his innards were going to spill out and collect at his feet. "You're not serious!" he finally managed to say.

"Mandraque children are vicious, my king."

"They're children!"

"They are vicious," repeated Phemus. "In some regards, more so than the adults. Mandraques are ready to fight from the moment they're hatched. In fact, in any Mandraque litter, at least two or three of the smaller ones wind up being killed and eaten."

"That much I can believe."

"By the time they approach adolescence, they are as vicious and deadly as they're going to be upon achieving full growth," Phemus continued. "The only thing that changes is that, as they grow, they become stronger. But one doesn't need all that much strength to kill Piri. One only needs determination, numbers, and the ability to break their necks like so many branches."

"You're telling me," Nagel said in wonderment, "that we should approach the Mandraques with the idea that they should provide us with a number of their children in order to wipe out the Piri? And they would do this . . . why? Out of the goodness of their hearts?"

"They would do it because Mandraques historically have never needed a reason to fight. Just a when and where. You tell them you wish to make use of their children in a battle situation, and the odds are that they will consider it a positive learning experience. I mean," he added in exasperation, "what else is there? Our own children? Perhaps we should just tell our people that all Ocular children are to be conscripted, trained in the ways of war, and sent into the caverns to root out the Piri. I somehow doubt our people would embrace the idea, don't you?"

"I . . ." Nagel shook his head, sagging into a chair. "I must think on this. I mean . . . I hear your words, honored Phemus. I even see the wisdom with which they are layered. But you are asking . . . a great deal. All my life, I have known that the Piri must not be feared, lest we give in to fear, and the Mandraques are not to be trusted, lest we leave ourselves vulnerable . . ."

"We *are* vulnerable, Nagel . . . *to* the Piri," Phemus said. He rested a hand on Nagel's sagging back. "My king . . . you have not slept. You have not eaten. I beg you . . . do the latter, then the former."

"I can't sleep. I keep envisioning Merrih. I see her being pulled down into darkness and despair, and I don't know how to help her."

"Yes, you do," Phemus insisted. "The only question is: Will you?"

Finally, Nagel nodded wearily. "I will eat something. Then I will sleep. And then I will decide."

"I know that you will make the best decision possible, one that is best for our people."

ii.

Nagel sat in the study, staring at the disarray for long minutes after Phemus had departed.

"The Mandraques," he sighed, shaking his head. He hated to say it, but Phemus had made a convincing case. And Phemus was his most trusted advisor, just as he had been for his father. What choice did the young king have but to depend upon the words of such a learned individual?

He could have assigned someone to put the books back and restore some order to the place, but Nagel couldn't bring himself to do that. He had, in his rage, been responsible for this havoc. So it seemed reasonable that he be the one to attend to it.

He gathered books together and placed them on the shelves, but his mind wasn't really on his work. Instead he was envisioning poor Merrih in the clutches of those animals, unable to get her out of his mind. He might be able to conscript children of the Ocular, yes, but he would knowingly be sending at least some, if not all, to their deaths. He knew that such decisions were an inevitable part of being a leader. Could he make such decisions? He was beginning to wonder if he was capable of it, or—

That was when he noticed something on the stone wall behind one of the shelves. Typically, books obscured the wall from view. With all the books out of the shelves, light was cast onto it, and he saw that one of the stones was protruding a bit from the others.

"That's odd," he muttered, and he pushed against the stone to try and shove it back into place. The stone moved easily, and he was startled by the sounds of unseen gears grinding against one another. He stepped back, looking around in confusion, and then gasped as the wall rotated inward.

Stunned into silence, Nagel hesitated only a moment and then stepped through into darkness. Naturally he could see perfectly and he looked around the chamber that stood newly revealed by the moving wall.

There were more books inside, and what appeared to be a writing table. A book sat upon it, a writing implement next to it.

Disappeared behind the stacks of books. His words floated back to him, and Nagel was amused at his own credulity. He'd tried to piece together the recollections of his youth and realized now that he couldn't have been more wrong. His father hadn't been behind stacks of books; he'd been behind the wall itself. This was some sort of hidden sanctuary where his father had sought privacy, an escape from the world around him. Nagel instantly felt a greater bond with his father than he'd ever known, considering the number of times that Nagel had likewise wished he could get away from the responsibilities that bore down upon him with crushing weight.

He went to the book, open on the stand, half-expecting to discover more Mort scribblings upon it. He was instead amazed to discover that it was Ocular writing. "A journal," he breathed. It was some sort of journal that his father had kept. For a heartbeat he considered closing it without reading a word of it. It was intrusive, invading his father's privacy in such a manner. Then he realized he was being ridiculous. His father was long gone, and his "rights" with him.

He paged through it and began to read with mounting excitement. His father had never been the most "giving" of individuals, and so Nagel hoped that he would be able to glean something of the way his father's mind worked from these writings.

And slowly his enthusiasm began to diminish, to be replaced by a building sense of rage. The words seemed to fly at him from all directions, arrows aimed at his heart, his soul . . .

> *I blame our son's mother for his weakness of spirit. Against all my wishes, she has coddled him, encouraged him to think far too much about matters of importance. I do not know how Nagel can ever lead . . .*
>
> *He spends far too much time with that sister of his. I begin to wonder if there is not something unhealthy in their time together . . .*
>
> *Took my son hunting today. He displayed no taste for it. He despises the notion of taking life. A ruler cannot be insensitive to such matters, but he has yet to realize that the lives of his subjects—be they animals or Ocular—are in his hands, to take or spare as he pleases. And it is not his ability to spare that concerns me . . .*
>
> *I do not trust Phemus. He speaks of forming alliances with those who I am convinced would destroy us. His words are soaked in honey but I believe the intent behind them to be sour. There are times I think I am standing in the way of his priorities. Either he, or one of his operatives. Phemus is very wise in that regard. No one should put himself at risk when he can use agents to do his bidding. I may have to have him disposed of before he presents a serious danger to me or my line. Would that I had someone to talk to about this. Would that I had a son in whom I felt I could confide. But I can trust no one. Not the children of my seed nor the wife of my bed. No one . . .*
>
> *The mother of Phemus has died, but not before telling me a very interesting tale. I have hinted to Phemus that I know. He denies it all, of course. I shall explore this in more detail before deciding how to proceed . . .*
>
> *Not feeling well this evening. I wonder if Phemus*

There had been more. Pages and pages and pages more, packed with suspicion and frustration and a growing sense of isolation. The line about not feeling well had been the last, and it had been left frustratingly incomplete. Nagel sat there, staring at the name "Phemus" simply hanging there. That, combined with hints of some "secret," was maddening.

He felt shocked, mortified, angered. Dozens of emotions warred within him. He had no idea how long he had been in there, paging through his father's journal, but it felt like a lifetime. A lifetime during which he was examining his own life-time, raging silently against his father's perception of him and knowing he would never be able to confront him.

He closed the book, resisting the temptation to tear it to shreds. Then he stepped out of the room and pulled back on the brickwork. The hidden chamber obediently obscured itself once more.

Nagel then replaced the books, dwelling on everything his father had written. Then he summoned a retainer, who came promptly and waited expectantly for his king to command him.

"Prepare an escort," he said. "I'm embarking on a journey."

"Where, O king?" inquired the retainer.

The Nagel he had been before he walked into the chamber would have replied immediately. But now he envisioned the retainer immediately going straight to Phemus and repeating everything word for word. The spider of suspicion about his advisor had crawled into his heart and was busy spinning a web within.

"None of your damned business," snapped Nagel. "Do as I order."

The retainer looked startled and then said quickly, "Yes, O king." He ran off to do as he had been bidden.

Nagel wished at that moment that his father was there so he could see, with pride, how Nagel was about to take action, and so that he could seek his father's blessing. Or his father's life. He wasn't sure which was more important to him at the moment.

FIREDRAQUE HALL, PERRIZ

Eleven races that walked or swam or crawled upon the Damned World quaked in fear of the Travelers.

One race did not. That race was the Firedraques. They were the smallest in number of the Twelve Races and yet, despite that—or perhaps because of that—they were among the most formidable. They feared very little in general, and not the Travelers in particular.

They only feared the Overseer.

And Nicrominus of the Firedraques did not even fear him.

Since Nicrominus knew very little of the Overseer, and not all that much more about the Travelers, he considered both of them merely subjects about which to learn. This separated him from many of his brethren and most of the other races, for others saw that which they knew nothing about as something to be afraid of, rather than a challenge to study.

So when word reached Nicrominus that half a dozen (or more, or possibly fewer) Travelers were visible upon the horizon and riding straight toward Firedraque Hall, he did not display any outward concern. All he said was "Hunh" in a manner that indicated he found the news interesting and unexpected, but nothing especially daunting.

Xeris, on the other hand, was more than daunted. "Preceptor," he said urgently, "we must get you to safety!"

At first his urgent plea didn't register on Nicrominus. Nicrominus was in the middle of eating his midafternoon snack, delicately pulling apart the small winged creature on his plate. It struggled feebly and let out a pathetic chirp right before he bit the head off, and crunched it between his powerful teeth. Nicrominus extended his tongue, running along the edges of his lips, not wanting to leave embarrassing feathers sticking to his maw. He looked up in polite confusion at Xeris and inquired, "Safety? From what?"

"The Travelers! Have you not heard!" Xeris came around the table and knelt near his mentor. "They are approaching! They will be here shortly! There's no time to waste!"

"And yet," sighed Nicrominus, "here you are wasting mine. I am getting far too old to run from things, Xeris. It is unseemly, to say nothing of being a waste of time since whatever might be chasing me is more than likely to catch me. What would you have me do?"

"At least make the effort! You have no idea what they intend for you!"

"But if I flee, how will I find out?"

"Preceptor!" Xeris scarcely knew what to say. He fumbled around, searching for the words that would impart to Nicrominus some measure of the situation's gravity. "How can you not . . . ?"

"Not what?"

"Not care!"

Nicrominus reached over and patted the top of Xeris's hand in a paternal matter. "Of course I care, Xeris. However, that which I care about isn't remotely the same as what you care about." He upended the plate and dumped the bird bones into a nearby receptacle. He carefully put the plate back on the table. His long, elegant tongue snapped out several times, clearing off the few remains of food upon the plate. "I care about learning, first and foremost. As my student, I should think that you would share that predilection. When faced with the unknown, the coward runs from it, while those who desire learning and knowledge run toward it."

"Fools run toward danger as well," Xeris reminded him, "for they don't know any better."

When he replied, his voice was surprisingly deep and angry, his brow scowling. "Are you implying that I am a fool?"

Xeris gulped deeply and then, steeling himself, said, "In some situations, in some things . . . yes, you can be a fool. Particularly when it comes to issues of your personal safety."

Nicrominus looked appalled that the subject even required debating, so clear to him was the course of action. He puffed his cheeks out several times as he usually did when he was worked up about something. "My personal safety means nothing to me. Less than nothing."

"Have you considered, Preceptor, that it means something to me? Or to your daughter? When she returns from her visit to the borderlands, how do you think she will respond if you are . . . are . . ."

"Dead?" Nicrominus, having thoroughly cleaned his plate, slid it aside, and placed his hands, long fingers interlaced, upon the table. "She will very likely say that I died as I lived: unafraid in the quest for knowledge. I had thought, Xeris, that you shared that same thirst to know as much as possible."

"I do, Preceptor, but not at the cost of your life while under my watch."

"Then tell me truly, Xeris . . . is this about my life? Or your supposed inability to protect it?"

Before Xeris could respond, several floors below the mighty doors of the hall slammed open. There were distant cries of shock and fear and supplications for the gods to preserve them. Nicrominus had found that such entreaties rarely if ever worked. The gods seemed to enjoy turning a deaf ear to the needs of those on the Damned World. The fact that they were on the Damned World to begin with certainly indicated that the gods were not sympathetic.

"It would seem," Nicrominus said softly, "that the matter is moot. You may leave me, Xeris."

Xeris's chin quavered, and then he drew himself up, squaring his shoulders. He turned defiantly to face the door of the chamber, his tail whipping back and forth. "They shall have to come through me to get you, Preceptor."

"Truthfully, I'm thinking they won't. But the fault is mine, Xeris. I was unclear. When I said you may leave me, that was not me putting forward an option. You will do so, now. This is my business, and the business of the Overseer and his agents. You do not enter into it. And so help me, Xeris," he continued speaking over Xeris's attempt to interrupt him, "if I catch you keeping nearby, listening in, or trying to insert yourself into this, I will personally see to your chastisement. It will not be a pleasant affair, I assure you. Now get gone with you."

Xeris looked for a moment as if he were going to endeavor to argue, but ultimately thought better of it. Instead he bowed stiffly and then exited the room through the far door. Nicrominus, his attention no longer split between the approaching Travelers and the petulant Xeris, turned to the main door of the chambers and waited patiently.

He did not have long to wait.

A chill moved through the room, radiating from the door, like an icy fog rolling in from a far-off ocean. Nicrominus shivered inwardly, but outwardly he was the picture of distant calm.

He had spoken brave words to Xeris, had talked of his desire for knowledge and how that superseded all other considerations. Now, though, faced with the reality of possibly impending doom, his thoughts were in turmoil and he was wondering whether Xeris had not been right all along. Perhaps he should indeed have fled when he had the chance. Lived to fight another day, to see his daughter once more. With his potential demise at the front door, departing out the back began to seem the preferable option.

"Too late now," he murmured, just as the door smashed open. He braced himself.

A Traveler was in the doorway, and he did not seem to stand so much as hover. There were others visible behind him. They were speaking to one another, but it sounded more like random, hoarse sighs than anything approaching language as Nicrominus knew or understood it.

The Traveler was dressed in billowing robes that, from a distance, always appeared black. That was the way Nicrominus had always espied them before: from a distance. It had always been more than sufficient for him. Now, though, with them near, he was interested to note that the robes were not truly black, but instead extremely dark purple. A purple hood was drawn up, making it difficult to see the Traveler's face clearly. This suited Nicrominus quite well, since some degree of superstitious dread convinced him that to see the unhidden face of a Traveler would be tantamount to instant death. What he was able to make out, however—the chin, the lower half of his face—was glittering silver, smoother, than Nicrominus had ever seen. The Traveler did not look like any one of the Twelve Races that walked the Damned World, or—for that matter—even from the great beyond where the Twelve Races originated.

The Traveler merely stood there for a long moment, and then slowly he entered the room. His billowing cloak swirled around him, although the origin of the winds that were moving it were a mystery to Nicrominus. It made it difficult for Nicrominus to get any real idea of how the Traveler was built, what his body type was.

"Greetings," said Nicrominus. "This is an honor."

"Is it?" The Traveler spoke with a flat voice that had a faint echo to it. It sounded unnatural to Nicrominus, soulless, as if the Traveler were somehow not even alive. But that obviously could not be the case, for here he was, and he was clearly speaking and living.

"Of course it is," Nicrominus said easily, hiding the anxiety that roiled within him. "What else would it be?"

The Traveler made no reply.

Nicrominus had no idea what to say. So he simply sat there and said nothing, reasoning that silence was preferable to foolish nattering. For all he knew, the

Traveler was assessing the best way to kill him. It made no sense for the Traveler to do so, but the gods moved in mysterious ways, and the Travelers were about as close to gods as it got on the Damned World.

Then the Traveler glided forward and Nicrominus braced himself. The Traveler reached deep into the hidden folds of his robe. *A weapon. He is about to hurl a weapon at me!* Nicrominus wanted to throw himself flat behind his desk, or perhaps even come out attacking and roaring defiance. Instead he just sat there, unmoving.

The Traveler extended his hand, which was clad in a leathery black glove, and he was holding something in the palm. Nicrominus leaned forward, curious in spite of himself.

"A hotstar," he said after a moment. He looked up questioningly, uncertain he'd given the correct answer. The fact that it was a hotstar was obvious, so obvious that he wondered what was to be gained by showing him one. "We do not have much in the way of tech here," he continued, since the Traveler was making no effort to fill in the silence. "So hotstars are not high on our priorities. Our vehicles are powered by them, but other than that . . ."

Placing the hotstar upon the table, the Traveler took a step back and said, "Look at it."

"Look at it," repeated Nicrominus, uncomprehending. He started to reach for it, hesitated, glanced at the Traveler to see whether he was doing something precipitous. But the Traveler simply stood there, so with a shrug, Nicrominus picked up the hotstar. He turned it over and over in his hand, wondering what it was he was supposed to be seeing.

Then he realized that it wasn't a matter of seeing so much as it was a matter of feeling. And he wasn't feeling anything. Not a damned thing. Hotstars were never scalding, but the warmth that radiated from them was part of what lent them their distinctive names. This hotstar had nothing. He studied it more closely as if truly seeing it for the first time. Another characteristic of hotstars was the small sparkles of light that danced within their center. They were not reflections of outside illumination, but instead originated from deep within, emanations from the power that the hotstars possessed.

"This is dead," Nicrominus said, squinting in hopes of finding something that he was missing. "There are no inner lights, no fire within. This hotstar has gone dead. I did not think it was possible, for hotstars to be drained."

"It's not," the Traveler told him.

"Ah. So this," and he waved the hotstar, "would be considered . . . what? An aberration?"

"No."

"What, then?"

"A possible trend," said the Traveler in his unwavering voice.

Nicrominus rocked back in his chair as if punched in the face. "Although, as I said, we here in Firedraque Hall have little use for such things . . . others depend upon hotstars very heavily. Hotstars, they . . . they have always been a source of boundless energy. Have they *all* run out . . . ?"

The Traveler shook his head. "This is the only one so far," he said in the longest sentence he'd formed since he'd arrived. Nicrominus did not feel any sense of relief upon hearing that pronouncement, as he correctly surmised what the Traveler's next words were going to be. "The Overseer believes there will be more."

"But why?"

"We have not been told."

Nicrominus was unsure whether the "we" referred to the Travelers in general, or if this one was simply referring to himself in an imperial manner. But that was a minor matter at best. Finally Nicrominus put the impotent hotstar carefully down upon the table and said, "What does the Overseer want of me?"

"Learn why," the Traveler told him.

It took a moment for Nicrominus to comprehend. "Learn why . . . this hotstar has gone dead? Why others are at risk? Is . . . that what you are telling me?"

"Yes."

Dumbfounded, Nicrominus stood. "But why me? What possible expertise do I—do any of the Firedraques—have in such matters? Certainly our resources cannot compare to that which the Overseer has at his command."

"Learn why" was all the Traveler said.

He turned and started to walk away from Nicrominus, leaving the stunned Firedraque there with the useless hotstar. Trying to find some means of grasping the situation, Nicrominus asked, "Is there a time frame involved? When does the Overseer desire me to provide him an answer?"

The Traveler paused a moment in the doorway. Without turning back to face Nicrominus, he intoned, "Before it is too late." As he moved forward, his similarly clad and eerily silent brethren closed in around him, obscuring him from view. As one, the Travelers headed away. Nicrominus could practically feel the chill air moving out of the room, following them. He moved quickly to the nearest window and looked out. Sure enough, moments later, the Travelers were riding their draquons away from the hall. The powerful creatures moved with a sound like rolling thunder. The streets of Perriz were deserted as the Travelers careened through the streets. There was no doubt in Nicrominus's mind that the Travelers would have run over anyone or anything in their way.

Nicrominus picked up the hotstar, regarded it thoughtfully, and wondered whether the Overseer would accept "I don't know" as a reasonable answer, and had the feeling that he most likely would not.

THE FIVE CLANS BORDERLANDS

i.

Zerena Foux could not recall the last time she had uttered a thanks of any sort to the gods. But she did so when the jumpcar roared to life, the hotstar powering it once more. She had tapped the hotstar several times, seeking to make sure that the energy couplings were secure. All the energy in the world that the hotstar might possess wouldn't make a damned bit of difference if it couldn't be fed properly into the jumpcar's engine.

The jumpcar had carried them successfully away from the battle plain of Marsay, and they had made camp near the outer edges of the Mandraque "borderlands," so called since the lands of all five clans were accessible from that particular point: a five-minute walk in any direction. The Bottom Feeders generally considered it a good place to catch their breath and plan their next move, particularly since the borderlands themselves were neutral territory. Cross over into any of the lands themselves and you were on the turf of specific Mandraque clans. But remain judiciously at the outer rim and none would do you harm. That was the theory, at least. There was always the chance of running into a Mandraque or Mandraques who had no appreciation for the concept of neutral territory or borders. If that occurred, it was then a matter of determining how fast one would run, and in what direction.

No Mandraques were appearing on the horizon at that point, and evening was just beginning to fall. The Bottom Feeders' flight of several days ago was nearly forgotten, for the Damned World was a place of constant change and challenges. There was little point in dwelling on that which had happened in the past, for the future was certain to bring enough hardships with it.

Still, the past held lessons that it could offer up. One of them, as far as Zerena was concerned now, was "Check your equipment." As the Bottom Feeders made camp in yet another rocky outcropping that provided some measure of protection, Zerena sat crouched on her haunches, watching Mingo go over the jumpcar's engine in order to make sure it was at peak running condition. Of all of them, Mingo was the one who was the most conversant in the mysteries of tech. Mingo insisted he was no techwiz, but that certainly wasn't the case as far as Zerena was concerned. It seemed there was nothing he couldn't do when it came to tech.

Mingo lay on his back under the jumpcar, studying the vehicle's innards with intense curiosity. Every so often Zerena would hear a clank or the brisk cranking of some metal tool against a fastener of some sort.

Unlike Zerena, who had no patience for this sort of work, Mingo Minkopolis could remain at such endeavors for an entire day. He never tired of it, his endless love for it bearing him up under inexcusable pressure.

Besides, Zerena's attention was elsewhere. She was watching her beloved Karsen and that suspicious girl, Jepp, huddled in a corner, legs drawn up, talking in intent, low voices and even laughing. It was actually Karsen who laughed. Jepp merely smiled indulgently at him. Perhaps she had no sense of humor. Or perhaps—and this was the more likely, considering what Zerena knew of the girl's background—she had been utterly brainwashed, depriving her of personality, interests, and all else that made her unique.

And yet . . . and yet . . .

"She could be useful," Zerena finally admitted aloud.

Mingo, under the jumpcar, hadn't heard her at first. With a confused "Hunh?" he hauled himself from beneath and looked up at her. "What did you say?"

"I said, 'She could be useful.'"

"She?"

Zerena, with a slight tilt of her chin, indicated a particular direction for Mingo to look in. He did so and saw Jepp and Karsen off by themselves.

"Ahhhh, I see," he said. Then he frowned and grunted, in that bullish way he had, before shaking his head, "All right, actually I don't quite see. But it sounded ever more profound to say that I did."

"I hate to admit that the human female might be a positive influence on Karsen . . . but there it is."

"There what is?"

She looked at him askance. "Are you being deliberately obtuse?"

"I don't believe I am, no."

Zerena sighed heavily, stroking her chin before admitting in resignation, "Karsen is ashamed of what he is."

"Ashamed of being a Laocoon?"

"No, you idiot," she said, slapping Mingo on the upper leg. He winced. Even a casual swat by Zerena had some power behind it. "About being a Bottom Feeder. He always has."

"Well, I couldn't remotely guess why that might be," said Mingo. "After all, to pursue a profession that is despised and looked upon by every single one of the Twelve Races, including yours and mine. To be at the very bottom of society's food chain. Why wouldn't someone be positively brimming with a sense of self-worth if they occupy that station in life?"

"You are not helping."

"I was not trying to."

"We," she said stiffly, "are part of the natural order. Ever since the first creature killed its fellow, our kind has been there to pick through the remains. Ours is a time-honored tradition."

"So is projectile vomiting, Zerena. But being a part of that is hardly anything that anyone wishes to boast about."

Now Zerena fixed "the scowl" upon him. It was a particularly fierce look that he knew all too well, having been on the receiving end of it countless times. "Am I to understand that you share the self-loathing that my son feels?"

"Not at all," replied Mingo easily. "However, I have no pretensions about my lot in life. I am what I am and I do what I do, and I am content in that. I simply don't ascribe any lofty ideals to it. If you wish to do so, and it's how you handle our turn-to-turn existence, then that is perfectly fine."

"I appreciate your permission to think what I wish to think," she told him with sour annoyance.

Mingo refused to be drawn in. "Think nothing of it," he said.

"But Karsen," Zerena continued, staring off at her son, whose back was to her, "shares neither my 'lofty ideals' nor your spirited fatalism. He actively despises what we do, and that mind-set informs all his actions."

"He does tend to carry an air of dispiritedness about him," admitted Mingo.

"It hampers him. It prevents him from achieving all that I know he can achieve. He could be the fiercest fighter, the proudest of us . . . a natural leader . . ."

"Perhaps. Then again, Zerena," he said, choosing his words carefully, "is it not possible that—as his mother—you have a less-than-realistic view of his capabilities? I mean, a fierce fighter? Honestly. In all my time as part of this clan, I have never seen a fight that Karsen could not either talk himself out of, or run from with all speed. So isn't it just as likely that—"

"You see that war hammer?" Once again using her chin as an indicator, she nodded in Karsen's direction.

"The one strapped to his back?"

"No, the one shoved up his ass," Zerena Foux snapped with impatience. "Yes, of course the one strapped to his back."

"Yes, I see it. What of it? He took it off a dead Mandraque, I'd wager."

"You'd lose. He took it off a live Mandraque, one of two. One of them he killed, and the other he beat senseless and left for dead."

Mingo's tiny eyes widened in surprise. "He did that?"

"Yes."

"Our little Karsen?"

"Most assuredly."

"I don't believe it," Mingo said. "What in the world prompted him to . . ." Then his voice trailed off as the answer presented itself. "Her. She did. She prompted him to."

"Just so," confirmed Zerena. "He hasn't exactly been forthcoming about it, giving me only the most terse of details. But the human did not hesitate to extol the virtues of my son's 'heroics.' The Mandraques were attempting to make off with her, and he fought back against them."

"That does not sound like Karsen," Mingo told her, making no attempt to keep the skepticism from his voice.

"The first thing he did was run away, leaving the girl to their mercy."

"All right, that *does* sound like Karsen." Mingo could scarcely process it. "Like any of us, actually. I mean, if trapped, we fight, that's only natural. But given any other option, we avoid conflict. Except Karsen, well . . . his fighting heart was always lacking somewhat, as you know. In a fight situation, on his own, he'd be killed in no time. But you're telling me that he not only fled the scene but then came back? And triumphed? Because of her?"

"So it would seem."

Mingo studied Jepp with newly found interest and appreciation. "Well, that's . . . puzzling. I mean, she's not much to look at, is she. Smooth and hairless, and not much meat on her."

"I wasn't planning to cook her up and serve her," snorted Zerena. "The fact is that she seems to be having some sort of an effect on him. What, I'm not sure. But I can tell you that I don't see Karsen running back to help just anybody. There must be something about her."

"She's a pleasure slave. Perhaps that intrigues him."

"Then why hasn't he had her pleasure him, if that's where his interest lies. She's been with us long enough. He could have availed himself of her at any time." She made a face. "I doubt she'd be offering any protest in that event. I don't know that she could, even if she wanted to. She's just this . . . this helpless creature, doing whatever males tell her to do. Gods, was the entirety of their race like this?"

"I wouldn't think so, considering the ferocity with which they fought against the Third Wave," said Mingo. "Although admittedly it was mostly males who did the fighting."

"So this may be characteristic of the female of the species, then. This pliability and refusal to stand up for their own interests."

"Could be. But it's all conjecture. And she seems to have little enough grasp of history to be of any use."

"I'm not sure she has sufficient grasp of anything to be of any use. Still . . . he appears enamored of her."

"Enamored?" He studied her thoughtfully. She was smiling at something that Karsen was saying. "Do you truly think so?"

"Honestly, I cannot be sure. I mean, he seems to be . . . but I've nothing to compare it to in his previous behavior."

"Nothing?" That was a surprise to Mingo. "You mean in all his years, he's never . . ."

"No."

"Not with any . . . ?"

"How often do we encounter others of our kind, Mingo?" she demanded. "Occasionally we come upon small, wandering tribes of Laocoon. That is the way of our people, to be vagabonds. And it is also their way to be insular and not kindly disposed to strangers."

"But what about your own tribe? I mean, I've only been part of your . . ." He made a vague gesture that included the gelatinous Gant a short distance away, and Rafe Kestor, who was absentmindedly sharpening his sword against a rock. "Of your 'clan' for a relatively short time. You were part of a tribe before, weren't you?"

"Yes. We were."

"And . . . ?"

"And now," she said tersely, in a tone that discouraged further discussion, "we are not."

"I see," said Mingo, who didn't entirely but chose not to pursue it. "And during the time that you were—"

"We do not need to go over this ceaselessly, Mingo," Zerena said, raising her voice slightly and getting a curious look from Karsen. She promptly brought her

tone under control again. "The point is, he's never been with a female of any
sort . . . not in any meaningful way. But this one interests him. Intrigues him. And
I don't see that I'm in any position to try and gainsay him, especially when the
female may well do him far more good than harm."

"But I still do not understand what he sees in her."

"It doesn't matter," Zerena insisted, "so long as she sees something in him."

"Then you are actively going to encourage this . . . this involvement?"

"I'm not going to encourage anything," she said, casting furtive glances in
Karsen's direction. "I shall simply allow matters to run their course. If she is of
benefit to my son . . . if she encourages him in her own strange way to reach the
potential I know he has . . . then she will have my gratitude."

"What if she hurts him in some way?"

"Then," Zerena said with a flash of teeth, "I shall rip her to shreds myself."

ii.

Karsen had a feeling that Zerena and Mingo were discussing him and Jepp, but he
was only able to catch a few words here and there. He decided there was little reason to be concerned about it, as they were not casting hostile glances in his direction, but instead simply looked interested.

"I can only imagine what my mother must think," he said, leaning back against
a rock wall. He swatted lazily at a passing fly.

"Think of what?" asked Jepp.

"Of us."

"We are an 'us'?" Jepp inquired, wide-eyed. "Are you definitely my new master
now? Am I to service you so it can be as it was when I was with the Greatness?"

He stared at her in bewilderment, all his mother's stern comments about how
Jepp needed to be a stronger person coming back to his mind. "Jepp . . . can you
imagine a life other than that which you had with the Greatness?"

"You mean a life where I serve you instead of him?"

"No, not at all." He shook his head, already feeling a bit frustrated and sorry
he'd brought it up. "I mean one where you are involved with someone . . . and it is
on equal footing. Instead of serving a master, you would be . . . well . . . as one
with a partner. Neither of you would be greater than the other."

"I've heard of such arrangements," Jepp said thoughtfully, "but not with my
kind. We are bred. We serve. We die. In some ways," she sighed, "we are to be envied for the simplicity of our lives."

"I couldn't envy it at all," Karsen assured her. "It sounds eternally awful."

"More awful than . . . than him?" Jepp pointed at Gant, subtly so he wouldn't see her . . . although since he was a large shapeless mass, she couldn't see where his face was and thus couldn't tell whether he'd spotted her pointing or not.

He looked where she was pointing and reluctantly nodded. "He has a difficult life, I'll grant you."

"I should think so," she agreed. "To live one's whole life in such a state . . ."

"Whole life?" Karsen looked taken aback at the notion. "You don't think Gant always looked that way, do you?"

"No?" She shrugged. "It never occurred to me otherwise. Well, then . . . if not always in that form, then what . . . ?"

Karsen glanced right and left to make certain none of the other Bottom Feeders were within earshot. Then, to play it safe, he leaned even closer in toward Jepp. Obediently she angled forward so that he could easily whisper to her.

"You did not hear this from me," he began.

"Really." This clearly puzzled her. "Then from whom did I hear it?"

That gave Karsen pause. He shrugged. "Very well, you did hear it from me. But don't repeat what I'm telling you. Have you ever heard of the Phey?"

"I've heard of many things, Karsen Foux," she assured him. "I know that you think me ignorant . . ."

"No!"

". . . and that your mother thinks me a fool."

"Ah, well," he sighed, "that much, yes. But if it's of any consolation, that is her usual opinion about all creatures that walk or scuttle or swim the surface of the Damned World. So I would not take it much to heart were I you."

"If you say so," she said uncertainly. "The point is, I was with the Greatness much of the time. He liked to show me off. And I heard many discussions about many things. So many, in fact, that I know more than I wish to. My knowledge invades my waking moments . . . worse, it invades my sleep. In the night, the visions come to me with such clarity I . . ."

She trembled, and Karsen stared at her in confusion. "Are you all right?" he asked, reaching over and resting one hand atop hers.

She pulled her hand away, still quivering, and then with a visible effort shook it off. "Yes. I am fine. I've never actually seen one of the Phey. They're one of only two races I've never seen with my own eyes, the other being the Serabim on their Zeffers. I would like to, though. I would like to have seen all of the Twelve Races. That's not always easy. There are many who have seen none but their own, you know. So seeing them all . . . that would make me . . ." She searched for the right word. "Interesting. I would be an interesting person if I saw all of them. I hope to."

"I find you interesting," Karsen said, smiling.

She returned the smile, and then concentrated on remembering all that she had heard, trying forcefully to pull the conversation back to where it had been. "The . . . Phey. The oldest of the Twelve Races. Older than the Firedraques, even. Some say that the Banishers feared the Phey more than any other of us. The Phey keep to themselves; even their homeland is unknown. They are tall and elegant and supposedly of such beauty that one can go mad just by looking upon them. Their beauty is so transcendent that whether you are Draque or Sirene or," and she nodded in acknowledgment toward Karsen, "a Laocoon, it makes no differ- ence. They will be fair in all eyes."

"Have you heard anything else?"

"Oh yes," she said, warming to the topic. "It is said they are powerful magic users. That it took all the power of the Banishers to send them here. That they are fewest in number of all the races, but because of their abilities, still the most dan- gerous. Although," she continued thoughtfully, "I have occasionally wondered if the Phey themselves put forward the tales of their formidable abilities in order to make up for their lack of numbers."

"No," said Karsen firmly, and then he cast a subtle glance in Gant's direction. "And he's living proof of it."

"What?" Jepp stared blankly at Karsen. "I'm . . . not following. Are . . . are you saying the Phey did that to him . . . ?"

"I'm saying he *was* one of the Phey."

Jepp gasped, scarcely able to credit what Karsen was telling her. "He was? He really was? One of—"

"One of a race of creatures so beautiful that you would have crawled across shattered stone, just to have him smile at you once and mean it." Karsen shook his head. "Poor bastard."

"But how . . . ?"

Karsen absolutely adored indulging in gossip even though he didn't have much opportunity to do so. With the air of guilty excitement that always accompani such chatty discussions, he said, "According to my mother—and she's never wrong about such matters—Gant was something of a rogue when it came to fe- males. He was involved with one young woman, fair of face and figure, but he could not resist and became enamored of the woman's younger sister. Frankly, I don't know what Gant could have been thinking, to play such a dangerous game as pitting sisters against one another. In any event, as anyone with a lick of brains would have been able to foresee, the sisters came together and exacted a terrible revenge on he who had been toying with them both."

"They turned him into *that*?" When he nodded, Jepp let out a low whistle. "How awful! That they could do such a thing to him. How did he wind up as part of this clan?" When she saw that Karsen was laughing in response to her question, she furrowed her brow. "Is that a funny question?"

"No, a funny answer. We salvaged him. Mother thought he was some sort of rare engine lubricant, and Gant was simply too depressed by his situation to make his status clear. It's a miracle we didn't destroy the jumpcar's motor with him."

Upon hearing that, Jepp laughed as well, and Karsen watched her closely as she did so. "I don't believe I've heard you laugh before."

Instantly Jepp ceased and lowered her head. "I'm sorry," she said contritely. "I won't do it again."

Karsen moaned. "Now, you see, that's exactly the type of thing you do that drives my mother insane."

"I'm sorry," she said in exactly the same tone. "I will try not to drive your mother insane."

"Yes, well . . . good luck on that score."

"Speaking of insane," and she glanced around but didn't see him, "what about that Mandraque? That 'Rafe Kestor.' What of him?"

"He was an aging Mandraque, a respected general, who came upon several others who were of lower order than he, surrounding my mother while she was on salvage. Truth to tell, she could probably have handled it herself. In case you haven't noticed, my mother is quite . . . capable." Karsen chuckled at that, but then grew serious. "He told the others to back off. That it was unworthy of them. They didn't listen, he stepped in, fought them off . . . but not before . . ." He thumped the side of his skull with the base of his palm.

"He punched himself in the head?"

"Nooo," he said with meticulously controlled patience, "he took a blow to the head from the sword of one of the Mandraques. Or maybe it was a club. Either way, he was downed, and Mother took him in with us. The wound took forever to heal, and even once it did, he was never quite right again. He has his moments of lucidity, as when he got into that argument about the Greatness. But much of the time, he's unclear as to where he is and sometimes even who he is. If he returned to his people, they'd eat him alive . . . possibly literally. So he stays with us. Face to the foe, he can actually be rather formidable, provided he remembers they're trying to kill him."

"That's so sad," she said wistfully.

Karsen noticed the campfire was beginning to die. He took several more pieces of wood and tossed them on, then smiled as it flared up again. "Sad? Actually, he's probably the happiest of us here. Every moment is a new surprise and a challenge for greater glory."

"So none of you is truly happy?"

"I didn't say that. The truth is that . . ."

Then he noticed that Jepp wasn't looking at him. Instead she was staring toward the sky in wide-eyed wonderment.

"I don't believe it," she whispered. "I . . . I just don't believe it."

He turned to see where she was looking, and when he saw what she had espied, his mouth dropped open in astonishment.

"Do you see it?" It was his mother, Zerena, calling out from a short distance away, and he had never heard that tone of pure awe in her voice. It took a great deal to impress Zerena Foux, but apparently this sight was capable of doing so. "Do you see it, Karsen?"

"Yes! Jepp sees it, too!"

"Not really caring about that," Zerena said brusquely as she approached, her gaze still riveted skyward. Mingo was right behind her, similarly impressed. Gant was undulating about, although it was impossible to tell if he was able to perceive reality the way others did. And Rafe Kestor continued obliviously with his sword thrusts at enemies that only he could envision.

High, high above, unimaginably high, sailed one of the few creatures left upon the Damned World that could possibly be referred to as "majestic." It floated with the carelessness of a cloud, and indeed could even be mistaken for one if the viewer was not sharp-eyed enough to realize what he was seeing.

Its body was like a vast dome, or even vaguely bell-shaped, billowing and shimmering. The color or colors of it shifted from one moment to the next, although it seemed to waver mostly between white and green. It undulated out and back, out and back, and from this distance it was impossible to determine just how large the creature truly was. Dangling from around its edges, harder to see but still visible, was an array of stringlike tentacles that wavered constantly in the winds on high.

"This is your lucky day," Karsen said to Jepp.

Zerena glanced down in confusion. "Her lucky day? Why?"

"Look! There's another!" Jepp suddenly cried out, and she was so excited that the hand she was pointing with visibly trembled. "A second Zeffer, coming from behind the clouds!"

"That's ridiculous," Mingo assured her. "They never travel in . . . oh, holy gods, she's right."

"She's right?" said an astounded Zerena, but the evidence of her own eyes was directly before her. A second Zeffer had joined the first, gliding just behind it and matching it in its pure, graceful undulations.

"Are there Serabim riding them?" Jepp could scarcely contain herself. She was hopping back and forth, clapping her hands in childlike glee. "I think I see one on each! I think! But it's hard to tell! But I think—"

"Quiet, girl! Gods!" Although Zerena's words were harsh, her tone was not. Karsen could tell that the sight they were seeing impressed even his hard-bitten mother. "Of course there would have to be Serabim riding them. They never go anywhere without each other. Everybody knows that."

They lapsed into silence. The only sound was Rafe's sword slicing through the air. He continued in his maneuvers, oblivious of all else.

Finally Karsen said, "Who else do you think is watching?"

"What do you mean?" asked Zerena.

"I mean . . . well, think of it, Mother. We're encamped here, waiting to see the smoke or receive word or smell the burning of another battle that we can then pick through for salvage once it's done . . . as is inevitable when one is discussing the Twelve Races. And surely the imminent future combatants, who will try to kill each other despite the Firedraque treaties they've all agreed to, are preparing for another pointless exercise in mutual extermination. But I'll guarantee you that, at this moment, all those involved in this endless cycle of violence are looking heavenward with slack-jawed amazement. We're sharing in the childlike wonder of it all. Can you imagine if all the Twelve Races could come together like that on a regular basis? Can you imagine what life on the Damned World would be like then?"

"Yes," said Zerena humorlessly. "It would put us out of business."

"Oh, Mother," groaned Karsen.

"You know, Jepp," Mingo spoke up, drifting over toward her while never looking away from the Zeffers. "To see a single Zeffer is rare enough. But it is said that when two Zeffers are seen, a time of great change is upon us."

"Who says that?" Zerena demanded. "People are always saying, 'It is said,' but no one ever says who did the saying. Damned foolishness if you ask me."

"I don't recall anyone, in fact, asking you, Zerena," Mingo replied archly.

Jepp shifted uncomfortably in place, suddenly looking very ill at ease in her own body. "A time of great change?" she asked.

"So I've heard."

"I can't say I like the sound of that," said Jepp.

"No one ever does, sweetling," Mingo sighed. "No one ever does."

ii.

She despises her dreams.

Oftentimes she has dreamt of images she can barely fathom. Images of creatures long past, long dead, being slaughtered at the hands and talons of the Banished.

Creatures that were so massive they could blot out the sun when standing fully up-right, and ruled the earth while her ancestors' ancestors cowered in trees. She watched them in their death throes, watched the beginnings of the Twelve Races es-tablish their collective toehold upon the Damned World long before it had its name, and then they themselves died out in their compulsion for mutual warfare that lasted to this day.

This night she does not dream of the past. This night she is anchored firmly in the present, or perhaps the future. She has not had a dream in quite some time. She has not missed them. She does not like them, for she typically wakes up from them trem-bling and terrified, and sometimes she requires as much as a full day to recover.

But one roars into existence now. It pervades her head and her soul, grips her firmly, and will not depart her without having its say.

She sees them coming. They are vast and frightening, and they are nowhere near as large as the Zeffers, but they are terrifying nonetheless. Yet she cannot get a true feel for their size, for one feature dominates above all. It is the eye, the large, unblinking, re-lentless, pitiless eye. It is fixed upon her, and it is invading her, and she wants to look away but cannot, for it is everywhere. And it brings disaster with its gaze. She knows that, as surely as she knows that matters are changing and not for the better, no, not at all. She wants it to stop, she begs for it to stop, but it will not, and she screams a name . . .

"Jepp!"

It is not the name that she had been crying out. The name is confusing to her at first, coming as it is out of nowhere, but then she recognizes it as her own and she fights back to consciousness, swimming through what seems a vast, viscous liquid, grasping toward the surface, certain she's not going to make it. The eye continues to stare at her, to surround her, to become her surroundings, and then it is no longer an eye, but a single great silver sphere, glistening and pulsing with an inner power that she cannot begin to comprehend, and suddenly light is cascading from every part of the ball, it has become the center of its own sun, and the word "Orb" burns itself into her mind, and then she is shaking, caught up in a quake . . .

"Jepp!"

Karsen shook her once more, her head snapping back and forth. The other Bottom Feeders, roused from their slumber by her shrieks, approached with vary-ing degrees of concern and annoyance. Foremost among the annoyed was Zer-ena. "What the hell is going on!" she demanded.

"They're coming!" Jepp cried out. "They're coming and . . . and they'll kill us . . . eye . . . eye . . ."

"You you what?" said Zerena.

"Eye!"

"*What about you?!*"

Frantically, Jepp pointed at her own eye with such insistence that she nearly jabbed her finger into it. "Eye! Eye! Huge and unblinking! Giant creatures!"

"You mean . . . Oculars?" asked Karsen.

"Yes! Yes, Oculars! The Greatness . . . he had a trophy of one."

"A trophy?" Zerena looked at the others. "What does she mean, a—"

To Karsen's surprise, it was Rafe Kestor who responded. He hadn't even realized that Rafe was near them or had stirred from his slumber, despite Jepp's howling. But he was quite awake, crouched nearby, and his eyes were dark as he said, "She means a hunting trophy. Before the Firedraque accords, it was not . . . unusual . . . for Mandraques to hunt up north for the specific purpose of tracking down and killing an Ocular. Then they would bring it back and preserve it. Stuff it."

Mingo, clearly appalled, asked, "How could they do such a thing?"

"Well, the process is quite interesting. First all the internal organs are—"

"I mean how could they bring themselves to . . ." Mingo was shaking his head. "Killing one another is one thing, but putting kills on display . . . that's just ghastly."

"It is tradition," Rafe Kestor replied, and he didn't seem remotely as put off as Mingo was. "It is what it is." He turned his attention to Jepp as if Mingo was no longer worth the effort. "And you dreamt of the trophy belonging to the Greatness?"

"No! No, it was . . . it was alive. Alive and terrifying they were. Terrifying! And now they are coming for us!"

Karsen settled next to the shaking Jepp and put an arm around her to steady her. He glanced toward Zerena to see what her reaction would be, but her face was a study in neutrality. If she was angry over Karsen openly displaying concern about Jepp, she was hiding it well. It made him wonder if somehow, for some bizarre reason, she was actually in favor of Karsen becoming involved with Jepp. Not that such a thing was likely. For some reason he found her utter devotion to him . . . off-putting somehow. And he doubted his attitude toward her was going to change.

"Jepp," he said soothingly, "it was just a dream."

"I don't have just dreams!"

"Well, you had one now," he assured her. "We are nowhere near the land of the Ocular. Isn't that right, Mother?"

"Yes, that's right." Zerena wasn't making any effort to sound at all reassuring, but at least she wasn't yelling or being belligerent, so that was certainly a plus. "The Ocular live far up north, in Feend, nowhere near here."

"Yes, and furthermore," Mingo continued, "they never wander away from

Feend because then they have to contend with normal shifts of day and night. And during the day they're blind, helpless. They may be the mightiest things on two legs in the dark, but give them a sunny day and they're easily dispatched."

"So rest assured," Karsen said, "that there's no—"

At that moment, the wind shifted.

It had been blowing away from them, but now the wind randomly changed direction. Mingo caught the scent first, his horned head snapping around, and an alarmed bull-like cry ripping from his throat. A few seconds later, Karsen and Zerena picked it up as well. They looked at each other in shock, blood draining from their faces. And Jepp sat there, her nose useless, sensing that something had abruptly changed in their situation, but not having the faintest idea what it was.

"Is there a problem?" she asked innocently, just before three gargantuan shadows emerged from behind a nearby circle of upright boulders. They moved as noiselessly as shadows, their silence belying their size. One of them stepped into the forefront, gazing at them with a single huge, unblinking brown eye.

"Well, well, well," rumbled the Ocular. "Zerena Foux and her clan. How convenient. My honor guard and I," and he said, as he indicated the other two male Ocular with a casual wave, "were just speaking of how we could use some fresh meat for dinner. And here you've done us the courtesy of presenting yourselves to us for our dining pleasure. Most considerate of you."

At which point Jepp fainted dead away.

THE CITY-STATE OF VENETS

i.

{At first the Markene does not understand what is happening. The Klaa is up ahead, but something is preventing him from getting to it. The fact that there's an obstruction doesn't initially register. He knows where he is, he knows where the Klaa is, sitting there in its coral bed in the cove, just out of reach. For some reason, he cannot complete the distance to obtain it.}

{Over time, other Markene drift over as well, for the same purpose: obtain the Klaa and continue to float in its comforting haze. They cannot reach it, either. Slowly, very slowly, just enough of the fog upon their brains begins to lift.}

{They see it, then. They see the obstruction, the mighty gate that blocks off the cove, that prevents them from getting to the Klaa. They have encountered the gate before. They know they cannot pass through it. Yet they try, gods, how they try. As their concern builds, they throw themselves against the mesh with head-rattling velocity and force. But the gate withstands their assaults.}

{They cannot pass. They cannot obtain the Klaa.}

{They know that means something. Somewhere in the inner recesses of their minds, they are aware that an inability to reach the Klaa indicates something of significance. And as the fog continues to lift, they will begin to remember what it is, and they will assemble, and they will learn, and they will perform, and then the Klaa will be theirs once more, and all will be well.}

ii.

"What are we being summoned for?"

Gorkon was floating just next to the Resting Point, which was where he had come to meet Ruark Sydonis yet again. They had rendezvoused there several times over the previous weeks since that day that Ruark had short-circuited Gorkon's attempt to kill himself.

The young Markene no longer gave any thought to ending his own life. In fact, he still felt a burning embarrassment that he had even considered it in the first place. Instead his attention and interest were entirely caught up in his meeting with Ruark. Ruark, for his part, had smiled and shaken his head in a slightly patronizing way and told him, "You have to find something else to live for other than me, son. I am old and not particularly interesting. At the very least, find yourself a nice female."

But the female Markene were just like all the others: content to live in their Klaa-induced haze. Gorkon had had sex with several Markene females in his lifetime. In each instance his partner had giggled and sighed and made billowy cooing noises, and minutes later seemed to have utterly forgotten the encounter. To a Markene male who was using females as an outlet for the release of urges so pounding that they managed to briefly penetrate the fog of Klaa, that was sufficient. (And female Markene, when they gave birth, were always surprised when they had done so. Fortunately Markene young were born largely self-sufficient; otherwise the entire species would have long ago become extinct. Unfortunately they were also born addicted to Klaa.) For a Markene male who wanted to make some sort of emotional connection, it was woefully insufficient, and Gorkon was unique in that respect. Unique and alone.

On their third get-together, when Ruark had made a casual slip in referring to the palace, Gorkon had figured out that this was indeed Ruark Sydonis, lord of the Sirene. Ruark had grudgingly admitted to it but then seemed disinclined to discuss it any further, and Gorkon had honored that obvious wish. He valued too greatly the discussions he had with Ruark about far-ranging topics. Matters of life and death, philosophy, history, all of them were fodder for their chats. Ruark and Gorkon had a spirited give-and-take that was almost like teacher and student, except often it seemed as if they took turns over who was student and who was teacher.

But this particular day, as Ruark bobbed up and down in his little one-man boat, Gorkon knew that he was not going to be able to ignore Ruark's station in life. Not when it came to providing answers that had potential significance for his people, as addled as their minds might be.

"Summoned?" Ruark raised his brow questioningly and stared at Gorkon with polite confusion. "I'm not sure what you're referring to."

"The gate is down."

"The gate . . . ?"

"The gate that blocks the cove."

"Ahhhh," Ruark said slowly. "*That* gate."

Gorkon swam around the Resting Point, studying Ruark scrupulously for some sign of duplicity. He had come to like the elder, there was no denying that. But there was also no denying that he was royalty and a Merk, and both of those factors had to be considered when it came to their interactions. "Yes, that gate. The gate that, when it is up, allows my people access to their precious Klaa."

"Perhaps you were responsible," suggested Ruark.

He gaped at the Merk. "Me? How do you possibly figure that?"

"Well, if your people were deprived of their Klaa, perhaps they would eventually become as clearheaded as yourself, and you would no longer require me for intelligent conversation."

Gorkon shook his head sadly. "Would that it were so," he muttered. "Besides, it's ridiculous to think that I would be involved. And you know all that," he added with vague irritation. "So why would you even accuse me?"

"I accused you of nothing," Ruark said mildly. "Merely floated a notion. It is from small, floating notions that great notions are born."

"Perhaps," admitted Gorkon. "But that still leaves me with my original question: Why are we being summoned?"

"You're certain of that, are you? That you're being summoned?"

"It is traditionally the reason, yes," Gorkon said. "My people are blocked from the Klaa. That means that the Merk want something from us. That your people do."

"We are all one people," Ruark corrected him.

"No," Gorkon said with such fierceness that Ruark rocked back in his chair, almost unseating himself and falling into the water as a result. "No. We are all Sirene, that much is true. But we are not one people, because if we were, one group of us would not so ruthlessly and shamelessly hold dominance over the other, relentlessly manipulating us as they see fit."

"If you believe that," Ruark replied, "then you don't know people at all."

"I suppose I don't," grunted Gorkon.

Ruark said nothing to that for a time. Instead, having steadied himself in his chair, he simply looked thoughtful. "Truthfully, my young friend," Ruark said at last, "I do not know. As I may have mentioned from time to time, my beloved mate is not always entirely forthcoming with matters of state. However . . ."

"However what?"

"However," he mused, "I think it may have something to do with the Travelers."

"With the Travelers?" That significantly piqued Gorkon's interest. "What could it possibly have to do with the Travelers?"

"I don't know. I suppose you will find out, won't you."

"Why do I have the feeling," Gorkon asked suspiciously, "that you know more than you're telling?"

"You would be wrong. I do, however, *suspect* more than I'm telling. I will not burden you with my suspicions."

"Why not? It would be no burden . . ."

"Because you are most likely right in that you are being summoned," Ruark told him. "The gate has been lowered, your people cut off. There can be no other interpretation, really. So they will assemble where they always go at such times, at the Great Pier, and there will learn just what is being asked of them. I think it would be best if you went with them without predispositions or preconceptions. Experience what is being said for what it is, and don't allow my thoughts to color yours. Decide for yourself. Utilize that brain of which you are so justly proud."

Gorkon looked at him askance. "You are acting very differently from when we first encountered one another."

"Am I?"

"Yes. You seemed vague, meandering in your thoughts. Unfocused and distant and even confused. Yet that no longer seems the case."

"Was I that way?"

"You were," insisted Gorkon. "And I am led to wonder whether you are elderly and your mind wanders in and out . . . or if you always know precisely what you're doing, and simply allow others to think you enfeebled in some way."

"Why on the Damned World would I do that?" asked Ruark Sydonis, sounding genuinely interested, as if they were talking about someone else entirely.

"So you will not be seen as a threat. So you can learn more when people who believe you their superior let down their guard. Or perhaps," and he swam right up to the boat, resting a webbed hand upon it, "you simply enjoy playing games and using others as your pawns."

"All valid reasons," Ruark said amiably. "I will be most interested to find out which one it is."

And with that, he turned his boat around and paddled off back toward Venets, leaving a thoughtful Gorkon floating in his wake.

iii.

Orin Arn Oran knew himself to be a decent Merk. A powerful and honest Merk. One who was interested in the best interests and goals of his people.

Long had he gone back and forth in his mind over what to do. The fervor of the lady Tulisia had been contagious, but doubts invaded the mind of the Warlord of Venets the moment he was away from her.

Madness. It's madness echoed in his head. He tried to see matters from Tulisia's point of view. She was right: Three-quarters of the Damned World was indeed water, and the Sirene were the only race alive that could rightfully claim to be masters of an environment that would repel any others. Even the vaunted Travelers couldn't survive in the murky depths.

Or could they . . . ?

That's what it kept coming back to for Orin Arn Oran. There were so many unknowns involved in all this. Tulisia had a very clear point of view of what would happen. She had laid out two possible scenarios, and she was content. Orin, on the other hand, wasn't concerned about that which could be predicted. Instead he kept dwelling on that which he wasn't able to foresee. It was the things that Tulisia didn't anticipate that could mean the destruction of everything. Which meant that it was up to Orin Arn Oran to figure out what it was she was overlooking.

What if the Overseer determined that Tulisia was behind it? That he, Orin, was involved? What if the Markene were believed when they claimed they were ordered to do what they had done? What if the Markene were successful in destroying the Travelers, but that defeat set an unimaginable chain of events into motion? What if there was some sort of failsafe device in existence in Venets that would cause the annihilation of Venets upon the defeat of the Travelers? What if, what if, what if . . .

His head was spinning with all that could go wrong. Not just could: he was convinced it would. Orin Arn Oran felt as if he was holding the future of his entire race in the palm of his hand.

"I will tell her 'no,' that's all," he finally said. "I will tell the lady Tulisia no." He was in his study, and his mate, Atlanna, had just brought him fresh water to drink. Atlanna had been a stunning young female when they had first met, and the years had been more than kind to her. Four youngsters had not taken a noticeable toll on her body, and on land or sea, she moved with a flawless grace that underscored superb upbringing and boundless confidence.

So it was all the more surprising when, upon hearing that pronouncement, Atlanna dropped the glass. It struck the ground and shattered. Atlanna did not even seem to notice it. Her yellow eyes were locked upon him with a frightened, stunned gaze. She brushed back wisps of her short seaweed hair even as she shook her head and said, "You cannot be serious. Is this . . . is this about the business with the Travelers that you told me about?"

"Yes, I . . ."

"You cannot be serious!"

He stepped around his desk, regarding his spouse with wonder. "But it could be suicide for our people, don't you see that?"

"And to refuse Tulisia is suicide for us! How can *you* not see *that?*"

Orin laughed at that. "That is just . . . just foolishness, Atlanna. The lady Tulisia will listen to reason . . ."

"The lady Tulisia will listen to the lady Tulisia," she corrected him sternly, "and she will listen to those who say what she wants to hear. If you are not among that number, then we are finished. Finished with her, with Venets. We would have to leave immediately. Or, if you prefer, you could just kill us all and yourself right now, and save us the time and trouble."

"You do not know what you're talking about," he said uncertainly.

"I know exactly what I am talking about, and you do as well, except you are not willing to admit it. Orin, listen to me," and her voice became supplicating. She stroked his arm. "The lady Tulisia turns to you because she believes that you will carry out her desires. You must. Otherwise she will strike back at us, get herself a new Warlord, and he will do what you will not."

"Strike back? I command the Markene. I command the royal guard."

"And she commands you. Ultimately, you don't know to whom the guard would owe its loyalty. And even if they were loyal to you, do you truly believe that brute force is the only weapon Tulisia has at her command?" She glanced around nervously. "She has eyes and ears everywhere! She has operatives everywhere! If you are out of favor with the lady Tulisia, if you defy her . . . do you seriously think an army of brutes will fall upon you one evening? No! You will be on your way somewhere one day, thinking of nothing save coming home to your daughters and me, and then there will be some quick pain in your ribs. You will look down and there will be more blood than you knew you had in your entire body, gushing from the wound from a passing knife and for the life of you—which will be quickly fleeing your body, rest assured—you won't have the faintest idea who it was!"

"Atlanna, for gods sake—!"

"Or me!" she said with increasing urgency. "Or your daughters! Did you even *consider* us in your . . . your orgy of concern? What if she decides simply to pressure you into doing as you are bid by disposing of us, one by one! How many of your daughters will have to meet with mysterious accidents before you do what you should have done in the first place!"

It was almost too much for Orin to process. "I . . . I never . . . she would never . . ."

She took each of his hands and held them so tightly he thought the fingers would break. "You must . . . and she would. You are a leader of males, Orin. There is none better. But you are no leader of females. In reading Tulisia's intentions, you have to trust me to be your mind and your heart. I am telling you that the well-being, the very fate, of your family, is hinging on the next decision you make. And if you refuse to believe that or accept it . . . then we're all of us doomed. All of us."

iv.

Gorkon was not among the first to arrive. By the time he got to the Pier, Markene were already there. They floated listlessly, staring at one another with glazed eyes. Gorkon could practically read their minds. They knew they had to be where they were, pulled there by some primal need, but their ability to connect their actions with the impetus that had brought them there was vague at best.

The Pier had been the traditional meeting place for as long as Gorkon could remember: a long, metal pier, extending from Venets hundreds of feet out into the water. This was because the residents of Venets itself, the Merk, disdained to look upon the Markene. They regarded their racial cousins as no more than a necessary evil. They were the beings of burden who did the jobs that the Merk did not want to have any association with. If the Merk were ever under attack, the Markene would be the first line of defense. The Klaa made them malleable, so that they would obey instructions even if they did not fully understand them.

Gorkon knew this, even though his peers did not. They were too oblivious to know anything except the bliss of Klaa. But Gorkon also knew the drawback of Klaa. While it made the Markene malleable, it also made their ability to act upon instructions hit-or-miss. With an enemy approaching them, usually only a few of the Markene were required to deal with the situation. The only practical means of attacking Venets was by water, and a handful of Markene could destroy an armada. So if a hundred of them received instructions and only ten of them actually had the presence of mind to remember them and execute them properly, still, that was enough. But if they were deprived of the Klaa, as was the case now, it meant something truly significant was going to be asked of them. Something that was going to require more than some Merk pointing in a particular direction and saying, "Go.

Go and destroy." The Markene were going to be required to hold an idea in their head for a time and then act as a coordinated force. Thus they were to be bereft of Klaa while the matter was explained to them. That way, even when they resumed their partaking of Klaa, the instructions would have sunk sufficiently into their heads that they would remember them no matter what. That was simply how their brains functioned.

Gorkon, naturally, was operating in possession of his full faculties. He was the first to see the distant form upon the Pier, approaching them as the unblinking eye of the moon gazed piteously down upon them. The Markene made no noise except for the sounds of bobbing in the water as they waited expectantly.

It was easy for Gorkon to tell that the individual approaching them was nobility. He had that confident air, the squared shoulders, the appearance of boundless confidence in the way he moved. He was someone who, once committed to a course of action, never wavered or doubted it for a moment.

The figure reached the end of the Pier and stared down upon the assembled Markene. Mounted on a pedestal nearby was a large bell that was sometimes used to summon the Markene to the Pier. The bell would produce a loud, sonorous ringing sound that could be heard both above and in the water, and the Markene were conditioned to come in response. In this case, it hadn't been necessary since they were already coming to the Pier, looking for answers.

Gorkon glanced around and saw that many more had joined the crowd. The sea was awash with them, several hundred of them at least. Enough to annihilate any fleet that might be sailing against the Sirene. And that, Gorkon was convinced, had to be the case. There was no other possible rationale for assembling the Markene. There had to be an imminent threat to the city-state, and the Markene were going to be dispatched to deal with it.

The noble looked down sternly upon them. When he spoke, his voice carried across the water, strong and true. Gorkon recognized him when he spoke. It was the Warlord, Orin Arn Oran.

"The Travelers," he said, "are preparing to move against Venets."

Gorkon was thunderstruck upon hearing that. The *Travelers*? He looked at the Markene nearest him. "The Travelers?" he whispered. "Why would they move against us? Or even care about us?"

The Markene simply stared at him in a tired manner and made no response.

Orin Arn Oran continued, "Even as we speak, the Travelers are coming in their mighty boats to survey our territories. To see where our defenses are weakest. We must not permit this to happen. We must not let them see any weakness. That, my dear Markene, is where you come in. We will restore your Klaa to you now, to tide you over until it is time for battle. But when you next hear the sound of the bell, you are to dispatch yourselves to the outer reaches of our waters. There you are to remain on station and wait. Wait for a sign of the Travelers. Sooner or later, their ships will approach. When that happens . . . you are to sink them. Show them no mercy. Annihilate the vessels, send them plunging to the depths."

"What?!"

The word had burst from Gorkon's mouth, surprising him almost as much as it did the Warlord. But in the sea of Markene, Orin had no idea who had spoken up. He peered out among them, squinting. "Who said that?" demanded the Warlord.

Gorkon was terrified. He had no idea what the repercussions might be for speaking back so to the Warlord, but fear gripped him like a dark fist around the spine. He glanced around at the Markene near him. None of them appeared to realize that he was the one who had spoken up.

His mother was there. He spotted her not ten feet away, and she was looking right at him . . . no. Through him. He could have been there or a hundred feet below the surface of the water, and it would have made no difference.

"Who was that?" Orin demanded once more, and still no reply was forthcoming. Finally he grunted in annoyance, no doubt realizing that the Markene were not of sufficient mental condition to answer the question, even if they knew it. Perhaps he even decided that the outcry was mere chance, some random Markene just blurting out an equally random word.

Slowly he paced the end of the Pier, returning to the original topic. "You will sink the vessels of the Travelers. However many there are, that is how many you will sink. You will pull the Travelers themselves under until they move no more, and then you will bring their bodies to the Resting Point. You will leave them there and you will not concern yourself about them any further. If any of you are captured . . . if any of you are faced with questioning by the Travelers . . ." He paused a moment, and then said, "You will cease to breathe."

It was all Gorkon could do to suppress yet another outcry.

For the Markene, the sheer act of living was a significant effort. No autonomic reflexes governed their respiratory system; they had to remind themselves to inhale and exhale. The most common cause of death among the Markene was simply forgetting to breathe, typically thanks to the effects of Klaa dulling their reflexes and self-awareness.

Death by failing to breathe, however, was just about the most agonizing means by which a Markene could die. It was usually swift, but the pain was excruciating and brutal as the chest collapsed. So awful a death was it that Gorkon, even when he had wanted to die, had chosen to beach himself instead.

Orin Arn Oran was instructing them to commit suicide lest they provide information to the Travelers as to who was the source of the orders.

The Markene processed this instruction and then nodded in a manner indicating that they more or less understood what was being asked of them.

"Are there any questions?" the Warlord demanded, but Gorkon could tell that Orin was looking in his general direction. The Warlord must have ascertained the area from which the earlier comment had issued, and was hoping that the speaker would make a repeat performance so that he, the Warlord, could determine exactly who was causing problems.

Gorkon wanted to remove all doubt. He wanted to swim right up to Orin Arn Oran, whom he had respected until this moment, and cry out, *What do you think you're doing? Attack the Travelers? You'll bring the wrath of the Overseer down upon us all! What sort of mad scheme are you concocting? Is this the bitch Tulisia's scheme? It is, isn't it! And we're to be your pawns in your grand scheme to . . . what? Test the limits of the Travelers' power? See just how much provocation the Overseer will endure before he condemns us to depths so low that we'll all be crushed? Or are you simply trying to get yourself killed and you've decided to bring company along when you go?*

Orin Arn Oran spread wide his arms, his voice rising in power and conviction. "The Sirene stand at the brink of their darkest time. Those who are intended merely to watch us are now on the verge of trying to annihilate us. We cannot allow this. You cannot allow this. The Sirene race as a whole is looking to you to save us. Are you up to the task?"

Nothing. Silence. The Markene were merely staring blankly at the Warlord. It would almost have been funny had it not been so depressingly ludicrous.

Clearly annoyed by the lack of response, Orin Arn Oran said, even more forcefully, "The Sirene look to you! Can you be counted on to—"

"Klaa," one of the Markene said. Gorkon couldn't see which one had said it, but it was with a mournful tone, pathetic and pleading. "Klaaaa."

The others began to take up the call. "Klaa, Klaa, Klaa," and now two, then ten, then most of them were chanting it. There was no demand to it. Instead they were lamenting its absence, as a child pining for a long-lost parent.

Orin stood there for a moment, his hands on his hips, shaking his head in disgust. For the first time the entire evening, Gorkon felt some empathy for him. Orin's disgust and impatience with the Markene was evident, and it mirrored Gorkon's own sentiment toward his people. They were so mighty, granted with greater strength than just about anything in the Damned World. Nothing, not even mighty warriors such as the Mandraques or Ocular, could withstand the crushing depths that the Markene could routinely survive. Yet the Markene were helpless, mindless, pathetic before their need for the seductive dreams of the Klaa.

"The Klaa," Orin Arn Oran called out, and that was all he said, but the Markene immediately lapsed into silence, waiting for him to complete the sentence. "The Klaa," he continued, "will be restored to you in small measure. Here. Now."

He shrugged slightly and Gorkon saw what he had not quite made out before in the moonlight, and that was that he was carrying a satchel over his shoulder. He reached into it and held up a fistful of the coral upon which grew Klaa, shimmering the telltale silver. The Markene moaned and reached for it. With a sweeping swing of his arm, he sent the coral flying into the midst of the Markene. The ones it landed nearest lunged for it, slamming into each other, pushing each other away in their desperate attempts to be the first to grab it.

Orin reached into the bag and threw out more, and more. Klaa did not float, but it did not have to. None of the Markene allowed it to sink more than a foot or so before grabbing it up in their eager, frantically grasping hands. There was a collective groan of sated joy as they snagged the coral and started licking it. Several Markene at once attacked each piece, engaging in communal caressing of the treasured commodity with their tongues. The entire scene was borderline orgiastic.

Gorkon drifted back in disgust, watching the water roiling in the feeding frenzy of the Markene as they threw themselves willingly and eagerly back into the comforting arms of the Klaa. "This much," Orin was calling out, "is being provided you by me. We will reopen the gate to you for now . . . but when it is shut once more, that will be the first signal to you that the time to mass against the Travelers is at hand. And when you hear the bell, that will be the signal to depart. We are counting upon you, our brothers and sisters of the Markene."

Brothers and sisters. Willing slaves, you mean. Fools in a grand joke, pieces in a sinister game, that is all we are to you.

The words seared themselves into Gorkon's mind, but he dared not speak, for he feared retribution. He had no idea what the Markene would do at Orin's request. If the Warlord convinced them that Gorkon stood between them and their precious Klaa, they would doubtless turn upon him and reduce him to a floating red carcass before he could offer the slightest protest.

"You!"

The single word echoed through the night, and Gorkon's head snapped around. There upon the Pier, Orin was pointing straight at him, frowning. He was looking, Gorkon realized, at the one Markene who was not indulging in the Klaa. The one Markene who was instead staring at him with unbridled hatred, humiliated on behalf of his people.

Immediately Gorkon dropped beneath the waves, plummeting down, down, praying that Orin Arn Oran had not been able to make out any physical details that would distinguish him from any other Markene. He left the mass of his people, enraptured in the glories of Klaa, far behind, and sought peace and solace in the inky darkness of the sea below.

THE UNDERGROUND

i.

"Faith . . . in ourselves."

It had been a good long time since Ulurac, the Spiritu Sanctum of the Trull, had given a service for the masses in the Hub. Mostly the spirit had moved him to outlying Trull lands, taking him from pocket to pocket where the words and ardor that pulsed within him would make themselves known to the scattered assemblages.

But Ulurac had begun to wonder whether he had been neglectful of the needs of the Hub. It was where he had grown up, matured to adulthood. He had told himself that his acolytes could more than provide for the spiritual needs of the local Trull, and his hand was needed elsewhere. He was starting to think, though, that that was merely an excuse to put as much distance between him and both his mother and his painful memories of his brother as possible.

Ulurac was trying to take this opportunity to reconnect with his own people. They were not making it especially difficult. Although he had come to believe that there was a growing rift between him and his people, here they were now expectantly gathered before him. Dozens upon dozens, packed into the Chamber of Spiritual Healing, looked up at him with eager, hirsute faces, hanging on his every syllable. Word had spread quickly that he would be holding services, and they had not hesitated to show up for his words of wonder.

It made him feel stronger, more focused, than he had in a very long time.

He walked back and forth before them, his long cape swirling about him as he held the edges of the cloak and moved them around subtly. "Faith in ourselves," he repeated, "is what holds us together. It is what elevates us as a race. Faith in what has gone before. Faith in the philosophies that bind us. It is that very faith that is lacking in most of the other races . . . and that will enable us to stay the course and survive while others fall."

There were nods of heads, rocking back and forth among the faithful as they heard his words and took them to heart.

"Above our heads, high above," he continued, dramatically pointing straight up, "there are races at war with one another who have not the faintest idea how to live in harmony. They attack each other, war with each other, kill each other. But we, my friends, my brethren . . . we know the true way of survival. The way that has been pointed us by our ancestors, and the way that we must point those who will follow us."

He saw young Trulls crouching in the front, eagerly hanging on his every word. Ulurac smiled down at them, reaching over to one particularly beaming young fellow and riffling his hair with his large hand. "We must make the next generation of Trulls respect the attitudes that have enabled us to survive. To prosper and flourish at a time when the numbers of other races have been seriously depleted.

"The underground is filled with lines, my people. Thin lines that are faults intrinsic to the construction of the Damned World. These lines cause the world around us to quake at random times. But we, the Trulls, walk those lines, so that where others stumble and fall and lose their balance during times of stress, we artfully maintain our balance."

"Tell us of the lines, brother."

The words reverberated through the chamber, and Ulurac scowled as he saw Eutok at the far end of the room. All heads snapped around to see who had spoken, and there were gasps and murmurs as they saw the Chancellor, in all his finery and battle armor, at the entranceway.

Eutok seemed genuinely interested in what Ulurac had to say. Ulurac, however, knew differently, and he growled in low irritation at the way in which Eutok had chosen to disrupt his service while seeming supportive of it. The onlookers were unaware that a philosophical battle had just been joined. Only the combatants themselves knew the truth of it.

It was an effort for Ulurac to continue. He had felt so comfortable in the fundamental principles he had been espousing. Now, as Eutok stood right there with a hint of a mocking smile, Ulurac was infernally self-conscious about every word that he was about to speak. A hesitation of merest seconds seemed a lifetime to him before he managed to recapture his thoughts and continue with his sermon.

"The lines," he finally said with effort, "serve to remind us who we are . . . and what we must be. We do not wish to fall into them when the ground shakes, but instead to ride them."

"Did you not just say something to that effect, Spiritu Sanctum?" inquired Eutok. He sounded almost solicitous, as if concerned that Ulurac were having difficulty and it was up to him, Eutok, to resolve it.

"Not in those exact words, Chancellor," Ulurac said stiffly. "Even if I had, it bears repeating, do you not think so?"

He was furious to see that now all eyes were upon Eutok. Eutok, walking around making grand gestures, speaking in a booming voice suffused with reassurance and swaggering confidence. Ulurac knew all too well that he could make the Trulls quake in fear . . . but beloved he was not. Eutok, on the other hand . . .

"By all means," boomed Eutok. "Taken to its core, you preach caution."

"I preach the ways that have helped us to survive."

"But is there not more to life than survival, Spiritu?" inquired Eutok innocently, thrown in a quick, respectful bow. "At least, I have always perceived it to be so. Are there not such considerations as living life on our terms?"

"That is what we are doing, Chancellor." A dim haze began to spot over his eyes. It was a sensation that Ulurac knew only too well. He had not experienced it for some time, but the moment he felt it, he knew what it portended. He focused himself, trying to push it away. "We dictate the terms and we live by them."

"Granted, but they are terms that are dictated by fear, are they not?"

He walked with that rolling swagger that so irritated Ulurac. The heads of the congregation were looking back and forth as if they were sitting and watching some sort of sporting event, with a ball rebounding between the two Trulls. This cause Ulurac's simmering rage to roil even more fiercely. "Fear does not determine our actions, Chancellor. Wisdom does that."

"Meaning we're wise enough to be afraid."

Ulurac didn't even know he was moving until he did it. He covered the short distance between himself and his brother so quickly that there were gasps from the Trulls around him. To them, it was as if he was a blur of speed. He was right in Eutok's face, and he snarled, "Sometimes it takes wisdom to be afraid."

"Well then," Eutok grinned broadly, "if that is the case, one is forced to the conclusion that you are the wisest of all the Trulls who live."

He turned to walk away, and Ulurac heard a voice howl, *"Don't count yourself among those who live!,"* and it was only belatedly that he realized the voice was his own. It was too late for such considerations, however, for Ulurac had already tackled Eutok from behind and slammed him to the rocky floor.

He didn't know he was doing it. The world was a haze of red to him, and all that mattered was feeling the flesh of his brother's neck being squeezed between his fingers. There was a collective gasp from the onlookers, which he also did not hear. The one thing he knew he heard beyond any question was his brother's mocking laughter, although later not a single other Trull would be able to claim that he had heard Eutok laughing, or making any noise at all other than a thudding sound as Ulurac kept banging his head against the stone.

Ulurac had no idea for how long his assault on Eutok continued. All he knew was that suddenly he was being lifted off his brother, and he was fighting like a lunatic against the hands that were grasping him. There were yells and shouts of "Hold on!" and "*You* hold on!" and he was sending Trulls flying everywhere. And suddenly the angry face of his mother, the queen, was in his field of vision. Her hand seemed to fly and then it was cracking hard across his face. He was halted then, not just by the impact, but by the realization that it was his mother doing the hitting.

A gasp rose from the assemblage, and Eurella bellowed, "Out!"

The Trulls who had been attending the aborted service did not need to hear a second edict by their queen. They practically stumbled over one another in their haste to vacate the chamber. Within moments the only ones left were the two brothers, Eurella, and the guards. Two of them were helping up Eutok, while the rest were holding back Ulurac. His body was quivering with tension. He felt as if his brain was disengaged completely, and his muscles alone were trying to determine whether he was going to take another swing at Eutok despite his mother's admonitions.

And then she was right in his face, her mouth twisted in contempt as she said, "Is this how you honor the memory of your loved ones? Of Shirella? Of Ulus? Is it? *Is it?*"

The words froze him. Even Eutok, who was several feet away and wiping the dripping blood from his nose, looked appalled at his mother's words. "Highness," he said, taking care to address her by her title, "I don't know that it's necessary to—"

"Quiet!" she hushed him. Eutok bowed his head slightly, pressing a finger against the side of his nose to still the flow. Although she had addressed Eutok, she had never turned her gaze away from Ulurac. "I am horrified by what I just witnessed. You are supposed to be the spiritual leader of our people? You? Yet the moment you are provoked—"

"And why should I tolerate such provocation," demanded Ulurac, "from my own brother? Eh? Tell me that! From my own brother!"

"If not from me," Eutok replied, "then from who?" Ulurac glared at him wordlessly, but Eutok didn't seem put off. "Your problem, Ulurac, is that you are far too accustomed to Trulls trembling at your every word, bowing and nodding and agreeing with everything you say, whether they understand it or not . . . and I'll warrant that more often than you'd think they do not understand it. Who else but a brother can make you think beyond the parameters of the dogma you spout? And you have to start thinking, Ulurac! And you as well, Mother," he said to Eurella. "The Damned World is changing, whether you wish to acknowledge it or not. And if we do not change with it, then—"

"You speak of things that you do not know," Eurella the queen informed him. "Should I lose my temper with you, I assure you the consequences for you will be far more dire than one of your brother's poundings . . . which, by the way," she added angrily, "I will not tolerate a repeat of! It is hardly conducive to the welfare of our people to see their two greatest advisors brawling like children! What do I have to do to prevent such . . . such stupidity?"

"Why don't you just use the Orb on us, Mother?" Eutok said defiantly. "Perhaps Ulurac and I are the excuse you've been waiting for all these years to employ it. The Orb will settle matters once and for all, would it . . . not . . . ?"

All fell silent at that. Eutok himself looked surprised that he had said it, and his mother's face darkened into a truly fearsome scowl.

"If you ever," Eurella assured him, "bring up the blessed Orb in such a cavalier manner again . . . Chancellor or no, son or no . . . I will kill you on the spot. Nor will I require guards to do it. With these two hands, which hauled you kicking and mewling into the world, I will dispatch you from it. Is that clear?"

Eutok slowly nodded, and then tried to rally his defiance. "If you were truly concerned about our people's welfare, Mother," he began. Then he saw the fierce expression on his mother's face and realized that now was not the time. His lips thinned and he fell silent.

"You were saying?" she growled in a warning tone.

"Nothing. I was saying nothing."

"You are quite sure?

"Very much so, yes."

She gave a curt nod. "Good. Ulurac . . ." She noticed that the guards were still holding him tightly, even though he was no longer fighting them. She gestured in annoyance and they released him. He smoothed his robes, casting an irritated glance at them for form's sake, even though they had been doing nothing but their jobs. "Ulurac," she continued, "you will remain in the Hub for a time."

"I . . . had thought to spread the word of Trull teachings to outlying colonies, as is my habit, Mother," Ulurac said.

"Yes, I'm sure you did. But I think it wisest if I keep a wary eye on the sort of teachings you're spreading."

"And what is that supposed to mean?" he demanded.

She gave him a look that could only be described as the evil eye. "The last time I checked into such matters, my dear son, there was no onus upon the queen to explain herself or her orders. So unless you are aware of something that I am not . . ." She paused. "Are you?" When his response was barely audible, she pressed, "What was that?"

"No," he repeated, louder this time, "I am aware of no such onus."

"Then we understand each other."

"And am I to remain in the Hub as well, Mother?" asked Eutok. The bleeding had stopped and he once more had that endlessly insufferable look upon his face.

"Come and go as you wish," she replied. "It would appear that you and your brother are incapable of sharing even a generous amount of space without coming to blows."

"In the interest of accuracy," Eutok pointed out, "most of the blows have been purely one way, with myself on the receiving end."

"That's as you deserve," Ulurac said.

Eurella made a severe "shushing" gesture, but Eutok took several steps toward his brother, a pleasant expression frozen on his lips that was not at all reflected in his eyes. "That," he assured his brother coldly, "is what I permit. Do not confuse my good humor, and my reluctance to fight back to any degree, with an inability to do so. I am Chancellor of the Trulls, brother dear. I am not without resources and an ability to defend myself. If I take offense at your offenses . . . it will not go well with you."

"Are you threatening me, Eutok?"

"I threaten no one, Ulurac. I merely advise. That is, after all, my station in life. I am an advisor. So if you were to consider yourself . . . lucky . . . thus far in our recent associations, why . . . then you would be well advised, and my job would be done. Be aware of this, though." He took one more step closer, and his voice was low and angry, permitting emotion to peer through for the first time. "The Piri are a blight upon this world. If you think they are going to be satisfied with tormenting the Ocular, you are living in a dream world. Sooner or later they are going to have to be disposed of. In the name of your beloved neutrality, would you provide them weapons to arm themselves?"

"No . . . of course not," Ulurac said, casting a glance at his mother.

"So you claim," Eutok sniffed, "although I'm not certain how much I believe your protestations. But consider that, even if that is the case, then you are not, in fact, advocating neutrality. You are willing to let arms be taken up against the Piri. The only question is, do you have the nerve to commit the Trulls, at long last, to doing it themselves? Or are you content to have others do the dirty work for you." He bowed mockingly, turned on his heel with a sweep of his cape, and walked away.

Ulurac took a step after him, but Eurella firmly set herself in his path. "You," she told him flatly, "do not wish to do that. Go to your residence, Ulurac. You do," she added after a moment of his silent glowering, "remember where it is, do you not?"

"Of course I remember. I burrowed it myself, didn't I?" he demanded.

Her response was the merest bored shrug of her shoulders. Then she turned and walked away, her guards scurrying after her.

He stared at the now empty chamber of worship, and couldn't help but see it as a metaphor for his life. In viewing it that way, he suddenly felt uncomfortable in a place that only moments earlier had given him solace.

He made his way out of it and wandered aimlessly through the tunnels, cursing his brother's name and actions. Some small part of him told him his ire was misplaced. That he shouldn't have let his brother's words get to him, and he had brought that . . . that debacle of a service upon himself. But he ignored that thought, tried to make it go away. After all, did he not have the right to—at the very least—have the thoughts in his own head conform to his desires?

Ulurac did not realize where his feet were taking him until he found himself standing in front of it. The burrow before him was typical of a Trull home. He knew very line, every crevice of it, for he had bored it himself, a lifetime ago. Once upon a time, it had been homey and comfortable, and illuminated by the comforting glow of hotstar lanterns within. Now there was nothing but darkness. Under ordinary circumstances, another Trull family would have moved into it, for it was truly quite fine in its depth and evenness. Plus there was a spring nearby that provided not only the convenience of constant potable water, but perpetual warmth.

A prime burrow in a prime location, the sort to which only the son of a queen would be able to lay claim.

It seemed an age that he stood outside it. He tried to command his feet to enter it, but they resisted. *This is absurd. It's just an empty burrow, no matter what happened there before. There's no reason for you to stand here paralyzed, as if you are not in command of your life.*

He forced himself forward, one unsteady step after the other. When he crossed the threshold he did so with a sharp intake of breath, as if something was going to come out of the darkness and stab him.

The warm smell of the place hit him first. Paradoxically, it caused him to relax as he was positive that he could scent his wife and son right there, right in front of him. His nostrils flared and he hummed softly to himself, a gentle lullaby that he had once sung to his son. There was no light, the lanterns long removed to be utilized elsewhere in the underground. But he had no need of light. His eyes closed, he could see ever so clearly his beloved Shirella standing before him. She reached out to him,

laughing in that lovely coarse manner of hers. His fingers brushed across the comforting stubble upon her smiling face, and little Ulus was there, calling out to him,
running up to him in greeting that way he always used to do. He threw his arms
around his father's leg and sighed contentedly, because his father was there and all
was right and all was perfect here, beneath the surface of the Damned World.

I will never let you go, his words echoed back to him across the years. There in the
darkness he reached out to them, and his fingers were so close, so close, and then
they passed right through the images of his life mate, of his child. Then they were
gone, reabsorbed into the air and stuff of memory from which they had come.

Ulurac let out a choked sob, sank to the ground, leaning his back against the
wall. In the darkness none saw, and in his isolation none heard, and in his depths
of despair, he would not have cared if either were not the case. His brother's
words floated back to him: *You're living in a dream world.* So be it. It was far more
comforting than the actual world provided him.

ii.

The tunnel walls whizzed past as Eutok rode in silence upon the Truller car. It
rattled and rolled through the subterranean labyrinth. Eutok steered it with
long expertise. He did not emit war whoops of pleasure at his speed, even though
that was typical behavior for him. In this instance, he desired to ride in silence.
After all, it was never wise to advertise one's presence when one wanted to avoid
detection.

The ride was rocky and inhospitable, since he was in sections of the Underworld that were relatively unpopulated. The Trulls had mined many places in the
Damned World that had been unproductive insofar as offerings of minerals that
the world had to provide. Such places, generally referred to as dead zones, were
unattractive, so most Trulls tended to steer clear of them. The tracks for the
Trullers, built while excavation was still under way, would routinely fall into disre-
pair and consequently were rough at best, hazardous at worst. Yet Eutok traveled
them with no less speed and no more caution that he used at any other time.

Once he had reached his destination, he pulled on the brake and slowed the
Trull car. As he did so, his thoughts flew back to the days when he would go
Trulling with his brother. He could scarcely credit his naïveté, his youth notwithstanding. During any such Trulling excursion, he would endeavor to impress Ulurac with his skill and his fearlessness. Truthfully, back then the act of Trulling had
terrified him, but he had been so determined to prove his bravery to Ulurac that
he pretended he loved every moment of it. The results of his endeavors had not

been remotely what he'd intended: He had, of course, failed to impress Ulurac, who continued to hold Eutok in contempt just as he had always done. He had, however, managed to convince himself of a love for Trulling that persisted to this day. So it had been a partial victory, albeit one that left a bitter taste.

Once the Trull car slid to a halt, he vaulted out of it, thumping noiselessly to the floor and removing a lantern from the place where it was affixed upon the front of the car. He wasn't sure if he was imagining it, but the light created by the hotstars seemed paler than he was accustomed to. He tapped it experimentally but no increase in brightness was generated. He stared at it for a moment more, then shrugged. There was always time to investigate the cause for this oddity later. It was probably nothing.

He held it up high before him and slowly made his way through the tunnels. Even if the hotstar had unthinkably given out completely, plunging him into darkness, he would not have been daunted. His vision was sharper than that of most Trulls, so even total absence of light was not the handicap for him that it was for others.

The silence around him was complete, the only noise being his own slow, steady breathing. His ears were so attuned to his surroundings that it seemed inconceivable that anyone or anything could possibly approach him unawares.

So he was understandably startled when a hand touched him gently upon the shoulder.

Despite all his combat training, despite all his confidence as a warrior, despite all that, Eutok still jumped and let out a most un-Trull-like yelp. He dropped the lantern. It hit the ground and rolled away, falling into some unseen hole or crevice. The light was gone.

"Oooo," a voice floated to him from the darkness. "And now you're helpless."

"So you would wish," snarled Eutok, and he lunged in the direction the voice appeared to be coming from. But there was a rush of air that might have been a random breeze, or might have been a body moving effortlessly past him. Even his superb vision needed a few moments to make the transition from some light to no illumination at all, whereas the creature in the dark with him needed no such adjustment time.

"Missed me," came the voice again, and there was a scraping of rock before he could turn, like clawed toes seeking and finding purchase. He started to turn back toward the voice once more, and then something hurtled through the air and landed on his back. His broad, flat feet maintained their position, so he was not knocked over. Instead he bent slightly under the impact, and then reached around and tried to grab at the creature on his back. But his arms, despite their length, didn't bend around quite that far back, and so he flailed in futility at the empty air.

There was movement on his back, and then a quickly darting tongue working its way into his large, cupped ear. He felt hot breath against it and moaned, his arms dropping to his side.

"The Chancellor of the Trulls," the female voice purred in his ear. "The mighty Eutok . . . so easily overcome. How fortunate your brother cannot see you now. Better that you're in the darkness now, eh."

There was a rustling of fabric, a tearing, and his leather tunic was ripped away from him. The hair on his chest and back was thick and matted, and thin, limber arms wrapped around him even as equally powerful legs locked around his waist. He felt the bare flesh of her against his, and he moaned once more. His hands sought and found her thighs and he stroked them, his fingers running the length of them until they were able to cup themselves around her small, firm buttocks.

Her voice hissed in his ear, and he squeezed, and she trembled. Her feet never touching the ground, she moved around him so that she was facing him.

He tried to move his face forward to smother her lips with his, but her head moved back on her slender neck. "Not yet," she said. "Tell me how it went."

"It went as it often goes," he replied and tried to kiss her once more.

Again she kept him at bay. "Have you convinced them to destroy the Piri?"

"It will take time . . ."

"I don't have time, Eutok," she snarled, the anger in her voice a stark contrast to the overtures her body was making and continuing to make to him. "I don't have time," she repeated. "What I have is a demented mother who would sacrifice my sexuality on the altar of her demented traditions."

"I'm doing all I can," he said in annoyance. "I lent you that digging equipment so you could construct secret tunnels to hide from your mother. What the hell happened?"

"She found me with it before I could hide it," she admitted. "I told her I took it off the body of a dead Trull."

"So now your people used it against the Ocular, and I'm under suspicion. Maybe this entire thing is . . ."

"Is what?" Abruptly she mashed her breasts against him, her breath a sharp intake against his ear. "Do you not find these worth a bit of risk? Or do you not care if my breasts are taken from me? Do you want that to happen?"

"No," he whispered.

"Should I be rendered incapable of enjoying pleasure?" She arched her back, and he felt the heat from her loins radiating through him, and it was enough to drive him insane with desire. His own need was becoming impossible to ignore. It was all he could do not to slam her down right there and thrust himself into her.

"No . . . that shouldn't . . . must not . . ."

"Then make certain it does not. We have barely begun, Eutok, to explore the full range of sensual delights available to us. No one and nothing should be permitted to put an end to it, ever. Ever."

"Ever," growled Eutok, and then he could not take it anymore. He fell atop her, devouring her skin, her scent, everything about her.

"Do whatever it takes."

"I will . . ."

"Stop the Piri. Annihilate them if you have to, if that's what it takes to save me."

"Yes, yes . . . anything . . . *anything* . . . "

She pulled away the last of his clothing, guided him into her, and gasped as he filled her.

The rest of the world fell away from him, even as Clarinda Redeye, daughter of the Mistress of the Piri, moaned beneath him.

THE FIVE CLANS BORDERLANDS

Jepp was not dreaming, which was preferable as far as she was concerned. Instead there was simply the cool blackness of her insensate state. Slowly, however, very slowly, awareness began to creep back to her. The black haze started to dissolve as she noticed the smell of cooking meat, then the crackling of a fire, and the chill of the night air. A fleeting burning sensation on her thigh told her that embers were being blown about in the breeze.

Tentatively, she opened her eyes. She was lying flat on her back, stretched out upon the rocky surface upon which they made their camp.

She stared straight up and the large, unblinking eye of an Ocular was gazing back down upon her. He was chewing on a long, angular bone that could easily have been a leg, ripping the last bits of meat from it with his sharp teeth.

"Oh, good," he rumbled. "Dessert has come around."

Jepp let out a scream that could have shattered glass, had there been any nearby. The Ocular had to drop what he was eating and clap his hands to his ears since the shriek was so shrill. "Thunderation!" he cried out. "What in the name of the Overseer is that noise she's making!"

"She's screaming," came a sardonic voice from nearby. "Her kind does that when startled. A fairly high-strung race."

"Well, make her stop!"

Jepp's focus was so completely on the Ocular looming before her that she didn't recognize the voice from nearby as Zerena's. But Zerena Foux's presence finally dawned upon Jepp when Zerena practically shoved her face into Jepp's and snarled, "Stop."

Jepp was sufficiently startled that she did indeed cease her screaming, her eyes opened so wide in wonderment that they seemed ready to bolt from her face. She saw Karsen standing some feet behind Zerena, shaking his head and saying, "Mother, go easy on her. She's having a rough time of it."

"You would be amazed, Karsen, how little I care for her rough time."

The brown-eyed Ocular had returned to munching the last bits of meat off the bone he was holding, but continued to regard Jepp with a degree of suspicion. The two other Ocular who had accompanied him simply looked bored. "The few Morts I've encountered in my time," he said, "none of them were like her."

"Lucky you," grumbled Zerena.

"I . . . I thought you were dead!" Jepp told Zerena, and now she could see the other Bottom Feeders dotting the encampment. Off to one side Gant was pulsating, while Rafe Kestor dozed and Mingo was making notes in some sort of small book. He glanced at her often enough to make her realize that whatever he was writing, she was the subject of it.

"Obviously, we're not," said Zerena.

"I . . . thought he ate us! Him and his—" She pointed a quivering finger at the Ocular. "He said he was going to!"

Now Karsen was at her side and he touched her face affectionately. "He was just having sport with you. No one thought you would pass out dead away like that. I was going to try and wake you, but you seemed so peaceful, so . . ." and he shrugged.

"So you just let me lie there?"

"You would never have come to any harm," the brown-eyed Ocular assured her.

"No?"

"No. You see, in order to guarantee your safety, I urinated on you so as to mark you as my property. None would dare touch you."

Jepp's first instinct was to let out a shriek and to run and keep running until she could find a body of water. But then she saw the studious deadpan expression on the giant, and Karsen's rolling of eyes, and the snicker and shaking of head from Mingo. And Jepp actually laughed softly then. "Very . . . amusing. I haven't . . . met many Ocular, really, but I can see you have a . . . a unique sense of humor."

"I have been told such." He turned his attention to Zerena. "Am I required to present myself, Zerena Foux? Or will you as head of your clan attend to the proper protocol of things?"

Zerena flashed a look of annoyance, but then obviously resigned herself to proceeding in an appropriate manner. "Jepp of the Damned World," she said, "I have the honor of presenting to you Nagel, lord of the high tower, the One-Eyed King, ruler of the Ocular. Honored Nagel, this is Jepp, an unremarkable creature."

"*Mother!*"

"*What?*" said Zerena in annoyance.

"Ignore her," said Nagel as he tossed aside the bone. "It is a pleasure to meet you, Jepp. I understand that you came to be with these Bottom Feeders as a result of having been salvaged."

"Yes, Highness," Jepp said, choosing a form of address that seemed appropriate. There was still a fundamental fear, down in the base of her spine, that the giant would reach over, pick her up, and pop her in his mouth like an after-dinner tidbit. But the more she studied him, the more she saw—or at least thought she saw—a basic sweetness in the single eye regarding her. "Karsen rescued me from a pair of Mandraques."

"Karsen did that?" The brow above Nagel's one eye lifted. "Truly? No offense intended, Karsen, but you never struck me as much of a fighter."

"I freely admit that," Karsen agreed. "But there is something about Jepp that— I don't know—brings out the aggressor in me."

Nagel snorted in amusement at that and looked at Zerena. "No wonder you keep her around. You always were the pragmatist, Zerena Foux."

"How . . . long have you known her?" asked Jepp.

"Oh, several full cycles around the sun it's been, has it not, Zerena?" She nodded. "We had some dealings, she and I, and I did her a favor at the time."

"What favor?"

"I allowed her to live," Nagel said, and Jepp looked for some sign that he was jesting. This time, however, there was none such. Jepp had the cold feeling that he was quite serious. That unease in the base of her spine began to return. "I felt," continued Nagel, "that she might be of some use to me in the future."

"And a solid instinct it was," Zerena assured her. "In fact, I'm going to lend some validity to that belief right now."

"How so?"

"By telling you that your mission to the Trulls is a fool's errand." She had been sitting near the fire, but now she stood and moved away from it, drawing closer to Nagel and speaking with conviction. "They turned you down once. They remain steadfastly neutral. What makes you think that you can convince them otherwise?"

"I will find a way," he said firmly. "I will barter. I will beg. And, if it comes to it, I will beat their thrice-damned ruler to death with my bare hands and take the digging technology that I require."

Zerena looked taken aback. "You would risk the wrath of the Firedraques . . . even the Travelers, perhaps the Overseer himself . . ."

"I will take whatever risks are necessary." He said it with what sounded to Jepp like a deep-rooted anger that was aimed not at anyone present but at someone who was nowhere around.

"I . . ." Jepp began, and when all eyes turned to her, she cleared her throat nervously. "I . . . don't understand what we're talking about. Or what you're talking about. I'm not trying to thrust myself into the conversation, you understand, but—"

Zerena groaned. "Why do you act so damned deferential all the time?"

"A lifetime of practice," she said without hesitation.

"My niece," Nagel told Jepp, "was kidnapped by the Piri. You know of the Piri?" When she nodded, shivering slightly as she did so, Nagel continued, "They dragged her away underground. If she is not dead by now . . . she may well wish she were. My people's lives and happiness are overshadowed by those animalistic scavengers, and I would seek help in finding a means of disposing of them. My foremost advisor suggested the Mandraques . . ."

Jepp laughed. Then she saw the look on his face and flushed in embarrassment. "Oh. Dear. That . . . was not another joke."

"No," said Nagel, sounding none too pleased, his words so frozen that they could have been formed from ice. "It was not." Then, perhaps feeling a bit sorry for Jepp, he continued, "For what it's worth, I never seriously considered it although he no doubt thinks I'm on my way to the Mandraques even now. I've elected this course instead."

"Certainly preferable," Jepp assured him, nodding briskly. "The Greatness always said he loved treaties and alliances, because it always gave his ally a false sense of security. Although," and she frowned, recalling, "I think he also said that any sense of security was always, by definition, false."

"The Greatness," Mingo called over, "sounds like one of the profound philosophers of our time. A pity I'll never get the chance to meet him and maybe, just maybe, rip his damned head off."

"A true tragedy, that," intoned Nagel.

Silence ensued. During that time, Jepp stared long and hard at Nagel, so much so that he noticed it and began staring back at her. She did not, as he might have expected, turn away or appear daunted by him. Instead she studied him with great thought, as if pondering something vast and ineffable.

"Would you care to share with me," he said finally, "what's going through your mind?"

Zerena cast a bewildered glance between Nagel and Jepp. "Why would you possibly care?"

"Because," Nagel said reasonably, "she seems to have something to say, and I find myself curious to hear it. Do you have a problem with that, Zerena Foux?"

"No, no . . . not at all," Zerena replied quickly. "It's your time to waste as you see fit."

"I just . . ." The seated Jepp took a deep breath and leaned forward, intertwining her fingers and wrapping them around her knees. Tilting her head slightly, causing her long hair to cascade around her shoulders, she said, "Tell me about the Piri. Tell me all you know about them."

Nagel did so. He spoke of their earliest encounters, of their animalistic nature, of their brutality, of their aversion to light. "It is said that light—sunlight particularly—can flay the very skin from their bodies," Nagel told her. "My people are blind in it, dislike it intensely, but the Piri supposedly cannot tolerate it at all."

Karsen was watching her with keen interest, and it was clear why. There was something different about Jepp in the way she was interacting with Nagel. It was as if her fear and her cowering had become secondary to her curiosity. In a low voice, Karsen said to Mingo, who was watching the proceedings with interest, "Why do you think she wants to know so much about the Piri?"

"Who can say?" Mingo said, shrugging. "Morts are a paradoxical group. But the one indisputable thing about them was that they had an insatiable curiosity about damned near everything. One certainly has to give them credit for that . . ." Then he thought about it a moment and amended, "Actually, no, I guess one doesn't have to give them credit for it since, in the end, it availed them very little . . ."

"Quiet!"

There was surprise on the faces of all the Bottom Feeders in earshot, because it was Jepp who had spoken. Even she appeared startled at the firmness with which she had issued an order. Nagel looked impressed. "She has more spirit than I initially thought, Karsen. I can see why you would be enamored of her."

"I'm not enamored of her," Karsen said quickly.

Jepp half turned and looked at him. "You're not?" There was no sound of disappointment in her voice. It just seemed as if she were inquiring.

"No! I'm not!"

"Oh." She processed that information even as Zerena stared at her son without knowing quite what to think about him. "Oh," she said again, and then she turned back to Nagel as if Karsen had not spoken. "My apologies, mighty one, if I have been asking too many questions . . ."

"No, no, that's quite all right," Nagel assured her. "One never knows where questions—"

"The Orb."

The two words were meaningless both to Zerena and to Karsen. Zerena glanced over at Mingo, who gestured helplessly in a way that indicated he had no clue what she was talking about.

That was when Jepp noticed, out of the corner of her eye, that Gant had ceased his random bubbling and was now oozing in their general direction. She didn't have the faintest clue why was he was coming over, or if he even was doing it deliberately. For all she knew he had fallen asleep and was merely seeping toward them without any conscious direction.

Nagel, meantime, was sitting straight up and Jepp had heard his sharp intake of breath. "The Orb?" he repeated back to her.

"Yes. The Orb. It is a source of . . . of great light," she said, choosing each word delicately. "I know that much."

"How do you know that much?" demanded Zerena.

"I don't know."

The Laocoon threw her hands up and stomped away, shaking her head in frustration. But she was back barely a heartbeat later. "You," she said, "are the most frustrating—"

"Zerena Foux," Nagel interrupted her, and his tone was different. Deeper, more threatening, and the change was not lost upon his guards, who clearly realized that something was up. "I will thank you not to speak to her again in that manner."

"But—"

"I will *thank* you . . . not to *speak* to her . . . in that *manner*."

Zerena was clearly about to toss off another dismissive response, and then apparently realized that matters had shifted in a way that she did not entirely comprehend. She did know enough, however, to defer to the huge, impossibly muscled creature that was more than twice as tall as anyone there, and backed up by two others of his kind even bigger than he. Her lips thinned in that way they had when she was impatient about something, but then she did something that Jepp had never seen: She bobbed her head and just sort of slunk away, like a whipped animal, although not before casting a furious look at Jepp.

Jepp felt an unaccustomed sensation, and she realized with a dim awareness that it was the feeling of triumphing over someone else. More . . . it was the feeling of being treated with respect. Granted, Karsen had been nothing but kind to her, but the others had acted as if she was someone to be barely tolerated. Even they were looking at her differently, their perception of her being filtered through the prism of the Ocular's attitude toward her.

Jepp was amazed at the turnaround. It was, to her perception, mere minutes earlier that she had been utterly terrified of the Ocular. Now she was starting to feel as if this Nagel fellow was perhaps her best friend in the whole Damned World.

Nagel studied her levelly for a full minute. One would have thought he knew great, deep secrets and was trying to decide whether or not he should voice them. None of the other Bottom Feeders dared to speak, although Gant had oozed even closer. Jepp had to think by that point that Gant was approaching purposefully. Perhaps even he was curious as to what Nagel was going to say next.

"You do not know much of your own race, do you," he finally asked Jepp.

"Very little," she admitted. "I cannot read our older writings . . . not that it would matter. The Greatness would always take care to burn whatever human writings he stumbled over. He spoke of how knowledge was power. He said it as if it were a very bad thing."

"To some, it's the worst thing of all," Mingo remarked.

Nagel nodded. "Certainly to those in power, knowledge is to be feared. At least, to those who have power but are insecure in it."

"But you," Jepp said slowly, "are not insecure. Are you, honored one."

"No," said Nagel, shaking his head, the edges of his mouth twisting just a bit. "No, I am not at all insecure. And I have acquired more books of Mort—of human," he amended, seemingly out of deference to Jepp, "writing than quite possibly anyone else in all the Twelve Races, or even the Overseer himself. And many of these writings I cannot read, but some I can, and some I have, to the best of my ability. And I have seen reference to an Orb that has some of the properties of which you speak. It is called something like 'the Orb of the Trinity.'"

"The Orb of the Trinity," Jepp repeated with reverence. It sounded so important. Then she frowned. "What is a 'Trinity'?"

"I am not certain," Nagel admitted. "As I said, my ability to comprehend the writings is not the most reliable. Many of the words are confusing to me, and there are entire segments, filled with numbers and complex statements and such, that are indecipherable."

"Is there only one of these Orbs? What does it do exactly?"

Nagel chuckled to himself. It was a very strange noise, a sort of deep wheezing, and the only reason she recognized it as laughter rather than, say, that he was choking on something was that he was smiling as it was happening. "You ask many questions for one who some believe is ignorant." He cast a glance at Zerena as he said that, but she made no reply.

"I *am* ignorant, great Nagel Highness sir," replied Jepp, adding as many flourishes to Nagel's title as she could. "How else to relieve myself of my ignorance except to ask questions?"

"How else indeed?" he concurred. "To answer your questions and banish your ignorance . . . there is more than one Orb. Or at least there were. Once upon a time, there were many of them. As for now? Who can say? As to the Orb's purpose: Well, there are more contradictions in my readings. Alternately, the Orb is described as being able to provide incredible, searing light . . . and yet, it can also bring darkness, producing a cloud so vast, so monstrous in proportion, that it can literally block out the sun. Some readings even talk about some type of 'winter' that would follow the use of an Orb. Me, personally . . . I like winters. Far prefer them. The cold air is invigorating, and the white particles that fall from on high . . . the snow . . . is most pleasant."

"A single Orb can do all that?" Zerena asked.

Nagel turned his attention to her. "You sound doubtful."

"I do not discount the notion that a device that accomplishes so many things—light, dark, warmth, cold, changes in season—that such a device could exist. But I very much doubt the humans could have made one, because it sounds magical in nature. And humans knew nothing about magic."

"Perhaps not," suggested Mingo. "Or perhaps they simply had a magic system that is unlike any we've encountered before. Is that reason to dismiss it? Or perhaps to, instead, fear it?"

"Not you, too, Mingo!" Zerena said with growing disgust. "You know the Morts are . . ." Then she became aware of Nagel's glare burning a figurative hole in her head. ". . . most resourceful, and so perhaps might have developed this . . . magic. Or tech. Or something."

"Can you imagine it?" Nagel said. He began pacing, and Jepp could tell that there was growing excitement in him which he was almost afraid to acknowledge. Jepp fancied that his every step caused the ground to tremble slightly. "One device that could solve all our problems. That could turn our lives around. It truly is tempting to think of it as magic."

"I'm not entirely sure I'm following, Highness," Karsen said. "How would it—?"

"He'd use it to destroy the Piri," Zerena told him.

He pivoted, moving so quickly that Jepp, even though she was seated on the ground, jumped back a little in concern. "Yes. Exactly. Hope for my people after all this time, to have our lives move toward a golden age. It seems too good to be true."

"It is my experience," Mingo said in his characteristic pedantic drawl, "that most things that seem too good to be true . . . generally are."

"You would dash even my slightest hopes, Minosaur?" demanded Nagel. "The incandescence of the Orb, projected into the hidey-holes of the Piri . . . the power of the sun itself ripping their bodies to pieces, leaving them scattered bits of ash there beneath the ground . . . followed by a cloud that blocks out the sun for the rest of my people so they can live happy, fruitful lives, free of being preyed upon, free of blindness . . ."

"Mighty Nagel, this is madness!" Zerena told him, unable to hide her obvious annoyance with Jepp. "This . . . human . . . is giving you false hope! I mean," she waved her hands aimlessly, "so you've read of this magical, mystical Orb that humans made. It still remains the stuff of legend, even though she makes declarations that one of them can make all your problems just go away! Where are you going to find one of these Orbs, anyway?"

"The . . . Trull."

The voice that had spoken was thick and syrupy. It was Gant who had spoken, having coagulated several feet away. It looked to Jepp as if he were trying to manufacture a body for himself in order to converse with them. A "projection" of sorts had emerged from the middle of the glob that was Gant, rising to about four feet in height, like a gelatinous stalagmite on the floor of a cave. It swayed gently in the night air. Jepp sensed that maintaining any sort of shape, even something as rudimentary and unappealing as this, was a huge strain for Gant. She couldn't even begin to imagine how he was manipulating his nonexistent tongue and vocal cords to form sounds, even in as slow and labored a manner as he was managing. But he was definitely doing so.

There was stunned silence, and then Nagel focused all the intensity of his single eye upon Gant. "The . . . Trull?" He was not deliberately mocking Gant's measured delivery, but instead was merely trying to accept the words that his hearing was telling him had been spoken. "The Trull . . . have . . . one of these . . . these . . . Orbs?"

"They did . . . at least," said Gant. His manufactured body shifted, as if he were settling himself in for the purpose of telling a long story. "Eurella . . . had one. She . . . treasured it . . . above all . . . other things . . ."

"Eurella? Their . . . queen?" Each word he spoke sounded harsher, trembling with barely contained fury, and then Nagel brought a fist around and smashed it down upon a rock. Jepp let out a little shriek, concerned for Nagel's welfare, and then she saw the rock—which was at least a foot tall and half again as wide—crumble into rubble. The impressiveness of the display was not lost upon her. "Their queen," continued Nagel, measuring each word, "the bitch who refused to help us search for my niece . . . it now turns out possesses a device that could exterminate them for all time . . . and she didn't see fit to mention it to me?"

"She mentions it . . . to no one," said Gant, his body twinging in sympathetic time to his voice. "It is . . . her treasure. She stares at her . . . reflection . . . in it, and . . . worships it . . . believing it to be . . . a gift from the . . . gods . . ."

"And how would you know of this, Gant?" Mingo demanded. "If Eurella mentions it to nobody . . ."

"I am not . . . or rather . . . was not always . . . a nobody . . . I was . . . of the Phey," Gant said, and he trembled a bit in what Jepp had to assume was sheer pride. "When one is of the Phey . . . there is no treasure . . . buried too deep . . . no secret . . . held too dear . . . that my people and I . . . could not find a way . . . to learn of it. None has secrets . . . from the Phey." Jepp could see that he was beginning to lose control of whatever "muscles" he had used to manufacture this form. He was starting to shake, and a low moan arose from him. "I was . . . I was . . . great . . . in my day . . ."

Nagel came in close to him, speaking anxiously, determined to learn all that Gant knew on the subject. "Did you see it yourself?"

"Yes. It was . . . beautiful . . . shining metal . . . she called it 'my light,' although it was not . . . illuminated . . . I heard her . . . whispering to it . . . tired . . ."

"She sounded tired?"

"I am . . . I do . . . so . . ."

"Thunderation, Gant! Do you know where she kept it?"

"I was Phey . . . went where I . . . wished . . . look at me . . . gods . . . look at me . . ."

And with that Gant gave up trying to hold his body together. The small upward projection that he had created dissolved down into itself with a low, long, drawn-out moan that almost sounded as if he was releasing his dying breath. He splashed down, sending small bits of goo flying. Some of it landed on Jepp's thigh, and she made a sound of disgust while trying to brush it away.

That was when the bits of Gant's body that had landed upon Jepp began to roll off of their own accord. Jepp, who by all guesses from her companions should have been screaming just then, instead gazed with fascination upon the bits of Gant that were departing her slender, darkly tanned body. Then they rolled off and away from her, being reabsorbed into the truly bizarre entity into which Gant had been metamorphosed.

"This is fate," said Nagel.

"What is . . . ?" Zerena asked, and then Jepp saw her face beginning to pale. "Oh, you cannot be serious."

"He cannot be serious about what?" asked Mingo, looking from one to the other. "About what can he not be serious?"

Jepp was confused as well, feeling she had somehow missed an entire section of the conversation. Nagel noticed her bewilderment, and then she let out a small "Eep!" as he reached over and placed one of his huge hands on each of her upper arms. Had he brought his hands together, he could easily have crushed her between them. His face drew closer and when he spoke, his breath washed over her. It was so powerful that it was everything she could do not to faint.

"Do you believe in destiny?" he demanded urgently.

"Nagel, please, with all respect, you cannot possibly—" Zerena started to say.

He ignored her. "Do you?" he asked Jepp once more.

Jepp's emotions regarding Nagel had seesawed back into the direction of intimidation. "Do . . . do you want me to?"

"I just want your honest opinion!"

"I haven't *got* one!" she wailed. "The only opinion I have that matters to me is that I don't want you to kill me!"

Nagel stared at her, then shook his head and released her. She sagged to the ground, and Karsen went to her and put an arm around her. It was comforting, but she felt confused and humiliated and not at all desirous of any sort of comfort. She shook off his arm and drew her knees up, peeking over them with trepidation at the Ocular.

"It doesn't matter," Nagel said at last. "All that matters is that I believe in destiny. I have believed in it for a good, long time." He looked up toward the stars, and Jepp could actually see their twinkling reflected in his large eye. "I believe that the Twelve Races were destined to take this Damned World from the humans, for your kind—no offense intended, Jepp—was not using it to its full potential. And I believe that destiny led me here, to the group of you, so that you could tell me what I needed to know. About the existence of the Orb . . ."

"Nagel, please—"

"And, Zerena Foux," he interrupted her, "I believe that destiny will support you as well, as you brave all odds to obtain the Orb for me."

"Uh, excuse me, Your Magnificence," Mingo said. He had been perched atop an outcropping, but now he hopped off it, thudding to the ground below, landing in a crouch. He tilted his head and "huffed" slightly through his oversized nostrils. "Did you say—?"

"I did."

"He did," affirmed Zerena, looking none too pleased. "As I had a feeling he was going to. I knew you were going to, Nagel," she continued, dropping all endeavors to add honorific titles to him. "I knew you, in your desperation, were going to try and do this."

"I am not going to 'try' anything, Zerena Foux," Nagel assured her. "I am telling you and you will do it."

"And I am telling you," she shot back, "that we are definitely not—"

He growled. It was a low and horrible sound, and it looked as if his eye were about to pop out of his head. Jepp could see a network of small red veins lining the edges of it. From behind him, his two guards rose, and they had pulled out monstrous clubs from holders on their backs. They were gently tapping the clubs in their open palms.

"—going to . . . eliminate . . . any possibility . . . without . . . discussing it," Zerena finished lamely. Trying to regroup, she spoke quickly, "But certainly you see the insanity of what you're asking."

"I see only someone who continues to live because of my generosity," Nagel reminded her. "I had you helpless, Zerena. I had you dead to rights, and the right to have you dead."

"What did she do?" Jepp whispered to Karsen. "What did she do that Nagel was ready to kill her?" Karsen simply gave her a look that said *You don't really want to be asking that.*

"But I did not do so," Nagel reminded Zerena. "I did not employ my right as ruler of the Ocular. On that night long ago, I didn't fully understand myself why something within me prompted me to release you. Now I know. It was destiny, preparing itself even then to dedicate you to a higher calling. I am issuing that call now, and you are sworn upon the honor of yourself and your clan to attend to it. You swore an oath then in exchange for my releasing you and your lot. You must honor that oath now, unless you desire to suffer the consequences of breaking it."

"The consequences?" Zerena was standing upright now, bravely facing off against Nagel even though Jepp knew the Ocular could annihilate her with minimal effort. Her build and weight might have daunted other Laocoon, and certainly humans such as Jepp, but they struck no fear in the heart (hearts?) of a towering Ocular. "What consequences? That I die at your hands? As opposed to what? Dying at the hands of the Trull? That will certainly be no pleasant experience, I can tell you. The Trull have no love for strangers in general and Bottom Feeders in particular. They like to pick and choose to whom they sell their weapons, and they despise the fact that we pick up their weapons from their fallen customers and take them for our own. We can't exactly go marching into the Underground, because they'll kill us as soon as look at us, and—"

"Sneak in," Nagel said easily. "Gant, after all, must know ways in and out. He said it himself: He is of the Phey, and nothing was hidden from him or his kind."

"But he's not his kind anymore, in case you haven't noticed," Karsen spoke up in exasperation.

"This is folly, most highly honored one," Mingo said. He tried to adopt a casual, chatting tone, as if he and Nagel were two very old buddies babbling about matters of no consequence. "Granted, Zerena owes you her life. Granted, she is bound by matters of honor for which even humble Bottom Feeders such as ourselves have nothing but respect. But why would you waste our debt to you on a . . . a suicide mission?"

"Suicide . . . ?" Jepp was definitely not liking the sound of that.

No one acknowledged her nervous repetition. "Whether it is suicide or not is up to you, Minosaur," Nagel said, his eye narrowing. Jepp had a feeling that Nagel had little patience or liking for Minosaurs . . . and possibly for Bottom Feeders as a group, or perhaps even for this clan especially. "But if you ask me, I do not believe that destiny brought us together in this time and place, simply so that you could die on my behalf."

"Destiny is a thousand laughs," Mingo said, unenthused. "And every single one of them is at our expense."

"Nagel." Zerena was trying her best to sound reasonable. "Putting aside for a moment our own skins—a consideration I do not diminish lightly—let us say that we succeed in this mad endeavor. Let us say that we obtain this Orb for you. Have you given any thought to the possibility that you are dealing with magicks or tech or whatever else that you may, in fact, have no control over? Poor Gant there," and she pointed in the direction of the seeping puddle of matter, "is living proof of how such power can be turned against one. You seek to unleash the power of this Orb and you don't know for certain if, once you do so, it is not going to rebound against you. You could," she gestured helplessly, "you could wipe out my people in your efforts to save them! Have you thought of that?"

"I have," Nagel said, although Jepp in listening to him wasn't entirely sure that he, in fact, had. "And I do not believe it to be a serious problem. Why in the world would the humans produce a weapon that could not, in some manner, be controlled? A device that would annihilate its user along with its victim. It makes no sense; no sense at all."

"They're Morts. They didn't *have* to make sense," replied Zerena.

"You haven't spent as much time with their writings as I have."

"And you haven't spent as much time with one of them as I have," and Zerena cast an irritated glance at Jepp. "Although if you'd like to remedy that by taking this one off our hands, I wouldn't say nay."

Nagel shook his head. "They were—are," he amended in deference to Jepp, "a people who believed passionately in life. That much I've gleaned. They spent entire documents pondering its meaning. I simply don't believe that they would create a device that would just obliterate all life around it, indiscriminately. Humans simply couldn't be that . . . that stupid."

"I actually think we can," Jepp said tentatively, but Nagel didn't seem to hear her.

"If it is a weapon," he said, "then there must be a way to aim it and focus its power upon a target. And I intend to aim it at the Piri and use it to the full extent of its abilities. And you are going to enable me to do that. You are going to obtain the Orb from the Trulls. You will bring it back to me at Feend, and even if our problems are not resolved in time to save my niece, gods forbid, we will have assured that my people will be forevermore spared the torments of the Piri."

"*We* will have assured that?" Zerena said in open astonishment. "The 'we' which is comprised of us will have risked their necks on a dubious mission for a questionable prize. What about us being spared torments by not having to participate in this potential debacle?"

"Your fates do not concern me," Nagel assured them, "except where they overlap with my needs, which in this instance is the case. Gant has been down there. He will lead you there, and can doubtless find hidden tunnels and secret passages that will get you where you want to go. Trulls love to tunnel. Find a tunnel and use it to your advantage. Find the Orb, get it, and get out. Do you have any questions?"

"Of course! But where to begin? How—"

"I said," he repeated, warning dripping from every syllable, "do you have any questions?"

She took a deep breath, the tone of his voice clearly not lost upon her. Nevertheless she said, "What if we refuse?"

"If you refuse," he told her, sounding quite reasonable, "then you will be in violation of the oath you swore to me. You will humiliate your ancestors going back ten generations, and your descendants running forward another ten."

"I can live with that," Zerena assured him.

"Also, my guards and I will devour you and your clan members, right now."

"That," she admitted, "becomes more problematic."

"No, but . . ." Jepp started to say, "he's joking . . . he—" Then she saw Karsen grimly shaking his head. "He . . . isn't joking?"

"Do I look like I'm joking?" he said.

"No," admitted Jepp, "but then, you didn't look like it before, and you were—"

"This time, I am not," he assured her. His level, piercing gaze swept the assembled Bottom Feeders. Then he held up both his hands, extending all ten fingers. "You have twice this many turns of the Damned World to penetrate the land of the Trulls, obtain the Orb, and bring it to me. If, Zerena Foux, you are interested in being a creature of honor, you will abide by this. If, Zerena Foux, you and yours are interested in not being hunted down upon failing to return, and subsequently being torn to shreds and served to my people in small, dripping chunks, you will abide by this. Do you understand?"

"May I speak candidly to you, Nagel . . . as someone who cares almost as much about you as she does her own skin?"

He gestured in a generous manner. "As you wish, Zerena."

"It is my opinion that you are being driven to the edge of madness over what has happened to your niece. Further, it is my opinion that you have not accepted the Way of Things."

"Really," said Nagel hollowly. "And that Way would be what?"

"That what you desire does not exist. You want everything perfect for your people, and such a thing cannot be. That is true destiny. Every positive must have a negative. Every light must have its dark. Attempting to bask only in the light will send you into permanent darkness . . . but not in the way you hope. Instead you will end up only with the darkness of hopelessness and oblivion. You must either accept the situation that you have, and live as best you can with the Piri . . . or you must relocate your people to someplace less advantageous, but that will leave the Piri far behind. Those are your reasonable choices. What you are foisting upon us, the situation that you are burdening us with . . . that is not reasonable. That is the unreasoning determination of the pathetically desperate. Of someone who is not rational. And have you not always believed yourself to be the most rational of beings?"

"Yes. Yes, I have," Nagel said slowly. His face darkened. "That was before I stopped sleeping."

"Stopped—?"

"Kept awake every night by the screams of my niece. They echo in my memory, and they will not stop, and I must stop them . . . which means you are going to stop them. You will stop them. You will do as I say, or you will die. Now, is there anything else to say?"

"No," Zerena sighed. "No, I suppose not."

"Excellent." He clapped his hands together so loudly that Jepp had a ringing in her ears from it. "I will return to Feend to await your good news. And Zerena . . . don't fail in your mission so that I have to go to the Trulls myself. Otherwise it will not end well for you."

"But why us?" It was Zerena's last, desperate gasp of frustration. "Why not just do your dirty work yourself?"

"Because," said Nagel, sounding amused, "no one should put himself at risk when he can use agents to do his bidding."

He smiled at her, displaying his rows of sharp teeth, and then he strode away, the ground rumbling beneath him. His guards followed him, glancing over their shoulders as they went, still tapping their palms with the clubs as if frustrated that they hadn't had the opportunity to utilize them.

The Bottom Feeders looked at one another in silence.

Finally Jepp said, "I thought he was kind of sweet, actually."

Zerena stared at her, then turned to Mingo, chucked a thumb in Jepp's direction, and said, "Be sure to kill her before we break camp."

The mighty Ocular runs from the pathetic "humans" . . . for that is what the pathetic denizens of the equally pathetic world choose to call themselves, apparently. He can barely sound the word out: "hoomun." Indeed, there are pronunciation difficulties for many of the creatures that populate the place to which the Banished have been exiled. The creatures, and the lands in which they live.

The Ocular does not know the name of the particular land through which he has been fleeing. But he does know that the natives are especially vicious, pursuing him with unrelenting vigor. He has no idea how many of them there are, but they seem to be coming from everywhere. No matter where he has hidden himself, no matter how far he has run, they always find him. Granted, his sheer size makes hiding difficult. Not for the first time does he envy the damnable Piri, who excel at finding small caverns or digging their way into catacombs within which they can hide. He has little doubt that the Piri who arrived the same time he did will manage to survive far longer than him or his kind. But even they will be flushed out and destroyed sooner or later. These humans are most ingenious at destroying that which they do not understand.

His breath heavy in his chest, the Ocular finds a group of rocks and flattens himself against them, trying to slow the hammering of his heart. He looks toward the sky, and imagines that the Banishers from his home dimension are looking down upon him, laughing and snickering at his dire straits.

"The final solution," he mutters to himself, shaking his head in disbelief that it has come to this. "Bastards. That the bastards would do this to us, simply because there are races that don't fit in with their grand vision of perfection . . ."

And now he is here.

Other Ocular were sent with him, and he assumes they are dead by now. For a time, he fell into the company of a Minosaur. Personally he could not stand Minosaurs, but he had to admit this particular one fought bravely and effectively. They had been a good team, until the Minosaur had fallen in a battle that the Ocular had managed to escape. From hiding, the Ocular had watched the vomitous humans as they had beheaded the Minosaur and pranced about, waving his horned head like a trophy. One of them had then plunged a knife into the Minosaur's chest and pulled out his mighty heart, holding that up as well in triumph.

Monsters. Monsters, the lot of them.

The Ocular suddenly feels the pain of a spear slamming into him, burying itself in his shoulder. It is small in comparison to him, because the creature who had wielded it was comparatively smaller as well.

He turns and sees them approaching. They are lightly clad, with scraps of cloth around their middles, some of them wearing pieces of armor that are no protection against the wrath of the far larger Ocular. He pulls the spear from his shoulder, wincing at the minor pain it causes, and then flicks it back at them. It lands squarely in the chest of one of the unarmored ones, who utters a shriek and collapses. Remarkable how little it takes to kill one of them.

Two or three more approach from different sides. In the distance, the Ocular hears water, the pounding of the surf. The sound gives him minute pleasure. In his old world, there was much water, and he loved to float in it for hours on end. But he is jolted from his reverie once more by the harsh reality of the humans with their spears. He is able to bat several of them away in midair, but one or two more thud into him. He lets out a yelp and the humans cheer, which is about what he would have expected from beasts such as these. He pulls out the spears but, instead of throwing them, breaks them disdainfully.

They charge him en masse, shouting war cries, and he meets the charge head-on. They clamber up him, swarming, and he grabs two of them in one of his huge hands and throws them to the ground as hard as he can. He hears a satisfying crunch as they strike the ground, their heads splitting, and what passes for their imbecile brains spills out upon the ground. He shrugs off the others, scattering them about, and then backs up to give himself some distance.

He is on a narrow incline, retreating, as more of them come from everywhere in response to the shouts of their fellows. The heat of the sun is relentless, beating down upon him. Does the very sky ally itself with these little barbarians?

The Ocular dwells briefly upon the First Wave, even as he continues to retreat. In the history of this world, they arrived long before these human creatures existed. Back when their ancestors, all but unrecognizable to modern humans, cowered in trees. But times passes very differently in the Elserealms than it does here. What was eons on this world was not much more than an eye-blink back in the place of origin of the Ocular and his kind.

Back then, the first of the Banished had it easy. In an orgy of extinction, they hunted the big, slow, stupid creatures residing on this world into oblivion. Then, bored, having conquered their enemy, they reverted to type and hunted each other. Brilliant move, that. Then again, the eventual climatic changes that followed their arrival, including a lengthy period of sheer frost, would have wiped them out anyway.

He almost envies them.

More of the humans advance on the Ocular now, and still more. How many? Hundreds? They chatter at him in their annoying language, a brutal cacophony, and he continues to back up. He can barely see, practically blind in daylight as are all of his kind. If only it were night, this would be a different story. But he suspects they're not going to give him that kind of time.

Some inner sense warns him at the last moment, stops him from retreating any further. The rushing of air, the closer sound of the water, tells him all he needs to know: He is at a drop-off. A very high one, judging from the echo.

He cannot retreat any further. Very well. Then he will attack. He will crush as many of them beneath his feet as he can manage. Who knows? Perhaps they will break and run when he charges them. Perhaps he may let live to fight another day.

Then he hears something. It is a faint "whup whup" sound, as if something is being spun around quickly. He shields his eye from the sun as best he can, squints so furiously that his eye is tearing up.

He is able to make out a human . . . a young one, it appears, smaller in size, curly hair that hangs about his shoulders. He is holding what seems to be a strip of leather in one hand, and he is whirling it about as quickly as he can. It is building up speed with every spin, apparently because there is a stone lodged in one end that is giving it weight. It's moving so quickly that the Ocular, already inconvenienced by the sun, cannot make it out at all.

"Give me that," snarls the Ocular, trying to reach for it. It is a desperate grab, and the boy moves lightly out of the way, twisting as he does so, and then unleashing the stone.

It flies across the intervening space and lands squarely in the Ocular's forehead, just above the eye. He staggers, uncertain and unaware of just how much damage has been done him. His first inkling is when he tries to take a step forward and discovers that his legs are collapsing beneath him. He no longer has command over his body. He mutters an exclamation of surprise, and then becomes aware that some thick liquid is trickling down his face. He touches it gingerly, reaches up, and feels the rock lodged in his head. Blood is oozing from around it.

He killed me. The little bastard, *thinks the Ocular in surprise, even as he backs all the way to the edge. He is uncaring of that jeopardy now. It is meaningless in comparison to his far more pronounced problem. The humans are cheering and shouting, celebrating the meaningless triumph of some pathetic child who attacked from a safe distance. Who knows what they'll build this incident into when they're through with the retellings.*

And he bellows at them even as he feels his right heel edging onto empty air. "Fools!" *he shouts at them. His voice is explosive, deafening, and they pause in their howling self-congratulation.* "Do you think this is the end of it? Do you think killing me and my kind will save you? You know nothing! We are but the Second Wave! Our oh-so-generous conquerors sent a few of us first, to test the environment! To see how we fared when it came to survival! They did not want our banishment to be a death sentence! And once they are satisfied that your world can support us, nurture us . . . they will send the Third Wave! And we will not be in tens or even hundreds of us then. That is when the rest of us will be sent through in all our numbers to reside upon your puny sphere! We will overrun you, and you will be as nothing to us! We will wipe you out! Those of you who do survive will be our willing slaves! Your race can enjoy its dominance of this world for a time longer—a few of your millennia at most—and then the Third Wave will destroy you! Do you hear me? Destroy you!"*

They hear him, but of course do not understand. To them it is merely roaring in an incomprehensible tongue. And when he stops, they advance on him, their spear points at the ready. But he is at the ready as well. He will not go the way of the Minosaur. He will not have his carcass brutalized, have his head paraded about as a trophy or his heart torn out. If he is to die, he will do so on his own terms.

When the humans, the great blurred mass that they are to his vision, draw closer, he steps back off the cliff. He hears several of them cry out, and is not surprised. They're about to lose their trophy, and they know it. They also know there's not a damned thing they can do about it.

Having delivered the only warning presented to humans about the eventual Third Wave, he topples backward. He falls in eerie silence, making no outcry, offering no protest. As he plummets, his mind races away to the ocean of his home, and he is floating in it and he is at peace. He is not even aware of it when his body strikes the jagged rocks, tearing him to shreds. The humans, standing at the top of the cliff, look down and howl in frustration, denied their prize. Using the hazardous paths that lead down from the cliff to the shore far below, they will never be able to get there before the strong currents drag the Ocular's carcass out to sea.

Still, the humans at least are able to take solace in their triumph. There are giants in these days, but the humans have overcome them. They have also, in various lands, slain dragons, killed vampires, beheaded Gorgons. It has been a busy time for humans, and a triumph of human resourcefulness and human imagination.

They are the lords of the Earth. They are God's chosen, placed there in order to have dominion over all those who crawl and walk upon the world, and burrow beneath it, and fly over it. Man, they will assure you, is the only creature with a soul, the only being in existence that is made as a reflection of God's own image. They will tell you, with conviction, that the sun moves around the Earth, and that mankind is the center of the universe. Although in years to come, they will come to know more of the reality of their own surroundings, that fundamental egocentricity will never really go away. It will simply mutate or evolve into other means of expression.

When the Third Wave is eventually unleashed, they will not be ready. That lack of readiness will cost them their world.

THE COUNTRY OF FEEND

Sunara Redeye crouched for a good, long time at the narrow hole that opened out onto the shore. The surf was rolling in gently, and the moonlight sparkled playfully upon the waves. Although she was content in Subterror, there was something to be said for getting out every so often. Still, she couldn't be too careful. Her nostrils flared as she inhaled the night air, trying to detect the slightest scent wafting toward her indicating an ambush.

There was nothing. Nothing at all. Not even the scent of the individual she was expecting, which annoyed her. She was there; where did he get off, keeping her waiting? Was she not Sunara Redeye? Was she not Mistress of the Piri? One did not keep the Mistress waiting. It simply wasn't done. She would have harsh words for him when he arrived.

Finally, overcome with temptation, and certain that she was unwatched and unattended, Sunara eased herself through the hole and landed lightly on the ground in a crouch. She stayed that way for a time, straining not only with her nostrils but with her ears as well. No sound, no movement, save that of the water.

Satisfied that she was alone, Sunara stood upright and raced toward the water. She moved so lightly that she made no sound upon the sand, although there was the slightest splash as her feet hit the water. She stopped at about ankle depth, not desiring to go any further. She knew the dangers that were incumbent if she undertook such a rash action. Sunara was as light-boned as any other Piri, and if she went in too deep, the current would yank her away as easily as it would a leaf. So she contented herself with splashing the water around with her toes, watching the droplets soar high and then rejoin the crashing ocean.

She had made certain that the breeze was blowing down toward her, so that the scent of anyone approaching would be readily detectable. If the wind had shifted, leaving her in a position where someone could sneak up on her, she would have hurried back to her place of concealment before anyone could get close enough to pose a threat. Fortunately the wind remained cooperative. So it was that when someone did approach, her sharp olfactory senses detected him immediately and she knew that it was the individual whom she was expecting. She knelt in the water, cupping it and splashing it upon her face. There was water available to the Piri through underground streams, but that was flat and lifeless compared with what she was currently gallivanting in. This was water as it was meant to be, free and unfettered.

She couldn't help but feel the water was a metaphor for the Piri themselves. There was no reason that they should have to reside in the dank and darkness of Subterror. It served as their home and their protection, and her kind would long ago have been wiped out were it not for their ability to seek refuge below the ground. But even so . . . why should other races, such as the Ocular, have the run of the surface, while she and her people were condemned to hide below?

"You are late," Sunara Redeye called out as the individual she was meeting drew closer. She remained with her back to him as he approached, an unmistakable sign of her confidence. She wanted to convey one of two messages: Either that she was certain she would not attack her, or that she was confident that if he did attack her, she would be able to dispose of him with facility. "I expected you some time ago, honored Phemus, and I do not like to be kept waiting."

"My apologies, Mistress," came the voice of Phemus of the Ocular. She turned to face him then, and was pleased to see that he was nervously glancing around. That was the difference between him and her. He was terrified of the consequences of their being seen together. She was not. "It is not always a simple matter for me to slip away from court. Important matters demand my attention."

"I am not an important matter?" she asked.

"I did not say that . . ."

She waved it off. "Don't be stumbling over your tongue trying to speak niceties to me, Phemus . . . although I admit I find it amusing when you do."

"As ever, I live for your amusement, Mistress."

He approached her tentatively and she reached up to cup his chin in her hand. She was tall for a Piri and he was diminutive for an Ocular, so they were quite close to the same height. She turned his head right, then left, and she made a soft humming noise as she did so. "How can they not smell it on you?" she asked finally.

"It?"

"The Piri blood that courses through your veins," she said. "It is muted by your mixed Ocular ancestry, but still, it is there for any who truly care to take a whiff."

He took her smaller hand in his much larger one and smiled, his one eye blinking rapidly. "There are none among the Ocular who share your discerning senses, Mistress. Oh, our sense of smell is sharp enough . . . but nothing compared to yours."

"And how lucky that is for you, wouldn't you say?" she asked.

"Indisputably lucky, Mistress."

"How long?"

"Mistress?"

"How long do you think you would last if they knew your secret?" She drew a single long fingernail across his cheek, and he gasped slightly as it cut into his face, leaving a thin bleeding line. "Quiet," she ordered him, and then she brought his face down to hers and drew her tongue across it, her tongue darting eagerly and licking up the fresh blood. He said nothing as she did so, although she could feel him trembling. She wasn't sure whether he was doing so in fear or in enjoyment, although either way didn't matter to her. She released him then and he stood, putting a hand to his face to stop the bleeding. "Do not concern yourself," she said casually, strolling several feet away with her hands draped behind her back. "I did not cut deeply and it will doubtless not be noticed upon your return."

"Why did you—?"

"Because," she told him reasonably, "I could. Why else?"

"No other reason that matters."

She leaned against a tree trunk and licked her lips. "Now tell me: Did you manage to 'encourage' Nagel to do as we desire him to?"

"Yes," Phemus assured her. "Even now he is on his way to the Mandraques, seeking an alliance for the purpose of wiping out the Piri."

Sunara laughed delightedly at that, clapping her hands in a small burst of joy. "Perfect! Perfect. And they will kill him, of course, leaving the Ocular leaderless. At which point you step in and . . ."

Her voice trailed off as she noticed that he was not looking particularly jovial about their prospects. "Is there a problem, Phemus?"

"Well . . . one can never know . . ."

"One had better know," Sunara said, her good mood beginning to evaporate. "If there is reason not to know, then it would be best if I knew that as well."

"The problem, Mistress," Phemus told her, pacing the area, "is that you are assuming . . . *we* are assuming . . . certain behavior on the part of the Mandraques."

"Assumptions that are perfectly reasonable," said Sunara, "when one considers the overall history of the Mandraques."

"So it would seem. But . . . what if matters have changed? One can never be absolutely certain. What if the scenario that I put forward to Nagel . . . the one that you and I both believe could never truly come to pass . . . did, in fact, happen? What if the Mandraques joined forces with us for the purpose of exterminating the Piri? Will we not have outsmarted ourselves? Brought death and destruction needlessly raining down upon us?"

"It will not happen," Sunara assured him. "I know the Mandraques far too well. They will certainly perceive Nagel for the fool that he is. If there is one thing that the Mandraques do not suffer gladly, it is fools. Mandraques do nothing in half measures."

"So I have heard."

"They will have no interest," she continued, "in allying themselves with a fool-ish young monarch who seeks alliances that he should not. They will destroy him and send his head back to us on a pike."

"Or they will seek to conquer us," Phemus reminded her. "It is not as if we're invulnerable. They could take advantage of the same power vacuum that you anticipate upon Nagel's demise, and storm in here. Then where would your plan be?"

"My plan would be defunct," admitted Sunara, but continued firmly, "How-ever, that is not going to be the case. Think about it from the Mandraque point of view. If they were to attack us, they would wait until the end of night. That is not for . . . what? Half a sun cycle? By that time, all will be attended to. You will be in-stalled as new leader of the Ocular. For your first accomplishment," and she let her fingers once more run lingeringly down the side of his face. He flinched automat-ically but she did not cut his skin this time. "You will create an alliance and treaty with the Piri. The Ocular will no longer live in fear. Instead . . . they will grow to understand us. To appreciate us. To offer us love, where before there was only hatred." She was speaking in a singsong tone, like a happy child.

"You expect a great deal, Mistress," said Phemus.

"I merely take the long view, Phemus. When one is Mistress, that is the only view it is possible to take. I must consider the long-term health of my people, and their best possible future." Her voice pulsed with enthusiasm. She draped an arm around Phemus's waist and spoke in the way a visionary would, describing some vast divine revelation that had just been unveiled for him. "Just imagine if we could finally, finally domesticate the Ocular."

"You've spoken to me of this dream of yours before . . ."

"It's no dream," she said firmly, drawing him tighter to her. He squirmed a bit at the closeness. This pleased her. "You know as well as I do, Phemus . . . the Ocu-lar are little more than . . . oh, what was the old name for those mindless animals? That simply followed when led and bleated when they were in trouble?"

"Humans?"

"No, the ones on four legs with white, wiry fur."

"Oh. 'Sheep.' "

"Yes, exactly. The Ocular are little more than sheep. They depend on their leader to guide them. That is particularly the case in daylight, when they wander about nearly blind."

"It's not as if the Piri are especially useful during the daylight either, Mistress," Phemus reminded her.

She shrugged it off. "That is not the point. The Ocular require someone to tell them what to do. To guide them and shape their destinies for them. They see us as predators, Phemus. More, they see us as parasites. But it need not remain that way. The Ocular and the Piri should be able to develop a more . . . symbiotic relationship."

"Symbiotic?" he said dubiously. "I don't exactly . . . how do you . . . ?"

"As it stands now," she said patiently, as if lecturing a child rather than one of the most important nobles of the land, "the Ocular see us only as creatures who suck the lifeblood from them as means of sustaining ourselves."

"Not an unreasonable way to view you."

"Perhaps," Sunara admitted, "but it is not the only way. We have much that we can give the Ocular in exchange for their being supporting of our needs. They don't have to think of themselves as victimized," she said, thumping a hand on his chest. "They can be partners instead."

"Partners in what?"

"In opening their eyes . . . my pardon, eye . . . to a whole new view of things. To seeing their world and surroundings in a way they hadn't before." She smiled, displaying her perfect fangs. "To see things with the enhanced senses of the Piri, rather than the muted perceptions of the Ocular."

"Make them more like *you*?" He laughed again. "Mistress, I know my kind. Both of my kind, the Piri side and the Ocular side. My own presence and mixed blood notwithstanding—and that was a freakish combination of events that resulted in my existence, as you well know—one cannot be made more like the other."

"You are wrong," she replied. "In old times, it was not uncommon at all. The humans were particularly susceptible to us. The longer one of them remained with us, the more they became like us . . . to such a degree that, save for their much shorter life span, one of them could become indistinguishable from us."

"That was the humans," sniffed Phemus disdainfully. "Hardly a fair comparison. It's foolishness to compare the Ocular to the Morts. Besides, much time has passed since those days. All beings change, and the Piri are no exception. The Piri no longer have the patience or interest to turn a vict—excuse me, a 'provider'— over to the Piri way of life."

"Oh, how certain you are of yourself," Sunara Redeye sneered. "How certain you are of the beings who compose part of your heritage. You would be speaking a far different opinion if you were able to see your king's beloved niece these days."

It took a moment for the full import of what she was saying to register. "Merrih?" he finally said. "You refer to Merrih?"

"The very same."

"She is not dead?"

"Not at all!" said Sunara, as if the notion was ridiculous. "She is very much alive."

"But I thought she would be long dead by now." A thought struck him and he began to sweat nervously. "Does she . . . know about me? About my connection with the Piri?"

"I don't recall it coming up in conversation, no. But if you wish," she offered, sounding as if she were truly concerned about his feelings, "I can mention it to her the very next opportunity I have . . ."

"No! I mean," and he steadied his voice, "I mean, no, that wouldn't be necessary. Or prudent. What if she escapes—?"

"She is not going to escape. She has neither the need nor the desire."

Phemus studied her a long moment with his unblinking, unwavering eye. "Are you serious?" Phemus demanded. "Are you saying that even if she could escape, she'd have no interest in doing so?"

"I'm saying that she is a remarkable test case for my theory of Piri-Ocular symbiosis. Just imagine how it will be, Phemus, when Nagel does not return and then the Ocular—at their most dispirited—are graced with the return of the king's niece. A young, popular Ocular who will speak highly of us and our way of life. Who will make the Ocular understand that cooperating with us, joining with us, will be mutually beneficial to all. She will be living proof that our way of life and that of the Ocular are not mutually exclusive.

"She will be a sensual being, oh yes," and Sunara made a soft, rumbling sound in her chest that any Mort of the olden days would have recognized as a purring noise. "That is another aspect that the Ocular do not truly recognize or understand: their potential for physical pleasure and erotic discovery. Those are being plumbed and released within Merrih even as we speak, and she is much the happier for it. She enjoys congress with the Piri, and is coming to think of them—not as predatory animals or parasites—but as companions on her journey to true ecstasy. Very soon . . . she will be drinking blood herself."

"I don't believe it!"

"Believe it," she told the stunned Phemus. "She becomes more like us with each passing day. Her skin is beginning to develop our sallow tint. When others feed upon her, she watches them closely and I see her unconsciously licking her lips, wondering what the taste of blood would be like. She craves our lifestyle. Whether it be out of morbid curiosity or long-suppressed desire, I could not tell you. But crave it she does, and I see no reason to deny the child."

"No, no, of course not," Phemus said, recovering from his astonishment. "I just . . . I find it so difficult to believe."

"That," she said, patting him gently on the face, "is the tragedy. I am aware you could not live among the Ocular—and thus would be no good to us as a spy—if they knew you for the mixed breed that you are. They would run you out of their settlement. We would not gain from that, and so your tongue is wisely held. But now you are offended—"

"Not offended."

"Concerned, then," she continued, "about my acquisition. About Merrih. About my assessment of the Ocular and your repressed society. Do not scold the messenger when you know the message to be true. Yours is a race that is blind to so much. Tragic that you are blind even to your own shortcomings."

"We simply have different priorities from yours, Mistress," replied Phemus, working to keep his wounded sensibilities under tight rein. "We concern ourselves with matters of the mind. You obsess over pleasures of the flesh. We are cerebral, you are tactile. We are—"

"Filled with nonsense, and we are not," said Mistress Sunara Redeye, thumping Phemus on the chest with a scolding finger. "Whether you admit to it or not, that's the truth. If there is one thing that I have learned, however, it is that within the heart of every sour pragmatist or high-flown intellectual, there is a sensualist positively screaming to be unleashed. We will loosen that leash upon the Ocular, and those who feared us, despised us . . . they will thank us. They will bow to us, and do whatever we wish. Whatever you wish as well." She looked him up and down, raising an eyebrow speculatively. "Certainly that must have occurred to you. You do have your own aspirations of power, do you not?"

He did not answer.

"After all," she continued, "what other motive must you have had for disposing of Nagel's father? You knew that the son would be easier to control . . ."

"I had no choice."

"You always have a—"

"*I had no choice,*" he repeated sharply. "He had just learned of . . . he knew what my mother had done . . . knew of her . . . of . . ."

"He had learned who and what your father was."

Phemus let out a slow breath. "Yes. You know that."

"Because your poor, dying mother, seeking forgiveness before she went before her gods, foolishly confessed her sin to her ruler, certain that he would understand and forgive." She laughed. "Trust a female with one eye to be shortsighted in—"

To Sunara's utter shock, Phemus was upon her. Her rank, her position, her status of having a person that was sacrosanct suddenly were of no relevance as Phemus's hand shot forward as if of its own accord. He grabbed her by the neck and collarbone and slammed her back up against a tree with such ferocity that the entire thing shook, dislodging a stray branch or two. She gasped, not just from pain, but from the pure incredulity of being treated in such a manner. "Have you lost your mind?" she hissed, her eyes wide. She grabbed at the single arm holding her with both her hands but wasn't able to dislodge it in the slightest. Her eyes widened as she saw his cocked fist hovering mere feet away, and she wisely ceased all movement. His face was impassive; he could have been cooking breakfast for all the emotion he was displaying. Phemus's voice was so low that she had to strain to hear it.

"Do not," he said barely above a whisper, "believe that, because I show due respect for your station, I am afraid of you. I respect you, Mistress. I am . . . intrigued by you. I display the same perverseness of spirit, I suppose, that drew my mother to my sire. But I do not fear you as your followers do. I do not quaver when you pass, I do not worship you, and—unlike the Piri—I can very easily imagine a world without you." Slowly his face moved in toward hers until it seemed to Sunara that the entirety of her world was one huge, unblinking eye focused upon her. "Do we understand each other, Mistress? Have I made my position clear? I sense that I have not. Just so you truly comprehend: Criticize me, display contempt for my king, dismiss the entirety of my race as sexually repressed buffoons. None of that means anything to me. However . . ."

"Your mother is out of bounds."

"Precisely," replied Phemus.

Despite the fact that he could have snapped her head off with a twitch of his fingers, Sunara nevertheless laughed. "How heartening in this day and age to see such loyalty from a son," she said.

Phemus growled a moment as if trying to decide just what he was going to do with her. Finally he released her, shaking her loose from his hand the way a dog would divest itself of fleas. They stood there for a moment, bathed in the moonlight, as if truly seeing each other for the first time. Sunara's hand idly rubbed the base of her throat. "Your . . . devotion . . . is admirable," she said at last.

"And your understanding is legendary," Phemus said with a slightly mocking bow. "You truly have a hold on Merrih's spirit?"

"Even stronger a hold than you had on me moments ago. Frankly, I am not entirely certain that, if and when we give her her freedom, she will wish to leave us."

"We shall have to see. You will keep me apprised of developments?"

"Of course."

He nodded in approval, turned, and started to walk away. She called after him and he stopped and glanced back at her over his shoulder.

"You do realize," Sunara Redeye informed him, "that at some point in the future, I will make certain that you die for the way in which you treated me just now."

"I realize," Phemus assured her, "that you will most definitely try."

"I suppose we'll have to see how that turns out then."

"I suppose we will."

She moved noiselessly backward, and was swallowed up into the darkness of the hole that led down into Subterror. Phemus remained, staring into it as if somehow the future was hidden within. When nothing presented itself, he sighed and headed back to the castle.

It was odd, though. As he had watched Sunara depart into the darkness, he could have sworn, just for a moment, that he saw another form within as well. Someone else moving about, hidden deep within. But it had only been fleeting, and then it had been gone. Sunara's senses were as sharp as anyone's, so if she hadn't reacted, then it had probably been his imagination.

But since Phemus knew all too well that he was singularly lacking in imagination, it was a consideration that did not sit well with him. He decided, however, to give it no more thought, if for no other reason than that thinking too much tended to make his eye hurt.

THE FIVE CLANS BORDERLANDS

Jepp knew of the Trulls, but not in much detail, so Karsen took the time to fill her in. She listened raptly as he gave as much background of the race as he knew, interrupting here and there with a reasonably well-thought-out question. While he did that, Zerena Foux and the others quickly and efficiently broke down the campsite. Several times Karsen offered to pitch in, but Zerena kept assuring him that they had everything under control. Meanwhile Jepp seemed happy not only for the explanations, but for the company, and Karsen was only too pleased to oblige her.

"So they remain neutral while selling weaponry to all sides?" Jepp said, tilting her head a bit so that she looked like a small animal listening carefully to the sounds of the wind. "Is taking all sides the same as being neutral?"

"That's just the point," Karsen told her. "They're not taking all sides. They're taking no sides."

"If they took no sides, wouldn't they refuse to make their weaponry available to anybody at all?"

Karsen paused at that, not entirely sure how to respond.

"From what you're telling me," continued Jepp, "they are bartering quite deftly, since their underground home provides no practical supply of, say, food. And that barter comes from trading with all sides that have farmlands and such, or can bring them slaughtered animals to feast upon. They take all sides and profit from all, rather than truly taking no sides and charting their own, much more difficult, course in the world."

"I doubt they think of it in that way," he told her.

Jepp hesitated for such a long time that Karsen noticed it. "Is there . . . something you want to say to that?"

"What? Oh . . . no," Jepp quickly assured him. "No, not at—"

"I think there was."

"I am telling you, Karsen, there was—"

He took a step toward her, scrutinizing her as if he could look right into the depths of her thoughts. "What goes through your mind, Jepp?"

"My mind? Nothing. There is nothing on my mind. Ever. I have no mind."

"At last," Zerena said, lugging a large crate under one arm that was filled with supplies, "something that we can agree on." She mounted it on the back of their vehicle, the rest of the Bottom Feeders already having climbed in and taken their customary seats. "Come on, Karsen. Let's go. Time to move out."

"All right," Karsen said guardedly, but he kept studying Jepp as they squeezed into the jumpcar. As before, there was some rearrangement and shuffling around required before everyone was inside. Zerena clambered into the driver's seat and fired up the jumpcar. At first it started up with no problem, but then it went dead.

"Now what the hell—!" Zerena cried out, slamming her fist on the dash. "Mingo! I thought you had this thing up and running!"

"I did. I thought I did."

She tried it again and this time the engine caught with more authority. She put the jumpcar in reverse, backed up, then rolled it forward and began driving it as quickly as it would go.

The ride was silent for a time as Karsen tilted his head back, looking up at the stars. Naturally he had no recollection of the Elserealm from which the Twelve Races had originally sprung. He had been born here, on the Damned World. Zerena claimed that she had, in her youth, an elderly relative who claimed to have been in the Third Wave. His recollections would alternate between wistful recollections of the Elserealm from which they had been banished, and chortling, colorful stories about the amazing depth and variety of salvage that had gone on during the time when the Third Wave had overrun the Damned World and mowed through the determined but, ultimately, outmatched humans.

"The best were the ones who would try to negotiate," he had said. "They were always the most entertaining, because the Mandraques, more often than not, although sometimes it was the Ocular would pretend that, yes, they were interested in coming to a reasonable settlement. They would invite the Morts to treaty meetings, and sometimes they'd just kill them outright, or other times they'd actually negotiate a treaty and watch the Morts run around and proclaim peace in their time while the races would move their forces into position and, sooner or later, do exactly what they'd intended to do the entire time. The Morts were *always* surprised. No matter how many times they were lied to, they were dumbfounded that they were then lied to yet again. It would have been funny if it were not so pathetic."

Karsen kept looking at Jepp and trying to see in her some hint of the determination, resourcefulness, and ingenuity that had enabled her kind to dominate their world for so long. He was forced to come to the conclusion that, before the Third Wave, whatever other races presented the morts possible competition for the very top of the food chain must not have been especially formidable. The Morts must have acquired their position of supremacy purely through default.

And suddenly, still gazing up at the stars, Karsen came to an abrupt realization. "Mother," he spoke up, and his voice startled Mingo and Rafe, who had been dozing. Jepp had been leaning against his arm, sleeping lightly, and she sat up and blinked in confusion. "Mother, which direction are we heading?"

"West," she said without hesitation.

"I thought so. Why?"

"Why what?"

"Why are we heading west?"

"Why wouldn't we be?"

Now the others were fully awake, and although Jepp and Rafe were confused (it was difficult to tell what Gant's state of mind was at any given moment, since he was little more than a puddle at the far end of the jumpcar), Mingo was not. "The nearest Trull hub point is due south of our previous location," Mingo said, rubbing the last of the sleep from his eyes. "We're heading away from where we should be going . . ."

"*Should* be going?" Zerena Foux was openly contemptuous of the concept. "I disagree. We're going in the precisely right direction that we should be going in . . . which is as far away from any of this insanity as possible."

"Mother!"

"You promised Nagel," Mingo said with a hint of reproach in his voice.

"I promised someone who was threatening to eat us if we didn't accede to his demands!" shot back Zerena. "You don't seriously, for one moment, think that such a promise is binding under that circumstance, do you?"

"Stop the jumpcar, Mother," Karsen said firmly.

"The hell I will . . ."

"Stop the car!"

"*The hell I will!*" Zerena repeated, her voice thunderous. The jumpcar was hardly the quietest of vehicles, but Zerena's bellowing response rose above the rickety engine. "Now, you listen to me, boy! I am the head of this clan, and I will make the decisions for us!"

"And the decision you made before was that we would do as Nagel asked . . ."

"Forced us to, Karsen. Don't forget that."

"I haven't—"

"I think you have. I know for my part that I would have said or promised anything if it meant buying us enough time to escape."

"But . . . what about—" Jepp began.

Zerena cut her off immediately. "You have nothing to say in this matter."

"It's her life on the line same as ours, Mother. I'd think that would give her plenty to say."

"Well, you'd think wrong."

Karsen ignored her, instead turning to Jepp and saying, "What about what?"

"It's nothing import—"

"*Jepp!*"

Jepp flinched back at the impatience and anger in his voice, and Karsen knew right then that she expected he was going to hit her. He moaned to himself, since he had no desire to have her think he was emulating the behavior of her previous "owner," the Greatness. But before he could soothe her or convince her that she was perfectly safe, Jepp told him, "Well, it's just that . . . from what you said, no one 'forced' Nagel to spare your life, Zerena. In that time past, I mean. He could have killed you then, but chose not to. So what you now perceive as 'forcing' you to do that which you have no desire to, is likely seen by Nagel as just insisting that you live up to the courtesy that he extended you by letting you live."

"I didn't ask for him to extend that courtesy," Zerena fired back, but even Karsen could detect the hint of uncertainty in her tone. "Besides, what it comes down to is what he wants versus what I want. Right now what I want to do is get as far away from the Ocular and their concerns with the Trulls as possible."

"But he said he would hunt us down . . ."

She waved dismissively. "Let him try," she said. "And even if he did, I'll take my chances of keeping so far away from the Ocular that they'll never find us, as opposed to braving the underground lair of the Trulls, anytime."

"But what of our honor . . . ?" Karsen asked.

"What of it? Who cares what the damned king of the damned Ocular thinks or says about us? Besides, have you forgotten? We're Bottom Feeders. We're seen as the lowest of the low anyway."

"So you're saying that we should not hesitate to live down to the expectations that others have of us?" asked Mingo, making no attempt to disguise his contempt for the notion.

"I'm saying it's not our fight!"

"What if it were?"

"It's not. And if it were, now that I think on it, we'd still be running away, because that's what we do. We're not warriors, you stupid Mort. We are merely the ones who pick up the droppings of those stupid enough to be warriors. I've seen enough rivers of blood and piles of bodies in my lifetime to know the futility of it, and I have no desire to see anything that's inside the bodies of myself or my clan on the outside. Whatever lunatic notion Nagel has come up with in order to eliminate the Piri, it's not something that need concern us!"

"Why not?" asked Jepp.

Zerena turned so violently in her seat that she almost sent the jumpcar clattering off course. "*Why not?*" she practically screeched, causing Mingo to cover his ears. "Have you heard nothing I've said? The enmity between those two races is their own! Of what possible profit would it be for us to meddle, especially considering that such meddling will likely get us all killed?"

"I . . . don't suppose there's any profit in it at all," Jepp admitted.

"There! There you go," and Zerena looked triumphantly, not at Jepp, but at Karsen. "Even your little Mort admits that—"

"But he did spare your life," Jepp reminded her.

Zerena's exultation turned to annoyance. "That," she said icily, "was his choice. Just as it is my choice now to get us out of harm's way. We are Bottom Feeders, Jepp. First of all, that makes us survivors. Now that I think on it, we are second and third of all survivors as well. Nothing supersedes that. Nothing. And if you find that philosophy so repugnant, then I cordially invite you to step out right now and I will most gladly leave you behind."

"You don't have to threaten the girl, Zerena," Mingo said.

She looked at him, incredulous. "You too now? What's gotten into you? You cannot possibly be hypocrite enough to criticize me for running away. You wouldn't be with us if you yourself hadn't fled a situation you found intolerable."

"It wasn't just the situation, it was the choice, and may I extend my heartiest appreciation for your pointlessly bringing up yet another painful memory," he replied.

"I'm sorry," Jepp said.

Mingo twisted around in his seat, staring at her. "What are *you* apologizing for?"

"For causing dissent and arguing," she told him. "I was . . . I was just trying to understand."

"What were you trying to understand?" asked Karsen, resting a hand on her arm. He was impressed, not for the first time, by the sheer warmth of her, the sleekness of her skin.

"I just . . . I mean . . . why weren't you moved?" Her question was clearly not to Karsen but to Zerena.

"Moved?" Zerena seemed bewildered, not having the faintest idea what Jepp was referring to. The jumpcar hit a bump and jostled all within, and Zerena gripped the controls tighter to keep the vehicle on course.

"By what the king told us. Nagel, the king . . ."

"I know which king you're referring to."

"Well . . . his whole situation. About his niece, about his people, living in fear and all that. It doesn't seem any way to live, and he wants to find some way to change it. I just . . . don't think that's such a bad idea at all. Do you?"

"No, it's not a bad idea," Zerena replied, "but it's an irrelevant idea. Irrelevant to us, I mean. If this is something Nagel wants to do, let him try and sort it out. Let him launch an assault on the Trulls rather than using us as his henchmen. There's no point in our trying to help him when we don't directly benefit ourselves."

"But maybe that's the point!" said Jepp.

"The point of what?" Zerena's exasperation appeared to be reaching critical mass.

To Karsen's surprise, Jepp didn't back down or flinch. "The point of . . . of everything! The point of living! What's the use of living in a world if you don't do everything you can to make it a better world just . . . just because you're there! And the benefit to you isn't something tangible or something you can trade or eat or . . . or copulate with. The benefit is knowing that you've done everything you can to try and make the world better for others."

The jumpcar skidded to a halt. The engine died.

Zerena turned and stared fully at Jepp. Mingo leaned over, looking worriedly at the controls. "Did it go out of commission ag—"

"I shut it down."

"You—?"

"I didn't want my focus split." Zerena licked her lips, apparently trying to form her thoughts. "You . . . are insane."

"I am?"

"Mother—"

"You're insane." There was neither anger nor heat in her voice. She actually sounded far more reasonable than she usually did. "I mean it. Seriously. You're insane. But you're also revelatory."

"I am?" Jepp said again.

"Yes. Because now I will never again wonder how it is that your species was unable to hold its own against our invading force. It's because you and your kind are actually capable of framing thoughts like the one that you just put forward."

"It's called 'altruism,' Zerena," Mingo said. "What, you never heard of it?"

"Oh, I've heard of it. I just didn't think anyone still sucking air preached it, because anyone embracing it was just too stupid to live. You have no idea, girl, of the needs of the real world."

"I'm beginning to," Jepp assured her, "but what's wrong with wanting to change parts of it?"

"Because it is what it is! You can't change it. You just have to live within it."

"I don't think even you believe that," said Jepp.

Zerena laughed roughly. "Child, you've only just now started stringing your own thoughts together. Don't dare to try and tell me what my thoughts are."

"But what if it were Karsen!"

She shook her head in confusion, not able to keep up with the jump in conversation. "What if what were Karsen?"

"Can we get out at least and stretch our legs?" asked Mingo. "It's silly to—"

"Stay where you are."

"All right," Mingo said.

"What," Zerena repeated, "if what were Karsen?"

"What if it were Karsen who had been dragged away by the Piri?" asked Jepp. "If he were the one hauled away, kicking and screaming, and you'd only been able to stand there and watch it happen. Would you want to do something about it? Do *anything* about it? Or would you just be saying, Oh well, that's the way the world is, and move on?"

"That's different," Zerena said, and she looked at Karsen and then away, which surprised him.

"How is it different?"

"Because then it's a matter of our survival, and it's not . . ."

"But it wouldn't be!" Jepp said, far more challengingly than Karsen would have thought possible. "He'd be gone. Nothing you could do would save him, presumably. And revenge doesn't have anything to do with making a profit either."

"At least revenge as a motive makes more sense than . . ." She looked to Mingo questioningly. "What was it . . . ?"

"Altruism."

"Altruism," she repeated.

Jepp stared unblinkingly at Zerena, and then she leaned forward and said, "You lie, Zerena Foux. If anything happened to Karsen, you would want to do everything in your power to make sure that no mother should ever have to be made to feel the way you did because your son was lost to you. If you knew of a way to safeguard all sons everywhere from the Piri, then you would do whatever it took. You know it. And I know it. So why pretend otherwise?"

Karsen scrutinized his mother. She looked as if her head were going to explode. "You don't know me," she said finally.

"I'm simply saying that—"

"You. Don't. Know. Me. If you pretend to do so again, I swear to all the gods there are, I will kill you. I will rip out your living heart and I will feast on it. Do you understand me?"

A range of conflicting emotions played across Jepp's face, but finally she simply said, "Yes."

Then Rafe Kestor spoke up. Not a word had passed his lips during the entire confrontation. He had simply stared off into space in such a way that it seemed he was totally removed from everything that was transpiring. Finally, however, he spoke, and it was hard to tell whether he was doing so in direct response to something that had been said, or if it was just a random comment from his addled mind.

"It's a good thing," he said softly, "to want to leave the world better than it was when you found it."

The aged Mandraque then lapsed back into silence, leaving all of them staring at him.

Karsen's mind was racing. He had rarely stood up to his mother on any sort of major topic. It was simply understood that she was the clan's leader, that her word was final, and that was all. The words she was speaking now, about the simple sensibility of watching out for one's own best interests . . . how, really, could that be called into dispute?

Jepp was an insulated creature, having been kept in the service of the Mandraque called the Greatness and isolated from the harsh realities of the world. There was no point in a selfless quest to benefit the Ocular when it would not help the immediate situation of the Bottom Feeders . . . even though it was true that Nagel had spared Zerena's life. Then again, the threat he had saved it from was his original intention to kill her, so how much credit should someone be given for saving someone from they himself? Yes. As fond as he was becoming of Jepp, in this instance she was in the wrong and Zerena Foux was in the right. Simple as that.

And then Jepp said, "Let me out." She began to ease her way past Karsen. "I wish to get out here."

"Why? Where are you going?" asked Karsen. "Do you have need to relieve yourself—?"

"I'm going to do as we promised. Zerena Foux, kindly open the door . . ."

"Oh, this is far too perfect," said Zerena, and she triggered the "open" mechanism. The large clear side door slid wide and Zerena hopped out of the jumpcar, sliding nimbly past Karsen.

The moment her feet were on the ground, Karsen was right after her. "What are you talking about?" he demanded as she began to walk, with Karsen pacing her. "Where do you think you're going?"

"To find the Trulls and their Orb of the Trinity device," Jepp said reasonably. "So that I can bring it to the Ocular and maybe make the world a better place."

"Mother's right, you *are* insane!" Karsen assured her, as he stepped around so that he was directly in her path. She tried to walk around him and his hoofed feet moved quickly so that she couldn't proceed. "You don't even know where you're going!"

"I'll ask someone."

"*Look* at you!" he said desperately. "You're dressed in flimsy garments! You have no capacity for self-defense. You have no weapons. Anyone whose aid or succor you would seek would simply take you prisoner and use you for whatever they wished!"

"Surely that's my problem, though."

"Can't argue with her when she's right," Zerena called.

He whirled and pointed accusingly. "Quiet, Mother! This is all your fault!"

"Your pet human decides to grow a spine. How is that my fault?"

Jepp took several steps in the general direction of the vehicle. "What did you expect me to do, milady? Ever since I've been part of your company, you've endlessly derided me for my lack of . . . of spine. Did you think I would not take your words seriously? Consider the truth of your comments? I want to have . . ."

"Have what?" asked Karsen.

She fixed him with her limpid eyes. "Worth, Karsen. All creatures have to have some kind of worth. For as long as I was with the Greatness, I believed it, but could never act upon it. And I was content not to, because it was so much easier. But I don't have that excuse anymore, do I?" She paused. "Do I?" she repeated, and she sounded quite sad when she said it.

"No," he sighed. "No, I suppose you don't."

"Maybe I'm just trying to make up for lost time. Or maybe I'm just tired of the excuses. But I like the notion of trying to do something in a cause that's greater than myself, which isn't all that difficult because just about anything in the whole Damned World is greater than myself. I should know, because my whole life I've been told how worthless I am, and how worthless my people are." She paused once more, and actually laughed. "Odd, isn't it. A lifetime of being putting down, of living with degradation. Yet such a relatively brief time with you, being made to feel that maybe, just maybe, I *am* worth something, and suddenly I'm ready to . . . to . . ."

"To throw your life away."

"It's a small enough thing. I've certainly had enough beings telling me *that*."

"But I don't want you to die."

"I should hope not."

"Yet you will."

"Then she dies!" Zerena called impatiently from the jumpcar. "It's her decision. You should be proud enough of her, Karsen. Take credit for her growth."

"Her growth is similar to a weed's," Karsen retorted, "and she will be cut down with about as much thought."

"That's her problem."

"Your mother's right. What matter that I die in service of the promise she herself made?"

That prompted Zerena to vault from the jumpcar. "Ohhh no you don't," she said, waving a finger angrily as she came around the front of the vehicle. "Don't you lay it upon me. I'm not asking you to do my job."

"No, but the job needs doing, and you won't, so . . ." Jepp shrugged as if that was all there was to say.

"My job is keeping this clan alive," Zerena said harshly, "and that's all that matters."

"Life should be about more than that."

"So say you!"

"Yes," Jepp replied. "So say I. And never before have I had people listening to what I said. It's exhilarating and I like it. I like it, Karsen, and I don't want to let it go. I feel . . . alive . . . for the first time in my life. If I die feeling this way . . ."

"It's not just that you'll die," Karsen assured her. "It's that you'll find yourself in a predicament where you'll wish you were dead. Mother," and he turned to Zerena. "This is your doing. So undo it. Stop her."

"I'll do no such thing," Zerena snorted. "If she wants to go, you're well rid of her. You wish to depart, girl? No one here is stopping you."

"The hell no one is," said Karsen, as he gripped her by the arm.

She made no move to pull away, but instead just looked at him sadly. "So all your grand words about how I have my freedom now are just words? When it comes down to it . . . I'm just serving a different master, aren't I?"

He stared at her, then let out an angry snarl and yanked his hand away. "Fine! Go! But I'm not coming with you."

"I didn't ask you to."

"You'll die!"

"Maybe." She brushed her hair out of her face and then put her hands on her hips. "Could someone at least point me in the right direction."

"You'll get lost. All right! Fine!"

"Fine?"

"Yes, fine." Karsen went around to the back of the jumpcar and opened it.

"Karsen, what are you doing?" demanded Zerena.

He pulled out the war hammer from their cache and slid it into the straps upon his back. "I'm going with her."

"*The hell you are!*" All the life was draining from Zerena's face. "You're not going anywhere!"

"Am I a slave? Are you my master now?"

"More than that! I'm your mother, and head of your clan, and I forbid it!"

"I'm your son, and a member of your clan, and your clan is obliged to fulfill an oath to the Ocular, and I'm not seeing a good deal of choice here." He walked over to Jepp and shook his head as he did so. "The things you get me into . . ."

"I'm not asking for your help in—"

"Oh, *do* shut up," he said irritably. "Come. It's this way."

"Karsen!" Zerena fairly howled. She covered the distance between them with one vault of her powerful leg muscles and landed squarely in his way. "Get back in the jumpcar. Right now."

"Or what?" asked Karsen. "Are you going to overpower me, Mother? Pick me up and throw me in?"

"If I have to. Do you doubt I can?"

"Actually, no," he said, looking her up and down. "But I doubt you can stay awake for the rest of your life. Sooner or later you'll sleep, which means that sooner or later, I'll be going after Jepp to guide her on her way. On our way."

"Then I'll tie you up—"

"Oh, honestly, Zerena!" Mingo called out, having climbed out of the jumpcar. Rafe Kestor was right behind him, watching the proceedings in a detached manner that made it difficult to ascertain whether he was truly following it all. "Is that to be your son's fate? That he be treated as if he were a prisoner of his own clan?"

"I'll do what's necessary to watch out for his best interests."

"I'm going with Jepp, Mother."

She stood there, gesticulating, trying to form words when none would come. Finally she took a step back, breathed in deeply and then let it out slowly in an obvious display of trying to compose herself. "What," she finally managed to say, "has she done to you?"

"Nothing . . ."

"No," Zerena shook her head furiously. "You cannot say 'nothing' when there's obviously been something. I've spent a lifetime training you to watch out for yourself, and this is what I get in return?"

"I *am* watching out for myself, Mother."

"Going on a suicide mission to satisfy the desires of the One-Eyed King! How is that watching out for yourself?!"

"Because it is I, myself, who am deciding to do so, rather than you deciding for me."

"Is something interesting going on?" It was Rafe Kestor. His tongue flicked out as if tasting the air, and he looked around expectantly at the participants in the little drama.

"My son is in open revolt against me, Rafe Kestor," Zerena said.

Rafe Kestor considered that. "Good," he said at last. "That's as it should be. Better open than behind your back. You should know that the knife is coming into your chest rather than between your shoulder blades."

"Thank you, Rafe Kestor," said an annoyed Zerena Foux. "That was very useful."

"I but live to serve," Rafe Kestor said graciously, bowing so that his snout almost touched the ground.

Mingo approached Karsen, moving with a slow swagger. "You know, you'll get yourself lost. You always had a lousy sense of direction. I'm just going to have to guide you there myself."

"Would you?" asked Karsen, looking relieved. "Truth to tell, I was going to guide her and hope for the best. With you along, we actually have a shot at not getting lost . . ."

"You cannot be serious," said Zerena. "Mingo, you cannot be serious. You cannot be planning to join them in this misadventure."

"You," Mingo told her, "should not have brought up things in my past that you once promised you'd never bring up."

"I was angry."

"So am I."

"You should never do things just because you're angry."

"And yet, here we are," said Mingo. He looked over to the Mandraque. "Rafe Kestor, will you be coming along?"

"*Absolutely!*" declared Rafe, and he yanked his sword out and whipped it through the air. Everyone near him stepped back, and anyone who wasn't near him stepped back as well, just in case. "Life is far too short not to do things that could make it shorter! Where are we off to, then?"

There was a "splat" sound, and Gant poured out of the jumpcar. He oozed over toward the others, and Zerena gaped at him with unfettered uncredulity. "You're going to die," Zerena said. "You're all going to die."

"True," agreed Mingo. "It's only the 'when' that's at issue."

"*All right!*" bellowed Zerena. She turned her back on them, stalked toward the jumpcar and climbed in without even bothering to close the doors behind her. "Go off on your suicide mission! See if I care!"

She gunned the engine, which started up obediently. She slammed the jumpcar into drive and it practically leaped off the ground in its urgency to depart. The others stood there and watched as the jumpcar sped away.

"Now what?" asked Mingo.

"Now," said Karsen, "we see if she cares."

The jumpcar made it approximately five hundred yards before grinding to a halt. It remained in place for a moment, and then backed up. Gears grinding in protest, the jumpcar hurtled backward, swerving from side to side as it came until it finally skidded to a halt, the vehicle's treads unable to grip the dry ground firmly.

The doors slid open and Zerena scowled fiercely at them.

"You're all idiots. I am the leader of idiots."

"And . . . ?" prompted Karsen.

"What sort of leader would I be if I were not the biggest idiot of all," snapped Zerena.

Without another word, the rest of the Bottom Feeders clambered into the jumpcar. Zerena didn't look at any of them. Instead her full attention was focused on Jepp. Jepp did not back down, returning the gaze levelly.

"This is all your fault," she said.

"Yes."

"This calamity will be on your head."

"Most calamities in this planet's history have been on the heads of humans," Jepp replied. "It's probably why we have hard heads."

"Don't get clever with me."

"Yes, milady."

And with that, Zerena whipped the jumpcar around and set the vehicle hurtling in the direction of the closest Trull hub.

THE CITY-STATE OF VENETS

i.

The evening that Orin Arn Oran addressed the Markene, telling them of their role in the planned assault upon the Travelers, Tulisia Sydonis was pacing impatiently within her private chambers. She had been expecting a particular someone, and had been extremely brusque with her husband, Ruark, telling him that she had no interest at all in seeing him that evening. Naturally her buffoonish mate had smiled and nodded vacuously. He was too great a fool even to be insulted by her rebuffs.

There was movement at her door and a tentative rapping. "Yes, yes, come in!" she called. The door swung open and the shift in her expression, from impatient to welcoming, was instantaneous. "My dear Lady Atlanna," she cooed, gliding across the floor, her hands extended daintily.

"Lady Tulisia," said Atlanna, the wife of Orin Arn Oran, Warlord of Venets. She went to one knee, touching Tulisia's extended knuckles to her forehead in solemn greeting.

"Up, please my dear, up," Tulisia urged her, helping Atlanna to her feet. "Come, sit with me. Are you hungry? Shall I have something brought up?"

"Not remotely necessary, Lady."

"Something to drink, then. I insist. I've already had it put out and it would be positively criminal to waste it," she continued when Atlanna tried to protest. "The Morts may have been inept in defending their world, but they knew what they were about in the production of their recreational beverages."

She waved Atlanna over toward a long couch, saw to it that she was comfortably seated, then sat herself at the far end. There was a low table in front of it, with two glasses and an open bottle of dark wine. Tulisia filled each glass with practiced expertise, took the nearest, and gestured for Atlanna to take the other. They sipped the wine, and a broad smile crossed Atlanna's lips. "You are most right, Lady. The Morts did have their uses, and this is most definitely one of them."

"Drink your fill. I have plenty." As Atlanna proceeded to drain her glass, Tulisia crossed her legs at the knees and leaned forward in an attitude that spoke of intimacy, of secrets to be shared. "Did you speak to him?"

"My husband? Yes."

"And . . . ?"

Atlanna let the suspense build just for a few moments. Tulisia knew perfectly well that was what Atlanna was doing, but didn't allow herself to become annoyed by such petty manipulation. Let Atlanna have her amusements.

"Even as we speak," Atlanna finally said, "he is addressing the Markene down by the Pier, or at least will be shortly as he makes certain they gather."

"He will speak to them of the Travelers? Of the great mission?"

"He absolutely will, yes."

Tulisia clapped her hands in delight. "That is excellent news, Atlanna. Most excellent news. Was he hesitant over it?"

"Oh, extremely so, Lady," sighed Atlanna, shaking her head in a way that showed her endless forbearance for her mate. "He conjured all manner of reasons as to why it was inadvisable. I daresay much of it was less than flattering insofar as you are concerned, Lady."

"I do not take the actions I do in order to garner flattery," Tulisia assured her. "I do it for the good of the Sirene. For the good of the Merk and, yes, even the Markene, although I doubt they've the wit to realize or even notice." She drummed her fingers on her knee for a moment, studying Atlanna. "How," she asked with a sly smile, "did you manage to overcome his reluctance?"

"Oh, I spun him some pretty considerations of my own," said Atlanna with clear amusement. "I put the fear of you in him."

"I can indeed be most terrifying," said Tulisia, barely able to suppress her smile. "Why, the very mention of my name is enough to make warlords tremble."

"So it would seem," Atlanna said. "In this instance, I told him that if he did not cooperate, the security of his wife and children could not be vouchsafed."

Laughing, Tulisia took Atlanna's hand in her own. "And he believed it? Truly?"

"I can be most convincing, Lady," Atlanna assured her.

"Come to me, then," said Tulisia, released Atlanna's hand and spreading wide her arms. "Come to me and let me embrace you as trusted friend."

Atlanna did so. The two women hugged each other, Tulisia patting Atlanna on the back. "What you have done for the Markene," she whispered to Atlanna, "shall be recorded in the annals of our triumph. When we have defeated the Travelers . . . when we stride his world from sea to sea, dominating it as is our right, songs will be sung about your name."

"About my name, perhaps," said Atlanna, "but not about me, certainly."

Tulisia released her, sitting upright, and gave her a scolding, reproachful look. "That you could think such a thing!" she protested. "Why not you?"

"For I am merely the vessel of your lady's will. If you have a fine wine, do you praise the liquid . . . or the cup that holds it?"

"Fair enough," laughed Tulisia. She glanced around once more, then, as had become her habit whenever she discussed matters of state. "You are certain," she asked softly, "that your husband does not suspect?"

"Suspect?"

"That we are sisters in all ways but blood, you and I. That I asked you to—"

"Oh, no," and Atlanna shook her head firmly. "No, not at all. He believes only that I fear you."

"But you do not."

"Certainly not, Lady." Atlanna chuckled, the idea clearly absurd. "Why would I fear you?"

"Because," Tulisia said, "an individual such as Orin Arn Oran would not take kindly toward believing that he had been manipulated by females . . . be it the female who rules or the female who shares his body and life. If he feels that anything he says to you is going to be relayed to me, he will not confide in you. For that matter, if he believes that wifely advice is actually words whispered by me into your ear in order to be relayed to him, he will certainly not desire to hear anything you have to say. In that event," and she calmly swirled the wine in her glass, "you would lose all future use to me."

Atlanna's eyes narrowed. "What . . . are you saying, Lady?"

"I'm saying that, in such an instance, your own status would be reduced to that of 'liability.' I have shared confidences with you, Atlanna, that I am not anxious to have relayed. I've done this because you are an intelligent and perceptive female, and you doubtless would have been able to see through any mendacity on my part. You would not have trusted me, and gaining your trust was, and is, essential."

"I'm afraid I'm still not following what you are—"

That was the moment Atlanna gasped. She clutched at her stomach, as the pleasant burning sensation of the wine became far less than pleasant. She looked at the empty wineglass in her hand, and it slipped from her grasp and clattered to the floor. Trembling, she stared at Tulisia uncomprehendingly.

"The reason I like you, Atlanna," Tulisia continued, as if not noticing Atlanna's suddenly desperate state, "is because we two are very similar. We have ambition.

We know how to maneuver others into doing things on our behalf. We desire power and will not hesitate to do whatever is necessary to acquire it. The problem is that, when dealing with someone who is very similar to you, there are often-times problems along the way. It's one of the odd truths that people who are *too* much alike can wind up destroying each other. They see in each other . . . oh, I don't know . . . the worst that they themselves have to offer, and it can be too much for them to bear."

Atlanna tried to speak, but the pain in her stomach became overwhelming and she doubled over, groaning.

"So here is the truth of it," and Tulisia leaned forward so that her eyes were on level with Atlanna, even though she was bending over and clutching her gut. "My concern is that, should the plan fail . . . should the Travelers withstand an attack and the Overseer comes seeking retribution . . . that you will tell all that you know in regard to my involvement. I do not believe that your husband would do such a thing, for he is far too noble. You, however, are a schemer, like me, and schemers can be quick to dispatch someone in their place if they feel the need. By the same token, if matters should proceed according to the way I am anticipating they will . . . well, power can be a very attractive lure. And I can easily see you doing whatever it took to snatch it away from me."

"No," Atlanna managed to get out, shaking her head desperately. "No, I . . ." and then she groaned loudly once more, in so much pain that she didn't know what to do with it all. "I . . . won't! I swear!"

"You might . . ."

"*No! No!*" By that point she was shaking her head so violently that it looked ready to fall off her neck. "I won't! I won't . . . challenge you! Please, Lady, I have children . . . a husband . . . please don't . . ."

Tunisia appeared lost in thought, as if unaware that Atlanna was even still sitting there. Atlanna tried to stand, to get to the door, although Tulisia hadn't the slightest clue where she could reasonably have gotten to. Ultimately it didn't matter, because the pain in Atlanna's gut was so overwhelming that she collapsed, lying on the floor and gasping like a landed fish. "If only . . ." Tunisia sighed.

"*Lady, please—!*"

"If only I knew for certain that I could trust you . . ."

"*You can! You can!* I swear—!"

Tunisia glanced at her over her shoulder, one perfect eyebrow slightly arched. "You swear? On what?"

"On my life! On my children's lives, my husband's . . . anything!"

Slowly she knelt next to the agonized Atlanna. Like a concerned mother, she reached over and brushed several strands of seaweed hair from Atlanna's face.

"What if," she said softly, "I asked you for the lives of one of your children in your place? Would you sacrifice one of them in order for you to live?"

Atlanna began to tremble, her arms locked around her stomach. "My . . . children . . . ?"

"If I gave you that choice, yes. If I told you that you could live in exchange for one of your own children dying . . . would you do it?"

"Tunisia, puh-please . . ."

"Would you?" Her voice was gentle, prodding.

"Don't ask me such . . . such a—"

"I simply wish to know. Would—"

"*Yes!*" The word was ripped from her throat, and Atlanna began to sob, hot tears rolling down her face, and the sobs became soul-wrenching howls of despair as she kept saying, "*Yes! Yes yes yes, anything, gods, please, I don't want to die—*"

"Oh, I'm afraid you are going to die, my dear Atlanna . . ."

"*Gods, no—!*"

"Well, yes," and Tunisia laughed as if it were the greatest joke in the world. "I mean, none of us are immortal, now, are we? Although I'll admit there is some debate about that insofar as the Overseer is concerned. But I'm afraid that, sooner or later, death must come to us all."

"*I don't want to die today! Like this! I—*"

"Atlanna!" Tunisia sounded astonished that Atlanna would even broach the subject. "Who said anything about your dying today? I know I never did." Her eyes were wide and innocent, her hand fluttering to her breast. "Are you not feeling well? Oh . . . you know what it is?" and she looked at the bottle of wine accusingly. "Some people—a very small minority—don't react well to his particular beverage. Gives them monumental distress. But it passes."

"W-What?" Gradually Atlanna was becoming aware that the pain was subsiding. It had already eased enough that she was able to sit up. "What are . . . it passes?"

"Oh yes. I see you were having a negative reaction to it. No more for you, young lady," she said in a scolding tone, and capped the bottle. "We shall make certain that you stick to milder concoctions in the future."

"I . . ." The pain was now almost gone, and Atlanna was getting to her feet. Her face looked worn and haggard, her hair hanging limply around it. "I thought . . . I was dying . . ."

"Did you?" Tulisia "hmmph"ed to herself. "How terrible that must have been for you—"

And now anger began to boil within Atlanna. She stabbed a trembling finger at Tulisia. "It wasn't the wine! You . . . put something into mine! You poisoned me! Gave me something to make me think I was dying—"

"I?" Her voice went up slightly. "My dear Atlanna, I am hurt. Yes, I am. That you could accuse me of such a thing, without the slightest bit of evidence. You test our friendship, my dear, yes you do."

"Our . . . *friendship.*" Atlanna choked back a derisive laugh. Her hands were flexing, making it look for all the world as if she wanted to put a fist through Tulisia's face. "Don't speak pretty words to me, Lady. I know you for what you are . . ."

"Yes. I imagine you do. Know that I see you as well, Atlanna," replied Tulisia evenly. "A woman who would sacrifice the spawn of her own loins if it meant saving her life. We see each other plainly now. We each see what the other is capable of . . . and we see where each other's priorities are. If I surpass your expectations of me while you live down to mine of you, well . . . at least matters are clear. And that can only be beneficial for everyone's long-term health and prosperity . . . don't you think?"

Atlanna's breath was ragged in her chest. She leaned on the edge of a chair for support, and then she managed to nod. "As you say . . . Lady Tulisia."

"Good." Tulisia stepped forward and embraced Atlanna, the oldest of friends. Atlanna went stiff, afraid to move, as if she were surrounded by poisonous fish and the slightest gesture might cause them to sting en masse.

"Go home to your offspring and mate," Tulisia whispered in her ear. "Treasure them as a good mother should. And promise me you'll never forget what transpired here this day."

"To my dying day, I shall remember, Lady."

"Good. Let us both hope that that day will not come for a long, long time."

She released Atlanna, and then stood and watched as Atlanna made her way out of the room on unsteady legs. Then she unstoppered the wine and drained the remaining contents, licking the last vestiges from her lips when she was done.

ii.

{Gorkon loses all track of how long he floats in the darkness of the depths. He could have been down there for five tides or five hundred tides, and it would feel exactly the same. He is down so far that even Markene eyes—capable of vision in far darker circumstances than a Merk could ever hope to duplicate—can discern nothing save a haze of ebony.}

{For a time he ponders what it would be like just to remain there. To turn the depths into a watery grave; that way he would never have to face any of his kind again. Never look at them with the sort of hopeless disappointment that pervaded any of his association with them.}

{But the longer he dwells on such a possibility, the more he rejects it. After all, has he not already dallied with the prospect of self-destruction? Has he not beached himself and waited for the inevitable, only to discover other possibilities in his conversations with Ruark Sydonis?}

{Yes, the two most obvious options for the course of his life are perpetual humiliation or death at his own hands, but is there not something else?}

{Ruark's face comes to him unbidden, staring at him with gentle disappointment. *Do you really have to ask that?* Ruark inquires. *After the time we've spent together, the discussions we've had . . . have you not yet learned to look beyond yourself? Must you really seek out only the simplest, quickest answers, rather than pursue the possibilities that are the hardest to achieve, but ultimately the most satisfying?*}

{But it is difficult . . . so difficult . . . }

{*That is how you know it is worth pursuing.*}

{He does not know how long he continues to float there after that, pondering those words. Nor does he make any conscious effort to head for the surface. All he knows is that he is moving. His body has made the decision before his conscious mind has done so. He heads toward the surface, picking up speed as the light from above begins to filter through, and soon . . . }

Gorkon broke the surface and glanced around, unsure of where he was. For all he knew, he was going to come up at the Great Pier, still surrounded by his fellow Markene, with Orin Arn Oran staring quizzically at him and perhaps even beginning to form suspicions about him. But he was not near the Pier. It took him a few moments to get his bearings, and as he did so, he sensed that time had passed. He sensed something else as well, and the instinct alone was enough to send him swimming toward the rendezvous point where he'd met up with Ruark Sydonis all those times.

He cut through the water like a spear, leaving a clean wake behind him, and it was not long before he reached the Resting Point, the location where he had first tried to take his life and had wound up encountering the wayward ruler of the Sirene.

Sure enough, just as he had anticipated—although he could not for the life of him explain how he had been able to do so—there sat Ruark Sydonis. As he had on all his previous encounters, Ruark was perched in a one-man boat and gave a wan smile upon spotting the approaching young Markene.

"I had a feeling you would be here," said Ruark.

"As I did about you."

Gorkon's voice was choked with emotion, and Ruark noticed it immediately. "What ails you, young friend?" he asked in his most solicitous voice.

Gorkon was about to respond . . . and then he stopped. Instead he studied Ruark for a long moment. Aware of the intense scrutiny, Ruark said, "What is bothering you, Gorkon?"

"You know, don't you." Gorkon was surprised to hear himself say it, but as soon as he did, he knew he was right.

Ruark continued to be confused, or at least to be feigning confusion. "I'm certain I don't know what you mean . . ."

"You said you were just guessing that there was something that was going to be happening with the Travelers. But you weren't guessing. You knew."

"My dear Gorkon," Ruark began, "you are giving me far too much credit for—"

Gorkon abruptly disappeared. He sank beneath the water without a word, leaving a puzzled Ruark Sydonis looking around, scrutinizing the water for some sign of the Markene. "Gorkon?" he called. "Gorkon . . . is something wr—?"

The surge of water caught him completely off guard. Ruark flinched back as Gorkon suddenly launched into the air, straight up, having swum down to some great depth and then blasted his way to the surface. The water undulated wildly around him. It was all that Ruark could do to hang on. Then Gorkon twisted in midair, plummeted straight down, and slammed into the water as hard as he could. The result was a most impressive wave that completely swamped Ruark's small ship, capsizing him and sending the monarch of the Sirene tumbling out of his boat and headfirst into the water.

He was not, of course, in any danger. A Merk could breathe in the water as easily as a Markene, although they couldn't begin to approach the depths that a Markene could reach. Nevertheless Ruark came up sputtering, more in indignation than anything else. Wiping the water from his face, he saw Gorkon floating not three feet away, looking deadly serious and indeed quite angry. *What the hell was the meaning of that!* he demanded.

Gorkon paused a moment before responding. "I might ask the same of you, milord. What is the meaning of the games you've been playing with me?"

"My dear Gorkon, I've no idea what you're talking about—"

Gorkon swam toward him, the gaze of his dark eyes never shifting. "Do not tell me that, for we both know it to be false. You are like the sea itself, Ruark Sydonis. What we see on the surface cannot begin to hint at what there is in the depths. You enjoy playing the pleasant, detached fool so that none will take you seriously. It matters little, or even not at all, to me. What does matter is the fate of my people, and I will not have that made the object of creative gamesmanship."

"How interesting," said Ruark. He swum backward easily and drew himself up onto the Resting Point. He proceeded to wring out his garments. "It was not all that long ago that you cared so little for your people that if you simply died, never to see them again, it would have meant nothing to you. I suppose things change."

"I suppose they do," Gorkon agreed. "So tell me now, Ruark Sydonis, and be honest with me . . . presuming that your meetings with me have some true meaning to you, and are not just mere diversions in whatever games are unfolding in your head."

"Yes, they have meaning to me," Ruark said. The water splattered out of his clothing in large droplets as he twisted the cloth. "Ask your questions then, whatever they may be. And be grateful that I am generous enough to ignore the ignominy of being dunked in the water by one such as you."

The comment was provocative, but Gorkon let it pass. Instead he circled the Resting Point warily as he said, "Orin Arn Oran met with my people. Do you know what he told them to do?"

"He told them," and Ruark sounded weary as he spoke, "to attack the Travelers, would be my guess."

"Yes. He said they were plotting against us."

"I'm sure he did."

"Are they?"

Ruark shrugged. "Not to my knowledge."

"Is it possible they are and you don't know about it?"

"Possible? Anything is possible, my young friend. Likely?" He shook his head. "No. Most unlikely."

"Then why would Orin Arn Oran send my people against the Travelers?"

"Why do you think?"

Getting angry, Gorkon said, "Stop playing games with me—"

But he was startled when Ruark tossed aside his avuncular persona and bellowed at him with a stridency that served to underscore just who it was who was truly the ruler of the Sirene. "That is what life *is*, you foolish little Markene! It is a game with players on all sides, each engaging in his own little maneuvers, and each trying to accomplish one simple goal: to be the only one left standing at the end of it, before he is himself swept off the board by the great gamesmen who look down upon us all and laugh at our foibles. If you do not start thinking . . . if you do not begin to play the game yourself, rather than wait for me to explain all the rules . . . you will be removed from play sooner than you could possibly anticipate. It will be done far more rudely and with far more finality than just being tossed in the water. Now answer me," he continued before Gorkon could recover, "why do you think that Orin Arn Oran wants you to attack the Travelers?"

Gorkon's mind raced, trying to put answers together with what little he knew of the Sirene warlord. "Well . . . he would want us to attack because he saw them as an enemy . . . except . . . except you said you did not know of any threat they posed. And they have not attacked us, not ever in our history . . ."

"So what can you discern from that?" asked Ruark. He sounded closer to his usual tone, but there was an undercurrent of iron to it.

"That . . . they are not a threat." He waited for Ruark to say something, but Ruark simply watched him. With a flip of his thick feet, he began to circle the Resting Point. "If they are not a threat, then Orin Arn Oran wants us to attack them . . . for no reason. Which is not consistent with what I know of Orin Arn Oran."

"Which would imply . . ." prompted Ruark.

"That attacking the Travelers is not Orin Arn Oran's idea. He is merely acting as an agent for someone else."

Ruark was about to ask "And who . . . ?" but Gorkon anticipated the question.

"Your spouse, the Lady Tulisia Sydonis," said Gorkon. "Only she ranks above Orin Arn Oran in the hierarchy of Venets. Only on her behalf would he order the Markene to do such a thing." It was all he could do to prevent the words from tumbling one over the other as his thoughts started to race faster than he could verbalize them. "And if we continue to believe that the Travelers pose no threat . . . if we take that as a given, as an unchanging fact . . . then the Lady Tulisia wants the Travelers attacked for one of two reasons: Either she wants to provoke something, or prove something."

"Does provoking something make sense?" asked Ruark.

"No, of course not. Why try to start a fight with the beings who are the right hand of the Overseer himself? Which would mean that she's trying to prove something instead."

"What would that be?"

Ruark could tell from the look in Gorkon's eyes that he had it even before he spoke. "She wants to prove, or at least find out if, the Travelers are vulnerable to attack. I mean, supposedly they are invincible, but no one in memory has ever tried to challenge that. But she wants to attempt it because, if Travelers can be challenged and defeated, then anything is possible . . . up to and including a complete shift in power in the Damned World. But she has no desire," he continued unprompted, "to commit any of the Merk to the campaign because, if it fails, she wants to be able to deny that she had anything to do with it. When questioned, she would merely claim that the Markene did it all on their own. No need to worry about the reason: She'll fabricate it. She'll claim we did it in a Klaa-addled haze. It doesn't matter. All that matters is, Tulisia Sydonis would take the credit for any triumph, while my people would take the blame for a failure."

"It sounds fiendish."

"It's diabolical!"

"Would it work?"

Slowly, Gorkon nodded. "It very well might. And there's nothing I can do."

"Nothing?"

Gorkon studied Ruark's passive expression. "Are you suggesting there's something I can do?"

"What do *you* think?"

Gorkon moaned very loudly then and slid beneath the water. Ruark thought briefly that was the last he was going to see of the Markene, but then Gorkon bobbed to the surface. He was, however, still moaning. "I was correct the first time. It is hopeless."

"Is it now?"

"Of course it is. As long as the Klaa holds the Markene in thrall, I'm helpless to do anything about it. I mean, I could always . . ." Then he shook his head. "No."

"No what? Say what you are thinking."

Snorting derisively in a preemptive dismissal of what was going through his mind, Gorkon said, "It's impossible."

"*Gorkon—!*"

"Well, it's obvious, isn't it. The only way to liberate the Markene from their addiction is to cut them off from the source of that addiction permanently."

"As the gate cuts them off, you mean."

"I was thinking more along the lines of destroying the Klaa supply itself, and I don't see how that's possible. It grows and regrows with determined stubbornness. Even if I ripped it all off the reef, there would be more of it in no time. The Merk have been far too efficient in cultivating it into indestructibility."

"So it would seem," said Ruark.

"Not 'so it would seem.' So it is," Gorkon insisted.

"Well, if you are so certain, than who am I to disagree with you." He gestured toward his boat, which was now floating upright but out of reach some feet away. "If you would be so kind . . ."

But Gorkon wasn't quick to return the boat to him. Instead he eyed him suspiciously. "Wait. You're thinking of something."

"Am I?"

"Yes. You're far too skilled at this 'game' to allow me to get ahead of you. I've only just now caught up with you, haven't I? You've a notion of . . . of something, I'm not even sure what."

"Possibly," said Ruark in a noncommittal manner. "However, I've no clue as to whether you'd be interested."

"Truthfully, neither do I." Gorkon dwelt on the immensity of that which he was contemplating. "I mean . . . let's say that I was able to manage it, with or without your help. Let's say that I was able to separate the Markene from their precious Klaa. I'm not even sure they could handle such a thing. It might . . . I don't know. It might destroy them. I can't even begin to guess the effect it would have. It could tear them apart, or they might tear one another apart. There's no way of knowing for sure."

"No, there isn't," replied Ruark. "But what *do* you know for sure?"

"That as long as Klaa exists, they will always be slaves."

"That's true enough. And although it's not my people and not my problem, I have to note that it certainly doesn't sound like much of a life to me. You, however, might feel differently about it."

"No, I really don't," Gorkon admitted.

He took a deep breath, let it out slowly, then put his hand against Ruark's boat and pushed it gently. It slid gracefully across the water and bumped up against the edge of the Resting Point. Ruark stared down at it but made no effort to board it. Instead he just shifted his gaze to Gorkon and waited for him to say exactly what Gorkon next said.

"You know the way to get rid of Klaa?" he asked.

"I know *a* way. That actually might be too generous; I know a *possibility*. Whether it's one worth pursuing, however, is up to you. We are, after all, discussing the future of your race."

"Yes, I'm aware of that."

"You may want to consider it further."

"I may want to, but I don't."

"Still, there might be other options to—"

"Milord, with all respect, talk to me or I'll tear your boat apart and you can swim home."

Despite the gravity of the situation and the magnitude of what they were discussing, Ruark chuckled at that. Then, his face growing serious, he said, "All right. Listen to me, then, Gorkon, for we have much to discuss. And since the Travelers might pass through at any time, it is hard to know just how much time there is to discuss it."

THE UNDERGROUND

i.

Several cycles of the sun earlier . . .

Eutok was going to make his mother happy. As a gift celebrating the anniversary of her ascension to the throne, he was going to bring her the head of a Piri.

Of all the races of the Damned World, the Piri was the only one that the Trulls had no congress with. They took no action against them, for the Trull code of neutrality was inviolable. But they did nothing to aid them, or provide them any sort of tech. The Trulls treated the Piri as the rest of the Twelve Races did: like the animals that they were. If the Piri had not been able to hide underground, in warrens and caves and tunnels that defied infiltration by other races, then they would have been wiped out long ago. On one occasion the Mandraques had obtained burrowing tech from the Trulls and had used it to go in after the Piri. That, however, had been a disaster, for the Mandraques simply dug their way into the midst of Piri mazes but, once there, were set upon and devoured by the Piri. Those few who had escaped the slaughter had described a terrifying and relentless foe, moving so fast in the darkness that none of their victims ever saw their doom descending upon them. They were there, they were gone, and so were the Mandraques.

This disastrous encounter had grown, in the retelling, elevated to epic proportions, and become a severe disincentive for anyone to make another assault upon the Piri. And that sale of equipment had been made before Eurella became queen. After that, she had forbidden burrowing equipment to be provided to anyone else, believing it should remain the sole province of the Trulls. "We do not sell that which makes us unique," Eurella had decreed.

But Eutok knew her antipathy for the Piri remained, and so he resolved to obtain the head of one for a trophy.

Eutok was Chancellor of the Trulls. He had vast experience with all manner of weaponry, and had no fear at all when it came to danger. So he outfitted himself with a formidable sword, and several daggers sticking out of various parts of his belt, and set out in a Trull car, or Truller, for the farthest reaches of the normally traveled Trull territory. There were tunnels that extended beyond that area, however, and once the Truller had taken him as far as the path permitted, he traveled on foot. He made his way through the passages, his bare feet large and leathery, capable of gripping uneven surfaces with his toes and padding noiselessly through the darkness so that none could hear him. In this way he hoped to be able to get the jump on one of them.

He knew that this could end badly. They could, after all, get the jump on him. Bear him down to the floor, tear him to pieces. Yet he was not at all concerned about that possibility. He had much confidence in himself as Chancellor, as warrior, as a chosen of the gods to be the instrument of their will upon the planet. An instrument of the will of the gods did not die so ingloriously.

He was able to discern the point at which he'd passed beyond the area where Trulls wandered. His broad, flat nostrils could no longer detect any scent whatsoever of his fellow Trulls. But the spoor of the Piri was not especially strong either. Eutok was in a sort of no man's land, where neither Trull nor Piri set foot often enough to make any impression.

It wasn't surprising that the Piri kept their distance from the Trull. One would have thought that the Piri would have targeted them since they were the only other subterranean race, but quite the opposite was true. The Piri wanted nothing to do with the Trull specifically because they had no advantage over them. There was nowhere the Piri could hide that the Trull could not follow. Whereas other races, such as the Ocular, concerned themselves with the Piri attacking in the dead of night and then scuttling away into their hidey-holes, the Trull could follow them wherever they went, hunt them down as they saw fit. It was the Piri's good fortune that the Trulls believed in neutrality, else the survival of the Piri race would have been questionable in the face of a true campaign of genocide by the Trulls.

Still, there was no reason that Eutok couldn't kill at least one if not more of them, so that he could parade their heads before his mother in order to curry her favor.

Although even as he continued to make his way cautiously through the caves, marking his way as he went so he could easily find his way back, he was bleakly aware that his endeavor to please his mother was very likely doomed. He was not the beloved son. Ulurac was. This was particularly galling to Eutok, considering that he felt he had done very little, if anything, to bring disgrace to his mother or the family name, whereas Ulurac's uncontrolled behavior—which had led to a tragedy that rocked the Trull community—was nevertheless countenanced. He could not comprehend it, and inwardly he railed against the unfairness of it all.

It was at that moment, as he dwelt on how supremely unjust it was that Ulurac continued to be the maternal favorite, that he heard splashing in the distance. And more, he heard a gentle singing.

He hugged the wall as he made his way through, crouching so low that he nearly bent himself double. His senses were extended to the maximum and, although he knew there was no one near him, nevertheless some part of him waited for a gang of Piri to drop down upon him and drag him to a terrible death. His hand remained firmly on this sword hilt, ready for anything.

The slow but steady sound of moving water told him there was some sort of underground spring ahead of him. Not only that, but he could detect a change in the temperature around him. It was getting warm. Perhaps it was some sort of hot spring.

And the voice . . . that was the most confusing of all. It could not be a Piri, certainly, for although he had not yet seen the person singing, he could tell from her voice alone that she was most beautiful and sweet, not some animal like the Piri. A Trull maiden, perhaps, having slipped away from the Hub to obtain some time for herself? Eutok supposed it was possible, but didn't seem very likely.

As the tunnel widened ahead of him, he saw a ledge that would give him a vantage point over the source of the water and the possessor of that lovely singing voice. He had been on his hands and knees, but now flattened to his belly. Obviously he could no longer have one hand resting on his weapon, so he pulled it from its scabbard, taking care to keep it slightly elevated so the metal would not scrape on the rock and give away his position.

Eutok edged his way forward, ever so slowly, not wanting to do anything that could conceivably reveal his presence. The closer he got, the more his curiosity swelled about the unseen singer. He got all the way to the edge of the drop-off and pulled his head forward so he could better discern what was transpiring.

What he saw staggered him.

It was indeed a Piri. A naked, female Piri. She was crouching in water that was only up to her knees, and splashing about in a carefree manner. Steam was rising from the water, and the song she was singing was an aimless ode to some long-dead Piri figure of heroic lore. This alone was surprising enough for Eutok, for he hadn't thought that the Piri had any sort of lore at all. They were just . . . animals. They existed, they survived, they hunted and they killed, and that was more or less it. Wasn't it?

The ledge he was perched upon was a good ten feet above the female Piri. He

*watched her, riveted. Dissimilar from the squat, stumpy bodies of Trull maidens—
even the loveliest of them—this female was tall and slender and curved in a way that
Eutok hadn't thought the female form capable of. He found it irresistibly attractive,
and involuntarily he wondered what it would be like to take such a female, to wanton her and make her his own . . .*

*It was with great effort that he shook such notions from his mind. It was disturb-
ing that his thoughts should even wander in such a direction. Every so often one
would hear hushed rumors about someone who had had sexual congress with a Piri.
Such individuals were sick. Everyone knew it. No normal individual could possibly
want to have any sort of physical involvement with a Piri. It was only slightly better
than having sex with a corpse, and there were some who might have claimed that
having sex with a dead Trull was more acceptable than with a live Piri.*

*But still . . . was she not . . . attractive, this one? She moved with such grace, as if
a true artist had designed her and loosed her upon the world. He couldn't take his
eyes from her. He watched her greedily, hungrily. She gave off some sort of marvelous
aroma, and it triggered sense memories for him. Rarely had he been up to the surface, but one of his most vivid recollections was the scent of flowers, which he had encountered when he was very young. He didn't know the names or species of them, but
he had stood in a field of them and the heady aroma had been nigh unto intoxicating. He had wanted to run among them, to sprawl in them, gather them up and
dump them upon his head. But his mother had caught up with him, grabbed him
firmly by the wrist, and, squinting angrily against the daylight, dragged him down
and away into the Hub and forbidden him from venturing to the surface and taking
such foolish risks again.*

*He had ignored part of her advice, gleefully indulging in foolish risks any number
of times, but he had remained away and withdrawn from the surface. He had forgotten the scent of flowers, forgotten what he had given up, but at this moment it all
came roaring back to him.*

*He must have gasped or let out a sudden breath in his recollection, for the naked
female Piri froze. He didn't move. Slowly she stood and then, without hesitation,
turned and looked full in his direction. Her clothing, what there was of it, was lying
on a nearby shore, but she made no move toward it. Her chin was tilted in a proud
manner, and her eyes were deep and red as blood, and challenging.*

*"Would you care for a closer look?" she asked. She did not seem afraid or threat-
ened. She sounded amused.*

*At first he didn't budge, but then he realized the foolishness of it. Still, this was a
Piri, and an enemy, and a thing of the night. He stood abruptly, gripped his sword,
and let out a bellow designed to freeze her where she was, to fill her with terror and
awe. As he did this, he vaulted from the ledge where he'd been hiding and landed*

heavily a short distance from her. He crouched in the water, the warm liquid burbling around his large feet, his gaze fixed upon her and his sword steady in his hand. Eutok tried to keep staring at her face, but he was not especially successful. Instead he looked at her body once more, and there was that smell of flowers again. It was so overwhelming that, because of the combination of the scent and the warmth of the springs around him, he almost toppled over. He caught himself at the last moment and snarled at her, but it was halfhearted. Nor did it help matters when her only response to his dramatic entrance was a lighthearted laugh.

"Stop laughing!" he warned her, waving his sword threateningly . . . or at least in a manner that he imagined was threatening.

She didn't appear bothered by it. Instead she cocked her head and asked, "You're a Trull, aren't you? I've never seen one of your kind, but I've heard stories and descriptions."

"You . . . tell each other stories?" he demanded.

"What an odd question," she said, regarding him as if he were deranged. "Of course we do. Why wouldn't we?"

"Well, because . . . because you're animals," he told her, although he felt foolish even as he said it.

"Are we?"

"Yes!"

"Of course," she said. "Thinking of us as animals makes it that much easier to try and exterminate us. Tell me, Trull," and she turned slowly in the water, her arms extended to either side. "Have you ever felt the need to stare at an animal bathing? Has watching that action ever given you pleasure before?"

"Never before," he sighed, and abruptly tried to regain his mental footing. "Not . . . that I derived pleasure from watching you here and now. No. No pleasure at all. I . . ." He cleared his throat, which suddenly felt as if there was too much blood within it. "I was simply . . . waiting for the right moment to—"

"To what? Kill me? Is that your plan?"

He nodded his head.

"Because I will be your . . . what? Hunting trophy?"

"Something like that."

"Well . . . if you are to be my killer, then you should know who you kill. I am Clarinda Redeye of the Piri." She knelt into the river and playfully splashed some water toward him. "Were you to kill me, you will have destroyed a very important member of the Piri race. For my mother is our Mistress."

"Your 'mistress'? Is that like your ruler?"

She shrugged. "I suppose." She cupped both her hands, collecting water in it . . .

. . . and suddenly flung the water in Eutok's face.

He blinked furiously, blinded for only a moment, but it was enough, for Clarinda was quickly atop him. She had almost no weight to speak of, but there was strength in her arms, and the heels of her feet dug down and in to the back of his knees. It was enough to throw Eutok's center of balance out of whack. He tried to cover, failed, stumbled, and fell backward into the water. Just like that, his head and face were submerged.

Clarinda looked down at him, visible in wavery fashion through the water. She was smiling and licking her lips. He tried to throw her off but she was straddling him firmly, and his attempts to bring his sword around were easily thwarted as, with one hand, she held his arm immobilized. She's going to drown me, *he thought frantically,* drown me and drink the blood from my lifeless body . . .

She brought her lips down and kissed him with a furious passion that took all the remaining breath out of him. Then she was gone. Eutok threw himself upright, coughing furiously, swinging his sword at empty air.

Once more her lightly mocking laughter reached his ears, and he saw her standing some feet away, still naked, still unashamed.

"You could have killed me just then!" he shouted at her, and even as he did so, he realized just how ridiculous his complaint must have sounded to her.

Nor did she let it pass. "As you would have me, had I given you the opportunity. Yet I didn't."

"No. You didn't." He lowered his sword and touched his hand to his lips. "Instead you kissed me. Why?"

"Because I've never before kissed a Trull."

"And that is all the reason you require for doing something? Never having done it before?"

"More often than not." She smiled. "You have a curious taste. You remind me of rock. And dirt. You taste of strength. It was . . . interesting. Was it interesting for you? How do I taste to you?"

"Like blistering heat . . . and ice cold. All at the same time."

"Hunh." She seemed to consider that briefly. "I like the sound of that," she decided. "Do your kind have names, as we do?"

"I am Eutok." He had no idea why, but he puffed out his chest slightly. "I am also the offspring of a leader. My mother is queen."

"Ooo . . . tuck." She rolled the unfamiliar name around in her mouth. "And what would you now with me, Oootuck, son of the Trull queen. Given the chance, would you kill me? Or would you kiss me?"

"I . . ." The aroma of flowers was even stronger to him than before, and he felt his heart racing within his chest. He was standing there, dripping with water, facing a

creature that he had come to kill as an offering to his mother, and all he could think of was the press of her lips against his. "I . . . don't know," *he said at last.*

"That is a start," *she told him.* "Come here again sometime. Perhaps I will be here." *She stepped back and the darkness swallowed her as even Eutok's sight was not able to discern her.*

"You forgot your clothes!" *he called after her.*

"Keep them!" *her amused voice floated to him from the gloom.* "Think of me fondly as you hold them close to you when you sleep."

He left then, picking up her garments and tucking them into his tunic. When he returned to the spot several days later, she was not there. But several days after that, she was. They met and spoke for a long time of their respective races, and learned of one another, and the kisses were prolonged, which led to other things that no Trull female had ever done to or for Eutok . . . probably, he suspected, because they had never conceived of such things or thought them possible. After they became lovers, Clarinda and Eutok were so attuned to one another that somehow he would just . . . know . . . when she was going to be at their place. And likewise, she could always find him. Eventually she even developed the knack for saying his name effortlessly.

So it went for a long time, for the darkness of the Underground provides generous cover for hiding a relationship that would certainly spell the death of either or both of its participants if discovered . . .

ii.

Eutok was stunned to discover Clarinda, crouched on the shore of the hot spring where they had first met. Her legs were drawn up tightly, her face was resting upon her knees, and her sides were rapidly heaving, racked by sobs.

Hardly a day went by when Eutok did not, in the privacy of his imagination, recall those first meetings with Clarinda. The thrill of discovery, the way she had yielded up her innermost secrets and pleasures to him. It was as if they were bonded in some primal manner that they could not fully understand, but that neither of them should ever question lest it turn to ash in the white heat of investigation.

And in all that time, he had never seen Clarinda in the depths of despair as he was seeing her now. Indeed, he wouldn't have thought her capable of being so morose. Yet here she was, mired in misery. Not only that, but from the very beginning they had automatically employed caution in all their dealings. Speaking in soft voices had been second nature to them, for although the places where they met were typically beyond the boundaries of both Piri and Trull habitation, neither of them desired to take any chances. Yet Clarinda was crying openly, making no attempt to modulate her voice or get her wailing under control.

"What's the matter with you?" he whispered as he drew near. "Clarinda . . . ?"

"You came." She drew an arm across her pale face, wiping away tears.

"Of course I came. I always come." He knelt before her, taking one of her slender hands and gently pressing it between his two large, meaty ones. "How now? Why the tragedy? Has someone died? Considering there is no love lost between you and yours, I'd almost think such a passing would be cause for celebration."

"I heard . . ." She took a deep breath and let it out slowly in order to steady herself. "I heard my mother speaking . . ."

"Yes?"

"I heard her speaking . . . to an Ocular."

"Really?" That development intrigued Eutok. "Which one?"

"I don't know," she said impatiently. "They were outside, I didn't get a good look, and besides, they all look alike to me."

"All right . . . but then what—?"

She gripped him firmly by the arm. He winced as her nails dug into his flesh, but tried to give no outward sign of his discomfort. "It's all heading in the wrong direction, Eutok. All of it. They were speaking of . . . of . . ." She was having trouble finding the words at first. "Of formalizing an arrangement," she said finally. "One in which the Ocular would be domesticated. Willing sources of sustenance . . ."

"It would never happen," Eutok said with a disdainful laugh. "The Ocular? Lining up to be meals on legs? The whole idea is ridiculous . . ."

"They made it sound not so ridiculous," Clarinda said. She had managed to get her emotions under control, but she was still obviously concerned about what she had overheard. "As if it might be something that the Ocular would agree to . . . even come to embrace."

"Never," he said even more firmly. "Nagel would never allow . . ."

"I suspect they are going to try and get Nagel out of the picture," Clarinda told him. She got to her feet and he tried to reach over to embrace her, but she shook off his grasp. Instead she paced furiously, although her weight was such that she made no sound as she did so. "One by one, I'm losing the best hopes I have for my so-called people being annihilated! The Ocular hate the Piri with a fiery passion! If you Trulls were willing to provide aid to the Ocular, they could wipe the Piri out!"

"Do you think I haven't tried to influence my queen mother?" demanded Eutok. "Because I assure you, I have! I've spoken to her about it so much that, if I bring it up again, she will probably try to tear me apart with her bare hands! We Trulls could overrun them, but no! We could aid the Ocular in annihilating them, but no! As much as my mother believes your lot to be animals worthy of no more consideration than we'd afford an insect, still she will not take the responsibility for genocide."

"Eutok, don't you see . . . ?" she started to say.

But he cut her off with an abrupt sweep of his arm. "Don't *you* see that it is not our way! It is the Trull way to maintain the balance of power. That way, we never have to worry about losing the business of any one side due to their being destroyed by our tech."

"So you perpetuate the violence, but never present any means of ending it one way or the other." There was clear disdain in her voice, something he had never heard from her.

"Well . . . yes," he admitted. "That's more or less the plan."

"It's a horrible plan."

"It's been working for us for a good long time now!" Eutok said, allowing his own annoyance with the situation to bubble over. He felt heartsick that she was upset, but at the same time, he felt as if she were singling him out for blame when he had done nothing to warrant it. "I don't think you have any right to complain about it. You have the sins of your own people to concern yourself with. So don't be heaping monumental piles of shit on me, all right?"

She stared at him, wide-eyed, and he felt instant contrition (although deep down he also still believed he was right). With a sigh, he reached for her to pull her toward him consolingly, but she batted away his hands. She had also, however, stopped crying, so that was something of a blessing. "Clarinda . . . Clar," he amended, using the affectionate diminutive. "I am sorry if I offended you."

"*If?*"

"I'm sorry that I offended you," he amended.

She shook her head woefully. "All the time you've known me . . . been inside me . . . and you still know and understand so little. All you Trulls, all the races . . . you probably think that we Piri only drink deeply of the blood of one of you. You know nothing of our day-to-day . . . rats."

"Rats?"

"Those gray, furry creatures. The Morts called them rats."

"Yes, I know what they are. What about them?"

"A rat is a typical Piri meal."

Eutok made a disgusted face. "Truly? Because they're rather repellent creatures . . ."

"On the outside. On the inside, their blood is as red as anything else's. Picture that, Eutok," she said. "Picture your lover, picking rat fur out of her teeth. Not a pleasant image, is it?"

"Why are you saying these things, Clarinda?"

"To make you understand how vile we are!" she told him. Whatever pity she had felt for herself had been mercurially replaced with intense self-loathing. "That we deserve to perish as a race. That maybe I deserve to as well . . ."

"Clar . . ."

"Maybe we truly are the animals they all say we are."

"Clarinda." He put his arms around her and drew her tight. He felt her trembling against him. "Things will work out."

"*How* will they?"

"Somehow . . ."

Her body tightened and she pushed him away, turning her back to him. "Nebulous 'maybe's, that's what you present me with, and you think that somehow can ease me. The problems I have to deal with are far less than nebulous, Eutok. You speak of how, at some unknown point in time, a solution will be found. Let me tell you the realities of the here and now, Eutok." She turned to face him, her chin pointed high, as if she were speaking to the populace of a vast chamber. "At any time, at any moment . . . my mother could decide that it is time for me to mate. There are no laws governing her decision, no guidelines. Nor is there any basis for appeal. Should the Mistress select a mate from the population of the Piri, I am his. He will mate with me, and I will produce a child, and the next thing you know, I will be made into the same genderless, pathetic creature my mother is. She, Sunara Redeye, acts as if she is a sexual being when, in fact, she can never enjoy true sensation or pleasure again. That is my fate, Eutok, unless something happens to change that. How attractive will I be to you then, Eutok? With these gone," and she cupped her breasts, looking at him defiantly, "and my main source of ecstasy nothing more than a hunk of scorched flesh."

"I won't let that happen . . ."

She moved quickly toward him, grabbing with fierce urgency at his shoulders. "How will you stop it?" she asked desperately. "Will you take me back to the Hub to live with you?"

"Of course not!" he said. "That would be . . . you know that's impossible, Clar. Interspecies relations of any kind are forbidden . . . save for dalliances with Morts, but they don't count."

"Forbidden, save for exceptions granted by rulers."

"My mother would never make such an exception."

"You don't know—"

"Yes, I do," he said firmly.

"You haven't asked . . ."

"I don't have to!" he assured her. "Clar, my mother . . ."

"But if you asked . . . if you only tried, at least—"

"*Clarinda, listen to me!*" Eutok felt as if this was the single most exhausting conversation he'd ever had in his life. "My mother can scarcely tolerate me as it is! Don't you understand that? It's not exactly as if she cares about my happiness under normal circumstances. Something as abnormal as us—"

"You think I'm abnormal?"

"I think our relationship doesn't exactly fall within the bounds of what most Trulls consider routine romance, yes!" he said in exasperation. "To say nothing of the fact that if she provided us sanctuary, the chances are huge that it will bring the wrath of the Piri down upon us. By remaining neutral, we have avoided a crippling war. That protection will be gone if you take up residence with me. How favorably do you think the rest of my people will look upon you if they see you as an invitation for the Piri to descend upon us? We Trulls do not shrink from fights, but neither do we seek them out. The Trulls would consider your coming to live in the Hub as most definitely seeking unnecessary trouble."

"You could explain to them—"

"Explain to them what? That due to my selfishness and a precipitous love affair, I've decided almost single-handedly to put the entire Trull nation squarely into harm's way? Something tells me they're not exactly going to embrace that."

Abruptly, she said, "Then we can strike out on our own."

"No."

"Eutok," Clarinda told him with mounting desperation, "you've no idea what you mean to me. I think of you constantly. I swear to you, we can be happy together! Why can't you believe that as I do?"

"I have responsibilities as Chancellor. I have obligations to my people. And I'll be damned," he added grimly, "if I leave the well-being of my people to my idiot brother, Ulurac the Spiritu Sanctum. They need me."

"And I don't?"

"I know you do." He took her hands in his. They were slim and delicate compared with his own hard, rough hands. "And I need you. But I can't be so selfish as to abandon several thousand Trulls just to pursue the happiness of two people, even when those two people are you and me."

"What then?" She pulled away from him. "What will we do?"

"I don't know. But something. I will find a way."

She nodded, biting her lower lip, and he was pleased she appeared to be believing him until he saw trickles of blood emerging from her mouth and realized she was actually tearing small holes in her own lips. "Clar," he said, reaching out gently and brushing the blood away. "Stop that."

"I need you to promise me something, Eutok."

"Of course. Anything."

"You shouldn't say that unless—"

"Unless I mean it, of course," he said with conviction. "Again, anything. Don't you understand? I cannot live without you. I would do anything you ask."

She stood several feet away from him, her back to him, and her arms were wrapped around herself as if she were feeling a chill but trusted only herself to keep herself warm. "I never," she said after a pause, "want to live as my mother does. I never want to be that person. Do you understand what I'm saying?"

"Of course," he said with a touch of weariness. "And I said I'd find a way, and I meant it—"

"No," she told him firmly, still not looking at him. "I don't think you're truly comprehending what I'm saying. There may come a time when I say otherwise. Who knows what could happen to my mind? My mother might induce a change of my point of view with potions I cannot even guess at. Or pure determination to live might overwhelm subsequent worries about the quality of that life. But I'm telling you, here and now, while my mind is yet clear, that I don't want to live like that. Be the creature that she is. I want you to promise me that you'll make certain I don't."

"I promise," he said with conviction. "I swear a blood oath, I swear on the lives of Trulls everywhere, I will make certain you don't live . . . like . . . that . . ." But the last three words were said with dwindling certainty even as he spoke them, for he finally, belatedly, realized exactly what she was asking.

"You're asking me to kill you." There was dull shock in his voice. "You're asking me to make certain that you die."

"It is the only way. I only ask that you make it quick and painless, if at all possible."

"Clar . . ."

"It is the *only way.*" She laughed bitterly. "I mean, that would bring it full circle, wouldn't it. You were, after all, intending to slay me when we first met. So it's not as if the notion is beyond your capacity for consideration."

"It is now."

"No." She whirled to face him, her gaze burning with intensity. "You promised. You swore an oath, upon the lives of your people. Do oaths mean nothing to you and yours?"

"They mean a great deal," he said, "but . . ."

"There can't be any 'but' about this. You promised. I hold you to it. If I ever stop coming to you . . . hunt me down."

"You want me to go into the stronghold of the Piri and probably throw my own life away in trying to kill you . . . ?"

"Why not?" she asked, sounding surprisingly reasonable about the whole matter.

"You did, after all, say you couldn't live without me. Or was that as meaningless an utterance as your blood oath?"

He opened his mouth, then closed it. "All right," he said, knowing he'd been outmaneuvered. "As you ask, my lady, so shall it be done. If the unthinkable should occur, I will find a way to separate your head from your shoulders. Will that suffice?"

"Yes. Oh gods, yes." She went to him then, pressed her body against his. "You are wonderful. You are all that any lover could ask. Take me."

"I'm really not in the mood right now, Clarinda . . ."

But she would not accept that, and she licked the inside of his ear and begged and teased and cajoled. Before he knew it, the matter was out of his hands as his body reacted to her urgency without the cooperation or willingness of his mind. He cursed his weakness of will, and resolved not to enjoy what was happening, but instead to be merely a mute and unhappy witness in the activity. Even that resolve, however, crumbled before her seductive power, and soon talk of death and beheadings was the farthest thing from his mind.

It would, however, come back to him later in the privacy of his own quarters, and would haunt him for many days and nights to come . . . not that day and night had all that much meaning in the Underground.

FIREDRAQUE HALL, PERRIZ

i.

"*Where is he?*"

Nicrominus heard her voice echoing through the hall, but it did not prompt him even to glance up from the text he was studying. His daughter bellowing over some damned thing or another was certainly nothing new. He wasn't about to let it distract him. Still, he knew that he was on borrowed time, in a sense, and so was determined to remain focused on his activities for as long as possible.

Which, as it turned out, wasn't all that long.

He did not hear the replies of whoever it was his daughter was bellowing at. If past occasions were any indication, that was likely because the assorted servants were busy cowering and replying in terrified whispers. Perhaps there weren't even audible replies, but just trembling, pointing fingers.

Whatever the case, it seemed not long at all before there came a repeated, angry thudding at the door of his private study. The door rattled beneath the power of the pounding, and Nicrominus had to admit to himself that—whatever else one might say about his offspring—she was remarkably strong.

"*Father!*" she was shouting through the door. "Open up this instant!"

"I am old and weak," he called to her, "and cannot muster the strength necessary even to cross the distance in this room to—"

"Spare me, Father, and open up!"

"*You* open up," he retorted. "It's unlocked."

There was a pause and then the door swung open. Evanne, his daughter, stood there, looking out of breath, with a film of sweat beading on her red, leathery skin. Her tail was twitching almost spastically, reflecting her agitation. She was so tall and slender that she might have passed for male on first glance. But when she walked it was with an almost exaggerated swaying of her hips that, Nicrominus occasionally thought, served as a sort of overcompensation.

Still, he loved looking at her. She had such grace, such confidence. Whenever he spoke to her, she always leaned forward, her gaze intent, making it abundantly clear that she was listening to every word. The intelligence that flickered in her eyes made her old father proud. He remembered when she'd first been hatched, and he'd been foolish enough to be disappointed because he'd thought only a male could possibly possess the sort of intellect he craved in an offspring. How wrong he had been.

"You could have told me it was unlocked," she said.

He felt constrained to point out, "I did."

"I mean before I began pounding like a fool."

"At what point did you give me the opportunity?" he asked reasonably.

She made a dismissive wave as she entered, as if the reasoning of Nicrominus was at fault. "I'm not going to discuss your door when there are for more important things to be concerned about."

"What a relief. So how was your trip to the border lands?"

"I don't want to talk about that now."

He set aside the texts in front of him. "This is stimulating," he said with false joviality. "If we go through enough things you don't want to talk about, we could actually wind up discussing nothing at all. Then you can go on about your business and I—"

"It's your business we need to discuss, Father!"

"Yes," he sighed, "I was afraid we were heading in that direction."

"The *Travelers*, Father?" She approached him with concern writ large upon her face. "The Travelers came to confront you and you simply . . . *sat* here?"

"If I am going to sit, here is as good a place as any," he said reasonably.

"They could have killed you!"

"It didn't seem terribly likely, since I had done nothing to them."

"Travelers don't require reasons."

"All creatures," he corrected her gently, "require reasons. It's just that sometimes the reasons they require are foolish ones. Still, I wasn't concerned . . ."

"How could you not be concerned—!"

He spoke over her protests. "Considering," he said forcefully, "that no harm came to me, as is evidenced by the fact that you're speaking to me now and I'm here with all my limbs and most of my faculties intact, it would appear that my lack of concern was well placed. Please, Evanne, do not treat me as if I were an imbecile."

She looked taken aback by the admonishment. "I would never treat you that way, Father. Nor would I think of you that way."

"Imagine my relief."

"Father—"

"They came to speak," said Nicrominus, coming around his desk. He made sure to play up his slowness of body to eke out what small dregs of pity his daughter might feel for him, if for no other reason than to get her to modulate her voice. "Actually, one of them spoke. The rest just stood there looking menacing."

Despite what she clearly saw as a situation that had been fraught with peril for her father, Evanne was also obviously intrigued. She tilted her head slightly, her forked tongue flicking out. "Of what did the one speak?"

He reached into his robes and held up the hotstar. At first Evanne barely afforded it a glance. "A hotstar," she said briskly. "What of it?"

"Look at it closely."

He held it out to her and she took it from him. Again she didn't seem especially interested, but he was pleased to see that she noticed it quickly. "Wait . . . it's not glowing," she said.

"Yes."

"It has no energy. It's dead."

"Yes," he said again.

She looked up at him. "Is that possible?"

"Apparently so."

"But how—?"

"Ahhhh," Nicrominus said, waggling a finger, "and now we come to it. The 'how' is what the Travelers came to me to discover."

"Came to you? Why you?"

"I wish I had a definitive answer for you, Evanne," he admitted. "Perhaps the simple truth is that they just had no idea who else to go to. Luck of the draw, as it were."

"So . . . what have you been doing?" She glanced at the texts upon his desk. "Studying up on hotstars?"

"Of course. What else *would* I be doing?"

"You could have Xeris doing it. He is your foremost student."

"If the Travelers had desired Xeris to do it, they would have gone to him. They came to me. Why burden Xeris with this, anyway?"

"Why burden yourself?"

"When a burden is assigned, you accept it and deal with it," he told her. "I'm studying the origin of hotstars, all available information as to how they function, plus any evidence—either scientific or anecdotal—that would indicate a time when they've gone dead or shown a diminishment in power. So far, it's been very educational. Very informative, oh my, yes."

"All right." She leaned forward, craning her neck so that she could see more clearly one of the texts that he had unwound upon his desk. "And what have you learned so far about the problem?"

"So far?"

"Yes."

"Nothing, actually."

Her head slumped forward and she shook it woefully. "Then how can you possibly tell me that you've found it educational and informative?"

"Because," he replied easily, "it is always informative to learn about the limits of our own knowledge. It certainly helps one to maintain perspective."

She looked as if she couldn't decide whether to yell at him or laugh, and finally she chose the latter. She chuckled softly and cupped his chin. "I never know what to make of you, Father."

"Neither do I." He patted her hand and continued, "Don't worry yourself about this hotstar business, Evanne. Just as importantly, don't worry Xeris about it. I have the matter firmly under control."

"Have the Travelers told you how quickly they desire your answer on this?"

"No," he said, "but I doubt they'll want me to take my time. So I'm to giving this the utmost priority."

"I have confidence in you, Father."

She turned away and, as she headed for the door, Nicrominus called after her, "It's good to have you back from the border lands, daughter."

"It's good to be back, Father."

He smiled at as she went out the door. "Such a delightful girl. If I'd realized the daughter was going to turn out so well, I'd never have devoured the mother. Ah well," he sighed heavily and went back to his reading. "Live and learn, I always say."

ii.

When Evanne told Xeris the news, he could barely contain himself.

"Running out, you say? Are you sure!?" They had seated themselves in a court-yard outside Firedraque Hall, and Xeris was actually bouncing up and down, much to Evanne's amusement. "The Travelers are concerned because the hotstars are running out of power?"

"Now, I didn't say that," Evanne reminded him, and then she laughed at his enthusiasm. "Xeris, please! I can scarcely stand to look at you, you're bobbing about so! Calmly!" She put out her arms to him and then folded him into her embrace. "You know," she said, "I would have thought that, considering I'm your betrothed, most—if not all—of your enthusiasm would be focused upon my return, not my father's research. Perhaps I should be jealous of him and his musty texts?"

"Of course not," he assured her. "There is nothing that is more important to me than you. But still, this development, it's—"

"It may be nothing," she said. "Remember, it's just the one hotstar that's gone dead. It could be some sort of . . . of fluke."

"No," he said firmly. Evanne was seated on a stone bench, and Xeris swung his legs around so that he was straddling it. Even though he was trying to contain himself, he was still bouncing slightly. He knew he probably looked ridiculous, but he didn't care. "No, I don't believe that. Where there's one, there's more, and it's not just that. If this is actually not isolated but, instead, a widespread phenomenon, it could completely change the balance of power."

"What are you talking about?" asked Evanne, her tail twitching in confusion. "That the relationship between the Firedraques and the Mandraques could—"

"No, no, no!" He swung his legs up and, with a hop, was now crouching on the bench, thumping it repeatedly with a fist. "You're thinking too small! Too locally! This is far, far bigger! How can you not see the possibilities?"

"Why don't you enlighten me, then," she said dryly, "considering that I'm obviously far too intellectually stunted to know what you're talking about without a detailed explanation."

The sarcasm in her tone went completely past him. "You have to know what hotstars are."

"They're power sources."

"And beyond that?"

She shrugged. "No one knows beyond that. They just . . . are. Both in the Elserealms beyond the rift, and here in this sphere, they simply exist. Some theorize that they are culled from rocks that fell from the skies, although that wouldn't explain the numerous . . ." Then she stopped when she saw him furiously shaking his head. "No? That's not right?"

"It's right so far as we know, but there's far more unknown than known."

"I believe I just said that. You know, talking to you can be as infuriating as talking to my father."

"I will take that as a compliment."

"It wasn't intended as such."

He scratched the back of his head, obviously trying to find the best way to approach the topic. "Hotstars have always been a sort of . . . of 'given' in the Else-realms. They were an energy source, and they were used there to power our tech. When the Twelve Races were dispatched here in the Third Wave, one of the things that our exilers sent along with us was a sizable supply of hotstars."

"Of course," Evanne said with not a little bitterness. "Because those who exiled us were ever so generous. Wanting to assuage their guilty consciences by provid-ing us with some helpful tokens of the home they were banishing us from."

"True enough. The thing is, no one in the Elserealms ever seriously questioned whence hotstars managed to derive their seemingly endless supply of energy. They were just always these . . . these sources of power that did what we needed them to do, fueled what we needed them to fuel. Those who did try to launch serious inquiries into the origins of hotstars . . ."

"Were rounded up," said Evanne. "In fact, most of the leading investigators into the origins of hotstars were convicted of heresy and included in the First Wave. Obviously hotstars are something of a sensitive subject . . ."

"Which makes it all the more curious that Travelers would come to your father to discuss them openly," Xeris pointed out.

Slowly Evanne nodded, looking thoughtful.

Seeing that he had her full attention, Xeris continued, "What was interesting was that those hotstars which were brought over here were even more potent than the hotstars were back in the Elserealms. That potency was one of the few bright spots—no pun intended—that the Banished were able to discern in the depths of their plight. Tech worked better here, with greater efficiency and power than ever it did in the Elserealms."

"But no one ever knew why."

"No," Xeris agreed, and then he puffed out his chest and said, "but I've devel-oped some theories in that regard."

"You've developed them?" she asked. "Or others developed them and you've just become thoroughly familiar with them."

He deflated slightly. "Some of both," he said defensively, and then leaned for-ward, his gaze intent upon her. "What I think," he said, "is that hotstars don't have any sort of internal generation of power themselves. I think they are channels for something. Energy conduits, if you will."

"You mean that whatever power comes from the hotstars, it's actually originat-ing elsewhere and the hotstars are . . . are linked to it somehow? And they funnel the energy through?"

"Yes, exactly," he said with growing excitement. "From some sort of a Primestar."

"Primestar?" She looked doubtful. "Did you come up with that term?"

He nodded proudly. "Do you like it?"

"Honestly? It sounds a bit inane."

Xeris didn't try to hide his annoyance. "No, it's not. It's not inane at all. In fact, it's the opposite of inane. It's . . . ane."

Evanne stared at him for incredulously, and then couldn't help but laugh with delight. "All right, you win," she said. "It's ane. So tell me about this Primestar then."

"That's the thing," he said. "My guess is that, whatever and wherever the Primestar is . . . it's here."

"Here? You mean here in Perriz?"

"No. Well, actually," he corrected himself, "maybe yes. I couldn't say for sure. The truth is that I don't know what this Primestar would look like or be like. I don't know anything about its nature. Maybe it's somewhere far off in the sky, or maybe it's sitting beneath our very feet or hanging invisibly between the two of us. Perhaps it's as gargantuan as a continent or as small as a dust mote. No way to say for sure. But my guess is that whatever the Primestar is, it's in this plane rather than the Elserealms. And that's why the hotstars are far more potent here."

"So you're saying that in relocating us here, the Banishers inadvertently gave us a tool that made us even stronger than we were back home." When he nodded, she smirked and said, "Well, that's a nice bit of irony."

"I think there's more than irony going on now, though."

She tilted her head slightly, her tongue snapping out. "What do you mean?"

"The hotstar that the Travelers brought your father."

"What about it?"

"He said it had gone dead?"

"That's right."

He scratched the underside of his snout, then got up and started to walk in a small circle. He didn't say anything for a time, and Evanne watched him until she grew bored. "Are you going to be coming to a point anytime soon?" she inquired politely.

"Why should they care?" he asked.

"Care about what?"

"About us. You said it yourself: Deep down, they know that exiling us here in their 'Final Solution' to the problem of the Twelve Races was a deeply unfair action. They provided us such amenities as hotstars as a sop to their guilty consciences. But if the hotstars here on the Damned World were running out of power, do you really think they'd be that concerned over it?"

"No, I suppose not."

"I suppose not as well."

"I'm still not seeing the signifi—" Then her voice trailed off and her eyes widened. "Ahhhhh," she said.

"You begin to see."

"The hotstar running out of power . . ."

"Yes?"

"It's not an isolated instance. More than that . . ."

"Yes?" he prompted her once more.

"It's happening back in the Elserealms as well."

He clapped his hands together once approvingly. "And there it is," he said with an air of triumph. "Exactly what I was thinking. It's happening back in the Elserealms as well."

"For all we know," she said with growing excitement, "it's happening more comprehensively there. I mean, here we're being handed one hotstar, and that may be the only one. But the Elserealms might be experiencing some massive sort of power shortage. They could have hotstars failing by the hundreds . . . by the thousands!"

"It's possible," he nodded. "Now, of course, we don't know for sure. But that might be the case. And if it is, that opens up some serious possibilities."

"You're saying they might *all* have to come here."

"That's one notion, yes."

Evanne laughed with almost childish glee. She leaped to her feet and threw her arms around herself, hugging herself delightedly. "Imagine it!" she cried out. "Our exilers, being subjected to the same treatment they inflicted upon us! The Banishers banished! Forced to leave the idyllic environs of the Elserealms to fend for themselves here on the Damned World. The advantage shifting to us for once! Not all the Travelers in the world would be able to keep us from them! It's too delicious!"

"There's another possibility that's even better."

"And that would be?"

His eyes flashed maliciously. "It's becoming clear that the power and properties of the hotstars are something that we haven't even begun to grasp. What if we're able to wield them in some manner?"

"Wield them? You mean . . . as weapons?"

"Exactly," he said. "What if somehow we were able to harness the hotstars, or even the Primestar itself, so that—even if the Elserealms are currently not experiencing any shortage of power—we were able to draw the power off from the hotstars they did have? Or, at the very least, find a means of blocking the energy flow from this plane to the other and thus cause the very outage that we're speculating about? If we were able to become masters of our own fate through manipulation of the hotstars, the Banishers would have to come to us for their energy needs!"

She gasped. "That's an even better notion than what we were just talking about!"

"Isn't it?" He smirked.

"But how would we do any of this? Find your theoretical Primestar. Gain control of the hotstars in the way that you describe?"

"I don't know," he admitted. Then his face took on a grim and determined expression. "I swear this to you, though, on my life . . . if it is possible, I will find a way to do it. It could mean a whole new life for us, Evanne. For you and I, for your father, the Preceptor, the Firedraques . . . for the Twelve Races as a whole. If we're able to harness the power of the hotstars to gain dominance over our exilers, it might well be what finally brings all the Twelve Races together and ends the constant cycle of violence."

"Because we would be uniting against the common enemy with an actual chance of defeating them?"

"Exactly." He paused and then added with a smile, "Failing that . . . if we Firedraques wind up using it to eliminate all other races save ours, well . . . I could easily live with that outcome as well."

"As could I, my love," she said as she stroked his snout affectionately. "As could I."

iii.

Nicrominus was far too old and experienced to allow himself to be startled by anything. So when a voice spoke to him from above, at least outwardly he didn't react in any discernible manner.

"She shouldn't speak to you that way."

He had been staring off into space, contemplating the hotstar, and so didn't react immediately. He waited to see if the speaker repeated herself. He didn't have to wait very long. "I said she shouldn't speak to you that way."

Very slowly he turned in his chair and looked up toward the rafters. The room had a vaulted ceiling and so he had to squint to see the highest part of it. There was a slightly movement in the shadows.

"So," he said with a trace of amusement, "my longtime lurker has chosen to speak."

As skilled as Nicrominus was at keeping his feelings and reactions to himself, his observer was incapable. She spoke with a mixture of surprise and delight. "You've known I was here? All this time?"

"Skittering about in the upper reaches of our hall? Of course, my dear. I'm elderly but not addled." He gestured for her to come down from her perch. Instead she hugged the shadows with even greater ferocity. "Who are you?"

There was a pause, and then she replied in a singsong voice, "My brother says I shouldn't talk to people. He says it's bad. Bad bad bad."

"I'm sure he wouldn't mind. Who is your brother?"

"He's the next king."

"Is he?" Nicrominus smiled at that. "That's his plan, is it?"

"Yes. But I'm not supposed to tell anyone that."

"I see. And who told you not to tell anyone that?"

"Arren."

"Ahhhh," said Nicrominus, although her words merely confirmed what he had already surmised. "So you would be Norda Kinklash."

She gasped as if he had performed an astounding conjuring trick. "How did you know?" Her tail whipped around one of the rafters and, releasing her grip with her hands, she allowed herself to dangle supported solely by her tail. "Can you read minds?" she asked with an impressed whisper, although her voice carried over the distance.

"It occasionally appears that way. I haven't seen you in some time. You're much taller than I recall."

Norda gently swung herself back and forth. "I growed."

"Indeed."

"And I hid. You didn't see me because I've been hiding. I like to hide. I'm very good at it."

"Yes, you are," he readily agreed. He tilted his head slightly, taking her in. "Yet you've come out of hiding now. Why?"

She stopped rocking. "I didn't like the way that female was talking to you. It wasn't nice."

"My daughter is very outspoken."

Norda started to climb her own tail until she draped herself over a beam, her front and back hanging from either side. "Would you like me to kill her for you?" she asked carelessly.

Nicrominus appeared to give the matter serious consideration. "Not at the moment," he finally said with a decisive air.

She shrugged, and it seemed to Nicrominus that she had forgotten the offer almost as soon as she had uttered it. He took a cautious step forward, although it didn't really bring him any closer to her since she was high up. "The way fathers and daughters speak to one another . . . that's very important to you, is it?"

Norda shrugged again, and folded her arms across her chest.

"I remember your father," he continued. "I remember him carrying you on his shoulders when you were very little."

She said nothing at first in response, but something told Nicrominus not to speak too quickly. Finally Norda said, sounding very far away, "I wish I did."

"You remember nothing of your father? How about your mother?"

Abruptly Norda vaulted from high above and plummeted toward the floor. Nicrominus, rarely nonplussed, barked out an alarmed cry as Norda fell with dizzying speed. Then she tucked her head down, her arms up and around, and when she hit the ground she came up in a perfect roll. It brought her to within inches of Nicrominus, who did not back up even though it was his impulse to do so. Norda hissed, her tongue flicking out, and then—to his surprise—put a hand to his face.

"Will *you* be my father?" she asked in a voice that ached of loss. "I would like that ever so."

"I . . . cannot be."

"My mother, then?" There was no trace of jest in her tone. Clearly she would have accepted either.

Despite the absurdity of the suggestion, or perhaps because of it, the edges of his mouth turned up slightly. "I think that even less likely."

She stepped back from him, looking him up and down, and then she stretched out her arms. There were thin bands of gold, bracelets, on the wrists of either arm. She extended them to Nicrominus and, once satisfied that he had seen them, she slid the one off her right wrist. "Here," she said, handing it to him. "My brother gave me these. I think he took it off the corpse of a Mandraque many years ago. I want you to have it. So we'll always be together."

"That's . . . very kind of you." Carefully he took it from her and slid it over his wrist. The cloth of his robe covered it. "I have to say, though . . . I'm still a bit unclear as to why you've chosen now to come to me, make your presence known, give me this . . ."

"Because sooner is better than later, and one never knows when someone is going to go away because nobody knows what the future will bring."

She pivoted, sprinted toward the wall, and leaped for it. She bounded straight up the side, her clawed fingers finding the tiniest of holds, and within seconds had made her way back to the rafters.

"That's true," Nicrominus called after her, hoping that she would come back down. "No one knows what the future will bring."

"Except me," she called down, and then laughed deliriously, and vanished into the shadows.

THE OUTSKIRTS OF FERUEL

i.

"She dreamt of the Ocular coming to us before they actually showed up, Mother. Certainly that has to have some significance to you."

The Bottom Feeders had made camp for the evening, and Zerena and Karsen were hunting. Zerena's spear, which she had thrown with her customary expertise, had just bagged the fourth rabbit of their outing. She shoved the limp carcass into the leather bag hanging from her belt. "That has no significance to me whatsoever, Karsen," she said.

"How can you say it doesn't?"

"Like this: Iiiittttt duuuuznnnnt."

Zerena Foux thought she was going to go out of her mind all the way back to the encampment as Karsen went on about Jepp's dreams and other nonsense. "Where are you going with this, Karsen?" she asked in exasperation as they neared the base.

"I don't know," he admitted.

"Then why in the name of the gods do you insist on bringing it up?"

"I just . . . I feel as if it's important somehow, that's all."

Zerena turned to face him, the rabbit-filled bag swinging about at her hip. "Then here's a suggestion, Karsen. If it's that damnably important, bring it up with her. Try to parse it all out in conjunction with your lady love, but don't—"

Karsen reddened when he heard that. "My . . . what? Mother, you don't think that I've . . . I mean . . ."

"What?" Zerena demanded. "Don't play games with me, Karsen. I know that you want this Jepp girl. I've talked to you about this time and again, and you keep denying it. It's insulting to me, and you're not making yourself look any too good either. She's trained to pleasure her betters. You're her better. Do I have to diagram it for you?"

"No, Mother," Karsen said coldly. "No, you've made your contempt for both her and me readily apparent."

He stormed away from her, his hooves digging up clods of dirt as he went. Zerena vaulted after him, easily covering the distance with one jump even though she was considerably heavier and older than he, landed behind him, and grabbed him by the arm. "Don't take that tone with me," she started to say.

Karsen both pushed and pulled away from her so violently that Zerena not only lost her grip but her balance. She was usually sure-footed, but this time gravity got the better of her and Zerena tumbled unceremoniously to the ground, narrowly avoiding squashing the rabbits in her bag.

"Mother!" Karsen called out. "Are you all—"

With a quick sweep of her furred leg, Zerena Foux knocked Karsen's own legs out from under him. He tumbled roughly to the ground as she sprang to her hooves and glowered at him.

"Karsen," she said tightly, "I have been more patient than I would have thought possible. I have been more patient than any head of our clan has ever been with any child. Thanks to you and your pet, we're heading straight into an insane amount of danger . . ."

"I'd like to think that Nagel of the Ocular had something to do with that," he pointed out, but made no effort to get up off the ground.

"*I don't care, Karsen!* I am no longer suggesting or cajoling. Now I'm telling you: Get your head out of your furry ass and back into the game of staying alive. It's enough that we're on this fool suicide errand for Nagel. I don't want to have any further discussions with you about the human! None! In fact, I barely want to have any conversations with you about anything! So if you are fond of the number of teeth currently in your mouth, you'll shut it and follow me back to the camp without saying *another damned word!*"

Karsen started to respond, but wisely thought better of it and said nothing more. Zerena stormed past him and he followed her with his head slightly lowered.

ii.

The scorched flatness of Marsay had given way to a far more forested area. They had camped amid a grove of trees, and the strong scent of them filled Karsen's nostrils, tingling his senses. Jepp was looking up at the trees in wonderment, running her hand along the bark, fascinated by the texture. Apparently the girl had never been beyond the small area that had been the stomping ground of the Mandraques. Or, if her master had taken her out of that immediate area, he had kept her locked away in his traveling tent wherever they had gone, so she'd had no opportunity to experience anything else of the rest of the world. Karsen, by contrast, had been all over the place many times, so he had become accustomed to it all. He found it entertaining, however, to discover the world anew through Jepp's eyes.

That evening the camp was unusually quiet and restrained. The only one who was at all convivial was Rafe Kestor, and Karsen figured that was because Rafe had completely forgotten where it was that they were going or what their mission was. Instead he regaled them with a detailed description of some great battle in which he'd taken a part. Karsen didn't know whether the fight had occurred in the real world or just somewhere in Rafe Kestor's head, but either way it was certainly exciting enough.

Jepp was listening raptly, actually gasping now and again when Rafe Kestor got to some particularly exciting bit. It was charming, Karsen thought, how involved she was in the narrative.

Later that evening, the Bottom Feeders settled down to sleep. Gant was on monitor duty, as he always was. Apparently, although he did possess some sort of state of relaxation, he did not actually require sleep the way the others did. Even when he was at his ease, the slightest vibration would bring him to full alert in a heartbeat (presuming he actually had a heart; it was difficult to know for certain with Gant). Since Gant's gelatinous mass was capable of enveloping any intruder—to say nothing of the fact that he could position himself so that people would walk right through him and find themselves immobilized—he was the ideal sentry.

In the stillness of the night, as the others slumbered, Karsen noticed that Jepp was lying awake, staring up at the stars. She did not appear to be perturbed by anything in particular. She was simply stargazing as the glittering orbs peeked through the foliage that formed a natural canopy above them. Nevertheless she did so with that same childlike wonderment with which she had listened to Rafe Kestor's adventures.

Karsen, who was lying several feet away, rolled over toward her. The movement caught her attention and she turned and smiled at him.

"Tired?" he whispered.

"Not really, for some reason," she said.

"Care to go for a walk?"

She shrugged. "If it's what you want," she said.

Karsen sighed, feeling a bit worn out with all the times he had told her that she could and should think for herself. She had shown flashes of determination, and had even threatened—in Mingo's words—to grow a spine. But every so often she would then revert to type and be almost insanely unwilling to express her own preferences. However, he had no desire to go into it at that particular moment, and so he just said, "Yes, that's what I want."

They walked through the woods in silence for a few minutes. She would glance shyly at him and then look away quickly when she thought he was looking at her. There was a full moon that night, so seeing was not a problem.

"How much do you know about your people, Jepp?" he asked.

"You mean the Mandraques and the Greatness? Well, let's see. They—"

"No, no," he said with a laugh. "I mean your real people. Your species. You know . . . humans."

"What do I know?" she asked. "I . . . don't think I understand. I mean, I know how our bodies work—"

"Your history, Jepp." He stopped walking and leaned against a tree, folding his arms. Small animals scampered about in the limbs high above, some of them chittering, offering token protest to the late-night intruders. Karsen ignored them. "Your people's history. Their accomplishments."

"We had accomplishments?" she asked.

"Well . . . yes. Obviously. I mean, the Orb of the Trinity . . . the bauble we're seeking to swipe from the Trulls . . . that was devised by your people."

"Yes, so I'm told," Jepp said. "But . . . I find that a little hard to believe. I mean, well . . ." She held her arms out to her side. "Look at us! At me, I mean. We are not as sturdily built as even the weakest of the Twelve Races. We are subjugated. I understand that we're nearly extinct. How much of what humans accomplished could possibly be considered of value or significance?"

"There are buildings," Karsen pointed out. "Great, tall buildings . . ."

"That the Twelve Races now inhabit."

"Yes, that's right."

She gave him a pitying look. "Then again, how much good did any of that do us in the long run? Or even the short run? All that we had was taken away from us, which could only indicate that we never wanted it all that much in the first place."

"Is that you speaking?" asked Karsen. "Or the Greatness."

She looked puzzled and even concerned at that. "The Greatness . . . is speaking through me?" she asked with obviously mounting fear. "Am I haunted . . . ?"

"No, not at all, I promise," he said, trying not to laugh in the face of her groundless concern. Then, adopting a serious mien, he took another approach. "I was just wondering whether you knew anything of your people's history."

"Nothing," she said brightly. "I once asked the Greatness about that, and he said there was no reason to clutter my head with it."

"Terrific."

"Do you know anything about them?"

"Only stories I've heard," he said. "And most of the stories, I'd . . ." His face darkened slightly.

"What?" she prompted.

"I'd rather not repeat them," Karsen told her. "I'm afraid that . . . well, they don't exactly portray Morts . . . humans . . . in the most flattering of manners."

"Oh."

"Are you insulted by that?"

"Me? Oh, no!" and she laughed at that. "Oh, Karsen Foux, do not concern yourself about that. If you don't want to repeat them because you're not comfortable with it, that's perfectly fine. But I promise you that, in all my time in the charge of the Greatness, I've probably heard all the insulting jests and tales that you know. I got used to them."

"Well," said Karsen, suddenly feeling like an idiot for having brought any of this up. "Be that as it may, it's probably best if I don't repeat them. I'd feel guilty about them, even if you don't hold me accountable."

"All right," Jepp said cheerfully. She turned around and started to skip away . . . apparently, just because she could.

But she was brought up short when Karsen called after her, "Do you know if your people were ever prone to prophetic dreams?"

Karsen knew that he'd hit upon something even before she turned and looked at him, a cornered beast sizing up her erstwhile prey and trying to decide whether she could tilt the odds back in her favor.

Then she laughed once more, except this time it sounded artificial and forced. "Is this about my dreaming about the Ocular? Because we've discussed it, and it's so . . . I mean, it was just coincidence . . ."

"Was it?"

"Yes. It was."

"Jepp, you can be honest with m—"

"Yes," Jepp said with greater force, in a manner that warned Karsen not to push the matter any further. "It was."

He put up his hands in an "I give" manner. "All right," he said. "It was just coincidence."

She nodded, seemingly content with the termination of the discussion, and then she flopped to the ground, lying on her back and staring up at the stars once more. She thumped the area next to her with an open hand, indicating that she wanted Karsen to lie next to her. He did so, and was surprised—but not too surprised—when she slid over so that her head was resting in the crook of his arm. The press of her body against his did not go unnoticed. He felt a stirring in the fur around his loins, and drew his legs together tightly to head it off before she spotted it.

"They say they're up there," said Jepp.

"Who says who's up where?"

She took a deep breath and let it out slowly. "You see how few humans there are now. And there were once so many more. Well . . . the story goes that, realizing the world couldn't stand against the Third Wave, many of my people simply left."

"Left? In what?"

"Boats. Boats to the stars."

Karsen snickered at that. "Boats to the stars? Jepp, I'm more than willing to admit that your ancestors had a considerable degree of wit and ingenuity, but . . . boats to the stars? Seriously?"

"Seriously," she said, "and by the way, I thought you said you weren't going to laugh at humans."

"I'm sorry," he told her sincerely. "I didn't mean to. You just . . . it caught me off-guard, that's all. Boats, you say?"

"Boats. Some of my people even believe there's one light in the sky for every human who survived and is hidden up there, in the blackness, waiting . . ."

"Waiting for what?"

"For the Twelve Races to destroy each other."

He blinked. "Hunh. Interesting."

"Interesting or inevitable?" asked Jepp.

She cuddled even closer to him. He was becoming intensely aware of the warmth of her skin, the scent of her. Remarkable how much difference time could make. Initially he had been put off by her human odor; now it was alluring. Perhaps his mother's comments were preying upon his mind, but all he could think of was taking her, plunging himself into her. And yet there was something deeper within him, some instinct telling him that he must not. That it would be a monumental mistake. He felt as if his brain was at war with itself, torn between sheer, wanton lust, and caution that was based in some sort of nameless fear. Karsen had always trusted his instincts, but now he had two different sets of instincts sending him two starkly different messages.

Unaware of Karsen's internal war, Jepp continued obliviously, "I mean, honestly, Karsen, you must see it. All of you must see it. The only time the Twelve Races were united was when they were driving my ancestors into oblivion. Once you all triumphed, the next thing anyone knew, you were back to trying to kill yourselves. If it weren't for the Firedraques endeavoring to impose some sort of rule of law upon you all, the lot of you would likely be dead by now. And even the Firedraque laws and treaties aren't sufficient. They're being violated all the time. I can't understand it."

"Can't you?" He realized his voice sounded strangled, and he coughed loudly to clear his throat. "My understanding is that we could have learned a few things from your ancestors when it came to war. I'm told they were bellicose, fierce, and unreasoning. That they destroyed anything they didn't understand, and since more often than not they didn't understand each other, they would have done themselves in had we not shown up to expedite it."

"Well, that just sounds silly."

"*Silly?*"

"Of course. I mean . . . look at me, Karsen. Do I look fierce and unreasoning to you?"

He tried to look anywhere but into those eyes of hers that threatened to consume him. "Uh . . . no. Not . . ." His throat was closing up again and he forced it open. "Not . . . at all, no."

"There you are, then."

She adjusted her position and laid her head upon his chest. "Do you mind?"

"N-No . . ."

Jepp sighed contentedly, and ran her fingers across the thick mat of hair on his chest. "To think I was so terrified when I first saw you. I wanted to run screaming, I . . ." She stopped moving her hand, letting it rest on his belly. He thought he was going to explode. "I don't know. Maybe there's something in what you say. I was scared of you because I didn't know you. I can see how fear of something can turn into hatred of it."

"Anything is possible."

She lifted her head slightly and looked up at him. "Do you think my people returning is possible? That instead of remaining hidden, they could come back, and I wouldn't be so . . . alone?"

"I suppose. After all, I just said 'anything is possible.' That certainly falls into the category of 'anything.' But . . ."

"But what?"

"But . . . you're not alone, Jepp. Not as long as I'm here."

She sighed contentedly. "I was so hoping you'd say that."

She continued to lie there for a time, staring up at the stars. She said nothing and Karsen, who wasn't much for filling up empty air with pointless discussion, said nothing as well.

He'd never quite understood the depth of Jepp's loneliness before this moment. In all his discussions with her, she'd always seemed so eager to please that, somehow, she'd never given him the impression that there was much more to her than that. Unaccountably, he started wishing that there was something he could do about her predicament. Some way to find other humans for her to interact with.

And then, even as the idea crossed his mind, he decided he hated it. What was he going to do? Hook her up with another human male? What a terrific notion. She could then fall in love with him and not feel anything for Karsen anymore . . .

What the hell am I thinking? Karsen wondered. He wasn't sure what he felt for her. He wasn't sure what, if anything, she felt for him. And there weren't other humans around of Karsen's acquaintance anyway, so why in the world was he going off on this tangent? It was . . .

He heard a gentle snoring in his ear. He angled his head around just enough to see that Jepp was sound asleep, her head on his shoulder.

Karsen considered the idea of trying to slide out from under her, pick her up, and carry her delicately back to camp. Finally he decided against it. He didn't want to chance waking her up. She was sleeping so peacefully, and considering how fitful her slumber had been since they first met, why risk spoiling it? Besides, he kind of liked just having her all to himself, even for a brief time. It felt as if the rest of the world had gone far, far away, and it was just Karsen and Jepp and a world that was empty of threat and war and anything that could keep them apart.

He gazed upon the stars and thought about humans hidden among them.

"Best stay in hiding," he murmured. "There's nothing for you here."

iii.

She has never seen a Trull before. Yet she sees one now—no, more than one, many of them—and they are shambling toward her, reaching out with their huge, meaty hands, grasping at her.

She sprints up, out from a tunnel, and starts to run across a broad plain. But suddenly those same hands burst up through the ground, grabbing her legs, pulling her down. She claws at the ground around her, trying to find purchase, some means of halting her descent. But she is unable to, and she screams but cannot make herself heard because her mouth is filled with dirt.

She falls into a tunnel once more, lit with glowing hotstars, except they are diminishing in strength. She is holding something. It is the globe. The orb. The Orb of the Trinity. Trull hands are grasping all around her, and suddenly they are transformed and they are Piri hands, they're trying to take it away from her. She shoves at them, trying to get away, and then looks down at the Orb and screams because it is now an eye, which she seems to remember from another incident, and the eye is that of an Ocular, staring at her unblinkingly and accusatorily. She wants to throw it away, but she is transfixed. The Piri are no longer clutching at her. Instead they are running, trying to get away, and in the dark center of the eye she sees an explosion of light that is widening, moving beyond the eye, filling the tunnel all around her . . .

Jepp woke up screaming. The scream was cut off a split second after it had started, so quickly that the sound of it would never have carried beyond a couple of feet.

She didn't even register where she was at first. Instead she was carrying over with her her dream imagery, and in her wild-eyed fear, she thought she was being grabbed by a Piri or a Trull. So it was that she fought wildly in Karsen's grasp without realizing who it was she was battling. Karsen, for his part, held on as tightly as he could. They were both seated, so he was wrapping his legs around her and keeping his hand firmly over her mouth. He certainly didn't need her shrieking to be heard by the others and force them to come running. Karsen doubted they would appreciate having their sleep interrupted in the middle of the night by a howling Mort.

Then she clamped her teeth down into the fleshy part of his hand and Karsen almost let out a yell that would easily have been as loud as hers. Fortunately he resisted at the last moment and bit his lower lip instead. This transformed his pain-filled shout into an inaudible whimper.

"Jepp!" he whispered fiercely, fighting to keep his voice down. "Wake up!" He shook her, more violently than he would have liked, but it was understandable considering the circumstances. *"Jepp, wake up!"*

She gasped, clutching at him, and her eyes locked upon him, looking like she couldn't believe he was there.

"Not again . . . I can't take them again . . . make them stop . . . they have to stop . . ."

"Jepp, what is—?"

She clutched at his arm and whispered, "They come true. When I have them, they come true. I lied. Oh, gods, make them stop coming, you have to make them stop coming . . ."

"I don't know how! I *can't*—!"

"You can," and her lips were against his, desperate and longing and insistent, and she would not be turned away. The pain he had been in before was forgotten, overwhelmed by the sensations that were flooding through him now. "You can," she said again, moving down and kissing his throat. "I never had them with the Greatness. He made them stop. You can make them stop."

"You mean . . ."

She fumbled at the clasps of her garments and they fell away as she clambered atop Karsen.

"Oh gods," he moaned as her breasts brushed against his lips. He had all manner of things he was going to say to her to make her stop, and he was going to push her away and tell her that this was just wrong, that he'd be taking advantage of her fear and desperation, and certainly there were other ways to handle this.

But somehow he managed not to articulate any of those thoughts. Instead the heat of her washed over him, and the scent of her was everywhere. And the next thing he knew he was in her, and more than just physically. He felt as if he were inside her mind, her heart, her soul as well.

He called out her name as she did his, looking down at him and smiling as her hips and buttocks moved hard against him. Then her head tilted back, her gasping building in intensity and depth, and if Karsen had felt earlier that the world consisted of just him and Jepp, that was as nothing compared to the same sensation now, only more so. There were no other living creatures, there was no one else on the planet, no one else in the universe. Just Karsen Foux and Jepp, and they were the entirety of the universe, their souls encompassing the whole of infinity.

"I am yours," Jepp moaned, "and you are mine, we are bonded . . ."

"Oh gods, yes, we are," cried out Karsen, and then the heat was simply too much for him, he could hold it back no longer, and ceased trying. She cried out his name once more, her legs rhythmically clamping around his upper thighs, and then she fell forward, collapsing upon him, wrung-out as a rag.

"We are bonded," she said again, and then began to sob very softly. "Thank you, thank you . . ."

And this time her words penetrated the haze of pleasure that had descended upon him and enfolded him like a gauze. "What . . . do you mean . . . by that . . . ?" he asked.

"By . . . what?" she managed to say.

"By our being 'bonded.' What does that mean?"

She raised her head slightly, looked down at him, and with a small bit of spittle dangling from one corner of her mouth, said, "I don't know what you're talking about." And with that, to Karsen's bewilderment, she sprawled upon him and fell into a deep and dreamless sleep.

THE DEPTHS

Undulating his great flippers, Gorkon propelled himself to the Depths. All around him was inky blackness, and yet his eyes enabled him to see in the murky surroundings. But even as he moved and saw with efficiency, there was nothing to be done about the pounding of his heart frantically against his chest.

The Depths.

None of his people had ever gone to that section of the waters that was called the Depths. The reason for it was simple: The Merk had forbidden them to do so. Really, that was all it took for the Markene to obey.

Gorkon's concern, however, wasn't rooted simply in the fact that the Merk had declared it off-limits. He was not exactly the greatest proponent of what the Merk had to say about anything, and had come to regard every Merk pronouncement with the utmost suspicion . . . especially recently.

No, the problem was that the Depths had been off-limits for so long that the Markene had spun in their own, addled heads all manner of tales about the Depths and attached them to that forbidden zone to explain *why* it was off-limits.

So although the actions he was taking had been suggested to him by none other than Ruark Sydonis, the ruler of the Merk, nevertheless there was a certain amount of trepidation that was hardwired into him. There was nothing quite as daunting as the imagination of someone who thrust himself into somewhere that he'd been told, since infancy, that he was not supposed to go. Throughout his descent, he imagined great, monstrous creatures lurking in the shadowy depths surrounding him. Twice he actually barked in fright when something brushed against his leathery skin, only to feel the total fool upon discovering that it was just some passing fish that was far more afraid of him than he was of it . . . at least in theory. Then again, there was every chance that he actually was outstripping the fish when it came to stinking fear.

He chided himself even as apprehension worked its way into his bones. *You wish to help your people. You even aspire to . . . what? Lead them? Yet you're so terrified of simple damned water that you can barely see straight. How can you get them to believe in you, to trust you, when you don't even trust yourself?*

He wondered if real leaders ever felt fear. It seemed unlikely. How could anyone grow to a position of leadership if they ever doubted themselves?

Then again, not all leaders were the same, were they? Ruark was a leader. Yet he chose to mask his abilities, allow his wife to take the forefront, while manipulating her without her even knowing it. Was that how leaders were supposed to act? Again, it seemed unlikely. Perhaps some leaders had an undercurrent of naked fear within them and they simply managed to overcome it. Gorkon thought he could be that kind of leader, presuming the opportunity ever presented itself.

He decided he was getting ahead of himself. At the moment, the Markene effectively had no leader. Their perpetual haze allowed little room for such things. They attended the words of Orin Arn Oran because he held control over their precious Klaa, but that didn't make him a leader. Instead he was just a biological extortionist. Leaders had to display principles, leaders had to concern themselves with the public good, leaders . . .

The blackness shifted.

Gorkon froze where he was, convinced that there in the depths, something large had moved. The murkiness that surrounded him was a challenge for even his eyes. He tried to remain absolutely still, but that wasn't possible. If he didn't move, he'd start to drift. Holding his position required movement of his legs or arms. Of the two options open to him, he decided on drifting, since he could always be mistaken for just some large piece of flotsam.

For long minutes, he did nothing. Since he'd been swimming downward, he'd halted in an upside-down position. Now, since he was making no effort to continue, he was slowly starting to turn right side up. The change in perspective didn't make any difference in his ability to make out anything. In all that time, nothing stirred.

I can't do this, I can't do this, he told himself, and he was about to give up and head to the surface when he suddenly spotted what he'd been looking for.

There, not far below him, were the remains of what appeared to be some sort of seagoing vessel. Obviously it had belonged to the Morts. It was said that Mort vessels were far more varied and impressive than anything the Sirene had to offer, but Gorkon found that a dubious boast.

With one final, cautious glance around, he twisted around and dove toward the bottom. He wasn't entirely certain he'd be able to find what he was looking for, but Ruark's description had been detailed, so ideally he could locate it.

Finally he got to the bottom and there studied the wreckage. At first he had no idea what could have caused the boat to wind up at the bottom of the ocean, but soon he discovered a sizable tear toward the back. He was reasonably sure it wasn't something that had occurred after the ship had sunk. This wasn't the result of its lying submerged for so long. Something had ripped a hole in the boat. Perhaps it had hit some sort of obstruction, like the top of an undersea mountain. Or an explosive device perhaps. Humans were alleged to have been quite skilled at creating suchlike.

No. No, that's not it, Gorkon realized as he studied the destruction more closely. There were metal plates in the hull, and there was clearly no explosion or accidental striking of a solid object involved. Something had ripped the plates apart, had literally torn a hole in the ship through brute force.

Had it been the Markene? His was certainly a strong race, and one or perhaps a couple of them could easily inflict this amount of damage. But the timing didn't seem right. Gorkon was hardly a scientist, but he had at least some vague idea, based upon the deterioration, of just how long the wrecked vessel had been down there. If his guess was correct, this damage had occurred long before the arrival of the Third Wave and, to the best of his knowledge, any Markene who might have arrived on the Damned World during the Second Wave were long dead.

Which meant that something else was involved.

But even if he was right . . . even if something had made it happen . . . that had surely been so long ago that it no longer mattered because whatever caused it had to be dead, right?

Right?

He tried to respond "Right!" to himself, but his brain didn't seem interested in accepting that as an answer. With an escalating sense of dread, Gorkon began to work his way along the hull of the sunken ship, and he mentally began to count down. If he reached "one" before having found what he was looking for, he was going to give up. He told himself it wasn't exactly giving up, though. It was simply the gods expressing their will that they didn't want him to find it, and who was he to argue with the gods?

As it turned out, no arguments were necessary. As his personal countdown passed "seven," he suddenly spotted the round shapes of what Ruark had sent him to find. He quickly made his way over there, drawing in close to see the large, round canisters piled up at one end of the ship. There were quite a few of them. Ruark had told him he would only need two, which was a relief to Gorkon because he didn't think he could conceivably carry any more.

He studied the canisters for a moment, looking at the words of Mort writing upon them. Naturally he could not read them, but some of the shapes were recognizable. There was a circle, and next to it was a single straight, vertical line of the same height, and next to that was another vertical line with a smaller, horizontal line at its base. Unless, of course, the canister was upside down, in which case it was all backward. But forward, backward, it made no difference to Gorkon. He was just going to do what he needed to do, and hope that he didn't get himself into even further trouble in the process . . .

Suddenly the darkness shifted once more, but there was more this time. There was a distinct movement, as if something of vast size and weight was displacing massive amounts of water. It was coming from above, large waves of pressure shoving down upon him. Nor was it just movement. There was some sort of soft, steady noise, like a humming.

Almost terrified to do so, Gorkon forced himself to look up. And when he did, he froze once more. This time, however, there was nothing voluntary about it. At that moment if Gorkon had wanted, with all his heart, to move so much as a fraction of an inch, he would not have been able to do so.

It was massive. Massive beyond belief. Massive beyond imagination. It cruised past above him, an endless shadow, and gods knew it was not waels because Gorkon knew what a wael was, he'd even seen waels from time to time. They were impressive enough beasts and could grow to considerable lengths.

But this . . . this was like nothing else. This was unsurpassed.

He couldn't make out any details. It was just so huge that there was room for nothing else in the field of his vision. In looking up, all he saw was blackness that was moving.

It passed with leisurely confidence as Gorkon hid in the shadows. As it slowed, Gorkon trembled. He felt something crawling ever so gently around in his mind. It was like tentacles that had no substance, and yet did, probing about, and for an instant there was some sort of connection that he couldn't begin to understand.

Was it trying to communicate with him? Or merely determine if he was there so that it could eat him? With great determination, Gorkon shut down his mind, shunning the contact.

Then, like morning mist, it evaporated, leaving no trace, and the great creature fell back into its leisurely forward movement. And finally, finally, it was gone.

Still Gorkon didn't budge.

He stayed rooted in his place for some time. Then he suddenly grabbed up two of the canisters and, with one under each arm, he leaped toward the surface.

He swam as fast as his legs would take him. He felt slow and leaden while clutching the metal barrels. Funny how it required an attempt at high speed to make one feel slow.

The entire swim upward, he was bracing himself, convinced that sooner or later that creature was going to come cruising in out of nowhere and devour him in one bite. Certainly based on the creature's size, there was no reason to think he couldn't do it.

But there was no attack from the water, unless one counted a jellyfish that stung him as he swam past. (He crushed the jellyfish with one hand. The other jellyfish in the area, seeing the level of the retaliation, promptly decided it was a good chance to be elsewhere.)

"I'm sorry," he whispered, even though there was no one around. He was speaking instead to his people, or at least the spirit of his people. "I'm sorry . . . that I must do this. Hopefully they will forgive me . . . and you will as well."

He ascended slowly, as Ruark Sydonis had warned him to do. Considering his biology, there was every chance that Gorkon would suffer no ill effects from a rapid rise from the depths. Considering his nervousness over a possible return of the giant whatever-it-was that had apparently overlooked him earlier, it was all he could do to restrain himself, since his sense of self-preservation was urging him to hurry the hell up. But with impressive control he managed to maintain a slow and steady upward course until finally he broke the surface of the water. Although he was just as comfortable breathing water, simple air had never tasted quite as delicious to him as it did right now.

The moon hung high above him in the night sky as he paddled slowly toward the Resting Point. There he waited, hanging just below the surface. He was ravenous from all his exertion. What he really would have liked to do was dump the canisters on the Resting Point and head out to the fishing grounds so that he could hunt himself up some sustenance. But he had promised Ruark Sydonis that he would come straight there and wait for him once he returned. Sydonis had warned him to wait until night so that he could operate under the shroud of darkness. Gorkon didn't understand the necessity of it. "Who will be watching me? Who will care?" he had inquired. Ruark had merely replied darkly, "You never know."

He wondered how Ruark Sydonis would know he was there, but decided he shouldn't worry about it. If Ruark was anything, it was resourceful.

It was not all that long before his confidence in Ruark Sydonis was validated. He heard a gentle lapping of water, and there, approaching in slow but steady fashion, was Ruark. He was steering his one-man boat, but Gorkon could see from where he was that there was some sort of towing hookup on the back. Clearly Ruark had shown up prepared for Gorkon's little mission to be a success.

"Do you have them?" he called softly to Gorkon as he drew nearer, and then seemed to correct his own thinking. "Why ask? Of course you have them. If you did not have them, you would not have yet returned, would you."

"No, I wouldn't," Gorkon agreed. "But I still do not know what is in these containers."

"Something that will solve your problems. The humans called it," and he paused, wanting to get the word correct. "Url."

"Url." Gorkon studied the canisters dubiously. "What did the url do?"

"Ah. Funny you should ask." He reached around behind his seat and drew out a small box. "I brought this from the Venets museum. I believe you'll find it educational."

He opened the lid and Gorkon eased over through the water to get a better look. When he did, he gasped, although it was as much in lack of comprehension as it was in horror.

There was some sort of small aquatic animal within, but it was long dead. Its remains had been treated in some manner so that it maintained the shape and look from back when it was alive. But there was still something horribly wrong with it. There were a few tufts of its fur still visible to indicate that it had once been gray, but it was covered with what appeared to be some sort of thick, black coating. Gorkon extended a webbed finger tentatively and looked nervously at Ruark.

"You can touch it," Ruark assured him. "It can't hurt you . . . anymore."

He did so and found that the blackness was hard and smooth to the touch. "This is . . . url?"

"Yes," said Ruark.

"Was this url responsible for the creature's death?"

"I believe so." Ruark examined the creature sadly, shaking his head and sighing heavily. "To think that the Morts would have done this to a helpless creature, one that was sharing their world. Mark my words, Gorkon, we took his world away from them not one moment too soon."

"You're absolutely right. Did they create this url just to kill other living beings?"

"I'm not entirely sure," Ruark admitted "It may have had other uses."

Gorkon thought about it a moment, and then decided, "It doesn't matter. Even if it had a use that was beneficial, that pales in comparison to the destruction of which it was capable. I take it that animal you're holding was not the only one to suffer from url?"

"Definitely not," said Ruark. "The museum was left over from the Morts, and this pathetic thing was part of an entire display. It showed dozens, perhaps hundreds of them, in pictures, washed up on a shore."

"They were boasting about their conquest of these animals?" Gorkon was horrified.

"Apparently so."

"Monsters," Gorkon said fiercely.

"They come in all shapes and sizes," Ruark said, commiserating with the young Markene. "Help me load this on."

He did so, making sure that the device Ruark had attached to his boat was secured to the canisters. There were flotation devices attached as well so that the canisters remained buoyant rather than threatening to break loose and sink back to the bottom of the ocean. Considering that prompted Gorkon to inquire about something that was puzzling him.

"How did you know?" he asked as he secured the last fastenings.

"Hmm? Know what?" asked Ruark.

"How did you know that the url was down there at all? It was below depths that a Merk could survive, wasn't it?"

"Yes, it was."

"So you couldn't have seen it yourself."

"No," Ruark agreed. "I could not have."

"Then how?"

Ruark smiled. It seemed a benign smile, but Gorkon couldn't be sure how much of a shark was hiding behind it. "I have friends."

"Friends? What kind of friends?"

"Friends," Ruark said, "in low places."

Gorkon had no idea what Ruark as talking about, and then the realization hit him. "That . . . thing . . . ? That huge . . . that . . . ?"

Slowly Ruark nodded approvingly. "Not much slips past you, does it, Gorkon."

And with that he paddled off into the night, leaving a thoughtful and utterly confused Gorkon in his wake.

SUBTERROR

"You sent for me, Mistress?"

Sunara Redeye rose lazily from her bed, not fully registering whose voice was addressing her. When she saw who it was, she came to instant wakefulness and clapped her hands together in delight—not exactly the most dignified reaction, she supposed, but an honest one.

"Yes, my dear! Yes, yes." She crossed the room to Merrih, her feet barely touching the floor as she went. Extending her hands, she cooed, "Come, let me look at you! My, aren't you looking exceptional."

And she was. Merrih had developed a lovely pallor, and her single eye was receding slightly into her head where it hadn't before. She was far thinner than when she'd first arrived, but did not look at all sickly. In fact, she appeared healthier, moving with a newfound confidence and grace that belied her giant form. "I knew it. I knew from the moment you came here that you were going to be special."

"Special, Mistress?" Merrih asked. She didn't appear to have any idea what Sunara was referring to.

"When we've captured Ocular before . . . drank from them . . . we never did so with intent to kill them. You must understand that. Do you believe me, Merrih?"

"Of course, Mistress."

Sunara ran her fingers through Merrih's tangle of hair. Merrih gasped in pain as Sunara's fingers became tangled in it. "We can't have this," Sunara said disapprovingly. "It was so pretty when you came down here. We must make you perfect."

"Yes, Mistress."

Moments later, Merrih was seated as Sunara used a basin to wash Merrih's hair clean and then applied oils to keep it smooth. As she did so she continued to speak. "Anyway . . . we never intended to kill them. What would be the point of that? To keep an Ocular alive means that we can continue to feed. And isn't that desirable?"

"Of course it is, Mistress," said Merrih. Her voice sounded very distant, even dazed, in a singsong manner that was not at all comparable to the strength and firmness in her tone when she had first arrived.

"Furthermore, just as we feed from a host, the host—if he or she remains alive long enough—learns to feed from us. Ours is not a parasitic relationship, as the upper world would have all believe. We are symbiotic. We bring as much as we take. Is that not so?"

"Yes, Mistress."

"You have been feeding, yes?"

"Yes, Mistress." Merrih absently ran her tongue along the underside of her teeth. "It has been . . . revelatory."

"Of course it has," said Sunara confidently, combing through the last tangles in Merrih's hair. "Would that others in your race could see that. But," she said with a heavy sigh, "that has not been the case. More often than not, they simply . . . oh, what's the best way to put it . . . ?"

"Die?"

"Well, yes, that, but I think 'gave up' is the preferable view," Sunara told her. "Their spirits were not strong enough for them to open their minds to new choices, new lifestyles. But you have a strong spirit, Merrih. The strongest I've ever encountered from an outsider."

"Thank you, Mistress. You are very beautiful."

"Yes, I know. And you are becoming so, especially as you appreciate the Piri philosophy of sharing all things: spirit, body, blood. We have no secrets from each other, for all that any of us has is had by all of us. True?"

"True, Mistress."

Satisfied that she'd untangled Merrih's hair, Sunara began to braid it with confident expertise. "You have grown close to Clarinda, have you not?"

"Yes, Mistress. Very close."

"She tells you secrets?"

Merrih hesitated. "I . . . suppose."

"I would like you," she said, "to tell me those secrets. For, as I just said, no Piri have secrets from each other."

"I should tell you those things which she tells me in confidence?"

"Of course. After all, not only am I Mistress, I am also her mother."

Merrih fell silent.

"Merrih . . . ?" she prodded.

"I . . . do not know, Mistress."

"Do not know what?" Her deft fingers continued to braid Merrih's hair. "What is there not to know?"

"I just . . . I value Clarinda's friendship, Mistress, and I do not know how she would react if I were to relate to you that which she tells me."

"Oh," Sunara scoffed, "that is no great problem. Simply do not tell her that you've told me. Why upset her?"

"But if that's the case, Mistress, then I would be keeping secrets from her, and your entire reason for my telling you is that secrets should not be kept. How would I justify one with the other?"

That caused Sunara's hands to stop their motion.

"Mistress? Did I . . . offend you?"

"No," laughed Sunara. "Not at all. That would be a contradiction, wouldn't it? My oh my, yes, it appears you have me there."

"I did not mean to upset you, Mistress."

"I assure you, you have not. That's what I value about you, Merrih. Because *you* think, you make *me* think."

"Is that a good thing?"

"Thinking is always good." She resumed the braiding, working her way toward the bottom of Merrih's long hair. "You have to understand, Merrih, I don't seek to know this merely out of some sense of voyeurism. The truth is, I'm concerned about Clarinda."

"Concerned, Mistress?"

"Yes," she said, and although Merrih could not see it, her mouth was drawn in a taut, grim manner, even as her voice continued light and casual. "She is not around for lengthy periods of time. She sneaks away. Some of my people have tried to trail her, but she is far too clever, too elusive. That is indeed my daughter: If she does not desire to be followed, one would have an easier time plucking a shadow off a cave wall. I do not know what she is getting herself into, Merrih, and it worries me. You see that, don't you?"

"Yes, of course I do, Mistress. If I were blind, I could see it."

"Well, then, we're at something of an impasse, aren't we?" She said it with the air of someone who carried upon her all the world's strife and a bleak sense that she was helpless to resolve any of it. "You wish to protect any confidences she might bestow upon you . . . while, at the same time, you are bound to serve my interests since I am your Mistress. Can you think of any way around this dilemma?"

Merrih frowned, considering the situation. Sunara finished braiding her hair and began to tie small bits of sparkling twine into it, just to add a bit of festivity to it.

"I suppose . . ." she began finally.

"Yes?"

"I suppose I could watch for certain things and tell you about those. It's only the things that Clarinda actually *says* that fall under the arena of confidences. But if I happen to notice something and she is unaware of it . . . why, then, I suppose I wouldn't be betraying any—"

"Yes! Excellent," said Sunara, who actually did not consider it excellent at all, but was willing to take what she could to start out. "That would be most helpful. And I can count on you, Merrih?"

Merrih turned and looked over her shoulder at Sunara. "For anything, Mistress."

"I shall reward you, you know. For any information you can provide me that will help keep my daughter safe."

"I have no need of reward, Mistress. Being with you, helping the Piri . . . these are reward enough."

"That may be. But still . . ."

And as Merrih watched, Sunara Redeye extended her arm and drew a long fingernail across her outstretched wrist. A thin line of blood welled up, and she extended it toward Merrih. Merrih looked amazed. "Are you . . . serious, Mistress?"

"Very much so."

"I . . . the honor . . . I'm . . ."

"Shhhh," Sunara softly whispered to her as if settling an infant to sleep. "Do not question. Don't offer thanks. Merely take that which is offered to you, freely and of your own will."

Merrih licked her lips at the glistening blood, and then she seized upon the arm. At first she licked it lightly, to get the taste of it. Sunara smiled and ran a hand along Merrih's long braid. And then, with gusto, she began to drink deeply and heartily. Sunara tilted her head back, basking in the sensation, glowing with joy, the sucking sounds that Merrih made easing her into a blissful state.

Sunara slid to the floor, keeping her arm upraised so that Merrih could continue to drink it. Her face was near Merrih's bare thigh, and she sank her teeth into it. Merrih gasped at the sudden pain, but that didn't shake her from Sunara's arm, while Sunara proceeded to taste the nectar of Merrih's blood, drawing it from her leg.

"Exquisite," moaned Sunara between bites.

ii.

When it was done, and Sunara lay upon her bed in a blissful stupor, Merrih walked out of the chamber of the Mistress, leaned against a wall with her mind whirling, tried to comprehend what had just happened and—once she did—ran and ran until she could find some private place to cough up Sunara's blood. It tasted bitter and metallic, and Merrih—mind and body torn—sank to her knees and sobbed.

Her heart pounded furiously, and she thought of Clarinda. She thought of the things that she had not said to Sunara. She thought of Clarinda's persistent desperation and fear at turning into her mother. When they spoke of the truth between them, it was in hushed whispers and with many fears that they would be overheard and observed.

And she thought of the fact that, if Clarinda became sufficiently frightened over the prospect of being mutilated . . . then Merrih might be able to convince her to do what needed to be done . . .

. . . to kill Sunara Redeye and, with any luck, escape in the confusion.

Nurse your hatred. Don't forget your hatred. Your hatred, and Clarinda's fear, will be your salvation.

She kept thinking that as she sensed the tendrils of Sunara's will insinuating itself into her thoughts, and she prayed to the gods that had abandoned her that—if she did manage to escape—there was something of her left that was recognizable.

THE UNDERGROUND

i.

The Bottom Feeders stood before the looming cave entrance, studying it with trepidation. Zerena looked around at her clan, saw the looks of concern on their respective faces, and then said, "All right. We've seen it. We're here. Now who's for getting the hell out of here before it's too late?"

The jumpcar was parked not far away, hidden in the shadows and rocky outcroppings at the base of a nearby hill.

In preparing for what she still considered to be a suicidal fool's errand, Zerena had strapped a sword around her hip. Karsen had the war hammer attached to his back, and Mingo was softly tapping into his open palm an impressive club with spikes rimming the top. A short distance away, once again seemingly in a world of his own, Rafe Kestor was whipping his sword through the air and making loud noises of "Ha!" and "Have at you!"

Only two remained unarmed. One was Jepp, who was watching the energetic Kestor with a mixture of amusement and awe. The other, of course, was Gant, who at that moment was nothing save a percolating pile of goo upon the floor. Jepp, however, was holding a glowstick. She was studying the green glowing device with great curiosity, apparently never having seen one before.

"Well?" demanded Zerena when no one responded immediately. "There's still time to turn back."

"And do what?" asked Karsen. "Spend the next twenty, thirty sun cycles watching our backs for fear that the Ocular will be after us?"

"At least we'll have twenty, thirty cycles," Zerena said. "Whereas if we embark on this insanity, the odds are very much against that."

"We said we would undertake this endeavor," said Mingo. "I do not see how we can turn away from it now."

"It's easily done," Zerena told him. "We place one foot in front of the other—"

Karsen's impatience was very noticeable. "Mother," he said, trying to overcome the frustration he clearly had in dealing with her. "We're going with or without you."

"Hah!" she snorted. "Without me, you wouldn't last," and she snapped her fingers in the air once, "that long."

"That is not true!" Jepp protested before he could manage to get a word out. "He would last beyond . . . that," and she snapped her finger in response to a bemused Zerena. "Why, he might even last *two* of these," and she snapped her fingers twice more.

"Thank you for the vote of confidence, Jepp," Karsen said, gently pulling her back. "All right, so . . . Jepp and I are going in. You others with us?"

There were mute nods from all concerned, and Zerena let out an annoyed sigh, the air of someone who knew beyond question that she was right, but had to suffer the folly of others. "So be it," she said in exasperation. "So . . . Gant. You led us here. You said you knew the ins and outs of the Trull Underground."

"Yes" was all Gant said in his heavy, warbling voice.

"Then lead the way."

"Do we have any sort of plan?" asked Mingo. His club was sounding a bit louder as he continued to *thwap* it against his palm.

Gant's body morphed upward into as close to a standard bipedal form as it was capable of achieving. "We must . . . look around," he said.

"That's *it*?" said Karsen. "That's the cunning plan?"

"I know . . . my way around," Gant said in his labored way. "This entrance . . . little used. Stick to . . . forgotten tunnels . . . get close in . . . then we steal . . . the Orb . . ."

"Perhaps we should just send Gant in, if he's so powerfully certain that this is going to work," Zerena said.

But Karsen shook his head. "If he doesn't come back, how long do we wait? And when we've waited long enough, what then? We go in after him, with no clue where he is and no idea ourselves how to get around in there? Or we abandon him? Neither option seems a particularly good one, does it."

"Karsen's right," agreed Mingo. "Our best chance is to stay together as a group."

"Excellent idea. That way we can all die together and save time," said Zerena.

She didn't even realize that Jepp was standing practically at her shoulder until the human said, very softly but with conviction, "We're not going to die."

"You know that for a fact, do you?"

"Mother," Karsen began to say, "Leave her b—"

Jepp put up a hand, quieting him. "It's all right, Karsen. I can answer her. Yes, Zerena, I know that for a fact. I know we'll succeed."

There was something in Jepp's tone, her conviction and certainty, that piqued Zerena's curiosity. "How do you?"

"Because . . . I know."

Zerena couldn't hide her disappointment. "That's it? That's all? You know because you know? That's ridiculous!"

"Why? It's called 'faith.' You swear to gods, yet you haven't seen them. Isn't that faith?"

"Why do you assume we haven't seen them?" Zerena was astonished. "Of course we've seen them. Back in the Elserealms, they were seen all the time . . . at least, so I'm told."

Rafe Kestor whipped his sword through the air, nearly decapitating Karsen, who barely dodged. "Enemies to the right and left of us!" he cried out. "And I, armed with nothing but a length of rope and three pieces of ripe fruit!"

"Well said, Rafe," Mingo deadpanned.

"Can we . . . go now?" asked Gant, who had not moved away from the entrance during the entire discussion.

"Yes, we can," Karsen said, looking challengingly at his mother. "In the name of honor . . . in the name of aspiring to something greater than ourselves . . . let's go."

With that, Gant oozed down into the entrance. Karsen promptly followed him with Jepp directly behind him. Mingo indicated to Rafe Kestor that he should precede him, obviously because he didn't want the addled Mandraque to be behind him and pose a threat.

Zerena rested her hand on the pommel of her sword and muttered, "The idiot things we do to keep our children happy," and descended into darkness behind them.

ii.

Karsen felt as if he were being buried alive.

He had never been underground before. Never had any reason to. He had no dealings with Trulls, and thank the gods had never been captured by Piri. So making his way through caves was a new experience for him, and he couldn't say that he was enjoying it. For all this big talk about aspiring to greatness and acting in an honorable way, there was enough of his mother in him that Karsen wanted to turn around and get the hell out of there.

Every time that thought crossed his mind, however, there would be Jepp, smiling at him approvingly. Every time he looked at her, he remembered her and her heat, and the softness of her and the smell of her, and he had to admit he would have been amazed if human males had ever let their females do anything other than gratify the males. Because if Jepp was any indicator, it was something that human females were exceptionally gifted at.

So he tried his best not to feel as if the cave walls were weighing in on him. Instead he focused all his attention on the form of Gant, who seemed to be moving with a great deal of confidence. Then again, Karsen might just have been reading something into Gant's movement, because really, all Gant was doing was oozing. *Maybe he oozes confidence,* Karsen thought.

He had expected that it would be dank and drippy beneath the ground, but that did not appear to be the case. The path they were following seemed to be angling down at a pretty fair rate of descent, and the air actually felt warm. "Are we heading toward some sort of heat source?" Karsen asked.

"The world . . . is a heat source," Gant replied.

The group was bathed in pale green from Jepp's glowstick. But there was additional lighting as well, from lanterns that dotted their trail. Karsen wondered if this was a natural cave that the Trulls had developed, or if they'd carved it out themselves.

Suddenly Gant stopped, and the others did as well. The path forked in front of them.

"In case anyone is about to say, 'Let's split up,' you can just forget it," Zerena announced.

"This way," said Gant, and he moved down the corridor on the left. Karsen turned, and followed him, as did the others.

Several more times along the way they came upon split-offs, and each time Gant chose the left path. If he was guessing, at least he was doing it consistently.

There was no small talk among the Bottom Feeders. Everyone seemed focused on their endeavor. Karsen lost track of how long they'd been below. Subjectively it seemed a very long time, but he had a feeling that it hadn't been that long at all.

Then Gant stopped moving.

Karsen didn't realize it immediately. Instead he almost stepped right into the gelatinous Bottom Feeder's mass, but pulled back his foot at the last moment. "Gant? What's wrong?" he asked.

"Not used . . . to moving this much," Gant said in his warbling voice. "Need . . . to rest . . . a little."

"What's wrong?" Zerena called from behind.

"Gant. He needs to rest."

"So we'll rest," Zerena said indifferently. "Whether we run headlong to our dooms or take a break along the way, the result is all the same, isn't it?"

Karsen wanted to lay into his mother for her incessant defeatist talk, but restrained himself. Instead he said, "I'm going to scout a little ways ahead."

"I'll come with you," said Jepp.

"I'll be fine on my own."

"I'll come with you," she repeated.

He shrugged and headed off, Jepp trailing behind him.

As they made their way, Jepp slipped her hand into his and squeezed it tightly. "You were wonderful the other night," she said.

Karsen felt a tingling in his face as he flushed from embarrassment. "I . . . You were upset. I shouldn't have taken advantage of you that way. But if it rids you of the dreams that torture you so . . ."

"It should," said Jepp. "Of course . . . anything is possible, I suppose. But even if it doesn't for some reason . . . I don't see how providing comfort and warmth could possibly be seen as 'taking advantage.'" She frowned. "You're not . . . sorry, I hope. I mean, do you regret . . . ?"

"Oh, no," he said with certainty. "Not at all. It was . . ."

"It was what?" She seemed eager to hear his feelings on it.

He stopped walking and turned to her, gently brushing a strand of hair away from her face. "It was like . . . while I was in you, you were in me. Like there wasn't a beginning or an end to us."

She smiled shyly. "That's exactly how I felt, too. It was a good thing, wasn't it?"

"Yes. A very good thing. It—"

That was when he heard and felt a distant rumbling. It seemed to be coming from ahead of them. "What . . . *is* that?" he wondered.

"A quake?" she asked nervously.

Karsen shook his head. "No, no . . . I don't think so. Come on." He started forward and she fell into step behind him.

The tunnel they were following curved around and then opened up a short distance ahead. There, Karsen saw what appeared to be an intersection, but it was very different from the split-offs they had encountered earlier.

First of all, this new tunnel cut directly across their path in perpendicular fashion. And second, whereas the paths they had followed thus far had been rough-hewn, Karsen could see that this new tunnel was absolutely, perfectly smooth, all the way around.

Except for the floor. There were twin indentations on the floor, long lines, perfectly parallel to each other, running the length of the tunnel in both directions as far as the eye could see. Each of the indentations was about as wide as Karsen's hand. He couldn't imagine what they were for.

He stepped forward into the intersection, studying the walls and floor. His first impression had been correct. Not only was it smooth, but it was precisely circular. "The Trulls took a lot of care with this one," he said. "I wonder why?"

Jepp was standing just beyond the threshold of the new tunnel, and she was glancing around nervously. "That rumbling hasn't stopped."

"So I've noticed."

"I think it's getting closer."

Karsen was kneeling, running his hands over the tunnel floor. "I think you're right," he said. "I just wish I could tell which direction it's coming fr—"

"*Karsen! Move!*"

Reacting entirely on instinct thanks to Jepp's outcry, Karsen vaulted toward her, his powerful legs easily carrying him the distance in under a second.

As it happened, that was practically all the time he had, for the instant he was clear of the tunnel, something large and black blasted past them, the rumbling so loud as to be almost deafening. Karsen had barely blinked and the thing was already gone, spiraling away down the tunnel.

Jepp was holding him tightly, her eyes wide with shock. "What *was* that thing?"

"I don't know," said Karsen. "But thanks for getting me out of there. If that thing had hit me . . ."

He heard rumbling once again, and Jepp pulled at his arm. "Come . . . let's go . . ."

"Yes, by all means."

They retreated to where the rest of the group was waiting, and told them what they'd seen.

"That was . . . a Truller," Gant said immediately.

"A what?"

"A Truller," Mingo spoke up. "It's a Trull conveyance. It moves through a network of specially crafted tunnels, on tracks carved right into the rock. Propelled through concentrated bursts of air or some such. Once one of those things starts moving, it can go at amazing speeds."

"So I've noticed. If it weren't for Jepp, I'd be in several pieces right now."

"If it weren't for Jepp," Zerena noted, "we wouldn't be here in the first place."

"Mother—"

"*What are you doing here!*"

As one, their heads whipped around and standing there behind them was a Trull.

Karsen gasped. He'd never seen one before. The Trull was a little over half Karsen's size in terms of height, but he was remarkably wide, and Karsen was sure that all of it was solid muscle. He was holding an ax so massive, Karsen was sure he would have had trouble picking it up. But the Trull was holding it with no problem in a most threatening manner.

"*No one intrudes in the Underground of the Trulls,*" he continued, bellowing with such force that his voice bounced off the walls in deafening fashion. "You will be ripped to shreds for this, and your remains dumped into the molten core of the Damned World!"

Not sounding the least perturbed, Mingo inquired, "Do you think you could possibly keep your voice down? Believe it or not, we were trying for stealth."

"*Intruders!*" the Trull shouted even louder in response as he advanced, swinging his ax. The problem for the Bottom Feeders was that the tunnel where they were was particularly narrow, and none of them had a lot of room to wield their weapons. The far shorter Trull, on the other hand, had plenty of room to maneuver, and he let out a war cry as he attacked.

He did not get very far, for Gant surged forward, literally vaulting over Mingo's head, and he completely enveloped the Trull. The Trull was halted immediately, and he tried to swing his ax and cut through the viscous mass that had covered him. But he could no more deter the amorphous Gant than he could keep back the ocean tide by chopping at waves.

The Trull reflexively opened his mouth to let out a cry of protest, and instantly Gant began to seep in. The Trull's eyes widened in alarm. However the most he could offer was a smothered burble of protest as Gant's entire mass inserted itself down the Trull's throat. "Gant, what are you doing?" Zerena shouted, but Gant made no response. Instead, seconds later, Gant had disappeared, the entirety of him having flowed into the Trull's mouth.

The Trull staggered, dropping his ax, his opponents apparently forgotten. Instead he was clutching at his throat, trying to cough up what had gone in there. He reeled and made deep hacking noises, but was unsuccessful.

The rest of the Bottom Feeders waited, poised, their weapons at the ready, as the Trull—who had fallen to his knees—slowly got to his feet. He looked at the thick fingers on his hand, then thumped his hand on his chest, apparently just to hear the sound his hand made. "All right," he said sounding satisfied. "This works."

Zerena took a step forward, cocking her head in confusion. "Gant?"

"Yes, it's me," he said, and although the general inflections sounded like him, he was speaking with a swiftness and precision that hadn't been available to him earlier. "I think we have to keep moving, Zerena."

She didn't appear to have heard him. "What did you do?" she demanded. "How long have you been able to do this?"

"I didn't know for sure I could until just now," Gant admitted. His voice sounded deep and gravelly. He tapped the side of his head. "I can feel the Trull rooting around in here, but don't worry. I've got him under control for the moment. But I think that—"

That was the moment that they heard shouting and the sounds of running feet from behind them, the way they'd come. "This way!" one was shouting and "Intruders!" called out another.

"Let them come!" bellowed Rafe Kestor, swinging his sword and clanging it against solid rock. "I defy them!"

"Rafe, please!"

He ignored Zerena, and swung his sword in the other direction, narrowly missing Jepp. "Let them come, I say! Or I shall go to them, and they shall swim in rivers of their own blood!"

And, thinking fast, Karsen shouted "They're that way!" and pointed at the path ahead of them, rather than behind them from where the shouts were originating.

Unaware of the fact that the noises of pursuit were coming from the opposite direction, Rafe Kestor shouted "Have at you, vile opponents!" and charged in the direction that Karsen had just indicated.

The rest of the Bottom Feeders immediately followed, moving as quickly as they could. Karsen's heart was racing. He had no idea of the size of the force pursuing them. All he knew for certain was that never in his life had he felt as alive as he did right then.

"Get him out of there!" Gant-as-Trull suddenly shouted.

Instantly Karsen saw what he was referring to. Rafe Kestor, sprinting on ahead, had taken a stand squarely in the middle of the tunnel through which the Trullers barreled at high speed. He was waving his sword, and shouting, "Come! Face me if you have the nerve!" To make matters worse, he heard a distant rumbling that indicated to him a Truller was on its way. The odds that it would stop before plowing through Rafe Kestor were nonexistent.

Mingo led the charge. Moving faster than Karsen had ever seen him go, the Minosaur shoved past the rest of the Bottom Feeders who were in his way and charged into the tunnel. He grabbed Rafe Kestor by the arm, and it was obvious to Karsen from both the increasing rumbling sound and the expression on Mingo's face that the Truller was nearly upon them.

There was no time for delicacy. Mingo twisted, yanked Rafe Kestor completely off his feet, and sent him tumbling out of the tunnel into the cross corridor, safe from harm. Then, to Karsen's shock, instead of trying to get out of the way, Mingo leaped forward, so high that his back was almost scraping against the ceiling.

The next thing Karsen knew, the Truller hurtled past. Then there came a horrifying screeching, the sound of metal on rock, perhaps, and then a crash. "Mingo!" he shouted, pounding toward the tunnel, Zerena right behind him.

Heedless of his own safety, Karsen ran out into the smooth Truller tunnel, looked in the direction that the Truller had gone, and fully expected to see the worst. Instead what he saw stunned him.

The Truller had come to a halt. The former passengers were lying in various places against the cave wall, mostly looking either stunned or unconscious. They'd been wearing protective headgear, which had probably been the only thing that prevented them from having their skulls crushed. The Truller, the vehicle itself, was bucking furiously, like a restrained animal, as if the thing had a life of its own. Mingo was gripping the back of the conveyance grunting with the effort of restraining the Truller. "Get in," he grunted. "It's on some sort of auto mechanism. It wants to keep moving."

"Get in?" Zerena said doubtfully. "I don't know if that's—"

The shadows of the Trulls in pursuit suddenly made themselves evident at the far end of the tunnel behind them. *"There they are!"* one shouted, and they charged with an earsplitting roar of challenge.

Offering no further words of protest, Zerena and the others piled in as fast as they could. There were no seats within the Truller. It was simply shaped like a large box, and presumably riders just gripped the sides for dear life. How one steered it or predetermined its destination, Karsen couldn't even begin to guess. The only thing he knew for sure was that Mingo had jumped over it when it had approached him and then, moving faster than Karsen would have thought possible, grabbed the back of it in passing, causing it to screech to a halt.

"Hurry!" Mingo called through gritted teeth.

"Gant, help me!" ordered Karsen, who was already inside. He grabbed Mingo's right wrist. "Get his other hand! Otherwise when he lets go, he'll be left behind!"

"Oh right, can't have that. Wouldn't want to miss the fun," Mingo grunted.

Gant did as Karsen instructed, gripping Mingo's left wrist. "We've got you, Mingo! Let it go!"

Mingo did so, relaxing the tension in his legs. Instantly, with Mingo no longer applying opposite force to it, the Truller leaped forward liked an uncaged wild beast. Mingo was yanked forward and, moments later, Gant and Karsen had helped haul him in. He tumbled into the Truller along with the others.

Karsen had a brief glimpse of a mass of Trulls charging into the cave behind them, several of them shaking their weapons angrily. Then they were gone as the Truller sped through the tunnel at teeth-rattling speed.

"You said this area was mostly deserted!" shouted Zerena at Gant, trying to make her voice heard over the rushing of the air. "You said no Trulls ever came out this way and we could skulk about unseen and undetected!"

"So things have changed!" Gant shot back. "I can't be expected to keep up with everything!"

"Forget that!" said Karsen. "The important thing is, where are we going now?"

"You're right," Gant said. "That is the most important thing!"

"Well?" Karsen prompted when Gant didn't continue the thought beyond that. "Where *are* we going?"

"Haven't the slightest idea," said Gant. Then he smiled mischievously, a smirk that looked very much out of place on the grim features of the Trull. "But at least we're getting there at a rapid pace."

"Wonderful," muttered Karsen as the Truller sped away, taking them deeper and deeper into the depths of the Trull world.

THE COUNTRY OF FEEND

i.

By the time Nagel, king of the Ocular, had repeated for the third time to Phemus exactly what he had done, he was beginning to get just the least bit annoyed.

Phemus had looked surprised when he strode into Nagel's study and saw him going over various documents. He had recovered quickly and greeted his ruler cordially, expressing surprise to that the king had departed without giving the slightest hint as to where he was off to. "Gone to seek an alliance with the Mandraques?" he said with smug self-assurance, certain he already knew the answer. His eyes widened as Nagel informed him he had conscripted a group of Bottom Feeders to obtain the Orb of the Trinity to wipe out the Piri once and for all. Nagel spoke with a sort of jaunty defiance, as if he were so proud of his actions that he needed to throw them in Phemus's face in order to get a reaction from him.

As Phemus stood speechless, Nagel repeated it twice more as if Phemus was so addled that he might not have heard. Every time Nagel did so, Phemus went redder and redder in the face.

Nor did the three times seem sufficient, as Phemus took several steps toward Nagel, and then several back as if he were dancing, and repeated, "*What* did you do?"

"I am reasonably certain, honored Phemus, that you've genuinely heard me one of the previous times," Nagel said, his eye unblinking. "If I must reiterate it yet again, you may want to give some serious thought to having your hearing checked."

"But I told you to—"

Instantly Phemus shut his mouth, but it was too late as Nagel fixed a deadly glare upon him. Slowly he closed the text he'd been perusing and stood, looming over the smaller Phemus.

"My king, I did not mean—"

"You *told* me!" he thundered. "And who are you to tell me, the King of the Blind, what to do!"

Phemus tried to rally. "I am your senior advisor," he said, "and your father trusted my advice!"

"Yes. He did," said Nagel in a low, angry voice. "And he's dead now. So a lot of good your advice did him, eh?" Nagel continued to glare at him. "It was a fool's errand. And I am no fool, even though you apparently consider me one."

"I swear by all the gods, my king, I do not," Phemus managed to say, his voice hoarse. "And if you wish to disregard my advice . . . that is your privilege . . ."

"How generous of you."

"But . . . *Bottom Feeders,* my king?" Phemus shook his head, unable to comprehend it. "You assign a group of Bottom Feeders to penetrate the lair of the Trulls and return you a device to dispatch the Piri? Certainly you can see how someone might consider such a decision to be . . . dubious. If I may ask, what Bottom Feeders did you conscript into this endeavor?"

"Zerena Foux and her clan."

"Zerena Foux," echoed Phemus. "Well . . . she is resourceful, I'll credit her that. Still, my king, you must realize the likelihood that they will not succeed."

"Then it is their failure, Phemus, and not ours. As for your skill as an advisor, I might say that—particularly in regards to the Mandraques—the advice of Zerena Foux and her family rang truer to me than your own words. Even the human who accompanied them made more sense—"

"A Mort!" Phemus could not have sounded more shocked. "You take the counsel of a Mort over mine!"

"I take my own counsel over yours, honored Phemus," said Nagel.

Phemus, squaring his shoulders, looked as if he were trying to present as dignified a front as he possibly could. "If I may say so, my king, it seems to me that perhaps I should consider tendering my resignation from your service. I mean, if you are taking the advice of Bottom Feeders and Morts over mine . . . then truly, my king, I'm not entirely certain of what further use I can be to you."

"You serve at my pleasure, honored Phemus," replied Nagel, "and the decision to depart from that service is not yours to make, but mine to give. Now, if you'll excuse me," and he headed for the door, "I'm feeling the need for some exercise. I think a bout of hunting should do it. If I come back with something substantial,

I shall be certain to invite you for when I have it cooked up and presented for consumption."

"I would be honored, my king, to join you."

"I knew you would."

Just before Nagel got to the door, Phemus added, "I am honored that my king believes I can be of some service to him."

"It's partly that."

"Partly . . . ?"

Nagel faced him and smiled unpleasantly. "If I keep you close to me, it makes it that much easier for me to keep my eye upon you." He tossed off a mock salute and left the room, leaving a very shaken high advisor behind him.

ii.

Let them try to ambush me. Just let them try.

The words kept going through Nagel's head as he made his way through the woods. There was thick cloud cover, so what there was of the moonlight couldn't shine down upon him. But that didn't bother Nagel; his night vision was unsurpassed by any of his kind, and the darkness held no terrors for him.

That was certainly not the case for others in his kingdom, though, he was certain of that. None of his people had recovered from the trauma of losing Merrih. As he and his hunting party had made their way through the streets of Feend, those few people he did encounter out and about gave him quick, acknowledging glances, bowed just as fast, and then got out of his way. He could hear "Merrih" and "Piri" on their lips as he passed. That was how they all saw him: as a failure.

Well, he thought grimly, they would be changing their tune, yes indeed. They would be seeing things very differently once the Piri had been wiped out forever.

He was armed with a quiver of arrows and a long bow, as were the four other Ocular in his hunting party, and a long knife shoved into its scabbard in his belt. When they approached the edge of the forest, he turned to the others and said, "We will split into three groups. We can cover more ground and have a more successful hunt that way. You two head that way, you other two in that direction, and I'll head forward on my own."

There were uncomfortable looks exchanged between the guardsmen in the party. "What?" demanded Nagel in annoyance.

"My king," said one of them, "that will leave you vulnerable, don't you think? Certainly there are less risky ways in which to go about this endeavor."

"Are you implying that I cannot handle anything that should come my way?" he asked, bristling. "Do you think that little of your king?"

"No, my king, I was just . . ."

"There is no need for you to continue that sentence beyond 'my king.' Understood?"

"Yes, my king," said the Ocular guardsmen, and the others nodded in agreement. None of them looked especially happy.

Nagel could understand why. Their first responsibility was to protect their king, not to hunt. If the king should die during this endeavor, they would seem derelict in their duty.

"Worry not," he said, his tone softening. "We will remain within shouting distance. So if any of you needs me to come to your rescue, you need but cry out and I'll attend to you."

This prompted a few self-conscious snickers from the guardsmen, and minutes later, Nagel was by himself in the forest.

Just in case, he had already removed an arrow from its quiver and nocked it, but wasn't drawing it tightly. His mind was racing with contradictory thoughts. The fact was, he knew he was putting himself greatly at risk by opting to hunt solo. He should have kept all his people together.

But he felt as if he needed to push his luck. To expose himself to danger, even to risk his life.

Let the gods test me, he thought. *Let them see me, alone and vulnerable, and send enemies descending upon me so that I may challenge them and myself. I want it. I need it.*

Granted it was reckless behavior, but he desired recklessness. The gods had chosen to sacrifice Merrih to the ravening Piri. He had felt completely impotent since that time. Although the nominal reason for this escapade was to hunt food, his real desire was to capture or kill—preferably the latter—a Piri. He wanted to murder one of the things and parade his capture before his people. To declare, "Here! Here is at least one that will never harm any of us again!" He didn't know whether that would make all that much difference to his people, but it would be a start. The destruction of all the Piri had to begin with a single one, and if anyone was going to achieve that goal, it was going to be Nagel.

But he was certain the only way it could be a clean kill, a worthy kill would be if he was out there in serious jeopardy, rather than surrounded by a squad of protectors. *The gods test us, and sometimes the tests are ours, and sometimes theirs, but we must always pass those tests when given us,* his father had once said to him, and he had never forgotten those words.

He was beginning to think that Phemus was one of those tests.

Ever since he'd encountered the Bottom Feeders and sent them on their errand, he had been dwelling on his relationship with Phemus, colored by the words from his dead father. He did not like the directions that his thoughts were taking him, and was becoming increasingly convinced that he should be seeking motives as to just why Phemus might be trying to send his people down the path to destruction. Motives that no doubt related to the "secret" his father had written about.

There was a stiff wind blowing into Nagel's face, which was fortunate. It meant that his scent would not be carried to anything that was ahead of him. This gave him an element of surprise over all manner of beasts, two- or four-legged, that might be roaming the forest this evening.

Nagel had never felt more alone than he did right at that moment, and it was for reasons unrelated to his solitude in the forest. One went to advisors for counsel, but when one needed advice about the advisors, where was there to turn? Then his heart hardened: This was the exact sort of thinking that his father had held in such disdain. He was overthinking matters. If there was reason to suspect Phemus, he should just take a sword and dispatch the bastard rather than take chances.

A crack of branch and a rustling of brush from ahead of him interrupted his thoughts, and he froze. Despite his size, he was well able to secret himself within shadows and watch unobserved.

Whatever had made the noise stopped as well. Perhaps he had been detected, even though he had done all he could to remain unseen. Nagel held his breath, keeping the arrow loose in the bow lest the creaking of the bow, when drawn, alert whatever it was that he was stalking.

Nothing moved. Until this moment he'd been hearing all the small, normal noises that one hears in the woods, but even they seemed to have vanished. It was as if the entire forest was holding its breath, waiting to see what would happen.

There. Movement again, in the brush, and sounds of something being pushed aside. A hidden door, perhaps? It was too much to hope for, because a hidden door in the ground could mean only one thing.

Sure enough, there it was. A Piri, big as life. A female, most definitely, and not at all what he had expected to see from a Piri. She was almost elegant in her appearance, with long, white, flowing hair. Her back was to him, but she appeared nude from the waist up; he couldn't see the rest of her, as it was blocked by the bushes.

He considered the impropriety of shooting prey from behind. Then his heart hardened. These vermin had stolen Merrih from him through pernicious means. They deserved no pity, none of them.

But still . . . it might provide a source of information as to . . .

Stop thinking. Act.

Remembering the potential warning that the creaking of the bow might produce when he pulled it, he knew he would have to move in one swift motion. He took a deep breath, held it, thought, *This is for you, Merrih,* then stepped away from the tree and into view in the same instant that he released the arrow.

It buzzed through the air, a fatal insect, and a second later the wailing scream of a female Piri sounded in the still night air.

SUBTERROR

i.

Once again he came to Clarinda in her dreams, just as she had told him he did.

In the exact style of dream that was difficult to distinguish from being awake, Clarinda was supine upon her bed, naked. She could hear everything; hear her own breathing, hear her heart beating. She was waiting for something, and she knew she was waiting, but couldn't quite determine what exactly it was she was waiting for. And then he was there, her amazing Eutok. Even in her dreams, she knew there was no practical reason she should be attracted to him. Her standard of beauty, was shaped by the standard of Piri beauty, and Trulls were about as far away from that standard as could be.

Perhaps it was what he represented: a possible way out from the life and race that she despised.

She called out to him repeatedly, and he came to her and embraced her, and held her tight and whispered to her. She felt comforted by him, and felt as if she wanted to hold him forever.

And suddenly Eutok jolted in her arms. His mouth dropped open wide, and she stared at him, not comprehending. Then he rolled off her, his dead body thudding to the floor, and there was her mother standing behind him, with a long wooden stake in her hand and her lips drawn back to reveal her formidable fangs.

"Join me?" Sunara Redeye asked. And when Clarinda simply sat there, paralyzed with both anger and terror, Sunara dropped to the ground, grabbed Eutok by the throat, plunged her fangs into him, and drank deep. And Clarinda kept sobbing and crying "Eutok! Oh, gods, Eutok!" as her mother drained him dry of blood . . .

She awoke with a start, trapped for a moment in that instant between sleep and wakefulness, where one has to mentally come to the realization that a bad dream was still just that: a dream, and not something to concern oneself over. Upon discovering that she was alone in her chambers, that her mother was not there nor, thank the gods, was Eutok, she let out a relieved sigh.

But the sigh caught in her throat when she spotted Merrih seated a short distance away. Naturally Clarinda's chambers were not designed for one of Merrih's stature, but Merrih had managed to find a seat on the floor and had her legs pulled up tightly so that her chin was resting upon her knees. She was watching Clarinda with her steady, unblinking single eye.

"Merrih," Clarinda finally managed to say. "I was not . . . what are you doing here? I . . ."

"I can feel myself . . ." said Merrih, her voice sounding haunted, "slipping away. Bit by bit, the person I was . . . the Merrih I was . . . is becoming someone I don't recognize. Someone horrible. Someone . . . like you."

Clarinda, sitting up in her bed, drew her covers around herself. "I can sympathize. I doubt you'll find anyone in this entire land who is as filled with self-loathing as I am."

"I have to leave," said Merrih.

"As do I. But I—"

"No," Merrih said, so sharply that it startled Clarinda and she reflexively brought her covers up higher on her body. "There is no 'but' here. I want to get out of here while I can still recognize myself."

"Don't you think I feel the exact same way!"

"Not enough," said Merrih tightly.

Clarinda's face twisted in cold fury. "Don't you dare. Don't you dare try to diminish how I feel. You have no clue the lengths I would go to—"

Merrih drew close to the bed and crouched, her single eye glowering down at Clarinda. "You talk a great game of wanting to get away from your mother . . . of the fear of eventual mutilation. But you won't take action to change your situation. You just complain about it or hope that someone else will attend to matters. Who is Eutok?"

ii.

The three words stopped Clarinda before she could readily respond. *Oh my gods. She knows. Mother knows. She must have told her. I have to . . .*

. . . kill Merrih. Kill my mother. Kill all of them. It's the only answer. It's happening too quickly, everything isn't in place, but I'm out of time, I'm out of . . .

Her eyes narrowed, her chin lowered, like an animal being backed into a corner, she said, "I know no one by that name . . ."

"Interesting you should say that, since I have heard you cry out his name in your sleep. And not just this night; other nights as well. You murmur of running off with him. You watch your words during your wakefulness, Clarinda, but you've no protection in your sleep."

Clarinda licked her lips, which were suddenly bone dry. When she didn't reply, Merrih said briskly, "Very well. If it's all the same to you, I shall see whether the name means anything to your mother then."

As she rose to leave, Clarinda's immediate impulse was to leap for Merrih, grab her by the chin, and snap her neck. She wasn't certain that she could manage it, but she was willing to give it a try. Resisting the notion, she shouted, *"Wait!"* She did it so loudly that her voice seemed to echo forever, and she clamped a hand over her mouth in chagrin. Merrih, meantime, looked carved from ice, unflinching, unmoving.

"Something jog your memory?" Merrih asked softly when the echoing voice had finally died down.

"Merrih . . . you have to listen to reason . . ."

Merrih dropped down to one knee, bringing herself in close to Clarinda, and speaking in a harsh whisper. "I don't know what 'reason' is anymore. I don't know the state of my own mind at any given time. Your mother unleashes cravings in me . . . darksome urges . . . that I never would have thought I had, and would have denied it if someone said I had them. I veer wildly between extremes. The longer I'm here, the more I'm being drained away, and I simply cannot allow it to continue. If I do, then even if I ever see my people again, I'll just be this . . . this hollow shell where Merrih once was, with my own spirit broken and reshaped into an image your mother finds preferable."

"But if we're caught—"

"Then let's make certain we don't get caught."

Trying to sound reasonable, desperately hoping to buy time—time to convince Eutok, time to come up with another option—Clarinda said, "It's not as easy as all that."

"Well here's an idea," Merrih shot back. "Let's pretend that it is. Let's pretend that we can actually get out of here with relatively little difficulty. Let's pretend that you're going to help me because you don't want me mentioning any uncomfortable names, such as Eutok's, to your mother. She's on to you, Clarinda," she continued as Clarinda tried to interrupt her. "She wants me to spy on you. She wants . . . I don't know what she wants. But she's going to get it from me, sooner or later, because if matters continue as they are, I doubt any of the female I was will remain to resist her."

"Merrih, it won't be like that, I swear—"

"It already is like that." Merrih put her hands to her head and gently thumped against either temple, becoming more and more agitated. "She's crawling around in there, and if she keeps up, it's going to be too late. It has to end." Encouragingly, she added, "You can come with me."

Clarinda knew at that point that Merrih was as desperate as she, if the Ocular was floating fantasies even less likely than taking up residence with Eutok. "No."

"Live with the Ocular . . ."

"We've been over this, Merrih," Clarinda reminded her.

"Yes, I know, and I know it's not a perfect solution, but dammit, Clarinda, no perfect solution is going to present itself. But the solution that doesn't work for me is that I remain here and wind up unrecognizable as myself. And that's what will happen if I remain here much longer, I know it. I *know* it. Time is not our friend."

"All right, *all right!*" Clarinda buried her face in her hands. She felt as if her world was crashing in on her. She knew that Merrih was right. Time wasn't on their side. But if she was running from her enemies, how was she advantaged if her course took her off a cliff? From that muffled position, she said, "Just give me a few turns to—"

"No," Merrih said firmly. "We leave now."

"Now? This instant?"

"Yes, now, this instant."

"You've taken leave of your senses."

"No. Not yet. But if we leave now, then with any luck I never will."

Clarinda stared at Merrih and, to her surprise, she felt herself drawing strength from the determined young Ocular. *Yes. We are parasites. That is my greatest problem. I am what I am, and I have no resources of my own . . . only what I take from others. Let me take her strength. Let my desperation feed into hers and together we can do this. We can survive . . . somehow. I don't know how . . . but somehow.*

"Let's go," said Clarinda.

iii.

Merrih could only marvel in amazement as she and Clarinda made their way through an intricate series of turns and tunnels, Clarinda in the lead. Not only did

Clarinda seem to know where they were with almost supernatural consistency, but they had yet to encounter a single other Piri along the way. Even more interestingly, the tunnels were accessible only for someone who knew where they were and where they led, for several times along the way they had encountered "switching points" where the path they wanted to take was hidden behind what appeared solid rock. It was only when Clarinda activated hidden triggers, causing the rocks to swing wide and reveal hidden entrances, that she discovered the hinges upon which the rocks were situated.

"Nice little arrangement you have here," noted Merrih as they made their way through one of the hidden passages.

"It's not my arrangement," Clarinda replied. "Believe it or not, these particular tunnels were originally built by Morts."

"You're joking."

"That's what my mother says. There's different theories as to why. Mother claims it was refugees hoping to hide from the Third Wave. But one of my teachers said it was from an even earlier time, when they feared some sort of calamity—war, an invasion, some such—and created them as an escape route or shelter. In their own way, the Morts were as warlike as any in the Twelve Races."

They reached another wall of rock which obediently slid aside at Clarinda's touch. They stepped out into another corridor and, as the rock eased back into its place, Clarinda turned and let out a startled shriek.

Merrih saw there was a Piri standing there, grinning toothily, clearly pleased with himself. He was tall and strong and appeared most amused with the situation.

"Kelliron," Clarinda said, clearly annoyed. "What are you doing here? Not your usual haunt, is it."

"Not at all, no," replied the Piri she'd addressed as Kelliron. "But your mother asked me to keep an eye on this particular area to see if you happened to pass through. She's been talking to quite a few of us lately." He glanced at Merrih. "Has she spoken to you?"

Merrih made no response. Her back was aching, since she was bending herself nearly in half to fit into the rocky corridor.

"All right, you've seen me," said Clarinda. "Now stand aside. Merrih and I are . . ."

"Are what?" He tilted his head with open curiosity. "What are you and Merrih up to?"

Squaring her shoulders and tilting her chin in a most regal manner, Clarinda said airily, "Now that I think on it, I don't see that it's any of your business, Kelliron."

"I have to disagree," replied Kelliron, and his smile spread even wider. There was something nasty in the way he was looking at her, so much so that Clarinda suspected what he was going to say before he said it. "You see . . . your mother has been rather impressed with me. She's spoken to me about being your mate."

Even though she'd been expecting him to say it, Clarinda was taken aback. She tried to shake her head, but she felt paralyzed. "No. She hasn't . . ."

"But she has. And she made it very clear that my opportunity rested upon just how vigilant I was in the assignment she gave me." He drew closer to her, and he reached out to touch her long white hair. She pulled back, muttering a curse. "You'll come with me now . . . you and your plaything," and he glanced at Merrih disdainfully, "and then you and your mother will have words . . . and, after that, I will very likely receive my just reward."

"Why wait?" Merrih asked.

The Ocular, as a race, were generally rather slow-moving. The Piri, by contrast, were incredibly quick.

Because of that, it never occurred to Kelliron that one such as Merrih could ever lay hands on him. So it was that Merrih's hands clamping upon him, one around his slim waist, the other around the side of his head, came as a surprise. He tried to break free of her grasp, but had no more luck than a rat trapped in the vise grip of a tiger's jaws.

Clarinda moved forward, realizing this was the moment to take him down. She had to dispose of him; there was no choice. And then, to her shock, before Kelliron could let out a shriek of protest or cry of alarm, his throat was suddenly between Merrih's teeth.

With one crunching, fearsome bite, she ripped out both his larynx and his jugular vein. Blood fountained from the Piri, but he had no voice with which to vent his screams. He struggled as Merrih drank deep of his blood. She was making pleased, gurgling sounds as she lapped up the thick, brackish fluid. Clarinda backed up until she was against the cave wall and could move no further, her eyes riveted to the gory sight as Merrih drained Kelliron dry with an expertise that suggested she'd been doing it her entire life.

And when his body stopped twitching, Merrih lowered him and, her eye, like a blood moon, gleaming red with the kill, glowered at Clarinda as she growled "Open that up again" in a voice barely recognizable as her own.

Clarinda did as she instructed and Merrih tossed Kelliron's body into the tunnel from which they'd emerged. Without needing to be told, Clarinda closed it, then turned and let out a startled shriek to discover Merrih's face bare inches from her own.

Merrih licked her lips, and then drew her arm across her mouth to wipe away the blood that flecked it. Then she fell to her knees, her stomach heaving, and she vomited up the blood that she had just ingested. Weakly she murmured, "Get . . . me . . . out of here."

"Yes. Yes," Clarinda said numbly, and she led the way, Merrih following her closely. The entire time she did so, she was bracing herself for the possibility of Merrih—seized with newfound bloodlust—falling upon Clarinda herself and draining her as dry as she had Kelliron.

Finally Clarinda halted. Merrih growled behind her. "Why have we stopped?"

"You'll see," said Clarinda, and she reached up and rapped on what appeared to be more of the rocky tunnel interior. But instead of the solid sound one would have expected, it sounded hollow.

"What in the—?"

"The Morts were ingenious, you have to give them that," Clarinda said with a grim smile. "This area where we're standing . . . it's quite near the surface. This is a secret exit. Undetectable from above."

"You go first," said Merrih.

Clarinda took a deep breath. "Did you really mean what you said?" she asked. "About my staying with you?"

"Clarinda . . . look at me," said Merrih grimly. "Do you think I'm unaware of what I did just a little while ago? I have no idea how my own people are going to react to me. Nagel will embrace me, I know, but until this condition wears off . . . it will wear off, won't it . . . ?" There was sudden nervousness in her voice.

"Of course," Clarinda, having no idea, assured her.

"All right. Then until that happens . . . you might well be the only friend I have in all of Feend. The only one who can understand what I'm going through. I will do my best to protect you."

"You are lying," Clarinda said with sudden heat. "I'm going to die. You're going to . . . to . . . ." She stopped, let out a choked sob, and then laughed bitterly. "As if I have a damned choice. I don't believe for a moment that Kelliron was the only one of my people that my mother was speaking to about being my mate. My time is running out . . . if it hasn't already, once they find his body. And they will, sooner or later. So . . . together, then."

"Together," said Merrih. "Lead the way."

Clarinda pulled on the trapdoor. It didn't open immediately, not having been used for some time. But in short order, she managed to yank it free and it dropped open. Cool night air rushed in, and Clarinda eased her way up into it and through.

Her head broke the surface and she glanced around, coming no farther than just enough for her to see her whereabouts. She sniffed the wind that blew against her face, but detected nothing. There were large bushes nearby that helped screen her presence, which gave her an additional feeling of security. *Gods, smile upon my endeavor,* she thought as she hauled herself to the surface. *I am damned. But I'm damned if I leave and damned if I stay. Let me die damned, then, rather than live that way.*

Without a word, she turned, reached down, and extended a hand to Merrih. Merrih gripped it and was so damned heavy that she almost yanked Clarinda right back down into the hole. Once Clarinda had given her sufficient leverage to get her hands up on the surface, she stepped back so that Merrih could pull herself up the rest of the way.

Clarinda stood upright, stretching her arms. Merrih, meantime, had pulled her waist through and was just bringing her feet up.

And at that instant, a strange "twang" sound split the night air . . . a small sound, but to Clarinda, deafening in the stillness.

She had no idea what it was.

All she knew was that barely an instant after she heard it, Merrih had emerged completely from the ground and was standing, facing Clarinda, and she was about to say something when she shuddered, staggered, and looked down in confusion.

There was some sort of point projecting from her chest.

Her mouth opened to speak, but blood was emerging from it, as it also was from her chest. Her eye widened. She clawed at the point, tried to pull it clear, and it was then that Clarinda realized what had happened and let out an ear-piercing screech of terror.

Merrih yanked hard and the arrow came clear through her chest and out the other side. Now blood was pouring down her front, and her legs trembled and began to collapse, and her eye rolled up in its socket as she started to fall forward.

With only a second to react, Clarinda did the one thing she could think of. She leaped back down into the hole, grabbing the hinged door and slamming it shut over her head as she fell through.

She landed hard on the cave floor, gasping for air, her hands over her mouth as she heard Merrih, like a great tree, fall so hard upon the ground that it shuddered from the impact. Clarinda could have vacated the area, but instead she crouched there in the darkness, listening. She heard pounding footsteps, and then they stopped.

"Oh gods," croaked a voice from above, "oh gods, oh gods, what have I done, *what have I done!*" And then the voice went loud, deafening, and it screamed "*Merrrrrrrihhhhhh!*" so loudly that, even from her subterranean hiding place, Clarinda could hear the sounds of hundreds of birds, startled from their slumber, taking wing from their perches in the treetops.

There was no further sound for a brief time, and then came the pounding of running feet. They were coming from several directions at once, and the ground was shaking so violently above Clarinda that she threw her arms over her head as clods of dirt were raining upon her.

Then came outcries of horror and lamentation, and they were saying, "What happened, my king?" and "Did you find her like this?"

And then came a reply that shook Clarinda to her core.

"The Piri," said the trembling voice that she had only moments earlier heard sobbing self-recriminations. "I . . . I found her like this. Look what they did to her, the bastards. Look at her skin . . . they made her like them, and . . . and then they brought her up here and they . . . they stabbed her to death in a final gesture of contempt."

That lying sack of shit! If it hadn't meant certain death for her, Clarinda would have thrown open the door and thrown his lies back into his face. *We didn't kill her! We loved her! We loved her! You killed her, you son of a bitch, you bastard, it was you—*

"No mercy for the Piri!" one of them cried out, and the others took up the shout as well. "Hunt them down! Kill them! Kill them all!" "This is the final insult!" "Poison them!" "Burn them out!" "Flood them out!" "They will die, they will die, to avenge the death of Merrih!" "We will force others to help us if need be, and if they don't, they will be our enemies as well!" "We'll destroy every race on the Damned World, if that's what it takes, to kill the Piri!"

Long after their howls of outrage and lamentations had faded, long after they had carried away Merrih's body while shouting their vows of revenge, Clarinda remained where she was, alternately laughing over the prospect of her race's possibly imminent demise freeing her from the tyranny of her mother, and sobbing over the loss of the only female on the planet whom she could even remotely call "friend."

That was the condition in which the other Piri found her.

THE CITY-STATE OF VENETS

i.

Orin Arn Oran got to the Reef as quickly as he could, summoned by messages that were confusing and contradictory, but hinted of some immense calamity. He hurtled through the watery streets of Venets in his personal speeder, leaving a considerable wake and a number of disgruntled Merks who had been standing about, minding their own business, and gotten themselves profoundly soaked as a result.

Under ordinary circumstances, he would have slowed, apologized, acted in the gentlemanly manner that he believed was expected of him. But the word had come from the Reef that an emergency was at hand, something truly horrific, and no time could be wasted. So it was that he got to the Reef faster than he ever would have thought possible. He killed the engine of his speeder and vaulted onto the Reef, where the Reefkeeper was waiting in great agitation, pacing back and forth and looking as pale as Orin Arn Oran had ever seen a Merk.

One of the keeper's assistants was there as well, and to Orin Arn Oran's confusion, he was patrolling the edge of the Reef with a harpoon. Orin noticed something else immediately, and that was that the gate that blocked the Markene access to the Reef, and its bounty of Klaa, was in the down position. He had no idea why; he was the only one who ever ordered the gate closed, and then it was only for the purpose of getting the Markene's attention in order to give them new directives.

Then there was a burble of water, and the assistant with the harpoon moved toward it, harpoon at the ready. There, emerging from the water, was a Markene—an elderly one by the look of it—and Orin Arn Oran gasped in shock.

The Markene was covered in some sort of huge, thick, black ooze. He was splashing about pathetically, only parts of his face and small sections of his body visible. The rest was obscured by the whatever-it-was that had enveloped him. And the truly pitiable aspect of it all was that the Markene didn't even seem aware of his condition.

"What in gods' name is that . . . that . . . *thing* on him?"

"I don't know, Warlord," said the concerned keeper, "but that it's on him isn't what worries me."

Before he could continue, the Markene surged forward toward the Reef, and he groaned "Klaaaaaa," even as the assistant stepped forward and shoved the harpoon toward him. The point went deep into the Markene's shoulder, as much from his own forward momentum as anything the assistant was doing. "Klaaaaaa," he moaned again, and then slid back into the water. For the life of him, Orin couldn't determine whether the Markene knew that he'd been stabbed.

"Well, what then—?" Orin Arn Oran's voice trailed off as he stared down at the water lapping against the edge of the coral reef. His eyes widened, and he felt a chill in his very marrow. "It's in the water, too. Along the edge, there," he pointed, "and there . . ."

"It's on the Klaa," the Keeper said tonelessly.

"On how much of it?"

"On it. On the Klaa," the keeper told him. Orin stared at him, not comprehending at first. "On all of the Klaa. This, this . . . gunk . . . it's washed up onto the whole Reef. The whole coral reef on which the Klaa is harvested." He spread his arms wide, as if he could encompass the entirety of the miles-wide reef. "There is no part of it, none, that is not covered in this. It's ruined the Klaa."

"Not all of the Klaa . . ."

"*All of it!*" The keeper's frustration was mounting, and Orin felt powerless to prevent the keeper from becoming upset, because he was having trouble processing what he was being told, and he knew it. He truly understood what the keeper was saying, but his brain wouldn't accept it. In his own way, he was just as deliberately blinded as the addled, gunk-covered Markene who was keening for his drug. "All of the Klaa! The entire harvest is ruined!"

Orin took a few steps along the Reef, as if he could—in that short distance—find a section that somehow had escaped damage. "How long?"

"How long . . . ?" Now it was the keeper's turn not to comprehend. "How long what, Warlord?"

"How long to remove this stuff from the Klaa?"

"It can't be removed."

"There has to be a way to—"

"Don't you think I *tried*!" Whatever decorum the keeper should have been displaying, whatever respect he should have been showing the Warlord, was gone. He had had far more time than Orin to come to grips with the situation and realize all the ruinous consequences. "It won't come off! We scraped, we scrubbed . . . nothing! It covers the Klaa like a black plague of death—"

"*Klaaaaaa!*" The Markene's howling was almost deafening.

"Where did that damned Markene come from, anyway?"

"The same place any of them come from. I found him in there. He was probably going to sample some of his beloved Klaa. They don't come on any sort of organized schedule—"

"I know that!" Orin did not appreciate being addressed as if he knew nothing of the Markene.

The keeper didn't seem to catch the irritated tone, or if he did, he ignored it. "And he got himself covered with the same garbage that's all over the Reef. As soon as I saw him, I lowered the gate so none others would get in here."

"You're sure there are none others here."

"Yes. But they'll be arriving at the gate before long. They'll hear him caterwauling about the Klaa. How could they not?"

Orin Arn Oran only had to give a moment's thought to the unthinkable. "Kill him," he said.

"But—"

"Look at him. The poor bastard's done for anyway. The last thing we need is for him to summon more of his ilk in his death throes." Orin made a throat-cutting gesture to the assistant.

The assistant nodded once, drew back his arm, and let fly. The harpoon flew truly, and it lanced the hapless Markene through the chest. The power of the throw sent the Markene twisting back, and he thrashed about in the water, still saying, "Klaa, Klaa," seemingly unaware that he had just been killed. The assistant and the keeper looked away. Orin Arn Oran wanted to do the same, but he forced himself to look and to listen to every last word the tragic dying creature uttered.

As a result, he heard the Markene's final word, spoken harshly over the death rattle in his throat. Then the Markene rolled over, limp, and simply floated there, unmoving. So thick was the coating of blackness around the Markene that, although the harpoon had penetrated, no blood was welling forth. Orin had to think that was a blessing, as the others might well have scented it in the water, and who knew the reaction they'd have then?

"Get him out of the water," he said. "Have him sent to the science hall immediately. I want to know what that . . . that substance on him, and on the coral, is." As the keeper gestured for the unhappy assistant to haul the heavy Markene's body from the water, and as the assistant went to seek out aid in doing so, Orin asked him, "If the Klaa can't be cleaned off—and I believe you that it cannot," he said quickly, intercepting the keeper's response, "how long would it take to grow more Klaa? To scrub the coral clean so that Klaa can grow upon it once more?"

"I have no idea, Warlord."

"Guess."

"Guess?"

"*Guess!*" said the irritated Warlord. "Give me at least some vague idea. Something I can take back to Lord Sydonis and give him something approaching an estimate."

"Hundreds of tides, at least."

"Hundreds?" Orin gasped. "Are you saying it could be an entire cycle around the sun before—?"

The Keeper nodded. "It could very well be, yes. Or longer."

"Gods." Orin sank down upon the Reef, staring bleakly at the blackness of the water as it splashed up. "You'll keep the gate down. Most of the Markene had their Klaa not long ago, correct?"

"Yes, Warlord."

"Then they shouldn't need it all that much. Not this soon. If any of them do start gathering, send them to the Pier. I will give them orders there."

"What will you say to them?"

"I'm still working on that," Orin told him. Seeking anything else to say that involved something other than the hopeless position they'd just been put in, Orin asked, "That last thing the Markene said. Did you understand it?"

"I did not hear it, Warlord."

"I could swear he said something like 'Gorkon.' Does that have any meaning to you, that word?"

The keeper thought about it, then shook his head. "Nothing, Warlord. Nothing at all. You might not have heard him properly . . . or perhaps it's the name of someone close to him. There's no way we can ever know now," he added, looking dismally at the Markene's corpse as it was hauled from the water.

"I have a very sick feeling, Keeper, that you are wrong," Orin Arn Oran said. "I think we will know. And I think we'll be sorry when we do know."

ii.

Having heard the entire story, the lady was having trouble believing it. "*All* the Klaa? *Gone?*"

Orin Arn Oran had arrived in the main council room to break the news to the lord and lady of Venets. Upon hearing the beginnings of it, however, Tulisia had whisked the Warlord to her private study, leaving Ruark Sydonis behind in the council room, smiling in his infuriatingly polite and perpetually confused manner. There she questioned the Warlord intently, until finally he called an abrupt halt to it, much to her surprise.

"My lady," he said sharply, "you keep asking me the same questions and I assure you my answers won't be changing." Then he took a breath, calming himself, before he continued. "Understand, I do not blame you. I was in the very same state of mind as you, unable to comprehend the breadth of our situation. I kept looking for ways for matters to be different than they are. But they are what they are, and we must begin coping with them."

"But . . . the Klaa is our club over the Markene," Tulisia said. "If . . ."

Again his impatience overwhelmed him, and this time he made no effort to apologize for it. "Yes, Lady, I know that, you know that, we all know that. The situation facing us is, what is to be done about it?"

"What will happen if the Markene are deprived of Klaa?"

"I don't know for sure, Lady," said Orin. "Certainly there will be a physical withdrawal. They will become far less placid. They may resist our orders, even refuse to obey them."

"It may be worse than that."

The unexpected intrusion of a third voice startled the both of them, and they turned to see Ruark Sydonis standing in the doorway. Tulisia couldn't help but think that he seemed unusually focused on the discussion. Still, out of long habit, she said dismissively, "This is none of your concern, Ruark . . ."

"With respect, my dear, I cannot help but think it is," Ruark said, shambling into the room. "If we are on the brink of losing control of the Markene, it will be of concern to all, isn't that so?"

"Yes, Lord," Orin Arn Oran said quickly before Tulisia could make some sort of biting response. She shot him an annoyed look but held her tongue for the moment. "You are aware of the situation?"

"I couldn't help but overhear the discussion, yes."

"And do you have any thoughts on the matter, Lord?"

Ruark seemed about to speak, but then looked in deference to his wife. "I wouldn't wish to speak out of turn."

Tulisia made that impatient noise with her lips that both Ruark and Orin had come to know all too well. "You are lord of the Sirene, Ruark. Obviously nothing you say could be considered out of turn. It's *always* your turn! So speak! How are we going to keep the Markene in check!"

"Well," he said slowly, thoughtfully, "perhaps the time has finally come for them not to be in check."

Orin and Tulisia exchanged puzzled looks. "I'm not following, Lord," said Orin.

"Warlord, unless I'm very much mistaken . . . the Markene are not animals."

"Of course they're not, Lord . . ."

"Nor are they slaves, even though it has been the traditional approach to treat them as either animals or slaves or both. So I was just thinking . . . and I'm sure there are perfectly good reasons why this isn't possible, but still . . . I was just thinking it might make sense to treat the Markene as our peers."

"Peers." Tulisia said the word flatly, with no inflection, not quite able to believe it had even been voiced.

"Yes," replied Ruark with a distinct cheerfulness that indicated he was clueless to her negative reaction. "If these are the first Markene in generations to have clarity of mind and vision thanks to the loss of Klaa, then perhaps we should regard this as an opportunity rather than a hardship. Don't you think?"

Orin Arn Oran, speechless, waited for Tulisia to speak. For a long moment, Tulisia was silent. And then she said, "You're insane."

"Am I?" Ruark sounded concerned, as if he'd just received a pronouncement of a fatal illness. "Are you sure? I don't think I'm insane. Then again, I suppose I would be the last one to be in a position to know, wouldn't I."

"The Markene," continued Tulisia, "are our servants. They perform simple tasks, are not required to think, and receive their precious Klaa as reward. The Merk will never accept a change in that status. That, Ruark, is insanity."

"You know . . . I thought as much. But I just needed to hear you say it."

"Well, now you've heard it."

He smiled beatifically. "Thank you for clarifying that for me, my dear. I don't know what I'd do without you."

"Yes, I've little doubt of that."

Orin Arn Oran clearly felt uncomfortable being present at such an exchange, and he quickly said, "That still leaves us with the question of what to do about the Markene. At the very least, we must cancel the . . ." Suddenly realizing he didn't know how much Ruark knew about Tulisia's plans, but having no elegant means of getting the lord of the Sirene to leave the room, Orin said delicately, ". . . the endeavor . . . that you and I discussed, Lady."

She looked blank for a moment, but then realized. Without giving him a glance, Tulisia said imperiously, "Ruark, leave us now."

"All right," Ruark said obediently, and he headed out the door, closing it behind him.

Orin was about to speak, but Tulisia put up a webbed finger cautiously, and crept over to the door. She threw it open and looked around. There was no sign of Ruark. Satisfied, she closed it again and turned to face Orin. "The hell we cancel it," she said.

"In five tides, the Markene will likely be in the full throes of withdrawal," said Orin. "Then, if not sooner. The last thing we need—"

"The last thing we need is for them to be anywhere near us!" countered Tulisia. Her mind was racing, trying to see all the variables. "Actually . . . this is perfect."

"*Perfect?* How—?"

"Don't you see?" she said eagerly, crossing to Orin and gripping his tunic. "This disaster, whatever caused it . . . it's given us total cover. Before, if the Markene attack failed, we would have been forced simply to disavow knowledge of it. Now, however, should things not go our way, we can point to the mishap with the Klaa and make clear that it was utterly out of our control. The Klaa was destroyed, the Markene went berserk. How are we then to be held responsible if the focus of their rage was the sailing vessels of the Travelers? Eh?"

"I . . . I suppose . . ."

"There is no supposing here, Orin. There is only certainty. Furthermore, if they are truly going through the sort of agonizing withdrawal that you are describing, then they will be uncommonly fierce, bordering on savage. Do not forget that our interest was in testing the limits of the Travelers' invincibility. The Markene will be in the ideal state of mind for what we need them to do. There are no negatives here. This is a blessing in disguise."

"If I may say so," Orin said, still doubtful, "it is a remarkably crafty disguise."

She released her grip on him, turning away and shaking her head. "You must look beyond your immediate concerns, Warlord. See opportunities for what they truly are. The best aspect of this is that the attack upon the Travelers will, at the very least, thin the numbers of Markene. Certainly there will be losses to the herd. No matter what the outcome, that will leave us less Markene to deal with, in a far more manageable number than before."

"Does it not bother you, Lady, that we've no clue as to how this situation came to pass? This substance that has washed up upon the coral . . ."

She shrugged. "A freak accident. Happenstance. Whim of the gods. Call it whatever you wish. Ultimately, the gods challenge us, Orin Arn Oran, and we must rise to those challenges. Can I count on you to do so?"

He bowed slightly. "Always, Lady."

She smiled, and then cupped his chin in her hand. "I knew I could." Then, to Orin's obvious surprise, she drew his mouth to hers and kissed him fiercely, her tongue thrusting into his mouth as she did so. He made no move to pull away, paralyzed as he was. Then she withdrew and, smile remaining upon her face, said, "Attend to the Markene. Send them against the Travelers now. Don't even have them wait on station; have them go out and launch the attack. Then return to me, tell me it has been attended to . . . and we shall see what we shall see."

"Y-Yes, Lady," he managed to get out, and then he retired hastily from the room, leaving a very satisfied Tulisia anticipating, in a most positive manner, the events of the next several tides.

Meanwhile, next door, Ruark Sydonis put down the listening device he'd had pressed up against the wall and smiled in a similar manner of anticipation. But those developments which he expected were very different from what his mate was looking forward to.

iii.

{Gorkon floats in a haze of grief.}

{He remembers recoiling in shock at the immensity of the destruction unleashed upon the Klaa, and seeing the thick, expanding area of blackness that was rolling off the coral, as the first fingers of dawn's light were caressing the water's surface. The shock stemmed from Gorkon's not knowing how to react. There was the sweeping nausea he experienced upon envisioning the reaction his brethren would have to the ruination of their precious Klaa. There was also an unworthy, almost evil glee at the expectation that finally, finally, his people would be freed from the shackle of this pernicious substance. It would be painful, it would likely be violent . . . but he would no longer feel alone.}

{Then he heard the word. The curious, ever-present question, "Klaa?" The inquiry came from behind him, and he recognized the voice even before he turned to see that it was his father, swimming up and looking with vague interest at Gorkon. "Klaa?" he said again, and headed toward the reef, bypassing his son entirely.}

{No! screamed Gorkon, and he intercepted his father, coming between him and the Reef. But the father fought him like a thing possessed, perhaps realizing on some level that the Klaa was threatened. Gorkon held on valiantly, but he could not stand against his father's greater strength. His father broke free of Gorkon's grasp, and when Gorkon lunged at him once more to hold him back, his father swung his feet around and kicked squarely into Gorkon's head. Gorkon tumbled backward, tried to right himself, called his father's name. His father ignored him, threw himself against the widening black pool, trying to get to the Klaa. Gorkon begged, pleaded with his father to forsake the Klaa, to come back to him, but as near as he could tell, none of his pleas came close to getting through.}

{Then came the rumble behind him, which warned him the great Gate was being lowered. He hesitated only a heartbeat, torn between fealty to a father who didn't even know him, and a desire not to be caught at the scene of the disaster, spurred by his guilty awareness of just exactly had transpired at the Reef this evening.}

{He turned his back to his father and swam like the devil for the exit. He angled down, down, and sped under the gate just as it slammed into its place on the ocean bed.}

{Now he floats, swathed in misery and mourning. He knows that there is much more to do. He knows the next steps he must take. He knows that if the moment is to be his, he must seize it now, aggressively. Yet never has he so wished for the sweet oblivion of Klaa that others bask in, so that it would numb the pain he feels for the father who, to the best of his knowledge, didn't even remember his name.}

THE UNDERGROUND

i.

"Dead end!"

It was Zerena Foux, sitting foremost forward in the Truller, who sounded the alarm. She was barely able to see anything as the walls of the high-speed corridor hurtled past them.

And then, through squinting eyes, she saw the end of the tunnel in the distance. There was nothing but a solid block of rock at the end, with no warning of any kind. There were tunnels leading off in a T-formation to either side, but the track didn't head there. Perhaps the Trulls who routinely made use of these mad conveyances knew their way around the tunnels sufficiently to be wary of such termination, but the Bottom Feeders were new to the "art" of Trulling. Considering what was waiting for them no more than a few seconds down the way, they weren't going to have the opportunity to gain much experience at it.

"Dead end!" she screamed once more. *"Gant! Make it stop!"*

"No idea how!"

"Leap out! Everybody leap out—!"

"We'll be torn to shreds, Mother!" Karsen yelled back.

"This should be interesting," said Mingo, five seconds before the Truller was going to slam into the wall.

Four seconds before the impact, there was suddenly the loud hissing of air, and the Trull car impossibly began to slow. Zerena knew of a certainty that it was simply impossible for the car to slow enough to avoid a collision.

And yet, with each passing second, the car's speed reduced by half and then half again, and the result was that the car bumped harmlessly against the far wall with the gentlest of taps.

Zerena sagged back against someone and realized it was Jepp, but at that moment she didn't especially care. "Son of a bitch," she breathed, her head spinning. She closed her eyes, having to make an adjustment to the fact that the world was no longer whizzing past her at breakneck speed. "Is everyone all right?"

"Can we do that again!?" Jepp asked eagerly.

"Gods, we should have fed her to the Ocular when we had the chance," Zerena muttered. "Karsen?"

"I'm fine."

"Mingo?"

"I think I left my stomach several miles back, but other than that . . ." said Mingo, climbing out of the car.

"Gant . . . of course, you're all right," she said before he could reply. "You're a lump of jelly riding inside someone else's body. Rafe?"

No answer.

"Rafe Kestor?" She turned around, seized with the fear that he had, in all the insanity, either been left behind or—even worse—fallen out. The others looked behind themselves and Mingo looked down at Rafe Kestor, who was slumped back in the car, his head lolling to one side.

"*Rafe!*" Zerena cried out.

Rafe Kestor's scaly head snapped forward, and he blinked in confusion. Then he let out a wide yawn. "Are we there yet?" he inquired.

"He fell asleep," Mingo said.

"I can see that he fell asleep. Maybe we're all dreaming and we'll be fortunate enough to wake up and discover this mad adventure was just a bad dream," said Zerena. As she and the others clambered out of the Truller, she continued, "Now the best thing we can do is put some distance between ourselves and this area before—"

"We have a problem," said Mingo, looking around, his nostrils flaring.

"Yes, exactly, before we have a problem."

"Mother," Karsen said, "I think Mingo is saying that we have a problem now."

"What are you—?"

Then she saw it.

In the tunnels on either side, glowering eyes were floating in the darkness. Slowly Zerena moved forward and she could see there were Trulls on either side of them, dozens. They had large stone axes or shining knives or short swords clutched in their large hands, and Zerena felt a chill in the air that made her tremble inwardly. Outwardly she maintained an air of casual confidence.

She immediately sensed one Trull in particular, standing to her right, was some sort of leader. He was watching her intently, his shoulders hunched and his head lowered as if he was prepared to charge. He was dressed in black and brown leathers, and he cradled a stone ax with the confidence of someone who knew how to use it.

"I suppose," she said to him, "you're wondering what we're doing here."

"Kill them," he told his followers.

"I guess not," said Zerena Foux, and then the Trulls charged.

ii.

Chancellor Eutok stormed through the tunnels as his squad of warriors hastened to keep up with him. His shoulders swayed and he had removed his ax from his sheath on his back. It was an act of greatest restraint that he was not burying it in the skull of the closest warrior, just to get some of the anger out of his system.

"Is someone trying to make me look incompetent to the queen? To look like a fool to my brother? Is that it?" he demanded, not really expecting an answer and not receiving one. "How the hell did a group of damned intruders get down this far?"

"Chancellor, it seems that—" one of the warriors began.

Eutok turned and in one motion punched the warrior in the face. He fell, unconscious, and Eutok turned back and continued walking. "I'll tell you how," he continued as the other Trulls stepped right over, or sometimes on, the fallen Trull. "Because I have people patrolling the outer rim who are thrice-damned incompetents, that's how! When this is finished, I'm going to have every damned one of them replaced! We've got intruders who elude pursuers, steal a Truller, are nearly to the damned Hub, and no one can even tell me who or what it is we're dealing with! All the early reports contradict each other! I hear one race is attacking, then it's another . . . it makes no sense!"

"I believe it's Bottom Feeders, Chancellor," said another warrior, and then his eyes went wide and he clamped his hands over his mouth, clearly wishing he could snatch back the words.

Eutok whirled to face him, his fist cocked, and then he paused. "Bottom Feeders? That's ridiculous. Why do you say that?"

The warrior was so busy flinching that it took him a moment to realize Eutok hadn't hit him. He straightened up, cleared his throat, and said, "Pre . . . precisely because the reports do contradict each other. The races don't normally mix. The only time you see any mixture of races is clans of Bottom Feeders, who are oftentimes varied individuals simply banding together for convenience and mutual protection. That would explain the conflicting reports."

"Yes. It would," Eutok admitted. The warrior let out a sigh of relief as Eutok started walking again, musing aloud, "But it wouldn't explain the presence of the Bottom Feeders down here. Bottom Feeders hang about scenes of battles and pick through the bodies for trinkets and supplies. They'd have no reason to enter the Underground. There has to be something in it for them."

"Does it matter, Chancellor?" asked the warrior, slightly emboldened.

"No," Eutok told him, "it doesn't. What's your name?"

"Klus, Chancellor."

"Klus. You have potential, Klus."

"Thank you, Chancellor."

Eutok arrived at the end of the tunnel where it let out onto the Truller channel that the intruders were supposedly traveling. He took a few steps back, putting up a hand to indicate that the others should hang back in the darkness. Across the channel he saw another squad of Trulls, also under his command, massing on the other side. The lead warrior there, a Trull named Gurnd, whom Eutok had trained personally, nodded in acknowledgment, indicating they were ready. "You've shut down the other channels?" Eutok called to him.

Gurnd nodded in confirmation. "This is the only place they can possibly end up."

"Good. It shouldn't be long now," said Eutok.

They waited patiently, and then heard and felt the familiar rumbling in the distance. They also heard loud screaming, which amused Eutok no end. For a moment it reminded him of the times that his brother, Ulurac, had cried out in their days Trulling together. Ulurac had never developed a taste for it, whereas for Eutok there was no speed too fast for him to try and attain.

Had Eutok been able to shut down the safety mechanisms in the Trullers, all the problems would have been solved, of course. The intruders—Bottom Feeders, if that's what they were—would have collided at full speed with the terminus point and that would have been that. But the Truller system had been built far too meticulously with too much attention paid to safety. It was impossible for anyone to sabotage it precisely because it had to be that way for everyone's sake.

So instead Eutok had to content himself with listening to the intruders' uncontrolled panic. Then he heard the familiar sound of the emergency air brakes hissing. Gurnd looked as if he was ready to leap out the second the car bumped to a halt, but Eutok wanted to wait until they were all out of the car so that there could be no chance of hidden surprises.

He watched in amazement as an assortment of individuals clambered out, looking sick and dizzy. A Laocoon . . . no, two of them, a male and a female. A Minosaur. A Mandraque. A . . .

A Trull?

Well, that explained it. There was a traitor working within the Trull Underground. Eutok recognized him instantly. His name was Crob, and up until this moment, he had been a reasonably trusted warrior with a spotless record. But for some reason he had fallen in with these Bottom Feeders. For a moment Eutok considered the possibility that Crob was some sort of hostage. But no, he appeared to be mingling easily with the others and didn't show the least sign of wanting to get away. They had turned Crob, that was all. He would die for his disloyalty.

Then Eutok's eyes widened as he saw what appeared to be a female of a race he didn't recognize at first. She was slender enough to be a Piri, and just for a second, Eutok thought that perhaps it was Clarinda having joined with these . . . these misfits. But it took him no time at all to realize he'd erred. Her skin was far too tanned for her to be part of the subterranean Piri race, nor did she possess any of the other Piri attributes.

Could it be . . . ?

A Mort? Was it possible? Were there any left? Eutok had never actually seen one with his own eyes, merely heard the stories of them.

This was becoming stranger and stranger. The combination of the apparently traitorous Trull in the company of a Mort was almost enough to make Eutok spare them. To bring them to the Hub and question them, learn more of what was going on.

But he quickly quelled the notion. Only strength was an acceptable response to such a brazen intrusion. Strength and decisive, terminal action.

The Bottom Feeders were talking to each other, and then the Minosaur was suddenly looking directly in Eutok's direction. He'd detected them. That wasn't too great a surprise to Eutok. Minosaurs had an exceptionally sharp sense of smell, even more so than the Laocoon.

"Mother," the male Laocoon was telling the female. "I think Mingo is saying that we have a problem now."

She demanded in irritation, "What are you—?," and then she looked at the tunnels and saw the ambush waiting for them.

Eutok strode forward. The warriors filled in behind him, and, taking his cue from the Chancellor, Gurnt advanced as well. Eutok wanted the Bottom Feeders to know just how badly outnumbered they were. He cradled his stone ax, trying to decide which one he was going to annihilate first, and decided it would be Crob.

"I suppose," the Laocoon said, "you're wondering what we're doing here."

She had nerve, he had to give her that. Or perhaps she was simply too stupid to realize just what sort of situation she was in. Well, there was no point in delaying her learning the folly of their intrusion. "Kill them," he ordered.

"I guess not," she said.

The Trulls converged from either side, moving with brisk efficiency, their weapons at the ready. The Bottom Feeders fell back and brought their weapons up. The female human was holding a short knife and looked to be the easiest prey, so consequently Eutok paid her the least attention.

The Minosaur suddenly pawed the ground, snorted loudly, bellowed, "One side!," lowered his head and charged. The Trulls tried to get out of his way, but he plowed through the midst of them, scattering them right and left.

Eutok was flat on his back and outraged to be treated so. He scrambled to his feet, shouted, "Take him down!," and turned to face the others. The two Laocoon were side by side, blocking Eutok's direct path to the traitor, Crob. Well, if he had to go through the two Laocoon, then he would do just that.

He roared a challenge, and he was aware that Klus was at his side, sword at the ready. They ran toward the Laocoon and the female swung her sword, which Eutok caught with the flat of his blade. He pinned her sword for a moment, but wasn't expecting her to lash out with her hooves. She knocked his legs out from under him, and he grunted in annoyance even as he snagged the back of her knee with his ax and pulled.

The damned female was nimble. She avoided being pulled off balance, vaulting over his ax, and she slammed her sword down right where Eutok's head had been. But Eutok was too quick, rolling out of the way and scrambling to his feet. He parried the slash of her sword with the ax handle, and then stepped in quickly and smashed a fist into her face. He heard the satisfying crack of her nose breaking under the impact and she fell back.

Then a war-hammer head swung in out of nowhere. Eutok reacted barely fast enough, ducking just in time to allow his helmet to catch the brunt of the impact. It was the male Laocoon who had assaulted him, and Eutok saw that Klus was down, his face a twisted mass of flesh, clearly having received a vicious blow from the hammer.

"*Get away from her!*" yelled the male Laocoon, and suddenly he let out what was, to Eutok, a most satisfying cry of pain. The Laocoon staggered, clutching his side, blood welling up between his fingers. Klus was there, and even though his face was a ruined mess, he had still pulled himself together enough to rally and bring his short sword slicing across the Laocoon's torso.

Behind him Eutok heard protesting roars as the Minosaur was dragged down by the overwhelming force of the attacking Trulls. The Mandraque was shouting defiance, waving his sword in the air and demanding to know if the Trulls were aware of who they were dealing with. The traitorous Crob was inscrutable, as if he didn't really care who won or lost, and the female Mort . . .

She caught the wounded male Laocoon as he fell against her. Her eyes were wide in shock, and she touched the blood that surged from where he'd been stabbed.

She screamed.

It was a sound such as Eutok had never heard . . . possibly such as no Trull had ever heard. It was a scream of distress and anger and challenge, and went on for what seemed an eternity.

Then the scream halted just as suddenly as it had begun, to be replaced by a seven-word battle cry that Eutok would hear in his nightmares for the rest of his days.

"How dare you try to kill him!"

The human's face was a mask of fury, and she came straight at Klus. He brought up his sword to run her through and she sidestepped it somehow, as if he was moving in slow motion, and suddenly she was behind him, one arm wrapped around his chest, the other around his thick neck, and she twisted it. There was a shuddering snap as Klus's neck broke and he went limp against her.

The Laocoon were forgotten as Eutok whipped his ax around to dispatch the human as quickly as possible. She didn't hesitate as she shoved Klus's dead body right at Eutok. Eutok's ax head buried itself in Klus's chest, and before Eutok could pry it free, she was upon him.

Her fingernails raked his face, and it was a miracle that she didn't rip the eyes out of their sockets. He cried out, staggering, trying to shove her off him, but even though he was using both hands to do so, she clung to him like a madwoman, shrieking incoherently and tearing at his face, sending pieces of flesh flying and blood spattering.

"Get it off me!" he shouted, and there was a thundering of feet toward him. Then she was gone, and briefly he thought it was because his warriors had pulled her loose.

That was not the case. Instead she was moving like a blur. Trulls lunged at her to no avail as she sidestepped them, ducked under their grasps, eluded the thrusts of their swords and the swing of their axes. And every dodge was then met with a counterstrike of blinding ferocity. She carried no weapon. She needed none.

Gurnd came at her with a club, slamming it down toward her. She crossed her arms, intercepting the strike, immobilizing it and him, and then drove a foot up into his crotch. He let out a gasp of pain and dropped the club. She caught it with one hand and swung it down so that it crushed his right foot. Two more Trulls were charging her and she flung the club at them, knocking one flat, causing the other to dodge to one side, barely getting clear. He then grabbed at her, and she jumped high and spun in the air, kicking the Trull in the throat. He fell, gasping, and she rebounded off his back and threw herself at yet another warrior, and he went down beneath her assault as well.

"You'll all die for this!" she howled, and then as she turned to face new assailants, Eutok yanked out the sling that hung from his belt. With one fast, practiced motion, he tucked a stone in the sling, swung it over his head, and let fly.

It was such a small missile that she didn't see it coming, and it struck the human female on the side of the head. It opened up a gash and she staggered. It was all the opening the warriors needed as they came at her from all sides, overwhelming her through sheer force of numbers, driving her to the ground.

"Kill them! Kill them!" howled Eutok.

"That order is countermanded! Capture only! Do not kill them!"

Eutok couldn't believe it as his brother, Ulurac, emerged from the tunnels, moving with brisk strides as if he were taking a walk through a party instead of the scene of a major battle. "No killing, I said," he snapped.

"This is not the business of the Spiritu Sanctum!" Eutok bristled.

Ulurac didn't slow. Instead he walked right up to Eutok, stopped several feet away, and snarled, "There are questions to be answered here. Questions are matters of the mind and of the spirit. That makes this my province and I say they live for now."

"And if I say otherwise?"

In a voice so low that only Eutok could hear him, Ulurac replied, "Then I kill you where you stand."

Eutok could feel his pulse pounding in his head, and part of him wanted to challenge Ulurac to try and make good his word. Instead his lips drew into a sneer. "And here I thought you reserved killing only for those who trusted you the most."

Ulurac took a step toward him, but before could attack, Eutok called out, "Intruders! Make one more move against us and your lives are forfeit. Come willingly and, for the moment, you live. Your choice," and he looked defiantly at Ulurac, challenging him to gainsay him, and almost hoping that the Bottom Feeders would instead press the attack, thus sealing their fate.

Instead the female Laocoon called out, "Mingo! Rafe! Stop struggling. Weapons down. Jepp!"

The one called Jepp, the human, was still struggling furiously in the hands of the half dozen or so Trulls it was requiring to restrain her. The Laocoon female went to her, grabbed her face with both hands, and shouted, "Jepp! He's going to be okay! Karsen is going to be all right! But you have to bring yourself back from . . . from wherever you are at the moment, or they'll cut you down where you stand! Do you hear me?"

Jepp's breath hissed through her teeth and then, very gradually, slowed. Her eyes seemed to clear, a fog lifting from them, and then she managed a nod. "Release her," said the female Laocoon.

"I give the orders to my people," Eutok informed her sharply, and upon the questioning look from his warriors, nodded. They let go their hold upon her and she stumbled away from them, paying them no mind and instead running to the male Laocoon. He was sitting up, using a cloth to stanch the wound in his side.

"It's going to be okay, Jepp, I swear," he told her.

Eutok looked at the body of Klus and then to Jepp. "You," he said darkly, "killed one of my warriors."

Jepp returned Eutok's glare, her chin upthrust, and she said defiantly, "If any others of your warriors cares to die, let them hurt Karsen, and I'll oblige them."

"Gods," murmured the female Laocoon, which was the first indication to Eutok that she was as surprised at the Mort's capacity for destruction as Eutok was.

"You will come with us," Ulurac announced. "You will offer no hostile actions. And then . . . we shall see what we shall see."

"Yes," Eutok said, staring murderously at his brother, "we shall indeed."

FIREDRAQUE HALL, PERRIZ

i.

Evanne, the daughter of Nicrominus, had never felt more frustrated with her lover, Xeris, than she did right at that moment.

She was practically dragging him down the corridor leading to her father's study, yanking insistently on his left arm, with several documents and rolled parchments secured under his right arm. "Evanne, will you be careful?" he whined. "My arm isn't like my tail. Pull it off and it won't grow back, I promise you."

Huffing in annoyance, she released his arm and turned to face him, her tail whipping back and forth as an indicator of her exasperation. "I promised you, Xeris, ages ago, to love you and watch out for your best interests. And I'm telling you, it's in your best interests now to talk to my father about your theories on the hotstars."

"I've offered my aid to him. He wasn't interested."

"As I've offered mine, and was likewise rebuffed." She took his free hand in both of hers. "But if we go to him together, we can make him listen to reason."

"Make the Preceptor listen to reason?"

"It's not unprecedented," she said dryly.

"But . . ."

"But what?"

"He'll yell at me," Xeris said.

Evanne closed her eyes for a moment, steadying herself, and then she forced a smile, her tongue flicking out and tasting the air. "Xeris," she told him, "you know my love for you is unwavering. But sooner or later, you're going to have to grow a spinal ridge."

"If it's sooner or later, can I opt for later?"

"Come on," she said with a sigh. She stood next to him, her tail wrapping around his waist, and she started walking again with the reluctant Xeris in tow.

They arrived at the large double doors that led to the study of Nicrominus, and Evanne thumped on them with authority. The sound echoed, catching the attention of servants who were wandering about on various errands. "See, he's not answering," said Xeris quickly. "We should come back later. Or not at all. It's . . ."

The left door creaked open and Nicrominus peered out. Evanne immediately felt a wave of concern. He looked haggard and burdened, not at all well. "Father . . . gods, when was the last time you slept?" she asked.

"Sleep is for lesser beings," he archly informed her in such a way that it was difficult for her to determine if he was joking or not. "I regret, my dear, it is not a good time . . ."

"Actually, Father," she replied, "it is the ideal time."

"Really." He seemed vaguely intrigued by the response. "I suppose it comes down to one's definition of ideal. How now, then?"

"Xeris here has been doing research into the hotstars," she said. Her tail was behind the small of his back, and she used it to push him forward a few paces. "He's developed some fascinating theories that he strongly feels you should be made aware of."

"Is that a fact?"

"He was positively insistent."

"I see." He looked from Evanne to Xeris, but continued to address her. "And here I would have thought he would be afraid that I would yell at him."

Xeris started to reply, but Evanne cut him off. "It never entered his mind," she said.

"Preceptor, please," said Xeris, "we tru—I truly feel that my theories might have some merit and could aid you in your own work."

"Tell me from out there."

"Out . . . here?" Xeris glanced around. "Not in there?"

"I am affording you a few brief moments of my time, Xeris. Say what you need to say from there or begone."

"Father," Evanne said, "this is really not—"

Now it was Xeris's turn to interrupt her. "No, Evanne. As the Preceptor wishes, so shall it be."

Evanne's eyes registered her surprise, but she said nothing . . . and even felt a small swell of pride . . . as Xeris proceeded to lay out for Nicrominus, as quickly and efficiently as he could, his theories regarding hotstars. His belief that hotstars were merely conduits, that there was some sort of "Primestar" that was the source of all energy, and that it was to be found in this plane of existence rather than in the Elserealms. Nicrominus, standing there in the half-open doorway, listened and nodded and Xeris grew more confident in his theorizing. He continued with his notion that the draining of hotstars might be something occurring back in the Elserealms as well.

"And then you see the possibilities *that* presents, Preceptor," he continued.

Something in Nicrominus's tone changed. "Yes, of course I do," he said hurriedly. Whereas before he had seemed genuinely interested, now he appeared determined to send Xeris on his way as expeditiously as possible. He began to close the door in Xeris's face, saying, "You've given me much to think on. Now if you'll excuse me—"

But Xeris was emboldened by having gotten this far, and he placed a hand against the door, bracing it, so Nicrominus couldn't shut it. "If the Elserealms are threatened, we can turn it to our advantage! Perhaps we can find a way to shut down the energy flow to the Elserealms altogether!"

"Xeris," Nicrominus said with growing urgency, "please, enough for now," and Evanne was beginning to realize that something was truly wrong.

Xeris, however, did not. "We can turn the tables on our jailers!" His voice rose with mounting excitement. "If we can regulate energy, we can make them come begging to us for it! Strike a deal! Or just shut them down completely! Force them to relocate to this plane, so we'll be exiled together! The Overseer, the Travelers, all those who sentenced us here, can be made to suffer as we have suffered! They can—"

The door to Nicrominus's chamber suddenly flew open, but it was not at the behest of Nicrominus. Instead he stumbled back and looked apprehensively upward as, standing there, looming over Nicrominus, was a Traveler. His eyes were invisible within the recesses of his dark purple hood, yet Evanne felt as if his gaze was boring directly into her own skull as the Traveler regarded both her and Xeris with silent gravity.

Xeris tried to speak, but nothing but vague sounds emerged from his throat.

Nicrominus sighed heavily. "I tried," he said.

Slowly the Traveler's arm rose, his shrouded hand extended toward Xeris, and suddenly Evanne was standing between the Traveler and Xeris, her arms spread wide. "He meant nothing by it!" she cried out. "He was . . . he's an academician! A theorist, that's all! And he was caught up in the excitement of a theory. He plans no treason, foments no revolt! He's nothing to you or to the Overseer, nothing!"

"Actually, he is," Nicrominus said mildly to the Traveler. "He's a source of intriguing ideas. Especially considering that the things he's said augment and expand upon some of the theories I've postulated. Theories I'm now prepared to present."

That prompted the Traveler to freeze in place, his arm poised but no longer reaching toward Xeris. "Are you?" said that Traveler in a whispery voice.

"Yes," said Nicrominus. He squared his shoulders. "But I will not present them if you harm any of my people. And I will not present them to you. I will speak only to the Overseer."

"Father, are you insane!?"

As if she hadn't spoken, he repeated firmly, "Only to the Overseer. You can, of course, try and compel me to speak, but I am fragile and will not bear up well under physical persuasion, I can assure you of that."

In the next few moments Evanne felt her life passing before her eyes as the Traveler remained exactly as he was, staring down at Nicrominus, his arm still outstretched toward Xeris. She stopped breathing. She was even convinced her heart had ceased beating.

Then the Traveler lowered his arm and stepped back. The door swung wide as the Traveler turned his back to them and glided toward the middle of the chamber, where he paused for an instant, and then moved to the large, stained-glass window at the far end. He faced it and remained there, as if communing with the moon.

Immediately Evanne entered the room, going straight to Nicrominus. She noticed that Xeris was holding back, remaining in the hallway, trembling, but she didn't have time to address that. "Father, this is madness! You told me the Travelers had left!"

"I thought they had," he replied mildly.

"When did this one return?"

"I asked him that when he showed up in my chamber moments ago. He simply said he had always been here. Truth to tell, I wasn't certain he meant 'always' as in 'since their last visit' or 'always' as in, well . . . always."

"But why—!"

"He seemed to know that I had come to some conclusions. He also seemed to know that Xeris was going to show up here with his own theories, which were very worthy, by the way, that was no lie on my part. If Xeris ever regains consciousness, I must be sure to tell him so."

"Regains . . . ?"

She looked back at Xeris and, sure enough, his eyes were rolling up into his head and he was collapsing in a swoon to the floor. She moaned softly.

"Quite a catch, your Xeris," Nicrominus noted.

Evanne chose to ignore her insensate lover. "Father, you're playing games with a Traveler! Issuing ultimatums! Wanting to be brought before the Overseer? *Wanting* to? It's certain death!"

"You'll find, Evanne, that the only thing certain about life *is* death," he said gently. "Everything else is up for negotiation."

"Father, this is—"

The Traveler abruptly turned to them and said, "The Overseer?"

Nicrominus nodded. "Yes. The Overseer."

Very slowly, as if he were moving under water, the Traveler gestured for Nicrominus to come toward him. Without hesitation, Nicrominus did so. Evanne followed him, saying, "Father, you must rethink this . . ."

"Must I?"

"Yes! There are too many unknowns!"

"How many is too many?" he asked reasonably. "Is there a certain number of unknowns that is considered acceptable?"

"Father, this is too important to play word games with!"

"I quite agree."

He drew near the Traveler and then stopped several feet away. His hands draped behind his back, he waited patiently. Evanne, for one of the few times in her life, had no idea what to do, and so did nothing except stand there and wait in agitation.

The silence seemed to drag on for eternity.

"Your wish," the Traveler finally said, "is granted."

The stillness of the night was shattered, along with the stained-glass window, as it blasted inward. Colored shards flew everywhere, as if a rainbow had exploded within the room. Evanne fell back, shielding her eyes, but Nicrominus stayed right where he was. And the night air was suddenly filled with screams from below, shouts of alarm from people in the streets.

Something long and black slithered in through the space where the window had just been. At first Evanne thought it was a snake, but it had no head, and then there were two more of them, and then a fourth. They reached for Nicrominus, who let out a startled gasp, but that was all the acknowledgment he made of the insanity that was unfolding all around them. He did not fall back, did not plead for mercy. He stayed right where he was, and then the . . . the things . . . wrapped around him. One encircled his waist, the other two moved in around either arm, and the fourth surrounded his legs. His walking staff clattered to the floor.

"Father!" screamed Evanne. She tried to clamber to her feet, slid on shattered glass, and suddenly something was holding her back. She let out a shriek, not knowing who or what had grabbed her.

It was Xeris, who had apparently come to, and he was shouting in her ear, "Don't move! Don't do anything! It'll get you too!"

"I don't care! *I don't care!*"

She struggled in Xeris's grip and watched helplessly as Nicrominus was lifted off his feet, through the air, and out the window. Absurdly, he tossed off a little wave just before he vanished from sight.

"*Fathhhhhherrrr!*" she screamed, and her tail whipped up and around and drove itself deep into the pit of Xeris's stomach. He gasped, lost his grip on her, and she leaped to the window. She caught herself on either side before she tumbled out, craned her long neck around, and looked upward in astonishment.

She had only ever seen them from a distance. But now, gaping at one of the creatures from relatively close up, she could only stare in mute stupefaction at its immensity.

It was a Zeffer. Because it was hanging high in the sky, its translucent skin billowing and shimmering in the breeze, she saw mostly its underside. Its tendrils were hanging down, too numerous to count, and she couldn't even begin to spot the Serabim that was doubtless sitting atop it, controlling it.

Several of the tendrils were still wrapped around Nicrominus, and they were drawing him upward. He was already little more than a speck, giving Evanne some vague idea of just how high the thing was.

"*Bring him back! Bring him back, you bastards!*"

Neither the Zeffer nor its unseen rider, naturally, made any reply. Instead the Zeffer began to move, slowly but distinctly, drifting in a generally westward direction. The winds seemed to hammer it at first, and it glided too close to the bell tower. Its tentacles slammed into it, and the bells crashed as if sounding an alarm. Then the Zeffer got its bearings and angled away from the Firedraque Hall. Within seconds it was moving across the Perriz skyline. Whenever she'd seen Zeffers before, they'd always seemed to move incredibly slowly, ponderously. It was only now, as close as this one was, that she realized just how fast the thing really was.

She whirled to face the Traveler, to repeat her pleas that sounded more like barked orders. But the Traveler wasn't there. Servants had come rushing in, and Xeris was standing there slack-jawed, as stunned by the presence of the Zeffer as she was. "*Where's the Traveler?*" she demanded.

Snapped from his inaction by her outcry, Xeris glanced around, looking rather stupid as he did so. The servants did so as well, although they didn't have any idea to whom she was referring.

"I . . . I don't know," said Xeris. "I was watching the . . . he must have . . ."

Having no patience for him, she turned back to the window, looking helplessly after the rapidly receding form of the Zeffer. She could no longer make out her father in the dangling forest of tendrils hanging below the vast creature, although she did think she could see—just barely—the vague outlines of a form atop the beast. But she couldn't make out any details and then, in moments, she couldn't see that clearly either.

"Evanne," Xeris said, putting a hand on her arm, "everything's going to be—"

She pulled her arm away from him and hissed in his face, "Do not talk to me. Ever again." With that, she turned and stormed out of the room, leaving a hapless, downcast Xeris staring at the floor.

ii.

Arren Kinklash had been on his way to Firedraque Hall when he, like many Firedraques all over Perriz, watched in shock and horror as a Zeffer wafted over the cityscape. Even from the ground, Arren was able to see Nicrominus dangling in the tentacles of the thing.

Naturally he felt a moment of pure terror, but he also felt a flash of glee. Obviously the long hand of the Overseer had scooped up Nicrominus, and there was every chance that he would never be seen again. This meant a power vacuum would come into existence, and Arren knew it was his chance to improve his own standing and position. He felt guilty over that notion, but fortunately enough, the guilt passed quickly and left no bad aftertaste.

He ran toward the great hall, and then slowed as he saw something that caused a faint buzz of concern. Apparently the Zeffer had clipped the bell tower in passing; a piece of the upper section had been shattered. He knew that the bell tower was one of Norda's favorite hideaways, and he was terrified by the thought that she might have been injured.

All thoughts of political opportunities faded in the face of possible danger to his sister.

Arren began to move at a brisk walk, but moments later that was insufficient and he was going at a full-out run. There was a growing crowd at the doors of the great hall, and those within were trying their best to close it against the pushing and shoving of the mob, demanding to know what was happening. Without slowing down, Arren leaped onto the shoulders and heads of the crowd and sprinted across them. There were shouts of "Hey!" and "Stop that!" and several grabbed at him. Arren made his way past them all and leaped through the doors just as they slammed shut.

He found himself staring at Nicrominus's daughter and a couple of retainers. Evanne started to demand what he was doing there, but Arren ignored her. Instead he ran past her, heading straight for the stairs that led to the bell tower.

Evanne's shouts followed him. He quickly outdistanced them as he sprinted up the stairs. In the past, he had always displayed the utmost caution in visiting Norda, knowing that having her perpetually hiding in the great hall was invaluable. Now he tossed caution aside. By the time he was halfway up, he was shouting her name. There was no response; nothing except the hollow echo of his own voice. By the time he got to the top of the tower, his lungs aching, he was convinced that he was going to find her crushed corpse lying in a heap to one side.

"*Norda!*" he shouted as he looked around frantically. "If you're hiding, this isn't the time! You need to come out! *Come out now! Now!*"

Nothing. No response.

The wind whistled in his face, and his mind raced desperately, trying to figure out where she might have gotten to.

Then his nostrils flared. He smelled blood.

He turned and saw it. It was on the wall, just under the section that had been broken away. He was certain the moment he saw it that it was Norda's. Nor was it an accidental spilling of blood. One of her bracelets was lying on the ground with blood on the edge. Apparently she had used the sharp edge to slice open some part of her body—her palm, perhaps—to draw blood so that she could create the image on the wall.

She had scrawled three simple lines to form an arrow, and the arrow was pointing straight up.

He looked up, but all he saw was the Zeffer drifting away into the distance.

"I don't . . ." he started to say, shaking his head, as if he were talking to her.

Then he realized, and he began to scream her name in total panic. But she was too far away to hear.

THE COUNTRY OF FEEND

The funeral pyre upon which Merrih's body lay blazed hot and high, a black plume of smoke twisting skyward and throwing a haze over the pale moon. The mourning and lamentations of the Ocular were almost deafening, and yet Nagel—who stood in the center of the great lawn, staring at his niece's body as the flames devoured it—heard none of it. He might as well have been alone.

He had spoken to other Ocular since Merrih died. He had interacted with them, barked orders, fought to keep his grief in check. All these had been things that the other Ocular had observed themselves. But inside . . .

Inside, he was dead.

Inside, he had not advanced beyond that horrible moment when he had released the arrow, seen it speed through the air, and then watched in stunned shock as Merrih had stood up, her back to him, between the deadly missile and its intended target. Although the entire incident had occupied mere seconds, at the time—and in all the subsequent rewinding of it in his mind—time seemed to stretch out infinitely. Certainly he'd had all the time in the world to cry out a warning. At that instant, he even felt as if he could have outsped the arrow in its flight and knocked Merrih out of the way himself.

Instead he had stood there, captured in a moment of terror like a fly locked in amber, and watched it happen over and over again.

When his guardsmen had come running up to him, when they had found Merrih's dead body, what had he done?

He had blamed it on the Piri.

Taking no responsibility, he had told them that the Piri had slain Merrih. That he had found her this way. So grief-stricken were they that none of them ever noticed the bloodstained arrow that Nagel had quickly disposed of beneath a bush.

He could feel his soul shredding, sin built upon sin. But even as he did, he desperately tried to rationalize it. Had the Piri not, after all, been the ones who took Merrih from him in the first place? And look what they had done to her. That pale shell of an Ocular was barely recognizable as Merrih. The truth . . .

. . . the truth . . .

(*The truth . . . you've finally been punished . . . for what you did with your sister . . . for who Merrih is . . . what she truly is . . . was . . . to you . . . the gods abominated her, abominated you, and she paid for that, she . . .*)

. . . the truth, as he began to construct it for himself, was that what had happened in the forest was a blessing. Perhaps even the hand of the gods themselves. Why, just looking at Merrih, it was obvious the Piri had made her like them. That the reason she and another Piri had shown up in the forest was because they were planning to attack others of the Ocular. Attack them, feed upon them, kill them. Nagel's killing of his

(*daughter . . . daughter, you sick monster, you . . .*)

. . . niece, as tragic as it was, was actually the best thing for all concerned. It was an aggressive action by him, Nagel, king of the Ocular, that protected his people from further assault. And . . .

. . . and . . .

. . . and . . .

The word hung in his mind in the same way that the smoke hung in the air. In the same way that the anticipation of his people hung in the air, waiting for him to speak, to address them with words of comfort and consolation, to tell them what in the Damned World they were going to do now.

. . . *and . . . I must continue to be aggressive. Yes. I cannot wait for Zerena Foux's clan to return, presuming they even do. I cannot simply accept what has occurred. I must take steps. Drastic steps. Now.*

And the words that Phemus had said to him, a seeming eternity ago, came back to him.

As Merrih burned, Nagel turned to his people and surveyed them with a steely gaze. There was still weeping and sniffling, but slowly it tapered off as they became aware their king was watching them, obviously preparing to say something of great import. He could see how they were watching him, with a mixture of fear and anger. Fear for what was going to happen next, and anger that he had failed to protect even his own flesh and blood from the ravages of the Piri. If he could not protect his own, what chance did he have of protecting theirs?

He looked at the children who were gazing up at him.

And he knew.

"You wish to leave, don't you," he suddenly said, his voice ringing out. "Oh, at first there were cries of 'Vengeance' and 'Death to the Piri in the name of Merrih.' But now, with even this brief passage of time, the fire within your vows has cooled. Instead you wish to leave Feend. You are saying to yourselves," and he began to stride around the lawn, taking in the entirety of the Ocular population with a sweep of his arm, "that our ancestral home is no longer worth the risk. That the Piri will keep coming. That we cannot win against them . . . and so we should leave instead. Who among you believes that? Raise your hands, show me."

A number did so, but only a few. Nagel had no doubt that far more believed it, but were afraid to admit to it. For such as those, he had no patience.

He nodded in acknowledgment of those who had displayed their desire to leave, and they lowered their hands.

"You live in fear," he said. "You wake up to it, eat with it, sleep with it. You stink of it." He made no attempt to hide his disgust. "We stride the Damned World as giants, and yet you fear the ground beneath your feet. You fear the Piri . . . or so you think. But I will show you what you truly fear. You," and he pointed to one Ocular at random. "Your name is Tansin, is it not?"

"Tansin, yes, my king."

"Tansin . . . you see the Ocular standing next to you?"

Tansin stared at the giant to whom Nagel was pointing. "Yes, my king," he said, not quite understanding what it was Nagel wanted. "I see him."

"Tansin . . . attack him."

The Ocular next to Tansin blanched, and Tansin looked uncomprehendingly at Nagel. "Pardon, my king?"

"You heard me. Attack him." Nagel took a few steps toward him, clenching his fists and shaking them. "Throw him down. Pummel him. Do whatever you can to lay him low. On my order. Now."

Bewildered looks passed between all the Ocular now. Tansin was staying right where he was, his arms at his side, his eye all but bugging out of his face. "But . . . but I don't understand, my king," Tansin stammered. "He has done nothing to me. He is my neighbor. It is against our laws to assault—"

"It is at my command and I pardon you in advance. Attack him."

"My king, I . . . it makes no sense," Tansin protested. "Why . . . ?"

Nagel saw that Phemus, standing nearby, was looking at him with as much confusion as anyone else there. Now other Ocular were also voicing their bafflement, asking what was happening, or murmuring to one another that the king had obviously lost his mind owing to his immense grief.

Part of him wondered if they were right. And yet he knew, with greater conviction than he had ever known anything before, that he knew precisely what he was doing.

Abruptly he turned on his heel and faced another Ocular . . . this one a youngster. The youngster looked up at the king with awe.

"You," he said to the youngster. "Who's that standing next to you?"

"My best friend," said the young Ocular, indicating a slightly shorter youngster standing next to him.

"Hit him. As hard as you can. Knock him down. Beat him to a pulp."

The young Ocular gulped nervously. "But . . . won't I get in trouble?"

"On my word as your king, you will not," Nagel assured him. "Now hit him."

Without hesitation, the youngster turned and punched his best friend in the mouth. His best friend went down, and the youngster leaped upon him, endeavoring to continue the pummeling. But the erstwhile victim savagely fought back, defending himself with impressive ferocity.

The parents of both young males involved in the fracas started to move to break them up, but Nagel put out a hand imperiously, fixed an angry scowl upon them, and they stopped where they were. Nagel then allowed the battle to continue for several moments before he called out, "All right! Halt! This instant! On your feet!"

Immediately the two youngsters rolled off each other and stood up. The young Ocular whom Nagel had ordered to attack his friend had a bloody nose and a swelling around the bottom of his eye. The other youngster had a split lip and various bruises on his arms. Neither, however, seemed excessively damaged beyond that.

"The problem," Nagel continued, raising his voice above the increasingly fierce crackling of the funeral pyre, "is not the savagery of our opponent! The problem is the lack of savagery in us! Somewhere in the transition from child to adult, we have been losing touch with the greatness within us! The joy of battle, the sheer thrill of crushing an enemy beneath our feet or between our fingers!

"The Piri, individually, are smaller than our children! More fragile! Weaker! And yet we cower at the sight of their latest travesty," and he pointed at Merrih's burning body, "and think of leaving our homes. Fie upon that! Fie, I say!

"Instead I will tell you what we are going to do. The youth of the Ocular will be drafted into training and service of our people! Our finest warriors will coach them and train them for a very specific mission: to invade the warrens of the Piri and exterminate them once and for all!"

Immediately shouts of confusion and protest rose up from the Ocular populace. Females clutched their children close to them, males started shouting that it was unheard of, unacceptable. A number of them advanced upon Nagel, not as an attack, but in order to make their protests heard.

"*Quiet!*" thundered Nagel. He grabbed a burning limb from the pyre and swung the torch around himself. The oncoming Ocular flinched back, squinting, shielding their eyes against the blinding flame. "This is not unprecedented! Previous generations of Ocular have gladly pressed their children into service . . . and for far less worthy causes than this! You have grown soft! Complacent! You have lost your thirst for battle. But it is not lost in our young ones. They hunger for it, yearn for it! We have merely to train them, point them toward the target, and let them go! The narrow tunnels in which the Piri hide will not deter our young Ocular. They will exterminate all of those parasitic monsters that they encounter."

"But what if they fail?" cried out one Ocular, and another took up the cry with "We could lose them all! We could wind up with nothing!"

"We have nothing *now*!" declared Nagel. "We have no pride! No security! No fire in our bellies! Day is as night to me, and I see clearly in both. You must be able to see clearly in at least one. We must restore what is rightfully ours! We will know peace in our lifetimes! Tomorrow all of you will send any youngster capable of wielding a weapon to the castle, where training will commence! When they have been trained to my satisfaction . . . then will begin the assault on the Piri. Then, my subjects, will your children do us all proud.

"Now go! Return to your homes! I wish to be alone with Merrih, to pray to the gods for strength, and to let her spirit know that she will be avenged.

"Go, I said. That is an order from your king!"

Nagel turned his back to them, keeping his ears sharp, aware that—for all he knew—someone might run up behind him and try to drive a knife into him. That, however, did not occur, and he listened as they shambled off into the darkness. There were mutterings, and angry comments, but also others were overheard saying things such as "Something must be done! Are we giants or are we men?"

Eventually he was alone, and then he heard soft footsteps approaching him. He knew who it was without having to turn to look. "Are you here, Phemus, to ask me if I am mad as well?"

Phemus stepped in next to him. "No, my king," he said cautiously. "But . . . you must know that some of your people are unhappy. Many of them."

"They will be happy when they can take pride in themselves. They've been missing it for so long, they don't even know it's gone."

"That's as may be, my king, but—"

"There is no 'but,' honored Phemus," Nagel told him, still without looking at him. "Especially when one considers it was your idea."

"*My* idea?" Phemus gasped. "But . . . no! Wait, my king, there's been some mistake. I was speaking of convincing the Mandraques to send their youngsters into battle on our behalf."

"You mentioned sending our own in as well."

"As an example of an unacceptable alternative!"

"In that case, honored Phemus," said Nagel, turning his glowering eye upon his chief advisor, "I strongly suggest you start accepting it, and actively backing it. Because I am going to be issuing a royal proclamation tomorrow formalizing the new draft, and I fully intend to state that it is by my order, but as per your suggestion. We are in this together, honored Phemus, and if you are concerned for my safety over our people's reaction to this new decree, then you're well to worry for your own." He noted with satisfaction Phemus's deep gulp, and then said, "This can and will work, and I suggest you strive mightily to help make it work. Is there anything else?"

Phemus gulped once more and then managed to say, "No, my king. Nothing else."

"Good," said Nagel. "Now, if you'll excuse us . . ."

Phemus nodded and backed away, leaving Nagel kneeling before Merrih's rapidly disintegrating body and apologizing to her for failing to rescue her from the Piri's vicious murder of her. His own complicity in her death was completely forgotten as his fragile mind labored to hold itself together against greater odds than more generous gods would have afforded him.

UNDERGROUND, THE HUB

i.

The room the Bottom Feeders had been led to couldn't really be called a "room." It was just another chamber in the subterranean world of the Trulls, with no furnishings. Nevertheless Jepp was doing her best to make Karsen as comfortable as possible. She was relieved to discover that the wound he had sustained was not as bad as she had first thought; the weapon appeared to have grazed his ribs and drawn a good deal of blood, but no vital organs had been punctured and she had managed to get the bleeding to stop by just applying some pressure.

She noticed, though, that the others were keeping a distance from her, and Karsen was looking at her warily, even as she bandaged him with supplies grudgingly accorded her by the Trulls at the instruction of that one, Ulurac, the "Spiritu Sanctum" (whatever that was). "Is something wrong?" she asked at last. "You're all . . . staring at me like you've never seen me before."

The others exchanged glances and then Zerena said, "How did you do that?"

"It wasn't difficult. I just pushed hard against the wound like so . . ."

"No, not that, you—" Zerena caught herself before she got too angry.

It was Mingo who picked up what Zerena had started to say. "You attacked the Trulls."

"They attacked us first." Jepp was instantly contrite. "Did I do wrong?"

"No! It's not a matter of right or wrong," said Mingo, "it was . . . Jepp, you were tearing into them. You almost single-handedly had them on the run for a moment there. I don't think anyone here thought you remotely capable of such action. I . . . suppose we're wondering how you did it."

"And why you're the way you are," added Zerena.

"The way I am?" Jepp had no idea what Zerena was talking about. "What way is that?"

Zerena approached her, hunkering down so she was at eye level with her. "Why in the name of all the gods are you so deferential, so timid, so . . . so afraid of causing any sort of offense and so eager to do whatever you're told, when you're always capable of handling yourself in that way?"

"I'm not."

"You're not what?"

"Always capable of it," said Jepp. "I barely even remember what I did earlier."

Zerena looked in confusion to Karsen, who simply shrugged. "What are you talking about? If someone attacks you, can you fight back?"

"No."

"Yes, you can! Why are you saying 'no'? It makes no—"

"It's Karsen." It was Rafe Kestor who spoke. He was standing at the far end of the chamber, leaning against the wall, eyeing Jepp with calm certainty and surprising lucidity. "It's because Karsen was attacked, wasn't it."

She nodded.

"And you," he shifted his gaze to Karsen. "She pleasured you, didn't she."

Karsen looked distinctly uncomfortable as Zerena stared at him. Running his fingers through his hair, he said reluctantly, "I . . . don't see that that's anyone's busin—"

Almost as one, the Bottom Feeders chorused in mutual realization, "She pleasured him."

"Karsen," Zerena said with a gentleness that surprised Jepp. "That development isn't entirely unexpected. When I allowed her to stay, I . . . but . . ." She shook it off abruptly, trying to regain her normal borderline-angry deportment. "Kestor, why should that make a difference?"

"It makes a difference," said Kestor, "because a Pleasurer, which is what she is, is more than just a sex toy."

"I'm so relieved," Jepp said sincerely.

Rafe Kestor ignored her. "She's a particular breed of human. A Pleasurer only has one master at a time. When she pleasures him, she bonds with him. And that bonding releases certain . . . tendencies . . . defensive tendencies . . . when her bondmate is threatened. Karsen . . . where did you find her?"

"On the remains of a battlefield."

"Bodies all around her?"

"Yes. Killed in battle with the Greatness . . ."

"Not all of them, I'll warrant. Were they all killed the same way?"

Karsen thought about it. "No. No, I remember thinking about the variety of ways that the Greatness had managed to—"

Then his voice trailed off and he looked at Jepp, his eyes widening.

And Jepp's own thoughts flew back to that time on the battlefield. Recalling the dizzying array of images assaulting her recollection . . . *blood flying, teeth tearing and ripping, terrifying and unrecognizable roars of defiance and death, death all around her . . .*

"Oh," she said, as if she had just recalled where she'd misplaced a necklace. "Yes. I . . . suppose I killed a number of them."

Karsen tried to speak but could barely get any words out. "*You . . . ?*"

"They were attacking the Greatness," she told him matter-of-factly. "He was my bondmate. But he died, despite my best efforts, and then you found me, and now you've become my bondmate."

"And if you are attacked, threatened in any real way," said Rafe Kestor, "she will enter a sort of . . . of berserker state. And gods help your enemies then."

"And you knew this?" Karsen asked Jepp in astonishment. "You knew you were capable of such mass destruction?"

"Yes."

"Why didn't you tell me?"

"You didn't ask," she said primly. "I was always taught never to speak unless spoken to, and never give answers unless asked."

For a long moment no one said anything . . .

And then Zerena Foux burst out laughing.

It was a very odd sound, a sort of nasal braying, and Jepp had never heard anything quite like it before. But there it was, Zerena's unbridled laughter, and she was clutching her stomach and continuing to laugh. To Jepp's surprise, one by one, each of the Bottom Feeders joined in . . . even Gant, still in the body of his Trull host, although his reaction was more of an amused chuckle than anything else.

"May I ask what's so funny?" inquired Jepp, eager to join in on the joke.

"I was wondering much the same," came a rough voice.

The Trull called Eutok was standing in the entrance, and there were several warriors in his company.

"Nothing," Zerena said stiffly.

"Good. The queen will see you now. And I warn you: If you make the slightest move against her, you will die where you stand."

"Personally," said Karsen, indicating Jepp, "I'm planning to stand near *her.*"

Jepp felt vaguely flattered by that.

ii.

Queen Eurella had not known what to expect when she had heard of the intruders who had penetrated deep into the stronghold of the Trulls, but the motley crew brought before her was not it at all.

Ulurac was standing next to her, looking stiff and formal. She was not entirely certain why he'd felt the need to bring the intruders before her. Simply disposing of them in combat was the appropriate way to handle it, and she had told him as much.

"With all respect, Highness," he'd said to her in a most formal manner, "if one simply addresses the symptom, one cannot comprehend the root nature of the illness. Do these intruders act alone? Or do they represent the first of many such incursions. If the latter, then the more we learn of them, the better we can prepare ourselves."

To her own surprise, she found the argument convincing. So it was that not only did she not condemn Ulurac for curtailing Eutok's efforts to kill the intruders, but she agreed to see them for herself, her curiosity overcoming her more bloodthirsty instincts.

Naturally the one who drew her immediate attention was Crob, a perfectly harmless Trull who, for some reason, seemed to have thrown in with these invaders. She studied them suspiciously as they were led in, and Ulurac called out, "On bended knee before the queen of the Underground, intruders!"

Obviously with great reluctance, each of the Bottom Feeders went down to one knee. The aged Mandraque seemed the least willing, but the female Laocoon muttered to him and, whatever it was she said to him, it got him to cooperate.

Only one of them remained standing: Crob. He stood there eyeing Eurella, and when Ulurac shouted, "Crob! Down! Now!," he still remained standing.

Eutok, apparently eager to back up his brother's angry command, started toward Crob, pulling out his ax as he went, but Eurella stood and put out a preemptory hand. Eutok stopped where he was and, as the assembled Trulls let out a startled gasp, Eurella stepped down from her throne and walked slowly toward Crob. He never lowered his gaze and, indeed, seemed to regard her with distant disdain. She stopped several feet away from him, dissecting him with her gaze.

"This is not Crob," she said at last. "This is a Phey."

Crob's only response was the startled raising of an eyebrow. There were rumbles of confusion among the Trulls, but Eurella continued, "I've met a few Phey in my time. There are no creatures walking the Damned World more arrogant than they, with the possible exception of Firedraques. But no Firedraques possess the ability to change their appearance, and although I've never witnessed it myself, this is most certainly an example of it. Am I wrong?"

Crob hesitated only a moment, then bowed slightly at the waist. "You are not wrong, Highness."

"Thought so. Never met the Phey who could keep from boasting about himself. As a race, they don't give a damn about anyone or anything but their own egos. Your name."

"I have many. Currently, it is 'Gant.'"

"'Gant.' And how came you, Gant, to be traveling with such as they?" She gave a disdainful glance toward the Bottom Feeders. "A bit low in rank, are they not, to be associating with one so self-revered as a Phey."

"If you know my people as well as you say, Highness, then you know we tend to keep our secrets to ourselves," he said.

Eurella "harrumph"ed at that, then said, "The rest of your 'associates' have names? Or is that, too, a secret to be kept to yourself?"

Gant shook his head and then rattled off their names, pointing to each as he did so. They remained on their knees, bowing their heads slightly in turn as he introduced them. Finally Eurella said, "Up. Stand. I'm tired of looking at the tops of your heads."

They stood upon her command and then waited.

Eurella drummed her fingers on the arm of her throne, and then said, "You're insane to come down here. You've realized that by now, I take it."

The Bottom Feeders remained silent, and then the one who'd been called Zerena Foux took a step forward and said, "Actually, Highness, some of us realized it before we started." She fired an annoyed look at the other Laocoon. "Others of us had other ideas."

Letting out a loud guffaw, Eurella said, "This one is your son, isn't he."

"Yes, Highness."

"I thought so. Only a mother could regard a son with such scorn." She looked significantly at Ulurac and at Eutok, but neither of them returned it. Settling back in her throne, Eurella said, "Speak to me, then, mother-in-scorn. For what insane reason did you foolishly brave our tunnels?"

"The king of the Ocular traded upon a debt of honor owed him," said Zerena.

"A debt of honor. Interesting. Bottom Feeders concern themselves with debts of honor?"

"It appears that, in recent days, we do, yes," Zerena said. "I understand your skepticism, Highness. I can scarce credit it myself."

"And yet, here we all are." Eurella was beginning to be pleased that she had agreed to meet with this misbegotten group of adventurers. It was providing more amusement than she would have thought possible. "Nagel, king of the Ocular. He sent word asking for my aid against the Piri, due to the tragic loss of his niece. He wished to exterminate them."

"He still does," said Zerena.

"I refused him aid. I told him we would not cooperate in genocide, but instead only serve to maintain the balance of power."

"Yes."

"And he sent you to plead his case otherwise?"

"No." It was Gant who spoke up now. "He sent us to steal something from you that would accomplish his goal. The Orb of the Trinity."

There was silence, then, a deathly silence. Eurella knew all too well why. "You dare," she said, her voice barely above a whisper. "You dare even to *speak* of it?"

"You said it yourself, Highness. The arrogance of my people is unbounded."

Eurella trembled with rage over his flippant audacity, so much so that she could barely string a sentence together. "The most sacred relic . . . the blessed . . . passed down . . . *you dare?*"

"Again, Highness, as you said—"

"*Shut up!*" shouted Eurella, on her feet. "You seriously thought that you could take it from me? My most perfect possession? And give it over to the grimy hands of the Ocular? Do you even know what it would unleash?"

Karsen spoke up. "Some sort of light, is what Nagel gave us to understand . . ."

"You understand nothing. Nagel understands nothing. You have no comprehension, none, of what the unleashed Trinity Orb can accomplish."

"If it will wipe out the Piri," said Karsen, "that is more or less all that matters as far as Nagel is concerned."

"Karsen is right," Zerena said. "For once, Highness, we are undertaking an endeavor that does not profit us. Whatever this power of yours is you guard, we do not want it for ourselves. We want it for someone else."

"Someone to whom you owe a debt of honor," Eurella said sarcastically.

The human, Jepp, spoke up. Sounding just a bit too chipper, she said, "If it means anything, he also said he would hunt us down, kill us, and eat us if he didn't get what he wanted."

"Did he?"

"Yes," said the Minosaur, Mingo. "You see the dilemma we were presented with, O mighty one. Death by being set upon and devoured by giants, or death by being set upon and . . . whatever . . . by 'not giants.' "

"I understand your dilemma," said Eurella with mock sympathy. "It has touched my withered heart. Truly, you have a difficult decision. But do not despair, because, fortunately, I am a ruler and thus accustomed to making difficult decisions. So I have decided that, for your crimes, you will be executed immediately."

Eutok snapped his fingers and the Trulls advanced, their weapons at the ready, upon the weaponless Bottom Feeders. The Bottom Feeders drew toward one another, forming a tight circle . . . all save Gant, who remained precisely where he was.

"I very much wish you had not done that, Highness," Gant said.

"Why?" she asked.

"Because then I would not have had to do this."

And suddenly Gant's mouth . . . or, more accurately, Crob's mouth . . . opened. Eurella leaned forward, looking confused, for there was some sort of thick goo bubbling in his mouth. "What in the Damned World is that?" she demanded.

That was the last thing she remembered before the gunk, as if it had a life of her own, leaped toward her, enveloping her face. Automatically she tried to let out a scream and suddenly it was down her throat, in her eyes and ears, and all went black.

iii.

"No one move!" shouted Eutok. It was the most unnecessary order he had ever given, for every Trull there was frozen in shock at what he was witnessing.

The queen's head snapped back and forth, and she staggered and fell against the throne, clutching it as she endeavored to gain her footing. Crob lay insensate upon the floor, making gurgling noises but otherwise not contributing anything to the proceedings.

And then, slowly, Eurella lifted her head and smiled in a sardonic manner that was most unlike the queen.

"All right," said Gant, speaking through her voice. "Now things have gotten interesting."

"Blasphemy!" Ulurac howled. *"Unhand the queen, you Phey bastard, now!"*

"Calmly, Trull," replied "Queen Gant." "Your shouting is hurting your mother's delicate ears."

Eutok did not hesitate. Before anyone could react, he grabbed Jepp from behind and brought a knife to her throat. "Get out of our mother, shapeshifter, or this one dies."

"Then she dies," Gant said indifferently. "Why should you think her life would be of any consequence to me? That any of theirs would be? You heard your mother. Phey care only about ourselves. What sort of son would you be to accuse your mother of lying?"

Eutok paused, then rallied. "Very well! Then her blood is on your hands!" and he started to put the point of the knife against Jepp's throat.

"And your mother's blood is on yours," Gant replied.

"Eutok, stay your hand!" commanded Ulurac.

But Eutok had already done so. His eyes narrowing in suspicion, he demanded, "What are you talking about, Phey?"

"My, you're slow to pick up on things, aren't you," Gant said in a pitying tone. "Open your eyes. I've assumed control of the queen. Her survival depends entirely upon my goodwill. At the moment, I'm wrapped around her brain . . . her heart and lungs. At the merest thought, I could contract upon them and crush them to pulp. While you're standing there helpless, I could kill your queen in a dozen different ways . . . although, honestly, do I really require more than one way?"

"You would not dare!" said Eutok.

"Of course I would. I've nothing to lose."

"Except their lives," and Eutok indicated the Bottom Feeders.

"You've already said they're forfeit anyway, so really, the result would be the same, wouldn't it? They die if I do nothing, or they die if I kill your queen. I might as well kill your queen so at least I can feel I had a productive day."

"Eutok!" Ulurac said sharply, before his brother could say anything else. Eutok fell silent, and Ulurac turned to Gant. "What do you want?"

"I believe the purpose of our quest has already been made clear to you," Gant replied easily. "Give us the Orb of the Trinity."

"You're insane."

"No, I'm really not."

"It is the queen's greatest treasure."

"Then I promise you, she will not live to enjoy it. So your choice is that she lives without it, or she doesn't live with it. Again, either way is acceptable to me."

There was a long silence then, as Ulurac clearly took the measure of who and what it was they were facing.

"Eutok," he said slowly, "get the Orb."

"Ulurac—!"

"On my authority, get it," he repeated.

"The queen will have your life!"

"And it is hers to take," replied Ulurac. "But her life is not mine to take, and if we do not do as he says, then we are responsible for its loss as surely as Gant here will be."

Eutok struggled where he stood, not wanting to do as Ulurac was instructing, but unsure of what other path to take. "There must be another way!"

"Not one that will leave your mother alive," said Gant. "This should really be a simple matter for you. All you have to do is ask yourself what is truly important to you: an Orb that is intended to wipe out a parasitic race . . . or your mother's life. I suggest you make your choice, right now."

"Eutok . . ." Ulurac began.

But Eutok nodded, his shoulders sagging. "Very well, Ulurac. I think you are wrong. I think what you are doing flies in the face of what our mother would want. But I will not take it upon myself," and he glanced around at the faces of the dozens of Trulls surrounding them, "to deprive our people of their ruler. I will get the Orb of the Trinity, and we will give it to these bastards, and may the gods have mercy on us all."

And as he turned away and headed off to get the Orb, his heart was pounding with excitement, and his mind racing with all the opportunities the situation presented him . . . provided he could turn them to his advantage.

THE CITY-STATE OF VENETS

{His people are writhing in torment.}

{He would be able to sense it if he were not seeing it for himself. Their state of perpetual bliss is being replaced by agony. He sees them fighting among themselves. He sees several of them trying to chew off parts of their own bodies for no good reason. He sees anger and petulance, bull males battling with one another by slamming heads or swinging their feet around in vicious arcs. He sees females berating their mates, who are striking back at them with burning fury. He sees cubs swimming in pointless circles, trying to understand why they feel the way they do, and why they cannot go back to feeling the way they did.}

{He knows the turning point is coming soon, Gorkon does, and he is correct. The turning point comes with the assault upon the gate. And he is there when it happens.}

{In the past, when the gate was lowered, they learned to respond by going to the Pier, where they would receive their instructions. But the gate remains down, they have gone to the Pier, and no one is there. Gorkon knows perfectly well why. It is because they do not yet know what to say. They are scrambling about like blind fish, trying to determine a plan, trying to figure out what to say. They presume, foolishly and wrongly, that the Markene will keep. That they will simply remain as they are, or perhaps simply become more and more confused and bewildered, but will do nothing beyond that.}

{They are very, very wrong, and Gorkon can see that clearly, even though the Markene cannot.}

{The assault upon the gate comes sooner than the Merk had expected, but more or less exactly when Gorkon anticipated. He watches from a short distance away with interest as the Markene begin to slam themselves against the massive steel barrier. It shudders under their attack, but does not give. The Markene continue to assail it, breaking their heads, breaking their bodies against the obstruction that prevents them from obtaining their beloved Klaa. First a few attack, then dozens, then hundreds. It is a sight to see, more and more Markene coming from all directions, all converging upon the gate, throwing themselves against it over and over, and the gate shudders and trembles but still holds firm against them. Nor is leaping over it a possibility, for it towers far too high from the water.}

{The Markene wail and bemoan their lot, and they are crying out. And Gorkon forces himself to watch from a place of mental detachment. He notices that the single, one-noted moaning of "Klaaaaaaaa" is being replaced by coherent thoughts and complex sentences. Granted, they are of the same sentiment, but there's more elegance to them. "Give us the Klaa!" "We demand you open the gate!" "We have done nothing to deserve this!" "Bring us Klaa!"}

{He allows this to continue for as long as he can tolerate it, until the howling of his people is not only deafening beneath the water, but also about as much as his heart can tolerate. And then he calls out a simple instruction: "*Listen to me!*"}

{Three simple words, but he repeats them, over and over and over again. It seems to take forever. The sun, which has just emerged above the horizon line, travels half its course through the sky as Gorkon continues to say, "Listen to me, listen to me." It takes that long for his words to break through the veil of despair that threatens to envelop the Markene, and then a few of them repeat the instructions, albeit slightly adjusted: "Listen to him!" They do not know why they should listen. They are not prone to questioning such things. All they know is that one of their own is demanding their attention, and this is such a rare event that it certainly must command notice.}

{Then even more time is required, for "Listen to him" is confusing and vague since no one is quite sure to whom "him" refers. So "him" is replaced in the repetition with "Gorkon," and then who Gorkon is must be further explained, and so on, and thus most of the day has passed before all the assembled Markene are finally, finally, finally paying attention to Gorkon.}

{It is an eerie moment for him. They are angry and twitchy and looking for someone or something to take out their ire upon, and all of them are now focused completely on him. He sees the building rage in their eyes as they float there staring at him, waiting for him to speak, and it is further clear to him that if they do not like what he says, they could turn on him and tear him to shreds in a matter of seconds. Which could be very problematic considering he knows that what he is about to say is not what they likely want to hear.}

{"The Klaa is gone," he says.}

{His voice carries under the water, and there is confused murmuring as the

Markene look at each other and repeat what he has just said, and he can sense a tidal wave of fury building and building. "The Klaa is not gone!" they are howling. "We want it! It is there beyond the gate! Bring us our Klaa!"}

{And Gorkon, miraculously, amazingly, shouts above the growing outcry. It is not difficult for him. All he need do is tap into the emotions built up during all those tides when he fumed and mourned and felt outrage at his own people for living in a Klaa-induced haze. Whatever anger his people may be feeling for him at this moment pales in comparison to what he feels toward them.}

{"The Klaa is gone!" he repeats, and before they can shout him down, he continues, "It is covered with a thick and deadly substance called url. It is dead. It is gone. You cannot use it, cannot enjoy it. The gate is in place because they do not want you to know. They think to fool you. They think you are fools. That is what the Merk think of the Markene."}

{"You lie!" cries one and "He is a liar!" shouts another.}

{And it is there and then that Gorkon gambles. "If I prove it to you . . . if I show you the ruined Klaa . . . what will you do for me then, my brethren? If I show you the truth . . . what will you do for me?" He does not give them the opportunity to come up with their own option. "Will you follow me? Will you attend me? Will you listen to my words and do as I ask?"}

{For a moment they ponder what he is saying, and then come a few cries of "Yes!" and then more and soon it is a chorus of hundreds of voices saying "Yes! Yes! We will follow Gorkon! Bring us to the Klaa!"}

{"I will open the gate," Gorkon says. "But when you see the url upon the Klaa, touch it not or you will surely die. Now . . . come with me, my brethren."}

{He brings them to the gate, picking a place arbitrarily, for one place is as good as any other. "We will go over the gate," he tells them.}

{Immediately they begin to protest, reminding him it is too high, reminding him that they are helpless in the face of it.}

{"We are helpless if we allow ourselves to be," he tells them. "If we are united, we cannot be stopped. Do as I now tell you to do."}

{He begins to pile them up. He creates a line of them, right at the place where the waterline laps up along the gate, and then he has more Markene pile atop those who are bracing themselves against the gate. And more piling atop of them, and another line, and another.}

{Gorkon does not know what a pyramid is. He does, however, know what a mountain is, for he has seen any number of them along the bottom of the sea. He creates a mountain now with the bodies of his brethren, and as he does so, their incessant chant of "Klaa" slowly is replaced by another chant. For they are beginning to realize what his plan is, and their minds are clearing enough to appreciate it. And the chant they begin to take up is "Gorkon, Gorkon." It makes Gorkon's heart sing, this acceptance, and though he knows that it is only because they are hoping he will bring them to their beloved Klaa, still it is enough to sustain him for the moment.}

{Soon the mountain of Markene flesh is approaching the top of the gate, and Gorkon, deciding it will suffice, selects a dozen or so young bucks to follow him. "Prepare yourselves!" he cries out, and he and the others begin to clamber up the bodies of their fellow Markene. There is slipping and sliding, as is natural considering how wet their pelts are, but Gorkon and his followers persevere. They clamber higher and higher, and the cry of "Gorkon! Gorkon!" is becoming nearly deafening even as it spurs him and the others on. They make it to the summit of the mammoth mountain of Markene bodies, and Gorkon pulls himself up to the top of the gate, up and almost over. The top is flat and wide enough that he lies upon it on his stomach, reaches down, and grabs the arm of the nearest of his followers. Muscles that can withstand the crushing pressures of the deep are more than enough to haul a Markene up, and then a second and third and soon all of the dozen are over the gate. They dive from the top, and it is a very long plummet, but Gorkon and the others hit the water cleanly, skim down about twenty feet, and then angle toward the Reef.}

{As they approach their goal, his followers begin to murmur "Klaa, Klaa," falling into their old habits. Gorkon is not concerned, however, and within moments his lack of worry is justified. The horrified Markene see their beloved Reef enveloped in the thick, viscous material that Gorkon had called "url," and their chants cease. "It's true," one of them murmurs, and another of them begins to sob aloud.}

{"We must show the others," instructs Gorkon briskly, not willing to give them any time to mourn that which they have discovered. "Come."}

{They angle toward the Reef, toward the controls that are set above on the Reef itself that control the opening and closing of the gate. At Gorkon's instruction, the rest of his people go deep while he himself skims the surface to see what awaits. Sure enough the keeper is there, and he gesticulates madly and bellows, "Keep back! How did you get past the gate? You are not to come here! Get back!" His assistant is there as well, armed with his harpoon, and he is waving it in a most threatening manner. Gorkon knows both of them all too well, and he fancies that he can see the blood of his father dried upon that harpoon.}

{He memorizes exactly where they are standing, jumping about along the Reef, and then he flips over and plunges down, down to where the Markene are waiting for him. The keeper and his assistant are looking down suspiciously into the water, trying to discern what is happening, and suddenly the waters begin to roil and then the Markene are hurtling out of the water, arcing ten, twenty feet into the air, Gorkon in the lead, roaring in fury. The assistant has the harpoon poised, but Gorkon twists in midair, angling around so that the harpoon merely grazes his side. He does not even feel it as, in his descent, he bats aside the shaft of the harpoon with one sweep of his powerful arm and lands squarely upon the assistant.}

{The keeper shrieks, turns, tries to run, doesn't make it, as two of Gorkon's followers land upon him. He is crushed beneath their weight, while Gorkon grabs the struggling assistant's head between his two mighty hands and smashes it firmly upon the coral. Instantly the assistant stops moving, his eyes going dead, as the Reef becomes stained with his blood.}

{The line has been crossed. Gorkon knows this. He does not care.}

{His body weight is an impediment upon the Reef, for he is not built to operate efficiently outside of the water. But he does not let it stop him, nor do the others. "Follow me!" he calls out, and they do, and within seconds three of them, including Gorkon, have reached the lever that opens the gate. It is but the work of an instant to drag it into position, and then they hear a rumbling and a familiar grinding of hidden mechanisms. The gate rises.}

{In the distance, a great wave pours forward, presaging the arrival of the rest of the Markene. They barrel toward their beloved Klaa and, as Gorkon expects, a number of them completely ignore his instruction and throw themselves against the Reef, trying to get their hands upon the Klaa. Fortunately for them much of the url has hardened, but a lot of it remains thick and sticky, and in short order there are Markene who find their hands or faces or parts of their body coated in the gunk. Gorkon has no pity for them. If they were stupid enough to ignore his warning, then they will be of no use to him.}

{The Markene cry out at their discovery, and Gorkon spreads out his arms and shouts, "Listen to me!" This time no repetition is required. This time his voice carries and this time they fall into silence. "See the world through newly opened eyes," continues Gorkon. "See the truth of how the Merk have treated you. See how they have used the Klaa to bludgeon you into serving them. And see how they have allowed the Klaa now to fall prey to this vile substance!"}

{"They did this?" the Markene demand, hundreds of voices shouting the same question.}

{"Of course they did!" shouts Gorkon. "Who else? Would we do this to ourselves?"}

{"No!" "Of course not!" "Never!"}

{"They did this because they want to destroy us! They are jealous of us! They despise us, because we are stronger than they!" says Gorkon. "They want to send us against the Travelers, so we will surely die. They want to deprive us of Klaa so that we will, in our throes of desperate want, turn upon each other. Are we going to let them do this to us?"}

{*"No!"* they shout, their voices carrying through the depths.}

{"Will we remain as slaves to the destructive whims of the Merk?"}

{*"No!"*}

{"Will we reclaim our rights as the truly superior race of the Sirene?"}

{*"No!"*}

{He blinks. "You were supposed to say 'yes' that time."}

{*"Yes!"* they chorus obediently.}

{Gorkon sighs. There is still a ways to go . . . but at least it's a start.}

THE SPIRES

i.

Nicrominus had lost track of how much time had passed, floating in and out of sleep. It might have seemed odd that anyone could possibly sleep at all under the circumstances: being cradled in gigantic tendrils that were dangling beneath a gargantuan floating creature that he had never seen before. But Nicrominus had hardly slept since the Traveler had first come to him with the mandate to discover what might be going wrong with hotstars. He had been pushing himself far beyond what was wise for one of his years, and could not recall the last time that he had slept more than an hour or so. Every time he had drifted to sleep, the urgency of the project and the haunting images of the Travelers would rouse him to wakefulness.

Now, though, secure in the grip of the Zeffer, Nicrominus felt oddly at peace. Perhaps it was the steady wind in his face, perhaps it was the continued swaying of the beast in that same wind as it glided along effortlessly. Whatever the reason, as Nicrominus gazed down at the lapping blue waves of the ocean far, far below, he settled into a deep and carefree sleep.

When he began to wake, at first he thought he was still dreaming, for what he saw before him seemed as if it could only possibly be the construct of a sleeping mind.

There was an island stretching out before him, as he hung high in the air, and the scope and breadth of it staggered him.

Nicrominus had been a young 'Draque when the Third Wave had arrived on the shores of the Damned World. Since he was still merely a student in the ways of Firedraque wizardry, he had not been at the forefront of the battles against the humans. For the most part, he had only heard about the thunderous wars against the Morts as they had struggled to maintain control of their dirtball world . . . and had failed in the face of the Third Wave's overwhelming superiority. Of course, once the Morts had fallen, the foolish Twelve Races had then turned upon one another, raiding and sacking each other's provinces. Nicrominus could still remember his first sight of the Piri, slithering through the streets of Perriz with— of all things—paintings snatched from a nearby museum. He'd wondered what creatures such as they could possibly want with them, and had come to the con- clusion that they were planning to burn them for warmth, or perhaps simply des- ecrate them to show their contempt for the Damned World's previous owners.

The sight of what he knew had to be the Spires at once thrilled and depressed him. Thrilled him for finally having the opportunity to see that which he had only heard about in whispers. Depressed him because he couldn't help but feel, just for a moment, that he had wasted his life cloistered away in one small section of the world.

The Spires. A largely intact city that was representative of what the Morts had created before the Third Wave came crashing down upon them.

Nicrominus did not know for certain how it was that the City of Spires had remained mostly untouched. By all accounts, most other similar cities had been leveled in the fighting. What he had heard was that the Overseer had taken an interest in the Spires, had descended upon it with his Travelers, and somehow— single-handedly—annihilated every human being who had resided there, with- out the concomitant damage to the terrain that one might have expected in such an endeavor. How the Overseer and his Travelers had accomplished such a feat could only be guessed at. But the fact that they had done it at all was the founda- tion for their reputation.

The Twelve Races had overwhelmed the Morts, true, but it had taken a hell of a lot of fighting, they had not gone down easily, and the races had certainly suffered their share of casualties. For the Overseer and the Travelers to dispose of the al- legedly millions upon millions of Morts who resided in the Spires without suffer- ing a single casualty, or even real-estate loss, hinted at abilities and resources of which the other races could only dream.

Nicrominus felt a sudden shift and, only for a moment, thought that the Zeffer was about to drop him. He was wrong. It was changing both direction and alti- tude, descending toward the Spires. It was at that point that he heard something he hadn't before. It sounded like—oddly enough—someone singing. It was com- ing from above, from the unseen controller of the Zeffer. At first he assumed that it was just some sort of idle tune to pass the time, but he quickly realized his error as each of the Zeffer's subsequent movements, however subtle, responded to a change in tone from the singer. He could not detect any individual words; just intonations. Those were apparently all the creature needed to be guided.

"Amazing," he whispered. He could not wait to return to Perriz and tell Evanne and Xeris of what he had experienced. It was only at that moment that he considered the notion that . . . perhaps . . . he might not be returning. After all, the Overseer was bringing him to the Spires to hear his thoughts about the hotstars. Once Nicrominus had told him, his job would be done. If the Overseer then felt that Nicrominus would be of no further use to him . . .

. . . that might well be the end of Nicrominus.

He resolved not to concern himself about it. He was too old to obsess about clinging to life, or how it might end. Every day was a blessing, and if he survived this one—which clearly was just beginning as the sun crept up over the horizon—then that was to be appreciated. If he didn't, well . . . at least he'd seen the Spires before he died.

ii.

The Zeffer set Nicrominus down upon a building with a large, flat top. There was a ring drawn in the middle of it which might have had some mystical, symbolic meaning to it. Then again, it might simply have been a targeting device of some sort. Either way, Nicrominus stood there, his robes flapping about him in the early-morning breeze, as the Zeffer wafted away from him, angling up and over the City of Spires in a manner that Nicrominus could only term "majestic."

Nicrominus had never been so high up in a building before. Slowly he approached the edge of the roof and looked down from the dizzying height. He realized belatedly that he was gripping the edge and stepped back, holding his stomach and fighting a sudden wave of wooziness. Odd that he would react that way now, considering how much higher up he'd been while in the grip of the Zeffer.

The rooftop door opened and a Traveler emerged. Nicrominus waited for the Traveler to speak, but he simply gestured for Nicrominus to follow. The Firedraque did so.

Once inside, the Traveler guided him to a small room, which Nicrominus stepped into obediently. The door slid shut noiselessly behind him and there, in the dim lighting, Nicrominus waited. He was clueless as to the nature of the room. Was he to meet the Overseer here? There was barely enough space for Nicrominus himself.

Suddenly the room jolted, and Nicrominus felt as if the floor was falling away beneath his feet. He heard an odd "whizzing" sound as if cable were being unspooled from somewhere. He put his hands out to either side, having the oddest sensation of movement, but not entirely sure what it was that was moving. Moreover, there was a series of small lights over the door that were blinking, moving consistently from right to left, one at a time, and a small triangle pointing downward that was gleaming red.

"Hello?" he called to the triangle. "Can anyone hear me?"

Long seconds ticked by in silence, with that strange sense of dislocation continuing. Then the floor shifted once more and the door opened.

There was a Traveler standing there waiting for him . . . presumably the same one who had led him into this odd room in the first place. He gestured mutely for Nicrominus to step out of the room.

It was only upon his emerging that Nicrominus realized that he was in a completely different place within the building: the bottom, apparently. The street that had been little more than thin black ribbon earlier as he had stared down from the roof was now directly outside a series of large glass doors. The amazing room had actually transported him from the top of the building to the bottom. Obviously something so ingenious, bordering on magic, could only have been put in place by the Overseer after his taking over of the Spires. It left Nicrominus wondering whether the same Traveler had somehow moved from the top of the building to the bottom, or if it was another one who had been waiting for him. Since one Traveler looked identical to another, it was impossible to tell, and he certainly wasn't about to ask.

Without waiting to be prompted by the Traveler, he headed for the large glass doors and tentatively pushed one open. He stepped out onto the road, which was quite wide, and looked up and down it.

There was no movement. Nothing.

It was as if the City of Spires was dead. He tried to picture humans, in their heyday, moving through the streets, but had trouble envisioning that many in one place. There were lights standing at intersections of streets, blinking red, yellow, and green intermittently, probably placed there for some sort of festival.

The air also smelled different. More acrid somehow. It burned his nostrils and throat a bit, and even made him squint.

The Traveler was now by his side and pointing silently down the street. Nicrominus started walking in the direction he had indicated, craning his neck to see the tops of the Spires as he did so. He wondered how it was that humans could have moved around in such a place. Were they not constantly tripping over their own feet as they looked up in wonderment at the mighty buildings, so high that their tops were not visible from the ground?

"Did this city have a name?" Nicrominus inquired. The Traveler, unsurprisingly, said nothing, and he wondered why he had even bothered to ask.

Then the Traveler stopped moving and instead pointed once more, this time to another building. It was substantially smaller than the building that Nicrominus had landed upon, but far gaudier. Large vertical lettering ran up the side of the building, spelling something that made no sense to the Firedraque. There was more lettering running horizontally around the building as well, but Nicrominus was even more fascinated by pictures that festooned the outer wall. He approached it, studying it closely. There were pictures of humans . . . a line of female humans, bare-legged, in red clothing, and each had one leg raised high in the air for no apparent reason. In the middle of the line of females was what Nicrominus took to be a male. He was also dressed in red, but he was far more corpulent, and had a bushel of white facial hair. He likewise had a leg raised in the air.

It was most curious, for back in Perriz, in his perusal of various texts, he had seen images of other human females also engaged in similar gyrations, in wall hangings and books and such. And he had seen the human male as well, often pictured with a sack slung over his back or crouched near green trees. But he knew he was nowhere near Perriz now, and wondered what the association could be.

Obeying the silent command of the Traveler, he walked into the building. Once within, he was overwhelmed by a sense of faded glory in the carpeting and furnishings. Unsure of where to go, he headed up a flight of stairs and finally found himself in front of an array of gold doors that were stood wide open.

He was surprised, upon entering, to discover a vast amphitheater, with hundreds upon hundreds of seats facing a vast, darkened proscenium. All was silence. He didn't know if he was in the right place or, if he was, what was supposed to happen.

Cautiously, he walked down one of the aisles that led toward the proscenium. The lighting was dim but adequate, although it was a bit cold in the theater. He marveled at the architecture, at the intricate designs on the walls and ceiling. It made him appreciate all the more the impressive ingenuity of humans, and regret that virtually all of his knowledge of them was limited to the histories and studies he had read about them. Granted many of them had been written by Firedraques who had made humans something of a specialty. Even Nicrominus had managed to learn enough of one of the human languages—the one most prevalent in Perriz—to read and comprehend the writings of some of their own philosophers and historians. Still, it was becoming clear from his recent intense study of humans, their history and their lives, that there was far more to them than any had suspected. Particularly when taken in consideration with—

It was at that moment that the lights in the amphitheater suddenly faded, plunging most of the vast chamber into near blackness. Then a single beam of light struck the proscenium at the front, and there was the sound of gears turning and something being lowered from overhead.

Nicrominus stood there in silent awe as the Overseer—or, at the very least, the being he presumed to be the Overseer—descended from above.

He was seated in a vast chair that closely resembled a throne, but was extremely square on all sides, and made from shimmering silver metal. He was at least two, perhaps three heads taller than Nicrominus and half again as wide, the Firedraque guessed, and he was clad entirely in gleaming armor from his head to his feet. The armor was designed in such a way that it was impossible to get any idea what the Overseer's body or face were actually like.

The Overseer remained completely immobile as the chair continued to be lowered on what Nicrominus could now see were several long cables. Finally the chair settled onto the proscenium, but the Overseer did not move. Nicrominus remained precisely where he was.

The silence continued to stretch to an uncomfortable length, until Nicrominus said, "You are . . . the Overseer, I take it?"

The head was helmeted, the front shield covering the face completely. It was solid except for a narrow slit at approximately where the eyes might be, but the space was dark within and Nicrominus could not determine the nature of his eyes, or even how many he had. He was even beginning to wonder whether the armor was occupied, until a very small, but distinct, inclination of the head in response to his question confirmed for Nicrominus that there was indeed someone in there.

"I am . . . Nicrominus. Which I assume you know. I thank you for agreeing to see me," he said, and he realized it was one of those odd moments where one just doesn't know what to do with one's hands. So he settled for holding his arms across his chest. "I am going to further assume that your Travelers have informed you of the preliminary thoughts and notions that I have developed, and which have likewise found grounding in the theories presented by my student, Xeris."

Again, ever so small, ever so delicate, came the slight inclination of the head.

"All right, then. I have developed some further notions about the matter, particularly in how it relates to human beings, the late masters of this world. I will admit at the outset that they might be considered . . . unorthodox. Nevertheless, I would ask that you give them a fair hearing, for they may well be true or at least have a grain of truth in them. Is that acceptable to you, Overseer?"

This time the mighty metal-clad figure didn't so much as move his head. Nicrominus, for no reason other than rank optimism, chose to take that as a positive sign.

"To understand our present situation . . . one has to understand the previous occupants of what has been named the Damned World. I am speaking, of course, about the humans." Nicrominus, despite the great number of chairs, chose to remain standing. It seemed only appropriate in the presence of the individual believed to be the most powerful on the planet. "It is undeniable that humans possessed a spectacular arrogance regarding their own status. According to our studies and their own histories, they took it upon themselves to befoul this world as they saw fit, with pollution and filth. They deforested entire sections, heedlessly slew other life-forms into extinction, without caring how such actions would affect the cycle of life. That arrogance carried over into subspecies interaction, as different subspecies believed that they, and only they, were the right and true rulers of the Damned World. They would often endeavor to hunt one another into extinction as well.

"The irony, of course, is that I cannot say that the Twelve Races are all that much better. Indeed, some would say that at some level, we and the humans deserved each other.

"Even more intriguingly," Nicrominus continued, "the humans had a tendency to be . . . how best to put this? 'Human-centric' in many of their philosophies. At one time they believed that the sun moved around the Damned World, rather than the other way round. Their answer for life on other worlds was to dismiss the notion out of hand since no planetary neighbors had made a point of coming by . . . as if the universe considered them anything other than one single mote of dirt in a vast universe of similar, undistinguished motes. Each group of humans believed its own particular god was responsible for the creation of the universe, and that they, the humans, held the divine truth of existence in their books and teachings. They believed that they alone, of all the creatures that exist on this world and possibly in the universe, were made in the image of their god. Just another of their divine truths. Naturally, the humans could never agree even on whose divine truth was most divine, since they all presented conflicts, and their tendency to go to war over those disagreements outstripped even the Twelve Races in sheer eagerness for conflict.

"In short, Overseer . . . humans foolishly believed themselves to be the center of everything in creation.

"The thing is, Overseer . . . my studies, the theories I've developed, my investigation of the diminished hotstar you gave me, or rather that one of your Travelers gave me . . . ends up posing a fascinating question. And that question is this:

"What if the humans were right?"

He waited for some sort of response and got none. It might have meant that the Overseer was being attentive. Or he might just have been bored. He might even have gone to sleep in that gleaming armor and Nicrominus wouldn't know.

"It's . . . this way. This realm that we're residing in right now . . . it's just one of many. Infinite realms there are, infinite dimensions. We know and understand that, even though most humans did not. And each dimension works in different ways, has rules that enable it to function. Rules that were put in place by the gods, blessed be they. Rules that are not handed to us, but instead we are expected to discern as we go.

"Different dimensions align more closely with some than others. As it happened, the Elserealms aligned closely with this one. 'Neighbors' is the way that the humans would have put it. When individuals are neighbors, that which happens in one realm can spill through to, or affect, what happens in the other.

"Part of the 'spill-through,' in our case, are the hotstars. They were rare here, but commonplace in the Elserealms. What we did not realize, I believe, is that the source of their energy was here, in this plane of existence.

"I believe that the source of that energy . . . was the minds of humans. Which," he said quickly, "may on the surface of it sound ludicrous. Then again, I should point out that it is documented fact that humans used, as their own source of energy, the fossilized remains of long-dead animals. So I don't think that one is intrinsically more ridiculous than the other."

Again he waited for response. Again he received nothing. He took a deep breath and plunged further ahead into unknown territory.

"Say what you will about humans . . . but they relentlessly used their imagination, their dreams, if you will, to shape this world to their liking. They thought, in their limited way, that this was simply a measure of their ingenuity. But it was more profound, much deeper than that. This plane of existence, for whatever reason—whim of the gods, if nothing else—was, and is, entirely shaped by the conscious and even unconscious desires of human beings.

"They thought that form followed function. They were wrong. The truth was the exact opposite: Function followed form. Humans would develop in their collective, dreaming minds the sort of world they desired. One that did not exist. This unconscious desire would then sit in a type of 'between' state, a 'limbo' or transitory condition. And so it would remain until enough humans dreamed the dream, at which point they would then . . . through bursts of industrialization, or visionary philosophers and leaders, or even wars . . . bring the unconscious desires to reality. They would think of it as ideas waiting to happen, and in a sense, they were right. They just didn't understand that there was an actual, metaphysical structure behind it. The concepts would develop a nebulous form, and then the functions would follow to actualize it.

"I even found one documented case where a world leader, all unaware, manipulated that ability. He informed his followers that, within ten cycles around the sun, they would land on the moon. An unlikely goal and one that would have been forgotten, save that he was then martyred. As a result the dream took hold with unusual fervor, function followed form, and the humans were on the moon in even less than the allotted time." He paused and said to himself, "Which now makes me think that humans might have been crafty enough to have made that moving room I was in."

And still the Overseer made no response.

"In any event, Overseer," Nicrominus continued, "here is the situation, and the problem. The human race has largely been purged from the Damned World. And if my theory is correct, those humans who do remain are remarkably dangerous. For energy cannot truly be destroyed; it simply changes form or concentrates elsewhere. Which means the pure power of dream and imagination, rather than being diffused over millions of humans, is now concentrated within the minds of a mere handful. Of course, they don't know it. They know of a time when humans dominated, but accept the status of their environment for what it is. But if they dream of greater things . . . if they take to imagining things not as they are, but as they could be . . . it could be disastrous for us. Through means we cannot begin to guess, they could set events into motion—affect probabilities, develop devices—that could spell the end of the Twelve Races.

"But we cannot simply destroy the humans in self-defense, because therein lies our quandary. You see, naturally this sphere, this plane of existence, far preexisted human beings. It was, however, chaotic. Unformed and void, almost unrecognizable. Humans were created to help bring it into sharper focus. They began as primitive specimens, but evolved over time. As they evolved, this sphere likewise evolved from the chaos that reigned to the relative order that now holds sway. The calamitous depopulation of humans has thrown this plane of existence out of whack. We are seeing, in the diminishment of the power of hotstars, merely the first step. If my theory is correct, if the few humans who are left should die off completely, the hotstars will not be the only things to give out. This entire plane of existence could come completely unraveled. It could well descend into the chaos that existed before humans were developed to hammer it into shape through their imagination, their will, their hopes and dreams and aspirations, and their odd obsession with ascribing names to everything. They even gave a name to the phenomenon: entropy.

"Nor will it necessarily end here. The nearness of the Elserealms, its dependence upon hotstars, and the effect the current energy depletion is having, indicates that the deleterious effects may ripple through to the Elserealms as well. Both the Banished and those who banished us may well share the same fate.

"The depopulation of humanity could be the single greatest calamity the Twelve Races has ever faced. There is only one solution that I can see: We must locate what humans there are and find a way to repopulate the species, all the while holding their dreams in check or turning them to serve us, lest they wind up—through sheer force of will—creating a series of circumstances that could lead to our utter destruction."

For a long moment, the Overseer said nothing.

Then came a deafening sound, like a crack of thunder, except it was within the enclosed amphitheater. Lights flickered wildly, as if a storm had actually sprung up all around.

Nicrominus staggered under the impact, the lights going from blinding to blackness and back again so fast that he threw up his arms to shield his eyes.

And then, if he'd had any doubts that the armor upon that high rise was anything other than inhabited, they were shattered as the Overseer slowly, menacingly, began to rise to his feet. Blue energy crackled all around him, and Nicrominus, who had told himself that neither the Overseer nor the Travelers held any fear for him, now knew pure, undiluted terror. It was not as if Nicrominus was without resources himself, but he could not focus any of his own energies. He was overwhelmed with stark, stinking fear, and he dropped to his knees and trembled and prayed to the gods to spare him. The Overseer was standing now, and he approached the edge of the stage, one great, clanking foot at a time. Each step echoed and the entire theater shook each time, and Nicrominus whimpered like a hatchling.

When the Overseer spoke, his voice was as overwhelming as the crashing of the ocean waves and the howling of the tornado, and he spoke seven words, slowly and ponderously, that would rip their way into the soul of Nicrominus, seven words that he would never, ever forget.

"YOU," thundered the Overseer. "HAVE *GOT*. TO BE *SHITTING ME*."

iii.

Norda Kinklash was exceptionally pleased with herself.

This had been her best hiding ever. *Ever.*

"You should have seen me," she sang to her brother, hugging herself with joy.

"No, but . . . you wouldn't have. My new daddy didn't see me. Not the scary trav-eling man. Not even the floaty thing I was hiding in."

For that, indeed, was where she had been.

The floaty thing—she had seen it coming. It wasn't always easy for her to dis-tinguish what she saw in her mind from what she saw in reality, so it had taken her a few moments to react. When she had, she had done so quickly, cutting open a vein and smearing a message to her brother, who she knew would come looking for her. Then she had stood and waited, waited for the floaty thing to float her way. When it had—when the long, dangling tentacles had been tantalizingly close—she had grabbed them and clambered up quick as lightning. Her new daddy hadn't spotted her, what with being reasonably distracted with looking around from his new perspective. She had insinuated herself among the tentacles, wrapping them around her arms and legs so that she could support herself. It felt good, oddly enough, even comforting. She felt as if her mother was cradling her in her arms.

There she had remained, and she had been sleeping when she was startled awake by the realization that the floaty thing had ceased moving. Looking down, she'd seen that Nicrominus had been deposited upon a rooftop and the floaty thing was moving away from him.

For the first time she was seized with a trill of alarm, but there was nothing she could do. The canyons of her strange surroundings yawned below her. She judged the possibility of surviving the fall if she simply released her grasp and knew she wouldn't have had a prayer. So she clutched on to the tentacles, looking around for a possible means of disembarking. Then she saw something, coming up fast. It appeared to be some sort of huge metal spike, projecting from the top of an im-possibly tall building. It was a short distance to her right, and at first she thought she wasn't going to be able to make it. Then, in a burst of inventiveness, she started throwing her weight back and forth, swinging on the tentacle in a wider and wider arc. She had no idea if the floaty thing noticed what she was doing, and she had neither the time nor the inclination to worry about it. Instead she was entirely too busy being pleased with herself over her ingenuity.

Just as she was passing the spike, she swung on the tentacle as far as she could and then released it. The momentum of the arc sent her hurtling through the air. She was fortunate. The winds this high up were fierce and buffeting, but they were blowing with her and helped carry her the additional distance over which she might otherwise have fallen short. She snagged it with her outstretched claws and wrapped herself around it.

She let out a cry of joy and sang a little song over the wonderfulness of being her. Then she watched as the floaty thing sailed away, oblivious of the fact that it had carried an additional passenger.

Norda clung to the spike for a while, swaying in the wind, because she realized a couple of things.

First, hunger was beginning to chew at her gut. Firedraques could go many days without eating, since they tended to digest their food at an incredibly slow rate. But Norda couldn't recall the last time she had consumed anything, and her stomach was starting to remind her of that fact.

Second, she didn't have the faintest idea where she was or how to get down from her perch.

But she wasn't concerned. She decided that, whatever sort of fix she had managed to get herself into, Arren would come along and get her out of it. That had always been the history of their relationship, and she had no reason whatever to think that recent events were going to change that.

So she clung to the spike and proceeded to sing herself little songs while waiting for Arren to show up.

THE UNDERGROUND

As the Truller hurtled through the tunnel, the Bottom Feeders holding on with all their might, Karsen kept staring at the gleaming sphere that Gant—or, more correctly, Gant inside the body of Queen Eurella—was holding tightly pressed against his bosom. On one particularly hazardous curve, the thing almost went flying from his, or her, hands, but Gant managed to hold on. Since he had both his arms wrapped around the Orb of the Trinity, Karsen and Mingo were each holding on to the side of the car with one hand while pressing down on either of Gant's shoulders with their free hands. It was, to say the least, a challenging endeavor.

"*Are you sure that's it?*" Karsen shouted into Gant's ear above the rushing of the air around them.

Gant nodded. "*Absolutely,*" he called back. "*I can feel Eurella screaming in my head. She's not happy at all.*"

"*Can you control her?*"

"*Yes. But it's not easy.*"

Zerena was in the back of the speeding car, along with Rafe, constantly looking behind themselves to make sure that no one was following them. And Jepp . . .

Jepp kept staring at the Orb. She was so fixed upon it that she was barely blinking, as if afraid to look away from it lest it do something untoward.

Mingo leaned in over Gant and called to Karsen, "*How do we know this thing is going to let us off where the Trulls said it would? Remember, we derailed it in order to get on!*"

"*We don't know,*" Karsen shouted back. "*We have to trust them!*"

"*Great plan! Because we know how interested in our welfare they are!*"

"*They don't care about us, but they care about their queen! That's all that matters!*"

Mingo nodded in grim agreement, and the Truller continued along its course.

And still Jepp wouldn't take her gaze from the Orb. Finally Karsen demanded, "What's wrong?"

She didn't reply, only shook her head slightly and continued staring at it.

Karsen was about to push the matter when the Truller suddenly jolted. Gant bounced upward but was promptly shoved back down by Karsen and Mingo. Karsen glanced behind along the path that the Truller had just traversed, and he saw what appeared to be some sort of raised device inset to the right-hand track. Apparently they had just run over it, and as the car continued to slow, he assumed that it was a triggering device—activated at some distant point—by the Trulls that was causing the vehicle to diminish speed quite rapidly.

"Brace yourselves," Zerena said, not having to shout as the noise level dropped. "I think we're about to—"

The Trull car suddenly jolted to a halt, throwing all of them forward save for Gant, who miraculously managed to stay exactly where he was.

"—stop," Zerena finished.

"Gods, I don't believe it." Karsen was looking around and saw an intersection of tunnels. "This is it. This is exactly where we first got on. That's just amazing."

"Yes, I'm very impressed," Zerena said, vaulting out of the Truller. "But what I'd really like is to be able to be impressed from a distance. Let's go."

"What about her?" asked Mingo, chucking a thumb at Gant. "I mean him? I mean . . . the her that he's in? I assume that Gant doesn't want to go through life as a Trull queen."

Gant gave him an annoyed look. "Right, because going through life as an amorphous blob is far preferable."

"What are you saying? That you want to stay that way . . . ?"

"No, no, it's fine," Gant sighed. "I just . . . it reminds me of what it was like having a real body. I miss it."

"We'll find a way to make it better for you, Gant," Karsen said. "I don't know how, but we will."

Not looking especially convinced, but clearly not interested in getting into a lengthy debate about it, Gant just half-nodded and started forward, continuing to clutch the Orb of the Trinity tightly in his arms.

Karsen had barely had a chance to get a look at the thing. It was fairly smooth, but there were small switches on it, and a flat red panel that was partly see-through. There was also a circle on one side of it that looked like a cylinder had been inserted into it. He had no clue what the significance of the cylinder might be or, for that matter, what the true purpose of the Orb might be either. Something that created light, something that would rid Nagel of the Piri. It all seemed so unsubstantiated. But it wasn't his place or even to his interest to determine the whys and wherefores of the thing. He and his clan were simply out to deliver the thing to the Ocular, aid him in disposing of a deadly nuisance, and save their own skins in the bargain.

Still . . . there was more than the skin saving, he realized. There was something about trying to help Nagel, to do something that would make someone else's life better . . . there was just such a nobility of purpose to it . . . it made Karsen feel . . .

He couldn't articulate it. He had never felt this way before . . . well, that wasn't true. When he had rescued Jepp from the marauding Mandraques, it was the first time he'd felt as if he were aspiring to something greater than simple survival. In some ways, he'd been wrestling with the feelings uncovered on that occasion ever since.

And still there was something going on with Jepp now that gnawed at him. She was moving stiffly, uncertainly, continuously casting glances at the Orb as if she expected it to somehow devour them. As they made their way through the tunnels, with Gant effortlessly retracing their steps, Karsen tried several times to engage Jepp in conversation about it. To find out what was bothering her. Each time she simply shook her head, smiled wanly, but said nothing.

Rafe Kestor had his sword at the ready, muttering, "Enemies to the right of us, enemies to the left of us . . ."

"Rafe, there's rock to the right and left of us," said Mingo, "to say nothing of above and below us."

Zerena was looking around suspiciously, and she gripped her sword tightly, her hooved feet moving cautiously across the stony floor. "Don't be so certain. I keep thinking they're following us. They know these passages in ways we can't hope to. They could descend upon us and . . ."

"And what?" said Gant from up ahead. "Risk killing their queen? You have no idea to what extent they will go in order to prevent that from happening."

"Yes, but here's a cheerful thought," Zerena replied. "We're bringing this thing to Nagel so that we needn't concern ourselves with the Ocular hunting us down and trying to turn us into a light snack. Has it occurred to anyone that now we have to worry about the Trulls coming after us? From now until the end of our days, for all we know, the ground will rip open beneath us and we'll go plummeting into their waiting hands."

"Thanks, Mother," Karsen said. "I needed that image in my head so I could sleep well at night."

"No complaining from you, considering you and your Mort got us into this."

Karsen didn't reply, mostly because he knew that to be true. Then suddenly he scented something and tilted his head back to make certain that he was getting it right. "Does anyone else . . ." he began.

"Smell fresh air?" Mingo interrupted. "Yes. Undoubtedly."

"Gods, we're almost back," said Zerena. "We are the luckiest bastards on the face of the Damned World."

There wasn't much light ahead of them. They had lost track of time down below, and so weren't all that surprised to discover that a dark and starless night was waiting for them. Gant in the lead, they emerged from the tunnel entrance that had led them down into the realm of the Trulls, and Gant called out, "There's the jumpcar! Waiting for us right where we left it! I can't believe it was this . . ."

And then, from around the back of the jumpcar, Eutok stepped out into plain sight with a grim smile upon his face.

". . . easy," Gant finished.

The other Bottom Feeders closed in tightly behind him, and Karsen was scouring the entire area around them, all the possible hiding places behind rocks or trees where additional Trulls were doubtless concealed, preparing to leap out upon them.

None were. None did.

"Satisfied?" Eutok said after a lengthy pause. He walked slowly toward them, his hands draped behind his back. "Check the area, have you? Satisfied yourself that none of my people are about to come jumping out to assail you?"

"How did you get here?" demanded Zerena.

Eutok continued to approach, swaggering in a gait that indicated excessive confidence. "There are none who can match me for my Trulling experience. Long-forgotten passages, shortcuts . . . I can go anywhere, be anywhere that our systems can reach long before anyone else can hope to make it there."

Gant, still cradling the Orb in one arm, pulled out the queen's knife and placed it at the throat of his "host." "No further, Trull, or I swear to the gods, I'll . . ."

"Kill her?" Eutok kept advancing, and he was smiling. "Go ahead."

"I'm serious . . ."

"As am I." Eutok spread wide his arms, like a showman playing to an imaginary audience. "I'm quite serious. We're the only ones here, you Bottom Feeders and I. I don't have to pretend now. Kill her. Go ahead."

"You're daring us to?"

It had been Karsen who spoke, and Eutok looked at him and said, "No, Laocoon. I'm not daring you. I *want* you to."

"What?" whispered Karsen. "You're not—"

"Serious? Perfectly so." He stopped several feet away. "I could not have asked for more ideal assassins, or a better situation. Kill the queen, my mother. I will discover her dead body, lead my people in appropriate wailing and moaning . . ."

"And then your brother, the elder, will take over the kingdom," said Gant. "That is the order of succession, is it not?"

"Just so."

"And where does that leave you, then?"

"One step closer than I was before," smiled Eutok.

Karsen was stunned by the cold-blooded calculation, although he knew that he should have learned by this point in his life never to be surprised at anything any members of the Twelve Races did. "What about the Orb of the Trinity?" he demanded suspiciously.

"Take the damned thing," Eutok said with a shrug. "That old relic was my mother's particular obsession. I've no use for it."

And then Jepp spoke up, and Karsen was thunderstruck as she said, "Give it to him. Give it to him and let's go."

"It?" All eyes had now gone to Jepp and Karsen continued, "What . . . 'it' . . . do you mean?"

"It. The Orb." She pointed at it with trembling finger. "Give him his queen mother or kill her, whichever, it makes no difference to me, but give him the Orb back."

"I'll kill her," said Zerena.

"I'm serious, Karsen," Jepp said. "Make him take it if he doesn't want it."

"I swear to the gods, Karsen, I'm going to kill her," Zerena warned once more. "If she says it again, right here, right now, I'm going to tear her head off with my bare hands and you won't have a damned thing to say about it."

"Jepp, you . . . it's *madness!*" Karsen said.

Eutok watched them with growing impatience. "You people really don't know what the hell you're doing, do you. Look, we need to move this along . . ."

"I know it sounds crazy, Karsen . . ."

"Not sounds! *Is!* You're one of the main reasons we undertook this, and we're not about to give back our prize now just because you . . . I don't even know what the because is!"

"It's just . . . it's a feeling I've had ever since I actually saw it." She was starting to tremble. "Things I'm remembering . . . except they never happened to me . . . but to others of my kind . . . is . . . is that possible? To remember like that . . . ?"

"You're right," Eutok said flatly. "She's insane. You're all insane. And if you think I'm going to stand here forever, you're insane. You," and he pointed, "Gant. That's your name? Gant?" The queen's head nodded. "Kill the queen. Now. In doing so, you'll earn my gratitude."

"The gratitude of a traitor who'd stand by and see his own mother die?" Gant said doubtfully. "Of what use will that be to me?"

"You'd be amazed. I overheard you before. A gelatinous mass is your natural state? I can help you with that."

"You can," Gant snorted. "You can overcome Phey magicks?"

"No. But I can craft you your own body. Nothing is beyond Trull tech. Your own body that will see, hear, feel, touch . . . it will take time, but I can do that for you."

Gant continued to look skeptical, but the touch of hope in his voice was unmistakable. "That . . . you could never . . ."

"I could. I will. And really, what have you to lose in the final analysis? Kill her, now, before—"

"Traitorous bastard!"

The Trull's eyes, normally locked into a perpetual squint, widened in shock as Ulurac emerged from the tunnel. He had his walking staff in his hand and murder in his eye.

"I *knew* it!" His body was trembling with barely contained rage. "I knew that you would do something like this. *Traitor! Murderer!*"

Eutok rallied, stepping around the Bottom Feeders. "Who are you to talk, brother! You have the blood of your mate and your child on your hands! Would you try to add your brother's blood to it as well—!"

"Yes! I would!"

Karsen saw that something within Ulurac just . . . just snapped. Any semblance of civilized thinking evaporated, and what came charging at Eutok in that moment was indistinguishable from the most brutish of animals that had ever trod the planet.

Eutok charged, swinging his ax, and Ulurac didn't slow in the slightest. The ax struck straight into Ulurac's chest, wedged in, doubtless caught between two bones in his rib cage, and he didn't even notice it. He twisted away, the action ripping the ax out of Eutok's hand, and Eutok blanched and backed up.

"*The jumpcar!*" Zerena was shouting. "Get to the *jumpcar!*" And the Bottom Feeders were moving as fast as they could. All save Jepp, who stood there, paralyzed, watching the unleashed mayhem between the two Trulls. Karsen bent at the waist and, without slowing, grabbed up Jepp and slung her over his shoulder, sprinting toward the jumpcar with huge steps.

"*Leave the Orb, leave the Orb!*" Jepp cried out as they piled into the jumpcar.

And Karsen, not even recognizing his own voice as he spoke, shouted in her face, "*We'll leave* you *before we leave it!*"

Instantly he regretted the words, but it was too late as Jepp recoiled from him, looking stunned, and she turned away and hid her face in her arms.

There was a thick, burbling sound, and Karsen turned just in time to see

Gant—having carefully placed the Trinity Orb in the front seat of the jumpcar—vaulting out of Eurella's mouth, like vomit, and enveloping the Orb with his protoplasmic body. "Go!" burbled Gant as Eurella collapsed to the ground.

"We're gone!" Zerena shouted back.

Karsen held his breath, expecting the jumpcar's engine to betray them for no reason except to make their lives miserable. But he was pleasantly surprised as the jumpcar roared to life on the first try. Zerena slammed it into gear and the jumpcar sped away from the scene at top speed.

Karsen twisted around, looking out the rear of the jumpcar to see what was happening behind them. Eutok had been knocked onto his back, and looked stunned, as a raging Ulurac ripped the ax out of his own chest, sending a vast spurt of blood flying from the wound. Karsen fully expected that he would try to use it to cleave his brother's head open. He could not have been more mistaken. Instead Ulurac tossed it aside and, in a fit of blind, uncontrolled rage—rage that, Karsen was sure, had been bottled up for who knew how long—fell upon his brother, even tossing aside his own walking stick as his hands balled into fists. He twisted him around, throwing Eutok flat upon the ground, clambering upon his back. "*See, Eutok! I remembered! So you can't slip a knife into me!*" He started slamming Eutok's face into the ground, and no more words were spoken by either as Eutok struggled in his grasp. The sounds of battle coming from the throats of the two Trulls were guttural, incoherent . . . undiluted primal fury.

Then the jumpcar whipped around the corner of the road, and the last sight in the deepening dark that Karsen carried with him was a pair of brothers, locked in a battle to the death, while their mother lay flat on her back, staring up sightlessly at the starless sky.

SUBTERROR

Clarinda Redeye could not recall a time when she was not in agony.

It seemed to her that she had always been stripped naked and tied to a rock, her arms and legs bound so tightly that she could no longer feel them. It seemed that there had always been great, racking pain upon her back, and that flames—or at least agony that felt like flames—was roaring up from multiple wounds.

Sunara Redeye, her mother, was standing a short distance away from her. In front of her was a large easel, and she was delicately applying colors to it with a paint brush. She was studying it with intense concentration, looking from Clarinda to the easel and back again as she dabbed at it with precision.

She sighed. "It needs a little more . . . something. The face is lacking, I think. Yerk, if you'd be so kind . . ."

"Mistress . . . please," Clarinda tried to say, but she barely got past the first "M" of "Mistress" before she let out a shriek as a lash whipped across her back. Tears poured down her cheeks and she tried to struggle against her bonds, but failed utterly.

"Yes! Perfect! Just hold that, dear," Sunara instructed, setting busily to work once more.

Sobs racked Clarinda's chest. *"Mother, please! Please, I'm begging you,"* she cried as the Piri named Yerk stepped back, lowering his whip and examining his handiwork in the form of the new welt across her back.

"Ah ah ah," Sunara corrected her, not even looking at her but instead focusing on the painting. "Mistress. Not Mother. If, after all, I were thinking of myself as your mother . . . I couldn't be engaging in this sort of action, could I. But as your Mistress, well . . ." And she glanced up and smiled. There was a hint of regret in her eyes, but she quickly covered it. "I have to deal with you in the appropriate manner, don't I. I have to make you understand . . ."

"*I'm sorry!*" wailed Clarinda. "I'm sorry Merrih was killed! I told you I was sorry. There's only . . ." She paused, a wave of pain washing over her, and she waited until it passed and forced herself to continue, "There's only so many ways I can apologize!"

"Merrih wasn't killed, Clarinda," Sunara corrected her calmly. "That makes it sound like happenstance. The truth is, you killed her."

"I didn't! I told you, it was an Ocular . . . he shot her . . ."

"You killed her," Sunara continued, making minuscule adjustments in her rendering, "because you tried to help her escape. You know it. I know it. Yerk knows it. And you insulted me—"

"I didn't—!"

"You did, because you thought you could come back here and lie to me and tell me that you and Merrih were simply hunting for prey when we both know that was not the case. In any event, you know you're not allowed to go to the surface hunting without an escort, so you were in violation of my rules either way." Her voice was calm, even slightly musical as it went up and down along the sentences. "These are things I'm aware of, as your Mistress. And you, who will one day become Mistress, must be made to understand . . ."

"*I understand! I understand!*"

Sunara, intrigued, put her brush down. "What do you understand?"

"Whatever you want me to!" Clarinda gasped.

"Ah. See, as I thought. I continue to fail."

"No . . ."

Coming from around the easel, Sunara studied her daughter thoughtfully. Clarinda tried to pull away as Sunara reached out toward her, but the ropes had no give, and she had no energy. The backs of Sunara's fingers caressed her blood-smeared cheek. "My failure," she continued, "is that I have spent so much of my life trying to give you a proper appreciation for pleasure . . . that I have done nothing to prepare you for pain. And that was a grave oversight, because without pain, you cannot appreciate pleasure. You're only half a being. Pain, my sweet, is vital. Pleasure shows us the outermost reaches of what we can experience . . . but pain shows us the limits. And if we don't know the limits, how can we appreciate exceeding them? True?"

"Yes, it's true, whatever you say is true."

"See, now . . . I know that everything I say is true, my love," Sunara told her, sounding sympathetic. "But I don't think that *you* truly know that, or even believe it. And that's what I'm trying to address, to make you understand. Pleasure breeds lies, and pain breeds truth. We believe the lies to heighten the pleasure, but we must know the truth even though it brings us pain. That goes for both of us."

Sunara then thoughtfully looked up at the fastening where the ropes that were holding Clarinda's arms were tied. She reached up and, very carefully, undid the ropes so that Clarinda's left arm was loosened from its bonds. The ropes around her right arm, her waist, and her feet all continued to keep her immobile. Nevertheless she began to cry tears of joy, even though her arm . . . having lost all sensation . . . simply dropped to her side like a sack of bone and meat.

"Thank you, Mistress," Clarinda said with a gulp.

"Oh, don't thank me," said Sunara. She took Clarinda's numb left hand between her own two hands, and then she said, quietly and lovingly, "I want you to answer me honestly, my dear. It's most important. Have you been consorting with a lover outside of our race?"

"No, Mistress, I swear I—"

Sunara's head speared forward, her teeth wrapped around Clarinda's left little finger, and she bit down. Her teeth sliced through the knuckle with ease and Clarinda screamed as she had never screamed before. Sunara spit out Clarinda's finger, and it plopped onto the floor with an ugly sound that was drowned out by Clarinda's continued howling. Sunara's tongue darted out and daintily removed the remains of Clarinda's blood from her own lips. "Yerk," she said calmly, nodding toward the finger, "pick that up, would you?" Then she held up Clarinda's hand close to her face so she could clearly see the blood seeping from her maimed hand.

"It pained me to do that," Sunara said in a low whisper. "But you pained me in lying to me. Pain is like pleasure in that it can and must be shared. Now . . . I will ask you the same question. If you give me the same answer, more pain will follow. And I assure you, it will hurt me more than it does you." She paused, thought about it. "But I can live with the consequences if you can. Now . . . Clarinda . . . did you—"

"*Yes!*" howled Clarinda.

"Ah. And wh—"

"Eutok! Eutok of the Trulls! We met and he was my lover and I did it because I *hate you, Mother!*" she screamed, all control gone, all caring gone. "*I hate you! I hate our race! I hate this life! I hate living in fear of mating and being mutilated and turning into a sick, twisted, perverted* monster like you and why not just kill me now and get it over with!"

She gasped, her rage momentarily spent, and then came the fear as she looked deep into her mother's eyes and saw terrible, terrible things within. And she was positive at that moment that her mother was going to rip her throat out, just sink her fangs into her and send her vital fluids spilling all over the rock and down her body and everywhere, and that would just be the end of it.

And then the anger slowly faded from Sunara's eyes, like a storm dissipating over the sea. "So that is how you see me?"

"Yessss," hissed Clarinda.

Sunara nodded once, then walked over to the canvas and picked it up from the easel, studying it. "This," she said, "is how I see you."

She turned the painting around and Clarinda stared at it, uncomprehending.

It was not an image of her tied to the rock, as she had assumed. Instead Clarinda was standing near a shore, water lapping around her ankles. She was smiling, but there was a hint of sadness in her mouth, her eyes. And her hand was resting upon her naked belly, which was swollen in the unmistakable manner of a female with a child within.

"Is the way I see you so horrible to look upon?" she asked.

"No," whispered Clarinda. "But . . . but I'm not with child . . ."

"Yes, you are."

"Mother . . ." and Clarinda tried not to weep, but she was unable to do so. She had no tears left, though, and her chest heaved with dry sobs. "I swear to you, I swear to whatever gods there are, I'm not lying, I . . ."

"I believe you're not lying," said Sunara, and she set the painting down and went to her daughter, cupping her chin in her hand. "But you are also wrong. You are with child. Your scent is already changing. I can perceive it, even if you cannot. You carry a child . . ."

"No . . ."

"And it is a half-breed. Is that what you intended . . . ?"

"No . . . no, I swear . . ."

"Clarinda . . . what you have done," she said gravely, "it is a crime against our people. It is a crime against our traditions. Do you understand the gravity of the penalty that awaits you?" Her voice dropped to a harsh whisper. "Do you understand the pain that will be the consequence?"

She walked away from Clarinda for a moment, then returned with a knife and handed it to Yerk. She nodded, giving a silent signal. Clarinda moaned, her body sagging against the rock, bracing herself, closing her eyes, knowing that she was going to be screaming until her throat was raw . . . provided she had a throat left to her.

Her right arm suddenly went limp. She opened her eyes in confusion, and suddenly the tightness was gone from the bonds around her waist. She looked down to see that Yerk, having sliced through the other ropes, was now cutting loose the restraints around her feet.

Clarinda staggered and almost fell, the world spinning around her. Freed of the rock, ironically she now again sagged against it. She stared uncomprehendingly at her mother. Yerk, without so much as a backward glance, walked away.

"For your crime," Sunara intoned, "you can never be Mistress of the Piri. Never take your rightful place as my heir. Never reach the level of greatness that I know in my heart you would have been able to achieve. Never . . ." Her voice caught, and her hands fluttered toward the empty place where her breasts had once been. "Never make the noble sacrifices that were made by your mother, and her mother before her, and so on down the line. You have disgraced your line . . . and will have to live with that disgrace for the rest of your existence. That is the decision . . . of the unfeeling monster that gave you birth."

The words hung there in the stillness of the chamber.

And then Clarinda whispered, "Thank you . . . Mother . . ."

Her gaze level, Sunara replied, "Don't thank me. You see . . . according to law . . . the life of a pregnant Piri is sacrosanct. But once your child is born, it will be taken from you, because it is a half-breed. And once the proof of your crime is evident in the child . . . well . . . it will be up to the Piri to decide what to do with you. I doubt we will be exceedingly merciful."

"I'll . . . I'll leave. Run away."

"You can do that. In which event, I can assure you, you will be hunted until the end of your days. You see? I told you it would hurt me more than you." And with that, she walked out of the chamber, leaving Clarinda gazing at the painting of herself with her hand resting upon her swollen belly.

THE CITY-STATE OF VENETS

i.

A light rain was falling that day as Orin Arn Oran stood out upon the Pier, ringing the alarm bell that was to send the Markene on their mission against the Travelers.

He had informed them that the closing of the gate would be the preliminary signal telling them the time was at hand. That was standard operating procedure, because if their supply of Klaa was not cut off, they would remain in too much of a haze to be effective. They needed to be deprived of it for just long enough that they could gain a fighting edge and accomplish what was needed. In this instance, of course, standard procedures had gone out the window. He'd never expected that the gate would have to be slammed shut prematurely in order to prevent them from discovering the ruination of their beloved Klaa.

But he was determined to make the best of it. Clanging the bell would signal the Klaa-deprived Markene that it was time to fulfill their mission. Some . . . ideally, most . . . would remember what that mission was without having to be reminded. Some others would show up at the Pier, looking confused, and he would have to reiterate for them what was expected of them. It was an inconvenience to be sure, but that was the price of dealing with their addled "cousins."

Sure enough, the Markene began to mass. He saw them moving through the water toward him. Orin registered mild surprise, because there were far more of them coming his way than he would have expected. Had *none* of them retained their instructions? Was it possible that the Klaa was beginning to permanently damage their brains? He resolved that, after he had sent them on their way, he would go and speak to the keeper of the coral and ask him whether the Markene might genuinely be getting more and more stupid. Indeed, a talk with the keeper was overdue, since he'd instructed the keeper to make sure he remained apprised of the cleanup efforts' progress. The keeper had failed to do so, which was puzzling, since he was usually very reliable.

More and more of them arrived, coming from all directions and moving right up to the edge of the Pier. Orin Arn Oran began to get a strange feeling, and he couldn't quite understand why. There was something different in the movement of the Markene. It was less aimless somehow, and their faces . . . they seemed more focused. Well . . . that was probably a good thing, was it not? They'd been deprived of the Klaa for enough of a time that they could properly concentrate on what he was about to say.

He felt a twinge of regret for what he was going to do. But he held firm to the things that Tulisia had told him. The bottom line was, not only had he sworn loyalty to her, but he knew that she was truly a female of vision. She was determined to fulfill that vision, and who was he to say that she was wrong? After all, were not visionaries often misunderstood by their own people? He was determined not to be too shortsighted to see things through.

He ceased ringing the bell, and the clanging tapered off. "My friends," he said slowly, "it is time. The attack on the Travelers is at hand. You must go to—"

The Pier abruptly shook.

Orin Arn Oran staggered, not understanding, and he looked around in bewilderment, simply assuming that there was some sort of subaquatic quake, or perhaps a design flaw, that was causing the Pier to shift unexpectedly beneath his feet. He regained his footing, and was about to resume speaking when the Pier shook yet again, even more violently.

He looked down.

Several Markene were slamming themselves full tilt against the support struts of the Pier. They were doing so on both sides, alternating at first, but then doing it in tandem once they managed to get their timing down properly.

"*What are you doing?!*" shouted Orin Arn Oran. He stumbled backward, fell, tried to stand. The Pier was rocking violently under the unceasing crashing of the Markene. He heard the metal groaning beneath the repeated impact. "*Have you lost your minds? Stop this at once! Stop—*"

The metal pier in front of him suddenly gave way. It flopped downward into the water, almost sending Orin Arn Oran spilling feet-first into the sea. At the last instant, Orin Arn Oran threw himself backward, getting traction on a more solid section of the Pier. But that started to rock and creak as well, and more Markene were coming in from either side, assaulting a structure that had simply not been designed to withstand attack.

And they were screaming. Not in pain, but in defiance, and it was that word, that same damned word, *Gorkon! Gorkon!*

"*Stop! I order you to—!*"

And then he saw the look on the Markenes' faces, really saw it for the first time, and Warlord Orin Arn Oran turned and ran as fast as he could.

He sprinted down the Pier, hearing the howling of the frustrated Markene behind him. In the distance was Venets, and it had never seemed so far away to him. But he was on a solid section of the Pier, one that the Markene had not gotten to, and already his mind was racing as to how he was going to handle this anomaly of an uprising.

And suddenly the Pier directly in front of him exploded.

At least, that's what it seemed like to him. An entire section was ripped away, just like that, as if it was nothing. He skidded to a halt, and Markene were leaping out of the water at him, springing up with powerful leaps. He sidestepped, tried to get out of their way, and yanked his sword from his sheath as he did so. It was long and curved and had a vicious hook at the end, and it did him no good whatsoever as three Markene, acting in perfect concert, barreled up and out of the water. He swung at them, missing them clean, and the force of his swing sent him off balance and tumbling off the Pier into the water.

He sank beneath the waves. He was in no danger of drowning, of course, for he could breathe under water as easily as any other of his race. He was still gripping his sword, and he brought it up to bear, ready to take on any assailant.

Suddenly a webbed hand grabbed him from below, yanking him down. He swung his weapon trying to snare the hand with the hook, and then he was pinned from behind. Arms that could have crushed his torso with no difficulty wrapped themselves around him, and a voice snarled into his ear, "Drop it or die."

Understanding spoken language under the water was not the easiest thing for the Merk, but this was certainly clear enough for Orin Arn Oran to comprehend, and he obediently released his weapon. He watched helplessly as it spiraled to the depths, and then he was yanked upward abruptly by the Markene who was holding him with bone-crushing force.

They broke the surface of the water, and the rain was falling harder now. Thunder rumbled across the sky as if to punctuate the gravity of the moment, and Orin Arn Oran was yanked rudely around to face the Markene who had assaulted him.

"This . . . this is . . ." Orin Arn Oran began to sputter.

The Markene drew him close, and any number of times Orin Arn Oran had seen the black fury that nature was capable of inflicting by way of the sea, but he had never seen anything as darkly frightening as what he saw in that young Markene's expression.

"Tell them," he grated. "Tell them their time is done. Tell them that I, Gorkon, and the rest of the Markene are coming for them. Tell them to clear out of Venets or they will surely die. Tell them. And make it fast."

Then he shoved Orin Arn Oran, spun around, and kicked him with the full force of his flippers. Orin Arn Oran sailed up out of the water, through the air, and landed on the Pier beyond the area that had been ripped apart.

"Gorkon," he murmured in shock, lying on his back, trying to pull himself together as the fury of the rain increased.

And then he heard a threatening, terrifying bellow that spoke of long tides of anger and resentment, all brought to the fore here and now. And the bellow was Gorkon shouting, *"Tell them, I said!"*

Orin Arn Oran staggered to his feet and ran as fast as he could along the Pier, slipping several times, but always getting back up and continuing. And as he did so, two things rattled through his mind. The first was that Tulisia was never going to believe it. And the second was that he had the deep, sick feeling that he knew exactly why the keeper had stopped keeping him apprised of what was happening.

ii.

{He plunges deep, deep toward the depths where even his most devoted of followers will not come after him.}

{That is acceptable to him. He knows there is only so much he can expect of them. One league at a time, that is the way to go about things. Besides, he knows that what he must do now, the others cannot help him with.}

{The darkness envelops him as it did before. He remembers, almost with a dim, amused nostalgia, how he had been so afraid the previous time. Much has happened since then. He has come to the slow realization that everything he feared . . . he had no reason to. That he has it within him to accomplish great things. That he is not alone. Not alone . . . }

{Not alone . . . in his head.}

{He senses it before he fully realizes what it is that he's feeling. It's back. That same strange, uncanny sensation of long, invisible tentacles encircling his mind. The last time it had happened, he had pulled back in fear. This time, he does not. This time he opens his mind, his soul to it. He welcomes it.}

{It is old, unspeakably old.}

{It speaks to him without words.}

{Gorkon cannot reply without words. He does not have ability. But he will, in time. For now, he forms words in his head.}

{*I need you. We need you. My people must be free.*}

{He has no idea what to expect for an answer. He is certain that his people can accomplish what is required on their own, but nothing that has happened to him in the past tides since he encountered Ruark Sydonis has occurred without a reason. He has to believe that his encounter with his behemoth of the deep falls into that same category. And what better reason than as an ally in his battle.}

{Or perhaps he has miscalculated. Perhaps he gone completely off in the wrong direction, and wherever the beast is, down in the deep, it will attack him, it will be offended at his presumption, it . . . }

{He perceives the shift in water before he actually sees the black mass of the creature approaching him. It is in his mind, sure enough, but now the beast itself is rising up from below. Closer and closer it draws, and he still cannot see its entirety, still can barely comprehend its size, and now he prepares himself for facing the distinct possibility that, in his misbegotten strategy, he has just doomed his enterprise . . . }

{And an eye the size of a small island, inset into a face too vast for him to take in, rises up to study him, and the voice sounds in his head, speaking in the vastness of eons long, long gone. And it says . . . }

{*I thought you would never ask . . .* }

THE COUNTRY OF FEEND

i.

"Thrust! Again! As if your lives depend upon it! Thrust! Thrust!"

Nagel of the Ocular stood with arms folded a short distance away as, in the castle courtyard, the Children's Crusade—as they had come to be known—stood in perfectly arrayed lines and jabbed their spears forward, again and again and again, under the guidance of the captain of the guards. Several dozen Ocular had already reported for duty, and he knew of a certainty that there were more. These were the ones whose parents had cooperated. For those whose parents sought to undermine the king's decrees, well . . . there would be serious consequences.

Phemus was standing at his side. "You disapprove," Nagel said.

"You already know what I think."

"That I've gone mad with grief."

"Yes, my king."

He turned to look at Phemus, his eye narrowing. "What would you have me do, Phemus? Nothing? And do not for an instant bring up the Mandraques again . . ."

"I wouldn't dream of it, my king, although maybe . . ."

He didn't immediately finish the thought, and Nagel sighed, knowing he shouldn't bother to ask, but unable to help himself. "Maybe what, honored Phemus?"

"Maybe there is one other option you haven't considered."

"Really," said Nagel. "I somehow doubt that. I mean, what possible means of response are left? We approach the Piri with an offer of truce? Search for volunteers, for the old or sick or dying, to present themselves as meals? What other . . . ?"

Then Nagel's voice trailed off as he saw the grim expression in Nagel's eyes. "You . . . were really about to suggest that."

"You see, my king, I knew that you would reject the notion out of hand—"

"Of course I reject it out of hand!" bellowed Nagel at such volume that the children froze in their place, gaping at him, their spears in an outthrust position. Even the captain of the guards looked surprised.

Annoyed, Nagel grabbed Phemus by the arm and pulled him into the closest room he could find, which turned out to be the armory. Phemus glanced around at the array of weaponry, looking somewhat uncomfortable. Stabbing a finger at his advisor, Nagel snarled, "And you accuse *me* of madness? Of not *thinking* clearly?"

"I accuse you of nothing, my king. But this might be the most reasonable way—"

"I am not interested in being reasonable, Phemus!" said Nagel, advancing on him until he could back up no farther. "I'm interested in obliterating them once and for all!"

And Phemus, his back literally against the wall, snapped back, "Have you considered the possibility that you cannot! Have you even considered the possibility that they have as much right to live as we? That they are not animals! That it is you, in your actions and obsessions, who is acting far more like a mindless animal than . . ."

Nagel grabbed for a spear and whipped it around, pointing it at Phemus's chest. "I could kill you right now and be within my rights as king," he said very softly, very dangerously.

There came an insistent knocking at the door. "Not now!" Nagel called as Phemus stood unmoving, not even breathing. "I'm in a conference!"

"But my king," came the voice of a steward, "there are people here who are insisting upon seeing you."

"Tell them I'm seeing no one."

"A wise decision, my king," the steward said from the other side of the door. "That was my instinct on the subject. They were just a pack of Bottom Feeders . . ."

Instantly Nagel dropped the spear, Phemus forgotten. He lunged for the door, grabbed it, and threw it open. The steward, who had just started to walk away, stopped where he was in surprise.

"Do they have anything with them?" he demanded.

The steward looked blankly at him. "'Anything,' my king? What sort of anything . . . ?"

"Never mind. Bring them to the reception room immediately. I'll meet them there."

Clearly confused by the abrupt turnaround, but not interested in getting into anything approaching an argument with the king, the steward bowed and went off to do as Nagel had ordered. Nagel, meantime, turned back to Phemus, who was still catching his breath at the nearness of his brush with death. "If they brought it, Phemus . . . if they accomplished their mission . . . but they must have! They wouldn't dare return here if they hadn't! They must have brought the Orb of the Trinity! It's miraculous! Come! Come and see it!"

"I . . ." Phemus straightened his clothing in an obvious attempt to restore some measure of dignity. "I . . . think it would be best if you spoke with them yourself, my king. I have . . . other matters to attend to."

"As you wish," said Nagel, not really paying any attention.

He exited the armory and sprinted across the courtyard. On the way, the captain of the guards intercepted him, saying, "My king, a moment of your—"

"Yes, yes, what is it?"

"I was considering taking the Crusaders on a training mission into the woods. We will exhibit caution, of course, but honing stealthy approach on some of the surrounding fauna . . ."

"By all means, Captain, splendid idea, go to it," and he patted the captain briskly on the shoulder and hurried on his way. Then he paused, turned, and called, "Captain!" The captain returned to him, eyebrow raised, and in a soft voice, Nagel said, "Do you, by any chance, have a trainee among your group who is . . . how shall I put it . . . already stealthy?"

"Young Turkin is quite an adept stalker, Highness, if that's what you mean."

"Yes, that's exactly what I mean. I was thinking he might be able to provide a small service for me . . ."

"Anything you ask, my lord."

"Good," smiled Nagel, and the smile had a hint of danger to it. "Very, very good."

ii.

The world seemed fuzzy to Jepp.

Having been escorted to the king's meeting room by a steward and several extremely suspicious guards, Jepp realized she was swaying slightly only when Karsen nudged her shoulder and whispered, "Pull yourself together." His caution garnered annoyed looks from the others of Zerena's clan.

She jammed the base of her palms into her eyes, rubbing them furiously to get them open again . . .

. . . light . . . blinding light, and heat, and bodies with the meat being seared from their bones, and then the bones themselves collapsing into piles of dust . . .

Jepp gasped and then staggered, sagging against a startled Karsen. "What's wrong?" he said in a hushed voice.

"I . . . was starting to fall asleep . . . just from having my eyes closed."

"I'm not surprised. You kept saying you couldn't sleep all the way back here."

"Not . . . not 'couldn't.' Didn't want to . . ." Then she fell silent.

All during the long trip back, she had ceased voicing her concerns about the Orb of the Trinity. Her plaints had done nothing to deter the resolve of the others, and only served to anger Zerena. Besides, the only one of the Bottom Feeders who'd made much of a point of talking to her at any time was Karsen, and the two of them were barely speaking. She knew deep down that he regretted the way he had spoken to her back during their escape from the Trulls. Nevertheless, it had hurt her deeply, and he didn't seem to quite know how to deal with that, and honestly, neither did she. So the gap of reticence widened between them, with only a few words passing between them every now and then.

Karsen shifted in place, then took a breath and began, "Jepp . . ."

But before he could continue, the doors burst open with an explosive thud, and Nagel strode in looking nearly childlike in his eagerness. "Do you have it?" he asked without preamble, and then added almost as an afterthought, "If you don't, I'll likely just kill you right here on the spot."

"I believe," Mingo said, "this is what you're seeking, oh mighty blinking one." He stepped forward, holding up the Orb of the Trinity.

Nagel gasped in amazement. "That's . . . it's exactly how it was pictured. I am . . . amazed. In slightly less than the time allotted, you have accomplished . . ." He put out his hands and said "Give it to me."

And the words burst out from Jepp. "You don't want it, sir," she said.

Zerena moaned loudly, and the rest of the Bottom Feeders reacted with similar impatience . . . all save Rafe Kestor, who looked a bit surprised and said, "He doesn't?"

"I don't?" echoed Nagel.

"No, you . . . you don't." She took a step forward and, in her exhaustion, her legs almost buckled. She caught herself at the last moment. "This . . . this device . . . it will not do what you think it does."

"Will it wipe out the Piri?"

"Quite probably."

"Then it will serve."

"No, but . . . you don't understand," she insisted, and came closer. Instantly one of the guards came between them, looking threatening.

But Nagel made a "tsk" sound and told his guard, "Calmly. I hardly think the tiny human poses a threat to me. Looking at her right now, I don't think she'd pose a threat to another tiny human." He eased the guard aside and approached Jepp, studying her. "It seems to me, human, that you can barely stand. Are you ill?"

"I have not slept."

"I can sympathize, more than you can believe. Then the solution for your predicament seems obvious."

"No, it's just—"

"She's a Mort, O King," Zerena said brusquely. "Not worth the time it takes to speak to her. Mingo, give him the Orb and let's be on our—"

"I haven't slept because of the dreams, sir!" Jepp said, forcing herself to speak through the haze that was threatening to descend upon her. "What I've been seeing now . . . comes to me while I am awake. Day dreams. Visions of . . . of that!" and she pointed at the Orb. "Visions of fire and death and . . . and more death! Agonizing death for all! I see it and . . . and it brings back memories of things I didn't even know I knew to forget!"

"I don't understand . . ."

"None of us does," said Mingo.

"She doesn't know what she wants!" Zerena told the Ocular, striding forward but stopping a respectful distance from Nagel. "She was hugely enthusiastic about this business! And suddenly she wants nothing to do with it! She's making no sense!"

"Indeed, human," Nagel said, not unkindly, "Zerena Foux makes a valid point. I mean . . . things you didn't even know you knew to forget? You're not sounding especially rational."

"That device is not rational," she replied, pointing once more at the Orb. "It . . . the power it contains, that it can unleash . . . it is not the product of rational minds."

"May I remind you, child, that it was human minds that created it?"

"Yes, Highness, I know," she said. "And I . . . I don't pretend that I'm being overwhelmingly convincing in what I'm saying. But I can tell you that I made a mistake. We all did. And I'm trying to fix the mistake before more people pay for it . . ."

"I assure you, child . . . I will not run blindly into the fray. I will study the device carefully. I will make no mistakes. And when I use it . . ."

"No," and it was all Jepp could do to choke back a sob as Mingo handed the Orb to Nagel. "Please, no . . ."

"All right," and she knew he was saying it merely to mollify her, which didn't help, but he continued anyway, ". . . if I use it . . . it will be with the utmost delib-eration and concern for the safety of all. I hope that will suffice for you."

"For me."

"Yes. For you."

Perhaps it was Jepp's utter fatigue, but she felt as if she were seeing the world through a thin veil of red at that moment. "It has nothing to do with me, you . . . you great blind fool! Nothing to do with me, and everything to do with you! You will die! Die! All die!" and she made as if to lunge toward Nagel. Instantly Karsen was there, holding her back, and she was pulling at him as she continued to scream in mounting fury, "All of you! Die at the hands of the humans you de-spised, because human hands created that and it will be your undoing! In fact . . . I should be glad! Glad you're going to die! You can *all* die! *You can all burn, Nagel! Burn! Burn as punishment, courtesy of the last, great death trap of the human race! Die! Die!*"

Mingo stepped in behind Jepp and clapped his huge hand across her mouth. Her voice was muffled and she struggled furiously in Mingo's unbreakable grasp.

And out of the blue, Karsen said—to the clear astonishment of everyone there—"Perhaps Jepp is right. Perhaps . . . sire, maybe it would be best if we—"

"You know," Rafe Kestor spoke up, "I likewise was thinking perhaps—"

"Perhaps . . . what?" Nagel said, and there was an electric air of danger in the room, a silent dare to the Bottom Feeders to challenge Nagel and his roomful of Ocular.

Zerena said abruptly, "This has been so much fun, we have to do this more of-ten." With a quick inclination of her head she indicated to Mingo to move back-ward, keeping Jepp under control. Jepp let out a smothered howl of protest. "We'll let you know next time we're in the area."

"Good speed to you, then," said Nagel, but he never took his eye off the strug-gling Jepp.

"And to you as well. Come, friends, let us away," Zerena said, and the Bottom Feeders—under the watchful eyes of escorts—hurriedly exited the reception room.

THE CITY-STATE OF VENETS

The rain had not let up. Indeed, the sky had grown even darker and was now a solid slate of black and gray clouds. As Tulisia Sydonis stood upon her balcony staring out on her beloved view of Venets, she fancied the clouds were taking the shape of fearsome, legendary monsters of the deep, roaring overhead in a manner symbolic of what the people of Venets were about to face.

Ruark stood within, looking mildly concerned. "Are you sure, my dear, that we should not perhaps do as the Markene warned? Evacuate the city?"

Slowly Tulisia turned to face him, and she had never felt more contempt for her husband than she did right then. "As pathetic as I know you to be, Ruark . . . I cannot believe you are seriously suggesting we abandon Venets."

"I am not," Ruark pointed out. "I was simply asking whether you were considering it."

"Come look at this," she said with an imperious gesture.

"Is it safe?" he asked timidly.

"Of course it's safe! Come here!"

Ruark walked hesitantly out onto the balcony. The rain was coming down fast and hard, but it was still possible to make out what Tulisia was pointing at.

Merk soldiers were lined up all through the watery streets of Venets. They were bobbing up and down in boats or standing upon floating platforms or were crouched on walkways. They were heavily armed with spears and harpoons, both ready to be thrown by hand and also with large harpoon guns aimed at where the ocean fed toward the city . . . the most likely point of entry for a Markene attack.

"We also have underwater nets strung all over, spring-loaded, ready to snap up entire herds of Markene," she said proudly. "And an underwater first strike force, standing ready on the seabed, prepared to send up signal balloons if and when they see the Markene approaching."

"If?" asked Ruark. "You think there's a possibility they will not attack?"

"A possibility?" she said with a sneer. "I consider it more a likelihood. They tried a pathetic bluff in hopes of convincing us to abandon Venets to them. Nearly scared the life out of Orin Arn Oran." She shook her head and stared into the distance, able to make out Orin Arn Oran standing atop one of the bridges that spanned the canals, looking out, waiting. "I have to say, as Warlord, he is a disappointment to me. When this is over and the Markene have been subdued, I am going to be giving serious thought to making some changes in key offices around here."

"You are?"

There was something in his voice that prompted Tulisia to look at her husband. "Do you have a problem, Ruark?"

"It's just, my dear, that I would have thought any changes to be made would have come through me, not you."

He was speaking to her in a way that almost sounded—could it be?—challenging. An aberration, surely, brought on by the stress of the moment. "Of course, my dear," she said without giving it any more thought. "Obviously I misspoke."

"Oh good."

Clearly he was mollified by that, and Tulisia couldn't help but think that the position of Warlord wasn't the only one that needed to be reconsidered. Ruark's usefulness . . . or rather, his lack of usefulness . . . as lord of Venets was coming to an end. The question wasn't whether he was going to be disposed of, but how and who was going to be trusted to do it.

Hell, perhaps she would attend to it herself during the attack. She was certain she was stronger than Ruark. Why, it would be a small matter to break his neck, cave in his skull with some sort of blunt object, and then claim that he fell during all the excitement and fatally injured himself. Who would question it? For that matter, who would really care?

Tulisia knew that she was the true power of the Sirene. There were none who could stand against her. If her plan to challenge the Travelers had not proceeded as she had hoped, well, there was always next time. And perhaps with more capable individuals than Orin Arn Oran in charge, and without having to worry about that fool Ruark stumbling into something and ruining it, then by the gods, she could make certain that things were done right. She would . . .

That was when she saw the waves churning in the distance.

They were about a mile off shore. Not only could she spot it from her vantage point, but the soldiers on the ground and in the water were ready as well. Granted, the Markene were the bulwark of Venets's army, but the Merk warriors were not exactly inept. The Markene were unarmed, having never been provided weapons. They hadn't been needed. Any surface-bound foe who was trespassing upon Sirene seas wouldn't be able to withstand a traditional Markene attack, so there had never been any purpose in arming the Markene. In this case, since the Merk could survive under water as easily as the Markene, the battlefield was level. The Markene were, pound for pound, Sirene to Sirene, far stronger, but the weaponry at the Merk disposal evened the odds and—in Tulisia's opinion—even tipped them toward the Merk.

Still, she wasn't entirely certain what was causing the waves. Her best guess was that the Markene were operating in concert, coming in one vast formation of bodies that was displacing some water. She shook her head, despairing of the poor creatures ever having a clue as to proper attack procedure. By causing the water to stir the way they were, they were giving advance warning of their approach. The sea-bottom guard wasn't even going to have to alert the—

"No, there they come," she said.

"The Markene?"

"No, Ruark, the warning balloons," said Tulisia impatiently, and she was right. The balloons of the submerged soldiers had been released and were popping up to the surface, an assortment of gray round spheres that informed everyone on or near the surface that . . .

Tulisia blinked in confusion. "What the hell . . . ?"

"Problem, dear?"

It was a sign of her concern that she actually responded to his question, rather than ignoring him while exuding disdain. "The sea-bottom guards . . . the ones issuing the first warning . . ."

"What about them?"

"They're surfacing. They're scrambling up to the docks . . ."

More than that. They were doing so in what even Tulisia could see was nearly blind panic. They were gesticulating wildly to the soldiers who were waiting, and several of them were sprinting straight toward Orin Arn Oran. Voices were beginning to rise. There were frightened outcries, soldiers looking at one another in steadily building fear that fed upon itself and spiraled more and more out of control as word spread of . . .

Of what? What in the world had they seen? What were they telling each other of that was so . . .

She couldn't believe it. The craven fools were beginning to back away. Soldiers who had been posted in boats or on platforms were vaulting off them, seeking to get to the narrow solid roadways and docks that lined the canals. Others were throwing down their weapons and flat-out running. Word was spreading like a plague, and Tulisia was hearing screams and outcries and sheer, stark terror was rampant.

And the wave was building. Growing higher, faster, and there was the distant roaring of building water that seemed far beyond anything the Markene could possibly generate.

"What's happening?!" she demanded, and she shouted down to Orin Arn Oran, *"What's happening?!"*

But her voice couldn't carry over the outcries of her people. Orin Arn Oran was no longer on the bridge. She couldn't believe it. She stood there, frozen on the balcony, gripping the railing so tightly that she bent the metal. "He abandoned his post," she whispered. "The Warlord abandoned his post."

"That can't be good," Ruark observed mildly.

Higher came the water, and higher still, and the wave was building upon itself, growing to an impossible height, rolling in with impossible force. From on high the rain poured down, soaking Tulisia to the skin, her seaweed hair flattened on her head, her clothing plastered to her body, and she continued to scream, *"What's happening! Someone tell me!"*

The canals and the roadways were now crammed with people, fleeing. Only a handful of soldiers had remained where they were, and as the wave, black with menace, barreled toward them, a mile high it seemed and growing still, they broke and ran as well. Tulisia had a brief glimpse of Orin Arn Oran in the masses. He was running, Atlanna and their children at his side. She screamed Atlanna's name. Somehow, amazingly, Atlanna heard her, glanced over her shoulder, spotted Tulisia, and made an obscene gesture at her before being swallowed up by the fleeing masses.

The door behind them burst open and one of Tulisia's handmaidens was standing there, looking stunned and panicked. She remained in the doorway, eyes wide.

"What's going on!" Tulisia demanded. "Tell me! Now!"

"You . . . you need to know—"

"Yes! I need to know what?!"

The handmaiden's face hardened. "That I have always hated you, you sea bitch." With that, she turned on her heel and fled.

Tulisia let out an outraged scream and started after the insolent handmaiden, but Ruark stopped her. The grip on her arm surprised her with its strength. "What's the matter, Tulisia?" he said challengingly. "Afraid of a little water?"

She looked at the oncoming wave, was almost overwhelmed by the earsplitting din of the howling crowd combined with the roaring of the impending deluge.

"You know! You know what's going on!" She grabbed at his clothes. "Tell me! I order you to—"

His hand swung so fast that she never saw it coming. It took her across the face and knocked her backward. She stumbled and fell, laid out on the floor, staring up in shock at someone she barely recognized.

Unbridled hatred burned in his eyes, and he seemed to grow in stature, looming over her. "Did you truly think I would let you do it?" he demanded. "Did you seriously believe I would let you bring destruction down upon Venets with your demented plans to challenge the Travelers and the Overseer? To dominate and rule the Damned World? You maniac! You would have destroyed us all!"

"So you're doing it instead?!" demanded Tulisia, trying to get to her feet.

"Yes," he snarled, and his foot lashed out and struck her in the face. It knocked her back down as he advanced upon her. "Because that is a lord's privilege. Because I have looked upon my people, and I have looked upon you, and I have found you all wanting. This is the only way to right it."

He reached down and grabbed a fistful of her seaweed hair. She screamed, batting at him, but he didn't even seem to feel it as he hauled her toward the balcony, yanked her to her feet. He shoved her forward against the rail, pressing his body up against her in a manner that—under other circumstances—would have seemed seductive. Now it was only forceful and brutal.

"*Let me go! Let me go!*" she shrieked.

"How's your knowledge of history, Tulisia?"

"*What are you talking about!?*"

"Almost all the Mort legends speak of a lord looking down from on high, finding his people unworthy, and washing their sins away with a flood. I am your lord. I can do no less."

She struggled in his grasp, but his astounding, unsuspected strength kept her immobilized . . .

And then she saw something within the wave. Not hundreds of individual Markene, as she would have suspected. No, there was one thing there, something vast and solid. Something that had remained unseen by anything upon the surface since it had landed in the First Wave.

"It can't be," she said, her voice broken in a whimper.

"It is."

"It's dead. Long dead."

"It's very much alive. And it likes the Markene. And it doesn't like you. You know its name. Say it."

"No . . . no," Tulisia Sydonis sobbed, trying with renewed, hysterical vigor to pull free of her husband's grasp.

"*Say it!*" he howled above the oncoming tidal fury. "*Say it! Say it!*"

"*Liwyathan!*" Tulisia cried out, invoking a name that was used to scare Merk children when they refused to go to bed willingly.

And Ruark cackled insanely. "There! That wasn't so hard now, was it?"

"Liwyathan sleeps! It always sleeps!"

Ruark shook her violently, and shouted, "You woke him, Tulisia! You and your schemes! Your infernal schemes, born of your insufferable pride. But the Liwyathan is the king of the children of pride, and the king shall have his due!"

The Liwyathan reared up, and it was gargantuan beyond Tulisia's ability to grasp. Not since that long-gone day when it had first encountered the mighty beasts that had once roamed the Damned World had the Liwyathan emerged fully from the water. It did not do so at this moment either, but what she was able to see of it was all slashing teeth and thick, black hide, water cascading down it, and eyes, many eyes, and tentacles, by the gods, it had tentacles whipping about that looked miles long.

"*I didn't wake that!*" screamed Tulisia.

"*The Markene did, Tulisia! One brave, despairing Markene, his mind screaming to it even though he didn't realize it at first! But I knew! Now he knows! Now everyone will know!*"

And suddenly Tulisia was in the air, thrashing wildly, Ruark holding her over his head with seemingly no effort.

The massive wave roared toward them, and the Liwyathan loomed everywhere she could see.

"*Bow down, Tulisia! Bow before your king!*" Ruark Sydonis shouted, and he threw Tulisia off the balcony, howling in demented laughter, seemingly driven mad by the sight of a force of nature unleashed. Tulisia twisted about in the air, began to fall, and then the swollen whitecaps hit, roaring into Venets. With a scream that was drowned out by the crashing of the waves, Tulisia vanished into the crush of the water. Ruark smiled, spread wide his arms, and the gigantic wave, majestic in its undiluted power, slammed into the buildings, blasting them apart like dead trees before the fury of a hurricane.

THE COUNTRY OF FEEND

i.

As soon as the jumpcar was a safe distance from the city of the Ocular, Zerena Foux halted the vehicle, turned to Jepp, and said, "I want you out. I want you gone. Now."

Jepp was seated all the way in the back, curled up in a ball, looking ashen. Karsen had watched in despair as, in the short time since they'd departed the castle, Jepp's physical appearance had substantially deteriorated. Her eyes appeared half sunk into her head, her lips cracked and dry. She was trembling as if an illness was coming upon her. "Mother, please. Can't you see she's ill . . . ?"

"I don't care about her excuses anymore, Karsen," she snapped at him. "Don't you realize what's been happening? Don't you get it yet? I should have realized it from the start. We all should have."

Even Mingo looked puzzled. "What are you talking about, Zerena?"

"The human girl is trying to gain revenge against us for the death of her Mandraque master."

"What?" Karsen gaped at Zerena. "But . . . we had nothing to do with it . . ."

"No, but we came through looking to benefit from the death of him and his ilk, and she resents us for it, and wants to punish us," Zerena insisted. "So she's sown discord into the clan from the moment she got here. Saying whatever was necessary to put us at risk. Filling your head . . . all our heads . . . with idiotic notions of heroism, and we were fool enough to listen to her, and it was only to put our necks on the line! And when that didn't work, she recanted right in front of Nagel, doubtless hoping we'd fall for it again so that Nagel would kill us!"

Jepp was shaking her head fervently. "No . . . you don't understand . . . I . . . I've seen it. I know. It's going to destroy the Ocular . . . the Piri . . . us . . ."

"The Orb is their problem!" Zerena said. "And why are you still in my jump-car? *Get out!*"

"It's our problem. You don't . . . I've seen it. Memories . . . flooding over me . . . not even mine . . ."

"You see? The girl's crazed," insisted Zerena.

"Karsen," Mingo said cautiously, "I have to admit, your mother has a point. The girl's become more and more unstable."

"Dump her," Gant burbled from the front.

"But . . . what if she . . . ?"

"Don't," Zerena said sharply. "Don't even suggest we should listen to her again. She'll say anything . . ."

"We won't be clear of it," Jepp rasped. "When they use it . . . we won't be far enough away. You've no idea . . . of its reach . . . we'll die . . . either quickly . . . or worse . . . slowly . . . the glow . . . the glow . . ."

Zerena started to clamber around to where Jepp was huddled. And to her clear astonishment, Karsen blocked her path, raising a hoof and placing it firmly against her stomach. She gaped at it, and him. "I should break that off at the an-kle," she snarled.

"You could," said Karsen. "But it wouldn't change anything. Mother, she's ill," he continued quickly, before she could interrupt. "You've been ill from time to time. You weren't always yourself. You didn't see any of us suggesting we abandon you to let the sickness ravage your mind and body. All I'm saying is, allow the same for her."

"Zerena, really, what harm would it do to allow her to stay a little longer?" Mingo asked. "It's not as if she eats a lot . . ."

"You were just advocating that we should get rid of her!"

Mingo shrugged. "What can I say? I blow with the prevailing winds."

Zerena made a sound of unfettered disgust, then shook her head. "Keep her silent," she warned Karsen. "Responsibility for her is on your head. And if I think for a moment that whatever's ailing her is contagious, I strap her to the roof. Understood?"

"All she needs is sleep, Mother," said Karsen, climbing over Mingo to get to Jepp. "Once she sleeps, it'll allow her body to heal."

Disdaining to reply, Zerena moved back behind the controls and, moments later, the jumpcar was rolling once more.

"Look at that," Mingo noted, tapping the dash. "The hotstar seems to be at full power. You notice that? It was unreliable at best, but the longer Jepp has been with us, the more dependable it's become. Perhaps she's a good-luck charm?"

"That, Minkopolis," said Zerena, "is the single most ridiculous thing you've ever said."

In the back, cradling Jepp in his lap, Karsen whispered to her, "I'm sorry. About . . . you know . . . when we were escaping the Trulls. When I yelled at you. It's just . . . you're my first human, and I truly don't always know what to make of you, even though we're . . . though you say we're 'bonded.' But what I know now is that you have to sleep. You must."

"Can't," she said, and she was trying to shake her head, but she didn't even have the strength for that. "The day dreams might . . . might follow me into sleep . . . I don't want to dream of fire and the light anymore . . ."

"Then dream of something else," he told her gently. "Dream of something better."

"Try . . . I'll try . . . but . . . have to stay awake . . . mustn't . . ."

Her eyes glazed over and for a heartbeat, Karsen thought she was dead. Then he heard a soft snoring, and her chest rose and fell slowly. He passed his hand over her eyelids, closing them, and Jepp's mind sank deep into a dreamless sleep . . . which did not remain dreamless for long . . .

ii.

Phemus, upon being told that that Nagel had brought the Orb of the Trinity to his study, made his way there with his thoughts racing.

There were things he was going to have to do, and he wasn't looking forward to it. But there was simply no choice. The Orb presented too great a risk to the Piri, and severe measures had to be taken.

No guards were standing outside the study, which was convenient for Phemus. It was going to make what he had to do that much easier. Silently he applauded Nagel's generous cooperation in his own demise.

He took a deep breath, preparing himself for the next few minutes, which were going to prove crucial for the survival of the Piri. He opened the door, which moved silently on its oiled hinges, and his heart leapt with joy.

Nagel was sound asleep at his customary reading table, his head literally buried in a book. There was a large mug of some sort of beverage near him, only partly consumed. And to his right, situated on the table, was the Trinity Orb.

It could not have been more perfect.

Slowly, stealthily, Phemus tiptoed across the room, watching for the slightest sign of stirring from the king. Nothing. He was so unconscious that Phemus suspected he could have walked in slamming rocks together and it wouldn't have roused him.

He reached into his robes and pulled forth a small vial. With a deft movement, he unstoppered it and then upended the contents—a tiny amount of clear powder—into the drink at Nagel's side. They settled in and promptly dissolved, as Phemus knew they would. Now all that was necessary was to come in far more loudly, "accidentally" awaken Nagel, and engage him in conversation until Nagel drank. Once that happened . . .

"You'd be free to make off with the Orb."

Phemus jumped several feet in the air, coming down hard and clutching at his chest in shock. The words had literally been plucked out of his mind and given voice, and the voice belonged to Nagel.

Nagel was sitting up and gazing at Phemus with cold intensity.

"I . . . beg your pardon, my king," Phemus stammered, trying to pull himself together and effect a casual air. "I . . . thought you were sleeping . . . I mean, awake . . . I . . ."

"I know what you thought."

Nagel said nothing. He simply stared at him, and Phemus, moved to fill the air with words, clapped his hands together briskly as if they were cold and said, "Well . . . I'll let you get back to your work. I can tell this is not the best time to—"

"You were going to wait until I was dead," Nagel said, slowly rising from his chair. "Then you were going to remove the Orb, knowing that I wouldn't wake up and sound the alarm. By the time my body was discovered, you would have safely delivered the Orb to the Piri and then returned here to share in the shock of my demise."

"My king!" Phemus affected astonishment. "I . . . I cannot believe . . ."

"The stuff you put in the drink . . ." and Nagel raised the mug, looking into its contents, "was it the same thing you used to poison my father? Make his death look like a tragic happenstance?"

Phemus gulped deeply. "My king . . . I do not know what . . . what dementia has seized you. Perhaps those Bottom Feeders did something to you, made you think—"

Nagel came toward him, holding the mug up, smiling a fierce nonsmile. "At my request, the captain of the guards had one of the members of the Children's Crusade follow you. A most deft little spy was he. He watched you just now go down, meet with one of the Piri, engage in what appeared a most interesting conversation. Did she ask you to bring the Orb to them, or did you simply volunteer? What's your connection to them? Are they paying you? Are you seeking power? Or is there something else?"

Phemus tried to speak, but no words came. He had been certain that his hurried meeting with Sunara, in which he had informed her of the arrival of this potent weapon, and she had told him to bring it to her, had been unobserved. How was it possible?

"Of course," Nagel said, "this could all just be some gargantuan misunderstanding. Fortunately, there's a simple way to determine that. Here," and he extended the mug to Phemus. "Drink this. Drink it, and all will be forgiven."

Phemus stared long and hard at the drink, the surface of which appeared so placid and inviting. Slowly, trying to stop his hand from trembling, he took the proffered mug.

"Might I suggest," said Nagel, "that you drink to the health of my late father."

"An excellent suggestion, my king. To your late father. What's the old Mort toast? Oh . . . yes . . ." He raised the mug. "Here's mud in your eye." And in one quick movement, he threw the drink in Nagel's face.

As much as he should have been prepared for it, Nagel was not. The drink splashed into his eye, and Nagel let out a pained cry as it burned him fiercely.

With strength born of desperation, Phemus leaped forward, tackling Nagel, and Phemus let out a furious shriek that was something torn from the throat of not an Ocular but a Piri. His lips drew back and his fangs, normally tucked up and back in his mouth, dropped down. It was the first time in his life that he had used his fangs, and he did so with assurance as he sank them into Nagel's throat.

Nagel, still in agony from the drink, was almost unaware of the assault on his neck. It took him only an instant to realize, though, and with a roar he started yanking at Phemus. Phemus clutched onto him, batlike, drinking deeply, and Nagel threw a fierce punch that smashed Phemus in the side of the head, jolting him loose.

Phemus crashed to the floor, but quickly recovered, and slithered past the staggering Nagel. The king of the Ocular clutched at his throat, feeling his lifeblood fountaining from the gaping wound that Phemus had torn in it. Phemus, meantime, sprang to his feet a mere arm's length away from the Trinity Orb, drawing an arm across his mouth to get the thick blood off his lips.

Just as Phemus threw his arms around the Orb, the doors were smashed open and two guardsmen were visible in it, demanding to know what was happening. His mind racing, Phemus cried out, "A Piri attack! They came in through the window, attacked the king, and got away! They're still on the grounds! I'm taking the Orb to safekeeping! Find them!"

The guardsmen nodded as Phemus started to move quickly past them.

Too slow. Nagel tried to speak, but his voice burbled within his throat, which was filling up with his own blood. Giving up, he settled for lunging at Phemus, slamming into him. The confused guardsmen watched as Nagel and Phemus struggled, each clutching the Orb, jockeying for leverage and position.

"They've infected the king! Pull him loose!" shouted Phemus.

Nagel kicked out, knocking the guardsmen back, and shoved the Orb hard right at Phemus, causing him to stagger off balance. Then he tried to yank it out of Phemus's arms, but the smaller Ocular held on. They pushed and pulled against each other, their hands all over the smooth surface of the Orb . . .

And they froze.

The small, red plastic piece had suddenly lit up, and there was a high-pitched whine accompanying it. The whine was coming from the Orb.

They had no idea what was causing it. They'd never heard any sound like it. Nagel was still blinking furiously, trying to overcome the burning of the poisonous drink, but Phemus could see clearly some sort of glowing runes appearing in the plastic.

They said "300" and then "299" and "298" and they kept changing with increasing rapidity, the internal circuitry long subject to deterioration, and as a result the timing device was speeding up exponentially as it counted down.

None of which any of the Ocular in the room knew. All they knew was that the high-pitched sound was annoying, and that each desperately wanted to see the other dead.

Nagel briefly got the upper hand, swung the Trinity Orb around, and smashed Phemus in the chin, staggering him. Phemus lurched back, and then the guardsmen—determined to get the Orb clear until everything was sorted out—endeavored to pull it away from Phemus.

And as they all struggled, the glowing numbers continued to speed toward "000" and detonation.

iii.

She sees it, so clearly.

It is as she has always known it would be. She sees the Orb. She sees it appear to collapse inward, and in a millionth of a second, the explosion comes, and it is loud beyond loud, terrifying beyond terrifying, of such power and magnitude as she has never known, as no one currently living upon the Damned World has ever known.

The surprised faces of the Ocular crumble like dead leaves, and the explosion ripples out, further and further, enveloping everything, and Zerena piloting the jump-car sees it coming toward them, and Karsen starts to tell her to drive faster but it's no good, the power sweeps them up and the last thing Jepp sees is Karsen's blood boiling alive before her own eyes boil and bubble over, and nothing can stop it, nothing can . . .

"It mustn't happen! Let it be them, but not us! Not us!" she screams, and she screams it in her sleep, and she screams it aloud, and Zerena completely lost control of the jumpcar. She cursed Jepp's name as the car skidded and slammed into a tree . . .

iv.

. . . and in the millionth of a second, as the circuitry triggered the explosion, and as the plutonium began to collapse in upon itself . . .

. . . something went wrong.

The detonation circuitry misfired. Instead, electricity ripped through the Orb, and there were small explosions from within, but not the implosion required to allow the fissionable material to fully detonate.

Smoke poured from the Orb, and it superheated, and Nagel and the guards yanked their hands away. "What the hell?!?" one of the guardsmen demanded.

The Orb clattered to the floor and there was more crackling, more smoke, and fire suddenly ripped upward from within. Fire and heat, and something else, some sort of liquid that was silvery white, except the moment it touched the air, it turned yellow . . .

. . . and the air seemed alive with burning, invisible fire, and Nagel staggered, grabbing at the air as if he could bat it away somehow.

There was still a high-pitched whining coming from the Orb, and Nagel suddenly felt ill, as if he wanted to vomit. He turned to his guardsmen, clutching at his throat, and was horrified to see that their skin was rotting away, their bones already peering through. They collapsed and there was Phemus, falling atop them, the blood vessels in his eye popping even as his body started to collapse in upon itself.

Nagel didn't understand what was happening, didn't understand why suddenly the floor had reached up for him and pulled him down.

He stared at the Orb of the Trinity, the device that was going to solve all the world's ills in one great stroke, and then, to his complete and utter shock, he saw Merrih standing a short distance away, and she was smiling at him, and he had forgotten just how beautiful his dead niece was. He wanted to reach out to her but he couldn't move, and the yellowish stuff was leaking everywhere, and he knew he should be in agony, but for some reason he wasn't.

I can still see, thought the One-Eyed King, and suddenly all his movements were unrestricted and free, and he knew as he reached for Merrih that everything was going to be fine, and then he knew nothing more.

v.

A silence hung over the jumpcar for a time, and then Zerena called out, "*Is everyone all right?*"

There were affirmative murmurs from everyone in the jumpcar.

"Everybody out. We've got to inspect the damage."

Obediently, everyone got out of the jumpcar, with Karsen the last one, helping a dazed Jepp out.

The second they were clear of the car, Zerena turned and hit Karsen in the face as hard as she could.

Karsen fell like a sack of rocks. Instantly Zerena turned to face Jepp and she had her sword out. "Now you die," she said.

Jepp's face twisted in fury, and Zerena belatedly realized—by injuring Karsen—that she had unleashed the berserker rage that dwelt within Jepp's heart.

And it was at that moment that Mingo shouted, "*Zerena! Jepp! Look!*"

Zerena risked a quick glance to see where he was indicating.

Her jaw dropped.

In the far, far distance, the city of the Ocular was glowing green against the night sky.

Instantly Zerena remembered all that Jepp had said. All of it. The description of what would happen to the Ocular . . . of what would happen to them . . . the flash of light, the glowing, the overwhelming wave of heat that would destroy them all . . .

There was a choked sob from Jepp, and Zerena looked back at her. So overwhelmed was Jepp by her nightmare made real that her deadly rage subsided. She was just standing there, staring. She was vulnerable to attack by Zerena . . . but instead Zerena, her arm numb, dropped her sword.

"Are . . . we all going to die now?" Zerena Foux asked.

It took Jepp a few seconds to process the information that Zerena was talking to her, looking to her for information. She shook her head, dazed, and murmured, "I . . . I don't know. I don't . . . think so. I don't understand . . . can . . . barely remember what happened . . . I . . ."

Suddenly there was a rumbling beneath their feet, the ground shaking, and a panicked Zerena Foux—who was not afraid of dying beneath the swing of a sword or a blow from an ax, but was terrified of meeting her death through some bizarre, unknown means that was comprehensible only to the tortured mind of a Mort—cried out, "It's coming! The wave of fire and light is coming, it's—!"

"No!" Mingo shouted. "It's not that! Don't you recognize it?"

And then she did, but too late, and even if she'd recognized it instantly, there would have been nothing to be done for it.

It was Travelers, a half-dozen of them, pounding across the terrain upon their draquons. The draquons let out defiant roars, and this time there was no uncertainty of their target. This time the Travelers were heading straight toward the Bottom Feeders, barely slowing down.

Zerena's clan scattered in all directions, desperately trying to get out of the way, and to Zerena's shock, the Travelers did not go through. Instead the draquons, at the command of their masters, whipped around the Bottom Feeders, herding them like cattle. Even in the face of a hopeless fight, Zerena wasn't about to back down, even from the Travelers. She grabbed up her fallen sword, looked for a target, as the Travelers hurtled around the Bottom Feeders, and suddenly one of them charged straight toward Zerena. She swung her sword and the Traveler effortlessly reached out and slapped it aside. Before Zerena could move, the draquon's tail lashed out and knocked her flat. She felt something break within her chest, probably a rib, possibly two, and she went down, clutching at it.

The others in her clan were being driven back as well, and then she saw one of the Travelers reach out, snag Jepp around the waist, and urge his black and terrible steed forward.

Obediently the draquon bounded away, and seconds later, the other Travelers were following him. Zerena, her arm around her chest, lay on the ground and watched in stunned silence as the Travelers departed, leaving the rest of her clan untouched.

Moments later, all was silent.

"Well, *that* was convenient," said Zerena Foux.

THE CITY-STATE OF VENETS

{Gorkon watches with vague interest, and only the slightest sense of irony, as a large sailing ship piloted by the Travelers cruises past.}

{He swims alongside them for a brief while, keeping a safe distance. He watches the deck with curiosity, hoping to catch a glimpse of one of these supposedly most dreaded of beings.}

{He sees nothing. The sails are billowing, aiding the strong wind that is propelling the ship along. But there are no crewmen on the deck running it that he can . . . }

{Then he sees someone. Someone has emerged onto the deck. He is cloaked and hooded, and it is impossible to see his face. Not only that, but he does not appear actually to be standing upon the deck. It is as if he is floating across it.}

{There is someone else there as well. This person is also wearing a cloak, but it is smaller, and seems more designed for protection than anything else. The hood is back, revealing the head and face, and he is not certain, but it appears to be a female of some sort. She is unlike any female he has ever seen, however. Her face is smooth and tanned, her hair billowing out behind her, and it does not look like seaweed at all. It is hard for him to be certain, but she appears both afraid . . . and yet confident. He does not understand how she can possibly be both, but she is.}

{"She is a human," says a voice from next to him.}

{He glances over to see Ruark Sydonis floating next to him. Floating is about all Ruark Sydonis can do these days, with his arms and legs having been shattered. Gorkon has fashioned a flotation device for him, and Ruark seems convinced that his limbs will eventually heal. Gorkon is dubious, but he defers to Ruark's wisdom on these matters.}

{"A human," says Gorkon. "I have never seen one."}

{"You haven't missed much," replies Ruark.}

{Gorkon considers the situation. "Do you think," he says slowly, "that the Travelers will notice that much of Venets is destroyed?"}

{"As they pass it? Perhaps."}

{"Will they care?"}

{"I very much doubt it," says Ruark. "Travelers only care about things that you and I cannot begin to understand."}

{"Such as humans? Why would they care about humans?"}

{Ruark Sydonis considered it for a time, and then said helpfully, "I hear they make excellent pets."}

THE COUNTRY OF FEEND

i.

The Children's Crusade of the Ocular huddled for mutual warmth and protection deep within the woods. They were cold and tired, and they could not stop staring at the distant green glow that emanated from the far-off city.

The children were looking to two of their own for guidance, the two oldest. One was named Turkin, a young, strapping Ocular lad. The other was a female, Berola. Berola had always been a precocious sort, and had far preferred to run with the males than associate with the females. Defying Ocular custom, she had actually shaved her head, which had infuriated her parents and made her quite the talk of the town.

Now she and Turkin were sitting a short distance from the others, and Berola was muttering, "This is ridiculous. We should just head back to the city, that's all."

"While it's glowing?" demanded Turkin. "Don't be ridiculous."

"So it's glowing. So what? A glow never hurt anybody."

"The captain said we wait here for him to get back," Turkin said firmly. "And here is where we wait. Did you all get that?" he raised his voice so the others could hear him. "We wait here until the captain returns." Then, once they nodded, he lowered his voice so that only Berola could hear and said, "Between you and me . . . I think this is all part of the training mission."

"Eh?" Berola looked at him skeptically.

"Yup. They come up with all sorts of ways to try and keep us off balance. Why, earlier the captain had me follow the high advisor himself, Phemus."

"Really?" Berola now seemed impressed, which pleased Turkin no end. "Did you find out anything interesting . . . ?"

"He was talking to a Piri."

"*No! You lie!*"

"Gods' truth," Turkin said fervently. "I told the captain, and that's why he went and left us here: to go back and tell the king himself."

"But why? Why would he have been talking to the Piri?"

"No idea. Not my job to—"

"Look!" one of the youngsters suddenly called out. "It's the captain!"

He was right. The captain of the guards was coming through the woods toward them. Berola and Turkin, who had been sitting, were promptly on their feet, shoulders squared, trying to look like capable members of the Crusade.

And then the captain began to stagger.

"Captain?" Berola said. "Is something wro—?"

"Stay back," said the captain, his voice thick and raspy. He'd been standing in the shadows of the trees, and the moon was covered by a cloud, but now it emerged from hiding and the children gasped. Even from the distance they were at, they could see his skin was blackened and peeling and falling off. His teeth were gone, and his eye looked like it was cracking.

"Don't . . . go back," he managed to say. "Nothing for you . . . everyone dying . . . all of them . . . all . . . dying . . ."

"Dying?" gasped Turkin. "Of what? Why? From what?"

"Humans," the captain of the guard managed to get out, and then he collapsed. Several of the children cried out as he fell, and they started to move toward him.

"Don't touch him!" shouted Berola, and the children froze.

They heard the captain wheeze horribly for long seconds, and then there was an ugly rattle, and then nothing.

"Is he okay now?" asked one of the children, and another one hit the first child upside the head and said, "No, he's not okay, he's dead, stupid!"

And then came wailing and sobbing and cries from all the children that they wanted to go home, that they had had enough, that this was all too terrible. "Shut up!" shouted Berola, putting her hands to her head. "We . . . we just need to think!"

"Think about what?!" Turkin was clearly starting to panic. "You heard the captain! We can't go back! Everyone . . . everyone is going to be like him—!"

"I want my mother!" cried one of the children, and they started crying all over again for their parents, and Berola and Turkin looked helplessly at one another. Because, really, all they wanted to do, deep down, was break down and start sobbing as well.

And that was when a voice shouted over all of them, "*You don't have mothers, you don't have fathers, and you're not going back!*"

They turned and stared, and Berola felt a surge of fear bubbling up in her throat. Turkin tried to control a similar sensation. It was all he could do not to bolt and run. Collective gasps were ripped from the throats of the remaining children.

A female Piri was standing there. She was tall and elegant, but had a haunted look. "All you have," she said softly, "is me."

"*You?*" said Turkin, trying to sound confidently arrogant. "You're . . . you're a—"

"I know what I am," she said. "But you don't know what I am. I'm your salvation."

"You're not serious," said Berola.

The Piri nodded. "If you come with me, now, I will protect you from the others of my kind. I can do this for you. And I will train you and help you . . . and, in time, you will help me. We will be able to protect each other."

"Us protect you?" asked Berola. "Why should we?"

"Because," said the Piri, "like it or not . . . you're the last of the Ocular. And you're in trouble. And I'm in trouble."

Berola studied her, tried to get some sort of sense of her. She noticed the Piri's left hand. "What happened to your little finger?" she demanded.

"Nothing. It's fine. It's just not on my hand."

"What's your name?" asked one of the younger Ocular.

"Don't talk to her!" Berola ordered.

But the Piri ignored her. "My name is Clarinda. What's yours?"

"Kerda."

"Kerda . . . will you come with me?"

"Will you hurt me?" Kerda asked guardedly.

"No. Never. I swear."

"All right," said Kerda.

Clarinda nodded, and started to walk off into the dark of the forest. Kerda followed her, and the others started to as well.

"Are you insane!" shouted Turkin. "We were being trained to kill her kind! You can't . . . this is crazy! Berola, tell them they're crazy!"

"You're crazy!" Berola called.

But the youngsters didn't stop, following Clarinda. And as the last of them disappeared into the woods, Turkin and Berola exchanged nervous looks, shouted as one, "Wait for us!," and sprinted off after them into the endless night of Feend.

ii.

Karsen Foux strapped the last of his provisions to his back as Zerena stood there, shaking her head. The other Bottom Feeders stood nearby, silent, unwilling to interfere.

"You can't be doing this, Karsen," Zerena said. "We need to have a discussion about this."

"I'm here, Mother. Discuss away."

"Dammit, Karsen. The Travelers wanted her. The Travelers took her. Who are we to say no to the Travelers?"

"We're no one," Karsen said. "We're Bottom Feeders. We're nothing."

"Exactly," Zerena told him. "The one time we tried to be something we're not, it was no end of problems, and even the stupid Mort who talked us into it recanted on it."

"I can't contradict a single thing you're saying, Mother."

"Then what the hell are you doing now?!"

"You don't get it, Mother!"

"Of course I don't 'get it'! Would I be shouting if I got it? That girl has done something to you!"

He steadied himself and spoke with a ferocity that he once thought he would never be capable of. "Yes. She has. And what you don't get is that she's done something to all of us, but you just refuse to see it."

"She sure as hell done something. She's driven a wedge between us."

"No! No, it's . . ." He put his hands over his face, searching for the words. "Mother . . . how can you go back to being nothing when, for just a moment, you were something?"

"We never were, Karsen. We were nothings pretending to be something. The way we are is the way to survive."

He shook his head. "I can't just survive, Mother."

"Well, you're in luck, because if you pursue this foolishness, you won't survive."

"I can't . . ."

"You can't what?"

"I can't . . . not know," he said in frustration. "The Trinity Orb . . . it was just part of one thing. But Jepp is part of something bigger. Somehow, in some way, she . . . she makes things happen. We've seen it. We've all seen it. I don't pretend to understand it. What I do understand is this: We've spent our lives sifting through the remains of great wars, picking through them and taking the valuables for ourselves. And we're always patting ourselves on the back for our ingenuity and our ability to take advantage of others' mistakes and see the rich prospects in that which was left behind. Well, Jepp is the remains of a war, and I'm not talking about the pointless Mandraque battle where I found her. I mean the war of the Third Wave. She was ours. She was . . . she was energy. She was light. She's all that we can be and more . . ."

"Oh, gods, all this rhapsodizing over a *damned Mort*!"

He came close to Zerena, look her in the eyes, and said, "We had one of the greatest riches in the Damned World right here, right in our grasp . . . and she slipped through our fingers. I may be a Bottom Feeder, but for a while, I was at the top, and I'm not going back to the bottom again. I want her for the way she makes me feel, and get that expression off your face, Mother, I mean for the way she makes me feel right now. Here," and he thumped his chest. "With her gone, I know that sooner or later, I'm going to stop feeling like this, and I won't let that happen. It's selfish and self-centered, but I don't care, because the Travelers don't win this one. I'm going to win this one. I'm going to get her back, and whatever she's going to make the Damned World into, I'm going to be part of it, so I might as well do something about it."

"You're not a hero, Karsen!"

"I dream of a world where I am, Mother. And if Jepp does, too . . . then anything is possible. If I stay on as I am . . . I know I'll never accomplish anything. It's better to try something that might happen than stick with something that never will."

Zerena's expression hardened. "You arrogant, judgmental bastard. You always thought you were too good for me, didn't you."

"No, Mother," he said honestly. "Not always. Only recently."

"Get out."

"As always, Mother," and he bowed slightly, "your obedient son. Mingo . . . Rafe Kestor . . . Gant . . . it's been an honor."

"Bring me back something," said Mingo chipperly.

Karsen bowed once more, then turned, adjusted his pack, made sure that his hammer was solidly upon his back, and started off.

The Bottom Feeders said nothing for a long time. They just watched Karsen bound away, his powerful legs eating up distance quickly. Karsen continued to move, faster and faster, until finally he was merely a speck.

With utter disgust lacing her voice, Zerena adopted a nasal tone and said mockingly, " 'She's light. She's energy. She's the center of my damned universe, Mother.' Of all the—"

"Do you . . ." Mingo hesitated, then said, "Do you think he might be right? I mean, there were things that—"

"He's thinking with his loins, Mingo. That's all."

"But what if—?"

"I don't believe in what-if."

"Perhaps," Mingo suggested, "that's the core of the problem, isn't it." She glared at him, but made no reply. He shrugged, then glanced off in the direction Karsen had gone. "He's heading northwest."

"Yes. I know," said Zerena.

"Which way do we go?" he asked.

Unhesitatingly, Zerena Foux said, "Southeast."

They piled into the jumpcar without another word. Zerena switched on the engine.

It sputtered and died, the hotstar going dark.

They stared at the gem, bereft of light and power, for a long moment.

"You know," Mingo finally said, "this is ironic on so many levels . . ."

"Shut up," said Zerena Foux.

ABOUT THE AUTHOR

In a career spanning more than twenty years, Peter David has written dozens of novels, comics, and screenplays. He has worked with both Marvel and DC Comics, and has penned many bestselling *StarTrek* books. In addition, he has written for several television series, including *Babylon 5* and *Crusades,* among others, and was the cocreator of the popular Nickelodeon series *Space Cases.* He lives on Long Island with his family.